BY MELANIE BENJAMIN

Alice I Have Been

The Autobiography of Mrs. Tom Thumb

The Aviator's Wife

The Swans of Fifth Avenue

Reckless Hearts *(short story)*

The Girls in the Picture

Mistress of the Ritz

The Children's Blizzard

California Golden

California
Golden

California Golden

Golden

A NOVEL

Melanie Benjamin

DELACORTE PRESS

NEW YORK

Published in the United States by Delacorte Press, an imprint of Random House,
a division of Penguin Random House LLC, New York.

DELACORTE PRESS is a registered trademark and the DP colophon
is a trademark of Penguin Random House LLC.

LIBRARY OF CONGRESS CATALOGING-IN-PUBLICATION DATA

Names: Benjamin, Melanie, author.
Title: California golden / Melanie Benjamin.
Description: First edition. | New York : Bantam Books, [2023]
Identifiers: LCCN 2022060484 (print) | LCCN 2022060485 (ebook) |
ISBN 9780593497852 (Hardback) | ISBN 9780593497869 (Ebook)
Subjects: LCSH: Sisters—Fiction. | California, Southern—History—20th century—
Fiction. | LCGFT: Novels.
Classification: LCC PS3608.A876 C46 2023 (print) | LCC PS3608.A876 (ebook) |
DDC 813/.6—dc23/eng/20230105
LC record available at https://lccn.loc.gov/2022060484
LC ebook record available at https://lccn.loc.gov/2022060485

Printed in the United States of America on acid-free paper

randomhousebooks.com

2 4 6 8 9 7 5 3 1

FIRST EDITION

Book design by Ralph Fowler
Floral background by PrintingSociety / Adobe Stock
Surfboard illustration by Iveta Angelova / Adobe Stock

To Emily,
the strongest woman I know

BOOK ONE

Mindy and Ginger

1

1964

The surf giveth, and the surf taketh away—thus said the Surf God every morning, noon, and night in his church, which was the universe, the planet, California, the beach, the waves. On this holy day, the surf would most definitely giveth.

The sand was cool and soft as sugar between her toes, the California sun tolerable, not blasting, because it was February. Yet the day was warm enough that the girls in their vibrant bikinis, and the guys in their board shorts, weren't covered in goose pimples as they danced to the wailing electric guitars of Dick Dale and His Del-Tones— twisting, shimmying, hand jiving. One girl's bikini was covered in long fringe that seemed to pulse with a life of its own as she gyrated so fiercely it was a wonder she didn't snap her pelvis.

Mindy laughed at the sight, then turned to do a groovy little two-step with one of the hunky boys who'd gravitated into her orbit, for today she was the sun itself, radiating joy and contentment. She danced a little Watusi, a little Pony with a side of Mashed Potato. Raising her face to her fellow celestial being in a sisterly salute, she turned her back on the waves lapping the generous beach of Paradise Cove, tucked between tall sandy cliffs and a spindly wooden pier.

If the sand was sugar, then gumballs and peppermint drops dotted the sky in the form of beach balls. Surfboards stood like totems in the sand. And Dick Dale and his boys—all clad in wild Hawaiian shirts, their crew-cut heads bopping up and down rhythmically—continued to give it their all as they cranked through the driving melody of "Let's Go Trippin'." The music—propelled by that wailing electric organ—almost drowned out the pounding surf as it hurled itself against the concrete pylons of the pier.

This is life, Mindy thought, grinning wildly at the other kids, who returned the joy, all smiling their blinding California smiles, teeth startlingly white against their suntanned faces. And why shouldn't they be happy? They were all gorgeous, all young, all dancing on the beach on a Wednesday afternoon. She caught her sister's eye; Ginger, with her curves, was naturally surrounded by guys with their tongues hanging out, but she managed to give Mindy a sly wink.

This should *be my life,* Mindy thought, correcting herself. Then, for the first time, the thin edge of the wedge:

Why can't this be my life?

"Cut! Print!" The director, high atop his lifeguard's chair, nodded decisively. The prerecorded music cut out abruptly, leaving Dick Dale and the Del-Tones strumming soundless electric guitars that were not plugged in.

"That's a wrap for the day, boys and girls," the director continued, his words garbled through the cheap loudspeaker. "See you tomorrow, same time, same place, wearing what you are right now."

There was an explosion of chatter and laughter as crew members started coiling cables, switching off the humming generators, and pushing the cameras back up the rickety wooden ramp toward the tent where they'd be protected from the salty night air. The two stars of the movie quickly headed off over the mounds of trucked-in sand to their trailers, assistants throwing terry cloth robes over their pocket-sized movie star bodies, which were coated in makeup, so different from the natural tans of all the locals, Mindy included. She snickered at the absurd hairstyle on the female star, a gravity-defying upsweep coated with hairspray so not a single hair was disturbed by the ocean breeze. Mindy's own hair was blond, bleached almost white by the sun, and conveniently short enough to style with her fingers.

As Dick Dale and his boys packed up their instruments, Mindy ran to grab a sweater she'd stashed behind a loudspeaker, pulling it quickly over her bikini; the sun was sinking fast.

"Hey, Mindy, where are you going?" Paula, the girl in the fringed bikini, came running up.

Paula wasn't an extra like Mindy and her crowd; she had an actual named part in the film. She was practically a movie star! Why was she talking to Mindy?

"I don't know, I usually drive back home or crash somewhere else," Mindy said. "Why?"

"Some of us have been camping out here on the beach," Paula answered. Her false eyelashes were mesmerizing, resembling black tendrils of seaweed, so long they almost grazed her eyebrows. Like the other extras, Mindy wore no makeup. She was never close enough to the camera to warrant it. And when she was out on the water, doubling the actual surfing for the female star, her head was encased in a smelly wig.

Paula giggled, for no reason at all; she was one of those Southern California girls who was all giggles and sunshine, always ready for a talent scout or a camera. "Why bother going back to a room, when we can build a fire and stay here all night? It's fun. You should join us. We might even hitch a ride to Whisky a Go Go. I know someone playing."

"I don't have anything to wear to that!" Mindy gasped, then blushed. But it was the truth; her wardrobe was woeful compared to the other girls' cute, trendy pedal pushers and miniskirts with matching headbands. And Whisky a Go Go? The club had opened a month ago, but already it was *the* place to be in Los Angeles. It was where starlets in white boots mingled with boys who drove convertibles. It was where all the kids of movie stars went.

It had nothing to do with the life that Mindy Donnelly lived.

"Oh, we'll just raid Wardrobe. I'll find you something cute. C'mon, it'll be fun. Then we'll crash here on the beach for the night and build a bonfire. Lots of kids are."

Mindy could see that; there was no rush to get to cars, the cast were casually pulling on sweaters and jeans or slacks, girls were combing the sand out of their hair, boys were hauling logs from a place Mindy hadn't noticed, and someone was loudly taking orders for hamburgers from the stand up the road. She thought of the long drive south and the long drive back up again in the morning—or the distasteful alternative she'd done her best to avoid—and bit her lip.

But on the periphery of her vision stood her sister.

Already the usual gang was gathering their boards to catch the last waves before heading to the disgusting shack farther down Malibu. Ginger waved at Mindy impatiently.

"Wait a minute, I need to talk to my sister. Don't go without me!" Mindy called over her shoulder to Paula, who flashed her sunny smile in agreement.

"C'mon," Ginger said when Mindy reached her. "We're gonna miss the waves."

"Some of the other kids are going to Whisky a Go Go, then camping out here on the beach. I guess they do that a lot—I didn't know that until now! They asked me to hang with them tonight." Even as she tried to say it casually, to keep her cool, Mindy Donnelly still marveled at the notion. The movie crowd, asking *her* to join them! "You should, too—it'll be fun!"

"Fun?" A masculine voice, dripping disdain like surf spray, caused

Mindy to tense. "You think going off with those kooks is fun?" Tom Riley challenged her, his dark eyes boring into her skin. "Jesus Christ, Mindy. You're a real surfer, you won Makaha. For fuck's sake, you're Carol Donnelly's daughter. It's OK to take their money and eat their food, but don't let them corrupt you. You're too good for that."

Even as Mindy flushed with his unexpected praise—Tom Riley was not known to praise any surfer other than himself, and she remembered a time when he hadn't been so impressed with her—she refused to allow him to spoil her fun.

"They're kids. Nice kids." *Real kids,* she wanted to say. *Teenagers— and I've never been a teenager, not really. Until now.*

Because this was what she'd been fighting all day, before finally giving in to it during the big beach party scene they'd just filmed. The feeling that she was being given a gift, even if it was a celluloid gift as fake as the thirty-year-old lead actors pretending to be seventeen. And the gift was the possibility of a *normal* life, a typical California teenager life like she read about in magazines, heard in songs, saw on TV and in movies like the very one she was currently working on. Dates at the drive-in, boys carrying your books to class while you looked perfect in a twinset and skirt, high school proms with silly themes, playing records in your room while your girlfriends painted their nails and tried out new hairdos and prank-called boys, picnics on the beach (real picnics with sandwiches in wax paper and potato chips, not stewed seaweed and fish caught at dusk, crudely scaled and cooked whole on a pan over driftwood). Parents who cared enough to ground you if you came home late after necking with your steady in a convertible—*fun fun fun 'til her daddy takes the T-bird away.*

Not the life she'd been leading. And suddenly, Paula had opened a door. Did she dare step through it?

"Jesus Christ, Mindy," Tom continued to rail, confident that she would want to listen because that was what people did; they threw themselves at the feet of the Surf God, begging for even the smallest crumbs of his endless philosophizing about himself, the waves, and life, in that order. "Don't cheapen yourself, chickie. Come with us; let's catch those last waves, then leave this place with our dignity intact."

"To go sleep in a shack that smells like a sewer, cracking coconuts to tide you over until you come back tomorrow to stuff your face at the craft table," Mindy retorted. "Yeah, that's what I call dignified."

Ginger's eyes widened at her sister's unexpected verve. No one talked to Tom Riley this way, especially not a girl.

"You talk of a life that is holy as if it were something to be ashamed of," Tom replied in his most seductive, reasonable tone. He could do remarkable things with his voice, Mindy had to admit; he used it as an instrument. "You, Carol Donnelly's daughter."

"Stop saying that. My name is Mindy. C'mon, Ginger." Mindy held out her hand to her sister. "Let's go with Paula. She'll fix us up with something to wear to the club. Something cute."

"Your mother would be disgusted," Tom pronounced. Even the Surf God held Carol Donnelly in reverence, and that reverence extended, occasionally, to her daughters. Tom treated most female surfers like shit. But he tolerated Mindy and Ginger, and now he draped his arm possessively around Ginger, who didn't shrug it off.

But she did look wonderingly at her sister.

Tom slipped his arm lower, circling Ginger's waist, while he continued to glare at Mindy. And Mindy was reminded of another time when they had been like this—adversaries, with her sister in the middle, the prize. Mindy had won the last time.

Or had she?

"Ginger, come with me," Mindy repeated. "It'll be fun."

"Ginger, don't eat of the apple your sister Eve is extending. The apple of the bourgeoisie. The kooks, if you will."

Ginger still didn't shrug off Tom's arm. She stood there, so pretty with her long blond hair just a shade darker than Mindy's, her curves spilling out of her bikini. The curves Mindy envied, except when she was on the water, where her own slight, slim body was an asset.

Ginger gazed pleadingly at Mindy.

"Come with us, Mindy, OK? I don't want to go back out there without you—come with us, like you always do. Let's just go."

The other guys were already paddling out. If Mindy abandoned Ginger, her sister would be alone. Mindy didn't fear being with the guys in the waves. She knew she could hold her own no matter what they might try out there—cutting in on a wave, plowing into her "by accident." But Ginger wasn't as good as she was.

"No, I'm going with the crowd. I'm going to have fun. I'm going to spend at least one night being normal and you should, too."

"See ya later, traitor." Tom dragged Ginger along with him as he sauntered toward his board.

"Ginger, come with me!" Mindy begged one more time. Was this one of those moments she'd read about in books—those moments that marked a crossroads in a life, that she would look back on later and recognize as the precise minute everything changed? She'd welcomed that feeling before when it applied to herself. But now that her little sister was tangled up in it, she panicked. As Ginger—after turning around to give Mindy one more look—began to paddle out with the others to catch the last wave before the sun set, she was far behind Tom, who attacked the water ferociously, selfishly. He wouldn't wait for Ginger, like Mindy always did; he wouldn't surf near her to protect her from her own timidity. Watching her sister trying to catch up, it seemed to Mindy that something precious was about to be lost forever.

The surf giveth, and the surf taketh away. Please, God, don't let it take away her sister.

Because it had already taken her mother.

"Mindy, come on!" It was Paula again, hands cupped around her mouth so her voice would carry over the surf. Mindy was still frozen, watching Ginger rise up competently but with her weight too much on her front foot, as usual. Had there ever been a time when she wasn't by her sister's side in the water? It was always the two of them together, paddling on their boards with Mindy in the lead, trying to catch up to someone bigger, stronger. Someone who had already forgotten about them.

That was the Plan, after all. And she'd never wavered from the Plan before; she'd never even considered it.

Until now.

Resolutely, she turned away from the ocean, walking toward the cheerful bonfires, the transistor radios blaring some girl group, maybe the Shirelles. Peppy young men and women, faces glowing with ruddy health courtesy of the California sun, either settling in around the crackling logs or heading out in groups to explore the neon Los Angeles night. She could join them.

Ten steps later, she did join them. It was as easy as that to trade one life for another.

"Do we have time to do our makeup before we go?" Mindy asked Paula, who was giggling as she pulled her through the sand, promising white go-go boots and her own set of false eyelashes that would make her eyes "look like Elizabeth Taylor's! You should be jailed for having eyes that violet blue!"

Mindy was so taken aback by Paula's effervescent praise—were her eyes *really* the same color as Elizabeth Taylor's? No one had ever told her that before—she forgot to turn around to see if Ginger had caught that last wave and was riding it in.

2

1957

Ginger couldn't really say when Mindy first came up with the Plan. All she knew was that it wasn't her idea, but there was no better solution for the Problem. That the ocean was the primary part of both the Plan and the Problem seemed inevitable, because the ocean was pretty much her first memory and she knew somehow, even when she was only a little girl just beginning to think of the future beyond what sandwich she was going to have for lunch or what television show she and Mindy would watch that evening, that it would be her last.

She hadn't had a choice in the matter. From the books she took home from the school library, books that were appropriate for a ten-year-old, the librarian said firmly, books like *Misty of Chincoteague* and *National Velvet,* she knew that some little girls grew up on farms and were destined to ride horses. Or there were other girls, like Eloise, who grew up in crowded cities in the East and ran around in big buildings with room service. But Ginger had grown up in California. So the ocean—the beach, the surf, the sun—was her destiny. Like it or not.

When Mom had come home from Hawaii—her leaving was the beginning of the Problem, although it took some time before Ginger was completely aware of it in the way Mindy was—they'd been enrolled in swim lessons at the YMCA after school. Mindy was older and a lot stronger, so she had zoomed ahead in these past two years, learning to dive while Ginger was still struggling to do a backstroke without swallowing gallons of chlorinated water. Mom dropped them off for lessons but didn't stay to watch, unlike the other mothers, who perched on the pool chairs and studied the lifeguards while chatting about regular mother things like laundry detergent and new appliances. Ginger's mother headed back to the beach instead, and after lessons were over and free swim was over and the lifeguards finally told them they had to get out of the pool, Ginger and Mindy would stand together, shivering, in the lobby of the Y, waiting for the battered old woody station wagon with the surfboard on top to turn in to the parking lot. And every time, Ginger always wondered if today was the day it wouldn't, because she knew for sure that day would come—but she never, ever wondered it out loud. And that was the Problem in a nutshell.

At least, Ginger didn't talk about it out loud, because that would be tempting something she didn't completely understand. But Mindy wasn't so afraid.

"We need to have a plan," maybe Mindy told her on one of those long evenings; it was only later, much later, that she thought back to this conversation, and then she couldn't tell if she had dreamed it or if it had actually taken place. It could have been one of many conversations the two of them had while waiting—fingers crossed—for Mom to show up, while the lights were blinking on inside the building and adults were arriving for night classes like pottery making or how to speak French. All the kids in their class had been picked up long ago. Strange how none of the other mothers ever once asked the girls if they needed a ride even when they made sympathetic noises as they passed them in the lobby.

Ginger shivered, her suit so cold and damp against her skin. Her mother had forgotten to pack them clothes to wear home; Mom wore her bathing suit all the time, so she assumed her daughters would, too. Except when they were at school, of course; Ginger's face grew hot whenever she imagined, as she did a lot, how the kids and teachers would react if she one day had to wear her bathing suit because Mom had forgotten to buy her new clothes, real clothes, like a plaid jumper, which Ginger wanted more than anything and planned to ask for at her next birthday. So far Mom had managed to buy the minimum amount of clothing—plain blouses and skirts for them, bobby socks (although not with little lace scallops, which Ginger longed for) and saddle shoes. A couple of pairs of shorts and sleeveless blouses for when they weren't in school, but mostly bathing suits. Practical one-piece suits, not cute ones with frilly skirts or lacy straps. Ginger's closet was pathetic, so many empty hangers, compared to the closets of her school friends.

"What kind of plan?" Ginger asked her big sister that day, whichever day it was, when they hatched the Plan.

"A plan in case she leaves for good next time."

"Daddy would take care of us."

Mindy cocked her head and squinted down at her younger sister; there was skepticism in her eyes.

"I don't think so" was all she said.

"He will! Daddy loves us more than Mom does!"

"Then why did he leave before she even came back?"

Ginger couldn't answer that, although she'd tried and tried to figure it out. How could their dad, who was the one who had remembered them when Mom couldn't seem to, leave? True, he'd been like most fathers, working all day, and then when he came home, he just wanted to eat dinner and watch television and talk to Mom, not the girls. Still, he had been the one who noticed if they were out of bread or peanut butter, or if the girls were wearing the same clothes three days in a row. He never did anything about it, but at least he noticed and told Mom to take care of it.

He only came over every other Sunday now, pulling up in his shiny new car and honking for them to come out. They usually went to Howard Johnson's for fried clams and ice cream. He smiled sadly at them, the two sisters sitting on one side of the booth, him on the other. He asked about Mom a lot and never seemed satisfied with their answers. He never asked about *them*, their schoolwork, what they watched on television, if they were still out of bread and peanut butter and wearing the same clothes over and over.

And when he took them back home, he sat in his car a long time after they kissed him goodbye and went inside; Ginger always watched him out the front window, hiding behind the lace curtain. Once, Mom came over and peeked, too.

"He's still out there? What on earth does he want?"

You, Ginger wanted to say. *We all do.*

But she shrugged and kept watching, until finally her father drove away.

"Maybe Dad loves you," Mindy continued as they waited at the Y. "Not me. And I doubt he'll keep coming around on Sunday for long."

"What do you mean?"

"Because, numbskull, he'll finally figure out Mom never loved him at all so they won't get back together, and then he'll marry someone else who does love him—he's a real catch, I heard Jennifer Carter's mother say that once—and have a regular life with new kids and he'll forget all about us. We'll just remind him of how sad he was with Mom. So we need to have a plan."

"Like what?" A car turned in to the parking lot, its headlights looking like two searching eyes in the gathering dusk. But it wasn't their old wagon. The car pulled in to a parking space and Ginger sighed. Her stomach growled; she was always starving after swim class.

"Like how we stay out of an orphanage."

Tears blurred the parking lot lights; Ginger wasn't hungry anymore.

"What about Grandma?"

Mindy snorted. "Grandma drinks."

"So?"

"Anyone from an orphanage would see that and take us away from her. No, we need to figure out how to at least get Mom to *like* us more so she'll let us come with her the next time she leaves."

This was the part of the Problem that they were afraid to talk about, of course. The next time. Because neither one of them believed it wouldn't happen again.

Oh, sure, Mom was nice to them. She smiled a lot and was so pretty when she did, so much prettier and younger than other mothers. But she never smiled at Ginger or Mindy in any special way; it was the same smile she presented to everyone—the mailman, the milkman, the boy who came around once a month to clean the windows. The same smile she presented to Grandma. To the neighbors. Smiling, always smiling.

But never letting anyone—least of all her daughters—know what was going on inside of her. And never wanting to know what was going on inside of anyone else, either.

No one—not even Mindy, at least not most of the time—ever asked Ginger what she was thinking about, or what her dreams were like, or if she wanted something special for Christmas or her birthday. The Problem was too big. It was all that the two of them could think about.

"What do you think she does at the beach every day?" Ginger asked. Because even if the Problem was always there, she herself was curious. She truly did want to know what people were thinking. If only so she could be sure that her own thoughts weren't weird or embarrassing.

"I don't know, other than swimming and surfing. You wouldn't think that would take all that much time, but I guess it does. So the way I figure it, we need to be able to keep up with her. Instead of being little kids, like we have been."

"But that's what we are! And keep up? With *Mom*?" Ginger's voice squeaked higher, as high as the voice of one of the Disney chipmunks, Chip or Dale. But she couldn't help it, because Mom was so, so—

Big. Out of reach. Strong. Ginger didn't really have any other words—no, she did. Mom was a giant. A *giantess*. No one else's mom was as pretty, as tall, as sporty. No one else's mom could open a jar of pickles with her biceps flexing in her sleeveless blouse. (No one else's mom *only* wore sleeveless blouses and dresses on the rare occasions that she wasn't in her swimsuit. It was like Mom was allergic to sleeves, Mindy had once said.)

One time, Ginger had opened a drawer in Mom's bureau, back when it was still her parents' bedroom and not only Mom's. She was looking for something, but she wasn't sure what. It was before the Problem, but maybe there was already a hint of it, like the big puffy clouds that appear before a winter thunderstorm. It was like Ginger had a question that needed an answer, but she didn't know what the question was, really. She simply needed *information*. A clue, maybe, to the ongoing mystery of "What's the Matter with Mom?" It could almost have been a television show, she sometimes thought. Like *What's My Line?* or *To Tell the Truth,* which she used to watch in the evenings with Dad. They could get famous movie stars to disguise their voices and tell them what was wrong with her mother, and maybe then they could be happy. All of them. Because even back then, before Mom had ever talked about going to Hawaii, Ginger had known Dad wasn't happy, and neither were she and Mindy, and for sure Mom wasn't, but there wasn't anything you could put your finger on. Nobody was sick, Dad had a good job, so they weren't poor, there hadn't been anything tragic—no grasshoppers raining down from the sky, like what happened in *Little House on the Prairie*. The Donnellys were all just kind of sad and on edge. All the time.

In that drawer of her mother's bureau, Ginger had found a treasure trove of certificates and medals and newspaper clippings. All about Mom. How she was a champion. How she was in a couple of movies. Which Ginger considered the most exciting thing of all because *she* wanted to be in the movies like Shirley Temple, whose old films she loved watching on television. She wished she could take dance lessons! A lot of her school friends did. But she didn't know how to ask for that, especially since Mindy didn't care about dancing and loved the ocean in a way Ginger never could. Mindy was so much like Mom, Ginger often thought, although she never said so because Mindy was always insisting that when *she* grew up she would wear pretty dresses, like in a fashion magazine—maybe she'd even be a model!—instead of just the same swimsuit every single day. Mindy was the one who hated it the most when they had to go to school wearing the clothes they'd worn the day before. Ginger didn't really mind; she liked it when her teacher looked at her in such a sympathetic way and gave her extra cookies at recess.

And Mindy wasn't afraid of the ocean like Ginger was. Ginger was sure that beneath the surface, there were things. Things she couldn't see. Dark things, things with tentacles and fins and sharp teeth and slimy tails.

Anyway. All those medals and certificates and newspaper clippings were part of her mother's *before* life. The one she didn't talk about, because she didn't talk about personal things at all. But still, maybe she missed it? Maybe that was why she was so sad most of the time, even when she smiled?

Unless she was at the beach. That was the only time Ginger saw her mother completely happy, joyful—playful, even. At the beach, she would run with the girls and tickle them and sometimes play games with them. At the beach, she would rush into the water, clasping a girl in each hand, and laugh.

But she didn't take them to the beach very often.

"So we need to push ourselves," Mindy continued to lecture. Ginger's big sister wasn't shivering even though her suit was as damp as Ginger's, although she did have tiny goose pimples all up and down her arms and legs. "You especially. You're not as good as I am, Ginger. You're better than some kids, but you need to try harder. You need to grow faster, too. Try to drink more milk."

"Will you leave me behind?" Ginger couldn't help her voice shaking. What if she couldn't keep up with her mother and her sister? What would happen to her? Would she be stuck behind on the shore, watching the other two swim off like mermaids, never to return, and since Dad didn't want her and Grandma was a drunk—something she hadn't even noticed before, but Mindy was right as usual; Grandma did fall asleep a lot when she came over to babysit, and her makeup was always smeared—would she be taken into an orphanage, then? All by herself?

"No, I won't leave you behind," Mindy said, and while her voice was as no-nonsense as before, she put a gentle hand on Ginger's shivering shoulder. "I promise. I'll help you. I'll pull you along with me. I won't ever leave you."

Ginger stopped shivering, and just then Mom drove up in the station wagon. As usual, her mother's face was relaxed, happy—until she stopped the car for the girls to get in.

"How was the lesson?" she asked. Like she did every time. But her face was already closed off as she smiled that sunny smile. She turned up the car radio so even if the girls did answer, she wouldn't hear it.

But they didn't. They shared a glance—Mindy in the front seat, twisting around to wrinkle her nose up at Ginger, trying to make her laugh.

She giggled. But only to please her sister, who was going to make sure they all would stay together. Her sister, who had come up with the Plan.

When Mom had gone to Hawaii that time, when Ginger was eight and Mindy was ten—when she left them behind—they all went to the airport and waved at her when she walked across the tarmac and climbed up the airplane stairs with her friend DeeDee. Ginger and Mindy had never met DeeDee before. It was strange, to think of Mom flying off with someone other than family, because Mom didn't have any friends as far as any of them could tell. She didn't play bridge or have coffee and Bundt cake in the middle of the afternoon with neighbors. It really hadn't occurred to any of them that when she was at the beach, she might be there with other people. And that those people—people Ginger had not even known existed!—were Mom's friends.

But DeeDee was nice, and she complimented Ginger on her pretty hair and Mindy on her long legs and smiled at Dad and even made him laugh a little. He and Mom had had a big fight the night before. Usually they didn't fight. They didn't talk enough for that. But the night before he had yelled at Mom and then he had cried, and it was the crying that bothered Ginger the most. It gave her a helpless feeling, like the whole house was in a twister, like in *The Wizard of Oz,* spinning out of control, and none of them could do anything about it.

Maybe it wasn't really a fight, though, because during all of it, Ginger never heard her mother's voice. And didn't it take two voices to argue? Two people to be angry enough to fight?

Mom had hugged both Mindy and Ginger at the airport. "Be good girls, but you always are," she said, and it surprised Ginger. Because she didn't think she was that good, although she supposed if you walked around quietly all the time and tried not to make anyone angry or take one step out of line, because that one step could be the one that capsized the entire ship and scattered your family in all different directions, a family no more—that could be mistaken for goodness. When actually it was just fear. And cowardly people weren't *good* people, were they? But if Mom thought she was a good girl simply because she was quiet and agreeable, then that meant something. It meant she really did love her.

Didn't it?

Then Mom had smiled at Dad—they were about the same height—and touched his face with her gloved hand. She was so pretty in a sleeveless dress with a full skirt, high heels, a pink ribbon around her ponytail. She didn't look like anybody's mom. Which was part of the problem—or the Problem—of course.

"I still don't understand why you're going," Dad had said, and there was a shakiness to his voice that made Ginger's stomach tense up. If he cried here, right now, in front of all these strangers and Mom's friend whom they had only just met, she thought she would probably die.

They watched the plane's propellers start up, turning faster until they were just a blur, then the plane carrying Mom—and her surfboard—turned and headed toward the runway and raced down it, lifting up. They watched until it was only a silver glint in the sky. They watched until that glint had disappeared.

Then they went home. To wait. Until the evening when Dad gathered the two of them together and sat them down on the sofa and told them he knew Mom wasn't going to come back.

"I've done everything I can," he said, so hopeless. He sank down into one of the living room chairs with a glass of Scotch in his hand. His eyes were small and red, and his hair was all rumpled. Ginger had never seen her father this way before.

Strange, how little a part he seemed to play in her daily life. He was in her thoughts, of course—her constant worrying about their family naturally included her father, who was always so sad—but he kept his activities to the garage or the yard, like all the other fathers. At least *he* fit in with the pattern Ginger saw on TV and in their own neighborhood: fathers who worked and mowed the grass and even played golf. Outside the house, he acted like Ozzie Nelson.

It was only inside, waiting for Mom like the rest of them, that he seemed so much smaller than anybody else's father.

"Everything a man could possibly do," he continued, swirling the liquid around in his glass. "I love her. I love her too much, I think. Do you? Do you think you can love someone too much?"

Mindy frowned and folded her arms.

"I'm not sure this is something parents usually discuss with their kids," she said sorrowfully but firmly. "We're not much help."

Ginger didn't have anything to add; all she could do was creep over to her sagging father and put her hand in his. He automatically enfolded her small hand in his own, but he didn't see her. And he let go of her hand right away.

"I love her, I do. I always have. The first time she really looked at me, it was a miracle. But I can't figure out how to hold on to her, no matter how hard I try. She's not going to come back, you know."

"Dad, really, I don't think you should talk about this with us."

"It doesn't matter. You're not just kids anymore, if you ever were. You two are the collateral damage."

Ginger didn't know what that meant, and from the blank stare Mindy gave her, she could tell her sister didn't, either. But it couldn't be good.

"Like in the war. Enemy fire. You two are being shelled, every day, from both sides."

"Tell us about the war, Dad," Mindy broke in before Dad could get sadder. And he did, and in the telling he sounded happier even though it was about icky things. He talked about crawling on his belly in slimy jungles, about the mosquitoes so thick he ate gallons of them but said they were better than K rations. He talked about not getting too close to anybody in his company because that was the only way to ever get past war once it was over, and he at least knew it would be over because he enlisted right after D-Day. But there were still people who would die, and while he didn't want to be one of them, he also didn't want to care too much when it happened to the guys he slept next to in the jungle every night.

"And I had a picture of your mom in her swimming suit, standing on the diving board, about to do a swan dive. It was a picture from one of her meets, and it ran in the local paper. I cut it out and took it with me overseas along with our wedding photo. The guys, they couldn't believe it, that I had such a goddess for a wife. I couldn't believe it, either. I told Carol that in all my letters home. Just knowing she was waiting for me—"

"And me, too, right, Dad?" Mindy piped in.

"Sure, sure, you, too. But your mother—knowing *she* was waiting for me. It was the happiest time in my life, if you can believe it. The damn war. Because I thought your mother—I thought she missed me as much as I missed her." Ginger couldn't help but see the sadness on Mindy's face, but it was only there for an instant.

Finally, Dad seemed to have talked himself out. Almost.

"Never fall in love with someone who doesn't need you," he finally said. Then he rubbed his face with both hands, like he was washing his face without any water. His eyes were teary as he kept blinking them. "You two never had a chance" was the last thing he muttered before Mindy finally pulled Ginger into their room, to try to go to sleep.

The next day, when the girls came home from school, Grandma was there. She was drinking a big juice glass full of the same Scotch that Dad had drunk the night before, and after one particularly long gulp, she said, "Your dad left. He's not coming back. I told your mother this would happen."

A few days after that, Mom came home from Hawaii. But it seemed to Ginger that only part of her was home; when she closed her eyes at night she saw an image of her mother forever standing on the edge of California, shading her eyes from the sun as she gazed west.

In 1957, an earthquake shook California. It wasn't the San Andreas Fault; it was a girl not much older than Mindy. A girl named Gidget.

The book—*Gidget, the Little Girl with Big Ideas*—was all anyone could talk about. The girl on the cover, with her dark ponytail and surfboard, smiled at Ginger wherever she went—the library, the Rexall, the big Broadway department store in the new Broadway–Valley shopping center. Suddenly everyone—not only weirdos like Mom—wanted to surf. This other, *crazier* world that Mom had been part of was now cool.

Before, Ginger had been embarrassed. "What does your mother *do* all day?" teachers asked when Mom forgot to show up for the school talent show or award assemblies. "I never see your mother at PTA, dear," other mothers sometimes sniffed.

How to tell them the truth? That Mom spent all her days at the beach with strangers, preferring to ride the waves instead of leading the Girl Scout troop? Nobody else's mom did that. Nobody else Ginger had ever *heard* of did that—until Gidget.

The neighbors, the teachers, found out what Mom did anyway—there had been an article in the local paper when Mom won her trophy in Laguna Beach—and then Ginger thought she would die of shame. Actually die, her cheeks burning so hot it was like she'd fallen facedown in a bonfire. "Oh, you're the little girl whose mother spends all her time with surf bums," Theresa Pope's mother said one day when Theresa invited Ginger home after school to have some cookies and milk and watch *The Mickey Mouse Club* on TV. And Ginger didn't know what to say; she wanted to disappear between the scratchy cushions of the Popes' corduroy sofa.

But then surfing became cool, all of a sudden. And the kids at school peppered Ginger with questions about her mother—"Does she know Gidget?" "Is Moondoggie really that cute?" "Does she say *bitchin*'? I can't imagine my mom ever saying a curse word!"

Still, despite the warm glow of unexpected popularity, Ginger couldn't help but think that, cool or not, Mom was simply too *old* for it all. Gidget—short for "Girl Midget," the nickname the surfer guys in Malibu had given to a girl named Kathy—was fifteen years old. Fifteen!

Mom was too old, because she was a mom. A mom shouldn't be running around in a bikini. A mom shouldn't wear her hair in a frizzy ponytail all the time. And a mom shouldn't be bringing home strange men—as scruffy as those described in Gidget's book—to sleep on the sofa. Ginger's stomach always knotted up when that happened, when a man who wasn't Dad was in the house, lounging around in long, threadbare shorts—board shorts, Mom called them—and dirty bare feet, and eating at the little metal kitchen table.

"At least they sleep in the living room," Mindy said once as the two sisters sat side by side eating their cereal, listening to one of those men snoring loudly on the sofa in the living room.

"Where else would they sleep?" Ginger asked.

"You're such a baby" was the reply as Mindy spooned sugar onto her Frosted Flakes.

Ginger, like every other California kid she knew, wanted to be like Gidget. But did that mean she wanted to be like her mother?

Because she hadn't before, not ever.

In that Gidget summer of 1957—there was a movie being made about it even, and Mom casually dropped the bombshell that some of the scruffy guys she'd brought home were going to do the actual surfing for the movie, one of them even wearing a wig to look like Sandra Dee, who was going to star—the Plan started to take shape: Wherever Mom went, whatever she did, Mindy and Ginger were going to do it, too. Gidget had shown them it was possible. Which meant that they were going to have to learn how to surf.

Most of Ginger's friends would have said that it wasn't the worst thing in the world to have to learn to surf. Because Gidget was one of them, in a way; she was a real California teenager who lived in the suburbs, maybe not Van Nuys but somewhere close by. Close enough to drive to the beach after school.

The beach had always been there, sure; it was always the edge of everything, you could only go so far west and there it was. Even when you didn't see it, you knew it was there, just like the mountains and desert to the east. You might go on the weekend to have a picnic, or you might take a school trip to look for shells. But only weirdos like Mom hung out there each day, like it was their backyard.

But once Gidget hit the scene, the beach suddenly was more popular than the roller rink or the ice cream shop. Now every teenager in California had to have a station wagon they could strap a surfboard to. And the idea of two young girls learning to surf in order to keep up with their mother so she would take them with her the next time she left on a surfing safari wasn't *quite* so odd or pathetic.

But in her heart, Ginger still wanted to be a girl who lived on a farm and rode horses or who took ballet with her friends or was a Girl Scout, something Mom had never even considered signing her up for. Even though Ginger thought Gidget was cute with her pony-tail and bikini, and she had a boyfriend, Moondoggie, the rest of it all seemed so—messy. Not to mention scary. The ocean—she shivered, thinking about it. About falling off a surfboard and getting hit in the head by it. About being sucked down, down, down, until she was strangled by all that lay within its depths.

She swallowed those other wishes, swallowed them whole until they were just a heavy stone in her stomach, and eventually it dissolved, and she forgot she'd ever had them. Mindy helped her forget. Mindy took their place, even—soon enough, the only desire that remained was the main one, to not be forgotten. By her mother, but even more urgently, by her sister. To be important to someone, so important that they would actually say it, like in old movies—say, "Ginger, you are so important to me, my darling. There is no one else in the world I would choose to be with. I would die without you, simply die."

Sometimes, when Mindy was asleep in her twin bed across the room, Ginger would leave her own bed and creep into her sister's, and when she woke up, she was usually holding on to a bit of Mindy's nightgown.

Being alone, she decided, was more terrifying than whatever lurked beneath the surface of the sea.

For her next birthday, Ginger did not get the plaid jumper she had circled in the Sears catalog, because Mindy told her to ask Mom for a surfboard instead.

And when she saw it, standing up against the kitchen table with a bow on it, a board Mom called a "Hobie," she squealed and jumped up and down. Just like Mindy had told her to do. While Mom—who smiled at Ginger in a different way, more intimate, with more genuine curiosity than she'd ever shown for her before, and that smile, that personal, unexpected smile, was Ginger's real birthday present—explained that the board was made of something new called polyurethane, instead of balsa wood like her own board, Ginger ran her hand up and down its glossy, smooth curves, oohing and aahing.

Just like Mindy told her to do.

3

1958

The first time Mindy surfed with her mother, she felt like she was a minnow chasing after a mermaid.

Mom took them to Malibu, the very place where the legend of Gidget had been born. Later on, they actually met her, Kathy, a cute teenage girl with brown hair. But she wasn't really part of the world that Mom introduced them to that first day. Kathy was a senior in high school by then, and despite the book—which she said her father had written, not her—she was concentrating on her studies and thinking about college. For her, surfing was just something to do on a weekend.

It wasn't a way of life.

Mom parked the wagon on the highway and led the girls—struggling to carry their new surfboards; Mindy had gotten one too, even though it hadn't been her birthday—down some crumbling stairs to the beach, where Mindy saw the strangest sight: a gray wall, like a castle wall, stuck in the sand. The wall had graffiti painted on it, and it didn't look in great shape despite the sagging chain-link fence around it; there were chunks of concrete missing or crumbling.

"This used to be private property," Mom explained, her arm gesturing to encompass all the beach that the eye could see. "Malibu. This wall was supposed to keep people out."

Now the wall was mainly used to prop surfboards up, as far as Mindy could tell.

That first day, at this strange beach—not the beach Mom usually brought the girls to for swimming, which was a little farther south in Santa Monica, a family kind of beach—Mindy wasn't sure that the Plan was a good idea after all. For starters, Mom had taken her and Ginger out of school, and that felt so wrong, even though Mom didn't seem to have any qualms about it. She'd been so breezy on the phone, lying to the school secretary, saying that the girls had dentist appointments that afternoon.

Mindy had not liked that at all, although Ginger had giggled gleefully, caught up in Mom's conspiracy. Mindy felt like the parent in the situation. She worried about getting her homework; she'd have to call her best friend, Sheila, to find out what she'd missed.

"Malibu is getting too crowded on the weekends," Mom explained matter-of-factly. "It's madness to go there then. But it's the best place for a beginner."

So she and Ginger were the only kids on the beach that Wednesday afternoon in late September. Mindy couldn't help but look over her shoulder now and then; were the truant officers on their trail? Her stomach was in knots, even though she told herself she should be happy that Mom was taking them along, that so far the Plan seemed to be working. Wasn't this what she wanted? To be included in Mom's world?

It hadn't occurred to her, until that day, that there was a price that would have to be paid. But at least they were with Mom, she told herself over and over that first afternoon.

There weren't any girl surfers other than Mom and them. There were girls hanging around, older than Mindy and Ginger but lots younger than Mom, and they wore makeup—Mom never wore makeup—and had their hair done in cute flips and wore fancy bikinis that Mom, in her practical suit, scoffed at. The beach bunnies—that was what Mom called them—hung around a shack that was tucked against a piling of the highway; it was made of half of what Mom called a Quonset hut, kind of like a cave. The front was covered with dirty, torn curtains and some palm fronds hanging from the roof.

A bunch of guys looked like they lived in the hut. Mom rattled off their names—Tubesteak and Pit Bull, Da Cat and the Surf God.

"Don't they have real names?" Ginger asked.

"I suppose," Mom said with a shrug. So Mindy understood that on the beach, real names weren't important. Maybe real life wasn't, either, but what *was* real life if it wasn't the life you were living? Mom's real life was here. But Mindy's and Ginger's real lives were back in Van Nuys at school, doing homework in the kitchen every evening. How could they ever be a family as long as Mom's real life and theirs weren't the same life?

It was so confusing. So the only thing that made any sense to Mindy was to change her real life—hers and Ginger's. Move it, as if she could pick it up in her arms and feel its contours—curved and smooth, like a surfboard—and drop it here, on the beach. Could she do it? By sheer force of will, could Mindy merge these two different realities?

All she knew was that she had to try.

"Surf Mama" was how the guys greeted Mom that first day, and she beamed. But when they saw that the Surf Mama had her actual daughters with her, they turned shy, and Mom looked a little disappointed. Mindy thought it was funny that these guys—all muscular and tanned so bronze their teeth were gleaming white—swaggered and strutted in front of the beach bunnies, but when faced with two young girls, they didn't know how to behave.

Mindy had often wondered how Mom was when she was at the

beach with these guys. She couldn't imagine her mother being romantic with them—she couldn't imagine her mother being romantic with *anybody*—especially now that she saw them up close in their own habitat for the first time. They were all kind of smelly, coated in sand, and needing a haircut.

Mom was weird, Mom was unlike any other mother Mindy had ever met—but she wasn't dirty or wild. And as she continued to observe her mother with these Malibu surfers, Mindy noticed that Mom seemed part of them, yet—not. Kind of aloof and above them. She smiled patiently at their antics—they snapped the tops of the bikinis of those other girls, and one of them, Miki Dora, aka Da Cat, started marching around with a Nazi helmet and uniform jacket, goose-stepping like the Nazis pictured in her history book. But they didn't goof off *with* Mom, only *around* her. It was kind of like Mom was Snow White and they were the Seven Dwarfs.

But as soon as someone shouted that there was a bitchin' swell coming in, they stopped their goofing, grabbed the boards that had been stacked against the wall, and plunged into the surf as if they couldn't help it. As if they were animals unable to fight some instinct to flee to the sea, like they'd been born in it. Like the baby sea turtles who, once hatched, marched to the ocean no matter what predators were nearby.

The youngest of them, the one called the Surf God, did stop to shake the girls' hands before paddling out. "I'm Tom Riley, it's nice to meet you," he said in a formal tone of voice that made Mindy want to laugh, but she saw that Ginger was impressed, so she didn't. He even bowed in an exaggerated way, like a waiter in a movie, before grinning at Mom and then running off with his board balanced on top of his head.

"He seems like a nice young man," Mom mused, watching him paddle out to the lineup. "He has good form." And Mindy wondered if the only thing Mom liked in a boy was his ability to surf—and if that was what she should like, too. Whenever she got to the age where boys would matter; she was thirteen now. She bet it would be soon.

Then Mom was all business. The first break at Surfrider, Mom explained, was the easiest and longest break in California—she pointed to the right where the beach curved out, a rocky outcrop, and then swept her finger along the cove to where the long Malibu Pier, on the left, cut off the waves.

"I learned to surf here," she said, and Mindy was stunned. She had never imagined her mother having to *learn* to do anything—especially surfing. "DeeDee taught me," Mom continued thoughtfully. "We were the only two girls here. For a long time, it was the two of us—and them." And Mom seemed to be sad that that time was over. That Mindy and Ginger were now part of this world whether or not Mom wanted them to be. At least, that was how Mindy heard it, in that little wistfulness in her mother's voice.

"Let's try paddling on the board," Mom said abruptly, and she carried her board about five feet into the ocean, then knelt on it and paddled on both sides with her hands.

Mindy ran after her, struggling with her own board, and Ginger trailed behind, dragging hers in the sand even though Mom shouted at her that she shouldn't do that, she might damage the fin. When the cool water was up to her waist, Mindy tried to kneel on her board but it bobbed and swayed, tipping her over a couple of times until she finally flopped on it on her stomach, then shifted her weight to her knees. Ginger flopped on hers, copying Mindy, but was too afraid to kneel, so she remained on her stomach like a beached whale and Mindy wanted to tease her, but she didn't. Then Mindy started to paddle out to where Mom was bobbing up and down in the gentle waves lapping the shore.

Ginger fell off when the first wave—A teeny one! A baby could have handled it!—reached her, and Mindy managed not to yell that she was ruining it, that she needed to try harder. Because Mom was already looking impatient, constantly watching the guys much farther out, riding in the long, regular wave. They came near the two girls but never bumped into them, giving them some space.

"C'mon, Ginger," Mindy said instead, enthusiastically. To her own surprise, she was excited that she'd managed it so easily and wanted to continue; she wanted to pop up on her board like Tom Riley was doing right now, one effortless, smooth movement. First he was on top of the wave, paddling toward the shore, then he was upright on the board and sliding down the wave, casually shaking his hands dry, barely even holding his arms out for balance.

He was so cool. Even Mom gazed at him with admiration.

Finally Ginger managed to stay on her board without it tossing her back in the water. So then they paddled a little farther out, and Mom showed them how to turn the board so that it pointed back toward shore.

"Now you wait."

"For what?" Mindy asked.

"For the right wave."

"How do you tell?"

"You learn" was all she said. Mindy tried to catch Ginger's eye, but Ginger was staring into the water, her big baby eyes huge. It was like she saw something terrifying, but when Mindy looked, all she saw was the sloshing, green-blue water, some kelp swirling around. She couldn't see the bottom, but that didn't bother her. She was a good swimmer.

Finally Mom said, "This is the one!" and the swell was a little more persistent—though still a baby wave, Mindy could tell that, because they were so close to the beach. But Mom started paddling her board along the crest of the wave, then popped up and rode it in about fifteen feet before she knelt back down and turned it around, paddling out to where the girls were still bobbing up and down, waiting. The wave had pushed them closer to shore, but not as far as Mom had gone.

Mom looked disappointed.

"You didn't show us how to get up on our board," Mindy reminded her, and Mom nodded.

"Of course. I forgot. I'm not very good at—this," she said, gesturing at the girls. Mindy wasn't sure what she meant, if Mom wasn't very good at teaching anyone how to surf, or if she wasn't very good at being a mother to them, period. Mindy would have agreed either way, but she was afraid to scare Mom off; she was afraid her mother already regretted taking them with her.

She wanted, in that moment—more than she'd ever wanted anything—for Mom one day to talk about this special time with her daughters in that gentle, wistful voice.

"You'll get the hang of it," she assured her mother. And Mom peered at her in a funny way—as if she didn't know whether to laugh or cry—before she nodded and started to teach them how to stand on the board. She beached her own board, then waded back out to hold the board for each girl as she tried.

"Hold on to the rails when you lean back on your heels," she instructed, and Mindy did so. Ginger slipped and fell back on her knees and would have tipped over into the water had Mom not been holding her board. Mindy sighed loudly, causing her sister to blush and hang her head, her tangled hair shielding her face, and Mindy wished she didn't look so pretty when she did that. Because she was just being silly, stupid, a baby. Ginger's face was soft, like a doll's face, her nose tilting up slightly, her lips kind of pouty. Mindy's face was all angles and splattered with freckles, and her nose had a little bump in it. Ginger's hair was always long and curly and tangled. Mindy had no patience for dealing with long hair, so she'd demanded a Buster Brown cut with short bangs a couple of years ago, a style she could take care of with a shake of her head. Ginger already had curves that Mindy knew she would never have.

At least Mindy was taller; maybe she'd get as tall as Mom. Although she couldn't really picture that.

"My pretty girl" is how Mom always described Ginger. "My athletic girl" was how she referred to Mindy. And Mindy was already wise enough to know which kind of girl boys preferred.

Anger and impatience surged through her as she watched Ginger floundering around while Mom tried to be encouraging; Mindy decided to paddle farther out. She could tell, by the way the lineup of men seemed to pulse with excitement, that a wave was going to break. She didn't dare paddle as far out as they were, but she paddled until the wave, not as big as it was when the guys caught it, reached her; she turned her board toward shore, paddling along with the wave as it lifted her up, held on to the edges—the rails—as Mom had told her to do, then leaned back on her heels and rose.

She was shaky, her feet straining for some kind of grip; her left leg wasn't as far in front of her as Mom's was when she surfed, but she did make it all the way up. And she felt taller than she'd ever felt as the wave pushed her gently toward shore. Her torso was leaning first one way, then the other, as she fought for balance; her arms circled wildly. The wax helped her toes grip the board; they curled in a way she hadn't known they could.

"Mom! Mom! Look at me!" She managed to wave shakily to Mom and Ginger as she rushed past them, thankful she didn't hit them, because she didn't know how to turn the board. It was all she could do to stay upright; there was spray in her eyes, and she couldn't hear what Mom said as she went past because of the whooshing of the surf against the shore. It wasn't a very long ride—maybe only about fifteen seconds—but she'd done it.

And she'd loved it; as soon as she fell off her board and paddled over to grab it, she couldn't wait to do it again. To feel the power of the ocean beneath her feet, the air rushing past, the shore coming closer as if she were flying.

Mom—leaving Ginger to flounder about on her board—swam over to her. She stood up—the water wasn't that deep—and hugged her. A wet, salty, fleshy hug, and while of course Mindy knew her mother had hugged her before, this felt like the first time. The first hug.

On the first day. Of her new real life.

As the months passed, the old Mindy would have hated how much school they missed, how many tests she flunked, how often her teachers pulled her aside to sternly ask what she thought she was doing these days, to say her head was always in the clouds, to ask what had happened to the straight-A student she had once been. She used to crave her teachers' approval.

Things were different now.

Mindy was a whiz on the surfboard. Better than Gidget, even— the guys at Malibu all agreed, and Mindy basked in their reluctant praise, ignoring the caveat "for a girl." What had started out as something she felt she *had* to do to keep her family together turned into something she *hungered* to do. That adrenaline rush of catching a perfect wave, riding it all the way in, seeing what else you could make out of it other than simply a clean ride—she hadn't expected it to be so addictive.

And that wasn't even counting the way Mom treated her now—

like an asset. Something to be proud of. Something that would only add, not take away.

Someone worthy of her attention, if not her love.

So school became perfunctory, necessary to keep the truant officer away. If the surf was going to be bitchin' that day—relayed up and down the coast with the cry of "Surf's up!," although living so far from the beach, they had to rely on one of the gang at Malibu driving to a pay phone and calling them, which made Mom talk, more and more, of selling the house and renting something closer—the girls just skipped. Mom had no qualms about calling in to excuse them.

"What you learn in the classroom," she once told them, "can't compare to what you learn from nature."

That sounded pretty cool to Mindy, although she wasn't sure how "natural" surfing was, since they never studied the marine life in any scientific way. She encountered seals popping up with their sleek gray heads and long whiskers, dolphins slicing the water in perfect arcs, and of course sea urchins, which stung if you happened to step on one. Reefs—while pretty—were something to be avoided at all costs. Once, she witnessed a nonlocal, a "kook," as Tom Riley called him with disdain, get a horrid red chest burn from scraping against a rocky reef. The guy actually cried, he said it hurt so much—earning him even more disdain from the Surf God.

Crying was not part of the surfing code, even when you were a girl—something that Ginger didn't seem to understand.

"I can't do it!" Ginger wailed one night when Mom was taking a bath and the girls were gobbling some peanut butter and jelly sandwiches; the surf had been bitchin' that day, so there wasn't time for anyone to cook. Mom had raced from the beach to pick them up from school; she was dripping wet, honking her horn impatiently, and the two girls hopped in and started changing into their bathing suits, crouched down between the backseat and the front seat out of view of the other kids, and that was maybe the first time Mindy felt truly outside of what some people called "society." Halfway through—her skirt down around her knees, her bikini bottom already on—her face burned with embarrassment; she hoped no one was looking in but she knew they were. Because gradually, inevitably, Mindy was being ostracized from her old school friends, who now wrinkled their noses at her bruised legs, her hair dried out from the salt and sun. Now it wasn't only "the Donnelly woman" who was scorned by the neighbors and PTA; it was "the Donnelly girls." It was one thing to read Gidget's book and watch her movie and surf with a gang of friends on the weekends; it was quite another to let it interfere with school. No more was she invited to birthday parties or sleepovers; as rarely as that had happened before, because every mother knew the Donnelly sisters could never reciprocate because of that crazy mother of theirs, the invitations now dried up completely.

"Those Donnelly girls are getting so wild," she imagined her friends' mothers whispering, those same mothers who had never offered to bring them home from swim practice, no matter how fiercely they were shivering in the lobby. Why did Mindy even care what they thought? But she did. She cared deeply. Even though Tom Riley told her, every day, that those other girls—"stuck-up little bitches" was his precise term—were the ones to be pitied. Not them.

But that was the one thing she hated the most about the Plan: that other girls felt sorry for her, even more than they had before. "What can you expect, with a mother like that? They've turned wild, poor things. Simply feral," she heard her former best friend, Sheila, sniff to the new girl who sat beside her at lunch now.

Mindy decided to eat her lunch alone in the library, after that.

"It's too hard for me," Ginger continued, sniffling into her Wonder Bread and Jif peanut butter. "You're so good out there. I hate you."

"No, you don't," Mindy replied resignedly. At least she also had someone to feel sorry for—her weak little sister. Somehow, that took some of the sting out of being pitied by those stuck-up little bitches. "You don't hate me. Remember, you're younger than me. You'll get better. I'll work with you."

"What if I don't, though? What if I try and try and I can't keep up with you?" Ginger couldn't meet Mindy's gaze.

"Then you'll go to an orphanage all by yourself because Mom and me will be together." Mindy hated saying it, but it was probably the truth and Ginger needed to hear it. This closeness with Mom was still too fragile, too new. It could still break, like an old piece of string, at the slightest tug in the wrong direction. Ginger had to stop being such a baby. She was going to ruin everything.

Ginger burst into tears and hiccups, and at that moment the water stopped running in the tub. "Shhh!" Mindy hissed at her sister, throwing down her sandwich with a sigh. She stood up and walked over to Ginger, shaking her head. It was up to her to keep Ginger from dragging them all down.

"I'm not going to leave you behind," she promised her sniffling little sister. "I promise. But you have to try harder. And pretend you like it even though you don't. I can tell. I'm not sure Mom can, but she might someday. Right now I think she's happy. But who knows how long that will last? She could always go back to Hawaii, you know. She talks about it all the time."

"Yeah." Ginger sniffed up some of the snot running down her upper lip. "DeeDee was over the other night and they stayed up late, whispering."

"I heard them. That's why I suggested we skip school the next day to go to the beach. We can't let Mom forget for a minute that we love this as much as she does—and that we can keep up with her. You *have* to get better, Ginge. You have to learn to stand up on your board."

Because Ginger hadn't yet, and it was so embarrassing—Mindy sometimes rolled her eyes at the guys, who didn't tease Ginger, but they probably would one day, because they teased everyone about everything and played all sorts of practical jokes on one another, like taking the labels off expired canned goods and making whoever wiped out the most that day eat them. These guys didn't tolerate weakness, and neither did Mom.

But Ginger did keep trying despite how terrible she was. Mindy had to give her that.

"It's so hard—aren't you afraid of falling off?"

"No." Mindy wrinkled her nose. "I never even think about it."

"I can't *stop* thinking about it! Did you hear about that surfer down in Laguna Beach who got bitten by a shark?"

"If you're on top of your board a shark won't get you."

"Tom Riley said that the shark bit the board! That the bite was about two feet long and you could see the teeth marks!"

"Tom Riley likes to hear himself talk."

"But I like to hear him talk, too. Don't you?"

Mindy went back to her seat and picked up her soggy sandwich. Did she like to hear Tom Riley talk? If she was being honest, yes. He was funny—like the time he teased Ginger into believing that he'd seen a real mermaid up the beach who looked exactly like her, so maybe she had a doppelgänger, and then he explained what a doppelgänger was. He goofed around a lot, like the other guys—borrowing that Nazi jacket from Miki Dora and wearing it while surfing, pretending to be a preacher and giving sermons using his board as a pulpit, lecturing them all about the Holy Trinity—sun, surf, and beach. Leading them in a parody of "Amazing Grace":

Amusing face, how freckled thou nose
That grinned a grin at me
I once was lost, but now I'm soused
By beer you gave to me

He'd pointed at Mindy while he sang it, and she blushed, surprised to have been singled out by him; she'd thought he considered her a baby like Ginger. Then she was mad because she'd never given him beer, so he must have gotten her confused with one of the beach bunnies who hung on him and the other guys when they weren't surfing.

"I'd never give you any beer, Tom Riley," she'd said, her nose in the air. "You act drunk enough without it."

As retorts went, she knew it wasn't very good, but the other guys laughed and teased Tom, and Tom glowered at her as she strutted away to wax her board.

So yes, she did like hearing him talk. Even if she didn't like being in the water with him. As sarcastic as he was on land, he was downright mean in the surf.

Nobody liked the crowds that—driven by Gidget's popularity—invaded Malibu, but nobody was as outright hostile to them as Tom Riley. He went out of his way to plow into less experienced surfers, and he laughed at their helplessness. He especially hated girl surfers, and he'd tried to plow into Mindy a few times when Mom wasn't looking. He always acted surprised and said "Sorry" to her, at least. But they both knew they weren't accidents.

And she thought it was a shame because he was the youngest of the group, only about five years older than herself. Maybe they could have been friends, in that other life. She wondered if he'd dropped out of high school, so one time she asked him.

"No, I graduated," he said, but he clipped his words; no longer did his voice have that soothing quality.

"Did you want to go to college?"

"My parents wanted me to. They wanted me to go east, to an Ivy League. Especially my mother. She was always showing me off, as a way to make her look better. Every good grade I got, she took credit for, told all her friends. And I *did* get into Harvard. I studied like a dog and I did. Then I told her I wasn't going to go, and it killed her—you should have seen the look on that bitch's face!—and it was the best moment of my life so far."

Tom's smile was terrifying, in that moment; he looked like a wolf, licking his lips before the kill. Before, she had tried to imagine his parents and couldn't; like the other guys, he seemed to have been born on the beach. Once, she did try to picture them all going to a restaurant up the highway, and she got the giggles. Imagine these guys in shirts and ties! With shiny leather shoes on their gnarly feet! Their hair plastered down with Brylcreem, like Dad used!

She couldn't. Just like she couldn't imagine Tom Riley, even now, wearing a high school letter jacket or studying for tests or going to football games or sock hops, like she figured all high school kids did. Like she had always thought she would, too.

She sighed again, glancing at the refrigerator, where she'd pinned a field trip permission slip with a magnet. Her class was going to the Griffith Observatory that weekend and there would be a test on it on Monday.

Mom came out of the bathroom, all rosy and sleepy, her hair not in the usual ponytail so that it fell down her back, tangled like Ginger's. She was wearing a fuzzy robe, but her feet were bare as usual.

Her nails were that pretty pink color she liked, and Mindy wondered when she'd be allowed to paint her own toenails, and if Mom would help her. Mom made herself a peanut butter and jelly sandwich and joined them at the table; Ginger sat up straight and wiped her eyes.

"What are we having for dinner tonight?" Mom asked with a laugh, and that laugh made the kitchen light brighter, the air sweeter, the soggy sandwiches taste like fancy meals. That laugh ironed away any of Mindy's doubts about the Plan. Mom appeared so relaxed and happy to be eating soggy peanut butter and jelly sandwiches with her daughters; it was just the three of them basking in the glow of the light hanging over the table, and everything outside of that glow didn't matter at all. They talked with their mouths full and laughed at how funny they sounded. Mindy couldn't remember ever being quite so happy.

"Let's go down to Laguna Beach on Saturday," Mom said dreamily as she picked up some crumb of bread with her finger and licked it. "Brooks Street Beach is less crowded than Malibu on the weekend. And, Mindy, I think you're ready for it if it's not too wild."

Mindy held herself still, letting the approval wash over her, soaking it in. Then she looked at the permission slip on the refrigerator. Her stomach tightened a little as she heard herself say, "That would be great, Mom!"

She made herself ignore Ginger's scared, pinched face.

4

1962

Mindy stood up, dropping her plate of food on the sand, but nobody noticed. She was trembling all over, her stomach in knots. She couldn't believe what her mother had just said to her—the Plan was a failure, after all. If a mother could say that to her daughter . . .

On this night, of all nights. How *could* Mom say that to her—even if Mindy had always known, deep down, that it was true?

Mindy stumbled off toward the other bonfire about fifty yards down the beach. As was tradition, now that the annual Makaha invitational was over and all the tourists had vanished, there was a big luau on the beach. But this year, there had been tension between the mainlanders and the Hawaiians about how to roast the pig; there'd been some scraps out on the water, too. One of the locals, the son of Jack Cho, one of Mom's friends, had been especially upset about the pig. Jimmy Cho was about Mindy's age—seventeen—and had come in second in the men's division; the locals grumbled he should have come in first but all the judges were mainlanders, haole. Mindy wondered if they were mad at her, too. Jimmy had glared at her when they all posed for a group photo, even though he'd hugged Mom with a warm smile that entirely changed his face, making it a face Mindy would have liked to gaze up into.

When she was between the two fires, so that the velvety blackness of the Hawaiian night fell lightly, softly, upon her shoulders, she stopped. She faced the beach, the surf pounding less intently now, but it was always there, that percussion always in her eardrums. The whitecaps glistened in the moonlight. There were so many stars—it was getting harder in California, even at the beach, to see them, but here they were abundant. She stood for a moment and took it all in, tried to reconcile the beauty of the place with the ugliness she had just heard in her mother's voice.

She forced herself to relive her second ride of the competition, the one that had cinched it for her—winner of the women's division in the 1962 Makaha International Surfing Championship. Her first championship ever.

The first time she had bested her mother.

The Fabulous Donnelly Girls had been competing together for a few years now, and of course Mom always placed ahead of Mindy and Ginger, and usually won. Carol Donnelly was a legend among competitive surfers, the first woman to win a competition on the mainland. She'd missed competing at Makaha by only a week the year she had run off to Hawaii, back when she had been on safari but had to come home because Dad left.

So Makaha was special to Mom, and this was the first year she'd been back—this time, with her daughters.

The girls had to compete on the day when the surf was mushy; the best waves had been yesterday, so that was when the men got to compete. It was always that way. The girls got the appetizers, the guys the main meal. But still, that second ride today—Mindy'd paddled out with her lineup, all of them wearing white T-shirts with numbers on them; she was twenty-two, her lucky number. As they watched the wave finally form and swell, she knew it was the best she would get; none of the earlier waves had held up as well. Mindy paddled furiously out to meet it so as not to drift into anyone else's potential path, then she waited a second after the first woman popped up; she knew it would pay to hold her breath a minute, not be in a hurry to be the first to the shore. Some of the other girls always got mixed up that way in a competition; even though they knew better, they couldn't help but try to race one another.

Mindy waited a beat more, paddling on top of the wave. Then she rose in one fluid, graceful movement, her surfboard reliably steady beneath her feet even as she dropped down the face of the wave, crouching slightly, her arms outstretched for balance, but they didn't wobble and jerk. She held her position for a long moment to let the judges up in rickety platforms on shore, their binoculars trained on the surfers, see that she had full control.

She walked up the board carefully, feet still digging in, thigh muscles straining to keep her steady. She walked back, still not wobbling a bit. Then she just rode it in, a huge smile on her face as she neatly navigated around the other competitors in her heat, not turning to watch as some wobbled and fell. She felt as if she were the only one, as if the wave were hers and hers alone, and it was such a smooth ride toward the end, it almost felt effortless—her board was a trusty steed being pursued by a wall of spray, sure-footed, never spooked.

It was a great ride. But Mom had ruined it for her. Not only today, but every day that had led to this moment. Every day that Mindy had engineered, given up so much to achieve.

None of it had mattered, after all.

"Hey, girl. Donnelly girl."

She jumped. That Cho boy—Jimmy Cho—had joined her.

"What?"

"I just wanted to say congrats."

"You did?" Mindy peered up at his face. In the moonlight his dark eyes gleamed, his sour expression replaced by a shy grin. Whatever beef he'd earlier had with her win seemed to have vanished. Maybe he'd had a little of the moonshine some of the guys were passing around.

"Yeah. I mean, you did good. You have great form out there. It reminds me of your mother's."

"Oh. Well, thanks." She knew he meant that as a compliment but it wasn't one she was eager to hear at the moment.

"I remember when I met your ma. I was a little squirt. She and the others sometimes came up to our house for dinner. I'd never seen anyone like her, so tall and blond. And out on the water, she was like a goddess. I didn't know any wahine could manage a big surf like that—I'd only really seen white women surfing in Waikiki, when Pa worked as a surf boy there. They were puny things, splashing around on their boards hoping the surf boys would rescue them. Nothing like your ma."

"Did you know—did she ever tell you then that she had us? A family? Back home?"

"Nah. She never said a word. But then, nobody ever talked about anything other than surfing."

"I guess." Mindy wasn't surprised to hear this, considering what had just happened, but still it stung. What Mom said earlier had flayed her wide open so that every little thing hurt. "You looked great out there, too. I think you should have won."

Jimmy's face hardened; his black eyebrows knit together, and that easy, generous smile vanished. "Yeah, well, thanks. I think I should have, too. But it's not like it used to be. . . ." He picked up a shell and threw it into the water.

"I'm sorry. . . ." But Mindy didn't know what she was apologizing for. For winning? For not being Hawaiian?

"You know we invented it, right? Surfing? We Hawaiians? You do know that?" Jimmy swung toward her, and his eyes were so pleading, so earnest. Why was this important to him?

"Well, yes—Mom told us about Duke Kahanamoku—"

"It was before him. Long before him. Before the missionaries came. *We* invented it—I'm hapa, mostly Hawaiian, some Korean. But the point is, nobody remembers that anymore. All you haoles, you Californians with your Beach Boys and Gidget, nobody remembers us. You come here to surf but God forbid we go over *there*. We're not welcome."

"Sure you are! I bet—I know you would be!"

"Nah. I've heard some things. Not that I'd want to go to the mainland. We have—this." And Jimmy turned back toward the ocean, arms flung wide as if he could embrace the waves of Makaha. Even when they weren't sharply defined, there was a powerful beauty to them Mindy had never seen in Southern California.

They were silent for a long moment during which she sensed he had relaxed, that his body wasn't so rigid. She was aware of his muscles, biceps like small grapefruits, his flat stomach, powerful legs surprisingly short for his body; his height was in his torso. And she was just as aware, as if for the first time, of her own body—the sweatshirt she wore over her bikini smothered any hint of breasts, so she took a deep breath and jutted her chest out as she sucked in her stomach.

Someone from the other bonfire shouted, "Hey, Jimmy! Dog, where'd you go?"

"Have you seen my sister?" Mindy asked, suddenly remembering that she hadn't seen Ginger since before the luau, when they were first starting the bonfire. "Her name is Ginger? I'm Mindy, by the way." She felt like she ought to put her hand out so he could shake it, but that seemed silly. She kept her arms dangling awkwardly by her sides. What were you supposed to do with hands? She appeared to have forgotten.

"I'm Jimmy. Sorry, I forgot my manners." He ran his hand through his black hair and grinned that grin that Mindy wanted to see again. And again. And again.

"Have you seen her, then?"

"Nah, but I'll tell her you're looking for her if I do."

"Thanks. I guess you should get back to your friends." Mindy nodded toward that other bonfire.

"And you should get back to yours." Jimmy did the same.

Mindy chuckled sourly. It was a little like they were Romeo and Juliet—they could be seen together only under cover of darkness. This night was just getting weirder and weirder.

She waved at Jimmy and reluctantly started to walk back to where Mom and the others sat, still eating and drinking and laughing. She was hungry and that roasted pig smelled delicious. No use letting her mother prevent her from eating. But she heard other voices, bottles clinking, behind a rowboat that was overturned on the beach. Its white bottom was visible in the darkness.

"Ginge? Ginger?" Mindy called out, softly at first because she couldn't imagine why her sister would be giggling with someone in the dark, forgetting that she had been doing the same. "Ginger?" she called more loudly as she got closer and heard laughter.

"Mindy?" Ginger popped her head up from behind the boat.

"The championship surfer in a stupid contest that was devised to legitimize something that is holy?" Mindy's stomach tightened as she heard Tom Riley's disdainful voice. Then his head popped up beside Ginger's, and her stomach did a somersault. Swiftly she took in the fact that while Ginger still had her sweater on, her hair was a mess.

"What the hell?" she heard herself saying too loudly. She didn't want anyone else to see what she was witnessing, so she lowered her voice. "What the hell are you doing, Ginger?"

"Just having a couple of beers with Tom."

"You're fifteen. You can't have beer."

"It's good!" Her sister had obviously had more than a couple of beers, because she collapsed in giggles, shoulders heaving in an exaggerated way.

"Jesus, Tom. How could you?" Mindy reached across the rowboat and yanked Ginger up by the sleeve of her sweater. At least her sister's bikini bottom was still firmly in place. Tom, too, still had his clothes on, although he sported a boner that made Mindy gasp in fascination, then look away in embarrassment.

Tom heard the gasp, grinned, and grabbed her hand and placed it on his erection like it was something to be proud of, and she felt sick.

"I'm offering you a gift, a gift I was going to offer your sister. But I changed my mind. I'd rather have you, it turns out—I don't know why, I can't predict these things. But right now you, Mindy Donnelly, are the one the Surf God chooses. This is your lucky night."

Her hand was still on his twitching erection, and for a second, she almost said yes. Almost wanted him as much as he obviously wanted her—she was proud of it, she was. Proud!

Then she saw his arrogant grin, so sure of himself. His dangerous eyes. Her sister, still giggling. Stomach lurching, she snatched her hand away and slapped him.

"Poor you, with that little old thing!"

His eyes widened, his nostrils flared; he looked like he was about to leap over the boat at her. Fortunately Ginger chose that moment to fall down, still giggling.

"Ginger, you're drunk. I'm taking you back to—" Mindy paused. Where should she take her? Mom?

Ha! What a joke—Mom wouldn't be any help. Mom was probably making out with George Downing by now, the guy she'd been whispering with at the bonfire before she decided to destroy her daughter. Mindy didn't even want to *look* at Mom. But Mom had the keys to the van that would take them back down the road to DeeDee's vacation house, where they were staying.

"I'll call DeeDee," Mindy decided. She could phone from the Chos'—her mind feverishly formulated a plan. Mom had said the Chos lived nearby. She'd go find Jimmy—instinctively, she knew she could trust him, that he wouldn't be as disgusting as Tom was. He would help her. None of the other surf bums would, that was for sure.

"Go ahead, surfing champ."

"Why are you even here?" Mindy spun around to face Tom, while keeping a grip on her squirming sister. "You hate competitions. You always say so, you think they're a sellout. Yet you're always around. You even give interviews saying how you're above all this. But you're always, *always* around."

"I'm here to convert the masses. To preach the gospel of surfing for surfing's sake, the purity of it. These contests are ruining it for the rest of us. I can't let that happen, because I am the Surf God. And I've converted at least one person tonight." He smoothed Ginger's tangled hair, and Mindy restrained herself from slapping his smarmy face again.

God! Had she ever thought he was cute? Harbored some idiotic notion that he might be boyfriend material? She couldn't imagine it now. First he strutted around brandishing his penis, then he sneered at her, belittling her. Like Mom had.

She'd *won* today! She was the very best female surfer! The best in the world!

Only Jimmy Cho seemed to remember that.

"You're full of shit, Tom Riley. If you were any good you would have entered the contest, but you were too afraid, weren't you? Too afraid that the Surf God wouldn't win!"

For a second, he looked stricken—found out. Then his eyes narrowed with hatred, and she saw his fists ball up before he took a step backward, away from her.

"Stay away from my sister, got it? Stay. Away. I can take care of myself. She can't."

Mindy yanked Ginger over the boat, ignoring her yelps of protest. Then she marched her sister toward the other bonfire. To find Jimmy Cho.

Tom Riley laughed softly as the two sisters walked away. Mindy heard him open up another bottle of beer.

She also heard him say, not so softly, "Bitch."

"I can't believe you," Mindy hissed at her sister, who was walking like she'd only just now discovered she possessed legs. "I can't believe you would go off with him! I'm always looking out for you, Ginger. I saved you tonight. Remember that. Because maybe I'm getting sick of being the only adult in this whole damn family. Maybe I'm sick of both you and Mom. Sick of these damn Donnelly Girls."

Ginger started to cry, then she leaned over and puked in the sand, her hands on her knees, her shoulders shaking.

Mindy only watched her, wincing at the gargled heaving sounds her sister was making. But she didn't go to her aid. She didn't even grab her sister's hair. Let it be coated with her own sick. Mindy didn't care.

Because nobody cared about *her*.

Mindy had *won*. And the only person who seemed happy for her was that moody boy she'd only just met and would probably never see again after tonight.

5

1966

"To surf is to know God—that is, to know me. I am God. I am the Surf God. You must bow down to me, worship me, feed me. Care for me. And in return I will cleanse you, wash away your sins, the sins of that other world, the dirty, grasping, striving world where kooks and idiots work for the man, not the water, not the surf, not the sun goddess. Not the rhythm of life, the actual rhythm of life. Listen to it, close your eyes, hear the waves gently lapping the shore or pounding it in anger, depending on their mood. My mood. The Surf God's mood. I give you this life, this real life, not the artificial one you have been conditioned to embrace since you were only an egg in your spectacular mother's womb. That life is not worthy of me, and I tell you it is not worthy of you. We live, we love, we eat, we sleep, to the cycle of the wave, to the power of it beneath us, behind us; we feed from it. The raw energy, the bounty of its waters. I take you as a woman—not my woman, only a woman. But a woman blessed. Among all others, blessed. Because you will serve the Surf God. You will know true enlightenment. You will leave that other world behind. There is only this—and only me. I anoint you my handmaiden. In the name of myself, I give you communion. Open your mouth, my chosen one. Open it and receive me."

Ginger, kneeling on the packed sand with her eyes closed, opened her mouth. Her stomach fluttered queasily—anticipation? Fear? Her breath was coming quickly; she didn't know what would happen, what he would give her today. It depended on his mood. Sometimes it was his cock. Sometimes a little white tablet.

She hoped it was the latter today, although she didn't mind the former. She was good at it, he'd assured her the first time. Some chicks had a gag reflex that made it impossible. Some chicks didn't know what to do with their teeth. Ginger was a natural, the best. The very best.

She heard a rustle in front of her—was he stepping out of his board shorts? Or was he unwrapping the tablet? She didn't open her eyes because it would make him mad and he might go find some other girl. But she didn't *want* to open them; she loved the anticipation. He was in complete control. She was his chosen vessel. All she had to do was—be.

It had been this way ever since that evening a couple of years ago when for the first time in her life Ginger was in the middle of a tug-of-war. She was wanted. She was prized. Her father and her mother hadn't fought over her, like divorced parents were supposed to do. Neither wanted her or Mindy when they split up, that was clear. Well, it was clear *now*, anyway.

Tom had explained it to her.

But that evening, after filming the big beach party in that silly movie—they were all silly movies, Tom explained that, too, but they would stick it to the man by eating his food and taking his money as long as the public—the kooks—kept demanding more. And it was fun to sneak into a matinee, barefoot because shoes were for civilians, as Tom called other people, never minding the sticky residue on the theater floor, the popcorn kernels surprisingly sharp, and watch these ridiculous movies, looking for themselves in the crowd scenes or doing the surfing for the stars. Although now that Mindy was being featured more prominently with speaking roles, her own surfing highlighted, Tom would no longer let Ginger be in them.

He still was, however. Sometimes he brought her food from the craft table for dinner.

Anyway, that evening when Mindy and Tom were fighting over her—it was the best moment of her life. Holding on to one of her hands was her sister, whom she loved and worshipped but who was always a step—or a wave—or two ahead, who had never really needed Ginger as much as Ginger needed her.

Who had started to look at Ginger, sometimes, like that time in Hawaii, as if she was weary of her presence, resentful, even. Just sometimes. But enough times.

And then there was Tom, grasping the other hand.

The Surf God.

Tom.

When had she fallen in love with him? Maybe that night on Makaha when he sought her out for the first time. When he saw that she was sad, sitting alone on a log while the bonfire was being stoked, forgotten by everyone as Mindy was being congratulated and Mom was huddling with all her Hawaii friends. Ginger hadn't come close to placing, not at Makaha. The surf frankly terrified her with its force, its size. The drop down—she'd barely held on, and then not for long. She simply fell to her stomach, clutching the rails for dear life, almost sobbing with relief when she made it safely to shore. But she would have gone back out again for her second ride—Mindy told her to—had Mom not pulled her aside.

"You don't have to do this, sweetie," Mom had said. She'd brushed Ginger's tangled curls back from her face and sighed. "This isn't your surf."

"But Mindy—we always compete together," Ginger had whispered, even as tears of relief sprang to her eyes.

"This is Mindy's surf. Not yours. She can ride it. You can't. You have to know your limitations as well as your strengths. You don't—you just—you're not good enough."

Mom didn't say she was worried about her; she didn't say she was afraid something bad would happen to her. No, it was simply that she was *embarrassed* by her daughter. Ginger nodded, let the tears block out the sun and the bright crowds and the water and her confident sister strutting about. She didn't go back out.

When Tom found her that night, he saw her. Really *saw* her. Not like the others—the guys who panted after her, who made her feel naked in her bikini, who whistled and hollered when she walked by. She was pretty, sure. She knew that, but it didn't seem like much of an accomplishment compared to what Mindy or Mom could do on a board.

Still, hadn't Dad always called her his pretty little girl? Back when he still came around to take her and Mindy out for Sunday dinner? But he'd stopped doing that as soon as he had his second family. Mindy had been right about that; she was always right. Except about Tom.

Tom thought she was pretty, too. "Damn, Ginger, the way you're growing up, I feel like a dirty old man sometimes," he'd said that night on Makaha, making her laugh. And that was the thing, the simple thing, but somehow Mindy and Mom both missed it. Tom had known she needed cheering up. Sometimes people thought beautiful girls didn't have anything to be sad about. Tom knew better.

Tom knew *everything*.

"Let's get out of here," he'd whispered that night, pulling her away from Mom and Mindy. As the two of them walked away, Ginger glanced back to see if her sister or mother was watching. But they weren't—they were in their own little world. The world of all the good surfers, the stars. Ginger had never felt like she belonged there, too, less than she did right now.

"Where are we going?" Ginger whispered back. She shivered, even though she was wearing a sweater. But she wasn't cold; a surprising warmth filled her belly.

"Just come with me. We don't belong here, you and me. We're better than them."

"We *are?*"

Tom grinned, and Ginger saw how his eyes were gray, and how finely chiseled his cheekbones were, how he had one crooked incisor that suddenly seemed adorable. And that smile—"cocksure," Mindy called it, but Ginger thought it was perfect. A little smug, a little boyish. His muscles were as sculpted as any other surfer's—rippling abs, rounded biceps—but Tom had a leanness that some of the other guys didn't. A coiled energy sparked out of him—Ginger could almost see electricity sizzling in the velvety Hawaiian night.

And that must have been the moment she fell in love with him. How else to describe the feeling that overwhelmed her—that this was the man only *she* could understand, of all the women in the universe.

And that he was the only one who could understand *her?*

"Don't fall in love with someone who doesn't need you"—wasn't that what Dad had said once? But what if you needed someone so desperately you couldn't remember living before you met him? Ginger was frantic to be rescued: From her failure, from the cold shadows cast by her mother and sister. From her abandonment by all the people who were supposed to take care of her when she was small. From herself, too. She was so weary of thinking about how anxious she was, how terrified of being left behind.

And here was Tom, who knew all that without her telling him. It was a miracle.

"I'll go anywhere with you," Ginger had said breathlessly as he pulled her along to a little sheltered spot behind an overturned rowboat. He sat down gracefully, like an Indian guru, folding his legs beneath him. Ginger—more awkwardly—fell beside him.

And then he was handing her a warm beer he'd uncapped with a church key, and the beer tasted sour at first but then it released its bitterness and tasted like—well, still like nothing pleasant, but soon enough she didn't care. It was warm, it filled her up, it made her laugh a lot, and Tom, too, giggled. Something she'd rarely seen. He had dimples! She was so surprised by this she laughed and touched those dimples with her forefinger, and Tom took the finger and put it in his mouth, and Ginger wiggled. Suddenly that warmth became a liquid gold that flooded her panties; she was so stirred, so anxious to be touched by him *everywhere,* her nipples tingled, and she envisioned his mouth upon them, sucking as greedily as he was now suckling her finger, and she gasped.

Tom gave her back her hand and grinned at her.

"All grown-up now, aren't you?"

All Ginger could do was nod. She possessed no words for what she was feeling. She would have followed Tom anywhere, done anything he wanted her to right then.

But he didn't go, and he didn't ask. She knew she should have been grateful—she remembered those pamphlets in school about how good girls behaved, and it certainly was not like this.

Instead, she almost cried with disappointment. She was so ready to be *necessary* to him.

"Yes," he said as he reached for another beer. "You're all grown-up now. You're not Carol's little girl or Mindy's kid sister anymore. You're special. You're better than them. We both are."

That she might be the same as Tom Riley—his equal—was too much to believe. Yet as he kept talking, she did believe it. She wanted to believe everything he said to her, ever. She made up her mind, right then, that she would.

He didn't touch her again that evening. He just kept talking, and as she listened, he rearranged her universe. Surfing was pure, but only if you embraced it as Tom did, as a way to live, a lesson, a holy scripture. Competition and commercialism were the worst things that could happen. Gidget was a Jew—Tom guffawed as he told Ginger he'd helped burn a cross on her lawn, back when the book came out. Ginger's idol went up in flames, then, too. It was as if she'd never existed, and Ginger vowed to throw the book out as soon as she got back home.

The Hawaiians, oh, sure. Maybe they'd invented the surfboard but they hadn't elevated its use the way the Malibu boys had. They'd brought purity to it. Purity that only people like Tom and a few ordained others who refused to compete, who were from California, who had no other job or identity other than what the kooks called "surf bum," possessed. But the joke was on the kooks. Tom and the others—and Ginger, too, she wished he would say, but he didn't, and she understood that she would have to earn her place among his apostles—*they* were the enlightened ones.

He didn't mention any other girls that night. So Ginger knew, then, that she would be the only one. Once she'd earned it, and Tom only needed to tell her how, and she would do it.

When Mindy found the two of them, the spell wasn't broken, not at all. It was strengthened by her sister's disgust. Because then it was, truly, only the two of them.

Tom and Ginger. Against the world.

She didn't see Tom again for a few months, because soon after, they moved to Laguna Beach. Mom didn't drive back to Malibu much;

she said it was too crowded, the surf too tame. But when Tom and the crew showed up at Huntington Beach for a competition, even though he was surrounded by other girls, all blond and pretty but not as pretty as Ginger was, Tom singled her out again. And she knew she hadn't dreamed it before.

It was the first contest Ginger had ever won—being chosen by Tom. So she had to choose him over her sister. And she didn't regret it.

Did she miss her sister?

Of course she did. She and Mindy had been closer than twins, Tom told her—and he made it sound like that was shameful. But this one time, she didn't agree with him. She would never tell him that, but she knew Mindy had saved her from the orphanage. That without Mindy, she would have been completely unloved and abandoned and never would have been rescued by Tom. Mindy never talked about love, she never hugged her or kissed her, but she was *there,* by her side, all those years. Mindy alone remembered Ginger, and nobody else in those days ever did.

Now, however, *Tom* was in charge of her, telling her what to do and how to think, and it was all so much easier. No more did she have to compete in surf that was too big for her. No more did she have to pretend she didn't care when she came in last. She wouldn't come in last ever again. Tom had assured her of that, cleansed her of failure—because only in competition was there failure—forever.

They lived in the hut, which they'd relocated farther up the coast away from the crowds, across the street from the beach in a vacant, sand-covered lot. Malibu was getting so popular—it had always been popular with the movie and surf crowd, but now it was popular with regular people. People who wanted restaurants and taco stands on the highway, people who wanted more police to patrol the beaches where they took their kids. They moved before they were told to, Tom and Ginger and some other guys and their girls.

Ginger took care of Tom—she fed him, fetched for him, once she even stole some bread and bologna from a grocery store because he wanted them and neither of them had any money at the time. She got odd jobs when he told her to—babysitting for frenzied parents on the beach, handing out flyers in her bikini for a sunglasses store, posing for cheesecake photos for a sleazy photographer friend of his. Some of those photos turned up in surfing magazines, the very things he hated because of how they popularized and commercialized surfing.

Somehow, if it brought in money, he didn't seem to mind it when she lowered herself in this way. Although he never did himself.

Mindy was busy with her new career. But their worlds, however different, still sometimes collided. Surfing was too small a sphere for that not to happen.

Once, Tom disappeared for the afternoon and when he returned to the hut he had showered, shaved, and was wearing new, unfamiliar clothes—clean jeans, a borrowed short-sleeve shirt. He looked kind of diminished, actually, like an eager little boy, not the Surf God. But she didn't say so.

"I'm going out," he said, and when Ginger asked where, he replied, "I don't have to tell you."

"I know, but still, I like to—"

"You like to what?" He sneered, and for the first time Ginger felt like one of the other girls hanging around the fringes. Not the chosen one.

"I like to know where you are, so I can worry about you," she answered with a weak little giggle, and he rolled his eyes and left. But when he returned, sometime after midnight, he smelled of smoke and booze, and he was high. He giggled in a strange, childish way and told her he'd seen Mindy at Whisky a Go Go.

"I went there to help her see the error of her ways," he slurred. "I saved you. But my work isn't done until I save her, too."

From what? Ginger almost blurted out, but she caught herself in time. Mindy was the last person in the world who needed saving from anything, but Tom couldn't see it. Mindy's disdain for him, for his proselytizing, for his entire way of life, bothered him. More than it should have. Ginger couldn't figure out why.

"She barely talked to me. All dolled up, in a sickening way—you should have seen her fake eyelashes, her ridiculous hair. She was with some kook who sings, I forget his name. She asked about you. I told her that you were not in need of her assistance. She got mad, the bitch. Almost slapped me, I think. I don't know. They threw me out."

Ginger soothed him, caressed him, opened herself up to him so he could lose himself in the safest way—the only way she knew how to keep him, if only for the time it took for a wave to crest and then throw itself against the resigned boulders that studded the cove.

But she couldn't stop thinking of her sister.

Sometimes she wondered what would have happened if she'd gone with Mindy and Paula that night after the filming, instead of Tom. Would she have gotten a bigger role in those movies, too, and become a movie star—*her* childhood dream, not Mindy's? Sometimes she felt Mindy had stolen that from her, her own thoughts and hopes. But that was ridiculous, of course; she wasn't sure she'd ever shared that with Mindy. Back then, they were forced to share so much—clothes and the last pieces of bread and even a lunch box at school—that Ginger had kept her most precious thoughts to herself.

Of course, Ginger didn't have any talent, not like Mindy. She was prettier than her sister, *that* she knew. But she'd still probably have been second fiddle to Mindy, who seemed to have leapt into this other, golden world with astonishing ease, straddling Hollywood and competitive surfing like no one else had. Famous—California famous, anyway. The table at Whisky a Go Go, the parties at the Playboy Club. Ginger kept the magazines that featured Mindy in a secret place between an orange crate and the flimsy wall, and when Tom was away doing whatever he did when he wasn't with her—he never would tell her exactly what—she searched for photos of her sister, studying them for some clue, some sign, that Mindy missed her, even a little.

But in those glossy photos—Mindy with her blond hair frosted, like Nancy Sinatra's, so much of it teased into a stiff bouffant it must have been supplemented with a fall of fake hair, cool, slim, and tanned in a sleeveless shift, or at the beach with her real hair, still frosted but more loosely styled in a flip, false eyelashes making her eyes look like Bambi's—Mindy's self-confident smile, brighter now with newly whitened and straightened teeth, told her nothing. It was Mom's smile all over again—sunny, uncomplicated. Fake and impersonal.

Just like California itself, Ginger sometimes thought. No wonder Mindy was so popular. She embodied the now-famous California Girl to a T. She was an ideal, not a person. And she didn't need a tagalong little sister anymore.

Only Tom needed her now.

Ginger felt Tom move nearer; a small disk was placed on her tongue, and she swallowed. She opened her eyes, and Tom was smiling down at her, giving her the sign of the cross, his benediction.

"You have received me, or the essence of me. Go in peace."

She giggled; sometimes she couldn't help herself, although he didn't like it when she did. He was so serious all the time. He rarely laughed. That night when she'd put her finger in the dimple of his cheek was long ago. Now he read books by someone named Dr. Timothy Leary. He paced the beach more than he actually surfed, ranting at all the kooks and foreigners who were dirtying it up. And when he did get on his surfboard, he targeted those kooks and foreigners, especially those with skin different from his; he would steer right into them, try to run them out of the lineup. The other guys who hung around the hut were his eager lieutenants, doing the same. Ginger felt uneasy about this; she would watch, hoping no one got hurt by Tom or the guys, but she didn't speak up. Tom was right, of course; she remembered Malibu when it was only her and Mom and Mindy and the small group of original surfers, when they had their pick of the waves, when it was their secret place. Now the beach was full of litter; you couldn't walk on it without piercing your foot on a bottlecap or piece of glass. Families with screaming kids parked on blankets, and people with no business being on a surfboard floundered about, not understanding the sanctity of the lineup. As far as the Blacks and the spics and the Japs—Tom's catchall word for anyone with eyes that weren't as round as his—Ginger didn't really have an opinion, but that's what Tom was for.

Did she, sometimes, gaze too long at some of those outsiders? It was her one power over Tom, she had discovered. He became enraged to the point of violence—not toward her, toward the guy. And after, he would make love to her passionately, more attentive to her than usual. He would tell her how precious she was, how special, how no Black or spic or Jap could ever—should ever—have her, and he would kill anyone who did. And then he would die, too, because she would be spoiled forever.

"Let us go in peace," Tom said to her now in benediction, and she took his hand, rose, and followed him outside the hut. It was dark, but they crossed the street in a trance as the LSD started whispering in their ears—she was aware of a car's brakes shrieking, a horn honking and descended the stairs to the beach, which was dotted with a few bonfires but mostly empty.

They lay down on their backs, no towels beneath them, and gazed up at the stars. The rushing sound of the waves was soothing; the tide was coming in but it was gentle. She smelled the comforting smoke from the bonfires, the sweet scent of sea lavender, and the musky, sourish smell of Tom mixed with her own funk; it was natural, Tom said, not to shower regularly. He wouldn't let her use deodorant or shave her legs or under her arms.

Ginger closed her eyes, feeling the LSD take control of her brain, piloting her to unknown lands. The waves were muffled now, but Tom's breathing was as loud as an airplane engine. Her own heartbeat sounded like a cannon. She heard people giggling from way up the beach, and then it was as if they were right next to her.

Eyes open now, she gazed up at the dark sky, and suddenly the stars and the moon were brawling, the stars gathering forces and racing to pummel the moon, the moon changing size, blowing up like a big yellow balloon before deflating to the size of a coin, inflating again as it charged the stars right back. Some of the stars broke ranks and joined the moon. It was endless, this fight, stars and moon chasing each other back and forth, back and forth, until Ginger got both dizzy and bored with it and shut her eyes again. She stroked her arm, and she'd never felt such velvety smoothness before, and she smiled, but then suddenly her arms grew scales, like a fish, and she was disgusted, and she tried to pick them off, one at a time, but then they fell off all on their own and her skin was velvet once more.

She sensed Mindy was with her. Where had she come from? She wanted to shout "Hi, Mindy!" and maybe she did. Her sister's body was lying next to hers, velvet skin to velvet skin. Mindy's hand took hers, their fingers intertwined, two hands making one strong, defiant fist. They gripped each other tighter, so tight Ginger's fingers hurt. But she didn't let go; she was too happy, overwhelmed with joy to the point of tears, to have her sister with her. In that moment she knew that if she was asked, again, to go with Mindy and leave Tom, she would.

"I don't need you," Mindy's voice whispered in her ear. "I'm better on my own. You were dragging me down. I'm like Mom. You're like Dad. You're the weak one."

"No," Ginger protested. But she knew her sister was right. She *was* the weak one. She could never be as golden, as bright and hard and valuable, as Mindy. She could never create a new life all by herself— she would always need someone to do it for her, to pull her along, as helpless as those stars above cowering in fear of the moon, which was gold now, too, and as radiant as Mindy's face in the magazine photos, and then the moon *was* Mindy, her sister had flown up there, leaving Ginger back on the beach, where she could only stare up at her sister's luminous face as it smiled at something else, not looking at Ginger no matter how violently Ginger waved her arms.

"Hey, hey, I'm here, I'm down here," she croaked, still waving, but Mindy's celestial face turned here, turned there, smiling, always smiling—but not at Ginger.

"I'm here," Ginger whimpered, and she guessed she was crying now because tears were running into her ears. Tom grunted something but he was on his own journey.

She was alone. Again. Left behind. Even the stars and the moon had vanished, and so had Mindy; the sky was a blank, black canvas of nothingness, just like her.

Ginger closed her eyes so she didn't have to see how alone she was—while at the same time, her hand reached out to grab on to Tom's ratty shorts, hoping he would take her with him.

Wherever he was going.

6

1967

Like a shark, she sliced through the neon night, cool and predatory in her white shift with matching coat trimmed with silver beading, her white stockings giving her legs an opalescent sheen. She held her date's hand, letting him lead her because he was a TV actor and all TV actors had fragile egos, but she knew her way. She knew this world.

This was her world now.

They slid through packs of strung-out kids and groups of older movie stars looking like waxworks, out of place but desperate to appear cool. They grinned when they encountered their own—other young people wearing minidresses or skinny sharkskin suits, with gleaming white teeth, skin glowing from the sun. Frosted eyeliner and fake eyelashes and teased hair. Go-go boots and Chelsea boots, Nehru jackets and Prince Valiant haircuts. Everything old was new again.

Just like Mindy. She was so new, the dew still clung to her shimmering skin, her giggle bright and infectious, her spirits reborn so that her smile was easy, not wary. She had recently emerged from an egg, a dazzling Fabergé egg to match her Fabergé lipstick, and she was *fabulous*. Simply fabulous.

The Whisky—after they'd pushed through the crowds waiting beneath the neon-yellow awnings outside—was packed as usual, but Mindy and her date were ushered right in and given one of the small tables that ringed the dance floor. It wasn't one of the coveted red booths, but it was still something of a status symbol.

Her date—Jack Daniels, a fake name to go with a fake heterosexual, because Mindy would have bet a hundred bucks he was queer—grinned and gestured toward the cages that hovered above the stage, where the go-go girls in their white fringed dresses and white boots gyrated above the band.

"Best scenery in all of California." He made the expected—extremely loud so anyone nearby could hear—joke. "Have you ever considered being one of those chicks?"

"I'd rather die," Mindy replied coolly. She twisted a Tareyton into her holder, held it out for a light. Since she'd done a Tareyton commercial—complete with black eye as she turned to the camera and snarled seductively, "I'd rather fight than switch!"—she was obligated to smoke them when she was in public. Then she settled back to watch the show for a few moments—let herself be seen, gaped at, envied—before joining it.

The first time she'd come to the Whisky, with Paula and some of the other kids from the beach movie, she'd felt like Alice in Wonderland, at once awkwardly big and timidly small for this crazy new scene. She'd literally walked out of her old life—there was still sand between her toes—into the new one she'd immediately decided was better. The life that she *deserved*—an urchin, an orphan, like Oliver Twist, suddenly learning that she had a wealthy family after all. The change in circumstances was *that* startling.

And that easy—all she had to do was step into it. It had been here all along. How had she not known it could be so easy?

That night, she and Paula and the kids mainly gawked. Johnny Rivers was playing, something soulful but electric. Between sets, a girl in the glass booth above the stage spun records—the Beatles, the Beach Boys, Jan and Dean. The girls in the cages didn't have official uniforms yet—the place had recently opened—so they wore their own clothes, mainly sheath dresses. Mindy and the other kids didn't get a table, but they stood on the fringes clutching sweaty drinks, gaping. There were movie stars there that night, too—Cary Grant was dancing the Frug, a dance Mindy had never seen before.

But mostly the Whisky crowd was made up of kids their own age, bright shiny things in their high school best, pretending to be grown-ups. Soon she and the gang were in the middle of the floor, losing themselves in the music, which was so loud, no one could carry on a conversation. And as she shook and shimmied—mimicking the other dancers because she didn't know that many moves, not yet—she savored the novelty of a world defined by walls, not beach and sky; glaring artificial lights and sounds; and kids her own age, kids in clothes straight out of fashion magazines, kids who laughed and chatted, when the music paused, about movies and records and restaurants and books and magazines instead of the size of waves or where the best swell could be found.

Mindy'd heard of hardly any of these things; at that point in her life she'd only ever eaten in a Howard Johnson's. As for books, well—as her mother said, who needed books (or television or movies) when the ocean was outside your door?

What a ridiculous life she had lived, she realized as she spun around, faster and faster, the room, the colored lights, and the amplified electric guitar all blurring into one crazy carousel of *now*, of potent urgency, of fantastical possibility. She was a high school dropout, she knew nothing of the real world. And who was to blame for that?

That night at the Whisky she tried a real drink, a cocktail, not warm beer or cheap wine. It was a sweet, sticky concoction—a mai tai—and she felt so sophisticated holding the tall, slim glass in her hands as she surveyed the dance floor. There was pure, blissful joy on every kid's face, an expression she'd never seen indoors, only outdoors on a day with bitchin' surf. The adults—including Cary Grant—were trying too hard to have fun, grimly smiling as they mopped the sweat from their brows. But the kids didn't care about sweat, they didn't need to force smiles; they were simply being young with no responsibilities, no expectations. And this moment, this place—this California, constantly reinventing itself—rewarded the young.

Mindy had never felt young; she'd never felt like a kid even when she was one. Always there was the responsibility for Ginger, the worry about being abandoned, the Plan. What would life be like without a plan? Without worry?

It was time she gave it a try, she decided, sipping that cool mai tai, putting the glass down on a table, and stepping out on the dance floor to take her rightful place with all the other glittering kids.

After that, things happened fast.

The director of the movie saw her on the dance floor that night—he was one of the old people there, at least forty, trying to look young and failing miserably; he saw her in real clothes and some makeup and her hair teased and sprayed courtesy of Paula. He didn't say much to her, only hello, but he watched her. And the next day, as she was getting ready to go out in the surf in that atrocious wig, doubling for the female star, he approached her.

"You're very good," he said. "Out there." He shrugged toward the water.

"I know. I mean, thanks."

"I have an idea. We could feature you a bit more in the next film. Do you have an agent?"

She laughed. "Of course not!"

"Get one, have him call my office."

So she did—for a pretty girl with an interested director, getting an agent was as easy as getting a suntan. All she needed to do was ask for some names. Soon enough, she was being featured in movies as the Girl in the Curl. She usually had one solo surfing sequence that was edited to look as dangerous as possible. The lead actor would be impressed and start to pant after her, which would cause the lead actress to get jealous and try the stunt herself (Mindy, still doubling in that wig), only to get in trouble and nearly drown, which then caused the lead actor to forget about the Girl in the Curl and run to rescue his beloved, who miraculously hadn't even gotten her hair wet.

They never billed her under her real name. One of the Donnelly Girls was now known as the Girl in the Curl, and Mindy only laughed about it. What was in a name, anyway, when she was booking magazine shoots and commercials, being featured on an album cover, getting a swimwear sponsorship—hovering on the fringe of real fame, not just California fame.

It was intoxicating. To be sought after, in a minor way—she had no illusions; she was no Annette Funicello in terms of fame, at least not yet; to be told she was pretty; to walk into Jax, where *everybody* shopped for the sleekest, tightest slacks, and be fawned over by salespeople; to go into a beauty shop for the first time (Jay Sebring's, the king of cool) and be shampooed and frosted and teased and sprayed, the stylist cooing about her amazing cheekbones, her long eyelashes— and those eyes like Elizabeth Taylor's; to have endless dates with handsome but dull actors who were more interested in looking into a mirror than at her, but she didn't really care, she was in it for the excitement of being seen, being admired, being envied.

It was all so much damn *fun.*

She was with normal people—that's what she told herself. Even though she was also aware that nobody in Southern California, especially not in Los Angeles, was what you could call *normal,* because they were all trying to be someone they weren't, aspiring to be *more*, to a perfection that was fake, but still, it was perfection, wasn't it? Perfect teeth, perfect breasts, perfect tans. They were golden, they were stars—they were on covers of magazines and record albums because they were California cool, California perfect. She and her female friends knew pasty-faced kids from the East Coast pinned up their pictures and wanted to be them.

California Girls, all of them.

She moved out of the apartment in Laguna, where she had taken to sleeping on the couch rather than share a room with her sister and mother. Mom had recovered from her accident, she seemed all right—at least that was what Mindy told herself. And if she wasn't, it wasn't Mindy's problem, was it?

Mom had absolved her of any responsibility or loyalty that night on Makaha.

She and Paula decided to share an apartment. It was small, two bedrooms and a kitchen and living room, on a road just off Sunset. One of those old apartment buildings from the thirties with a motor courtyard, a series of little bungalows. In addition to the Ford Mustang convertible she bought after her first movie as the Girl in the Curl, she drove a little Triumph motorcycle, cherry red, bought at a discount because she promised she'd mention it in every interview. She also had a new board with her own name on it, and Hobie was talking to her about an entire line of Girl in the Curl boards.

She was envied. No more the urchin changing into her bathing suit in the back of a car. Now all those old school friends wanted to *be* her, instead of pitying her.

She was a Surfer Girl—capital S, capital G, covered in stardust. Not a surfing girl, lowercase, lower-class.

Covered in sand.

She didn't surf all that much anymore, though, except for the movies and shoots or contests, where her presence was now a sensation even if she didn't always place; she was there to be seen, her agent told her bluntly. That was the only thing that mattered.

There was a lesson here. Probably. But then she shrugged. *Hollywood.* Wasn't that what happened to all of them, these bright, shimmering young people? Once they became famous for something, the fame prevented them from doing the thing, or at least, from doing it as purely and perfectly as they did in the beginning. It happened to musicians. It happened to actors.

It was happening to the Girl in the Curl.

Were there times she missed the old surfing days? Sure. No matter how much fun this all was, still she would think of that moment in Makaha, that exquisite ride when she was one with the ocean yet also master of it, and she was alone in a way that wasn't lonely, a singular star in the universe. She had never experienced a moment like it since. And it called to her, sometimes. The waves, the seagulls—they all seemed to call her name when she was surrounded by the cameras and the crew. A few times, she swore she heard, like a siren's song, *"Mindy, Mindy,"* coming from beyond the break.

Her life, for all the sheer fun in living it, was complicated now, in the way she'd always longed for it to be complicated—with dinner plans and parties and picnics and what shift should she wear tonight, what earrings, did she have a scarf that matched?

Life before—even with all the Mom stuff—had been simpler. Slower. She always seemed to be looking at a clock now. When before, they didn't even own one.

As far as the old gang, well—the less she saw of them, the better. They still straggled up to be extras, crash the craft table, or hang around the fringes of competitions to hoot and holler their disdain. Tom sometimes deigned to compete—no question, he still displayed the coolest style on a board, dancing up and down it like a cat. The crowds delighted in his cruelty when he steered right into another surfer's path. He once mooned the judges, which made everybody scream with delight. But it got him banned from competition. He proclaimed, loudly and arrogantly, to one and all, that this was the point. Surfing was corrupted; his gorgeous ass was the most beautiful thing about it.

Every time Tom pulled a stunt like this, Mindy's cachet went up with the sponsors. She was practically given engraved invitations to compete; *she* was the ideal they were pushing. Enviable, pretty, civilized, skilled, yes. But the skill wasn't quite as important as the other things.

Ginger was the biggest complication. Or, the absence of Ginger, the guilt but also the relief of abdicating responsibility for her. Mindy thought of Ginger often—in interviews, someone always brought up the Fabulous Donnelly Girls and asked about her mother. She was glad they hardly ever asked about her sister, because she wouldn't have known what to say—*I have no idea, I haven't seen her in a while, she's with these guys. She's smoking pot, and the last time I saw her she needed a bath.*

Because this is my *life now, finally, mine alone. And she doesn't fit in.*

Mindy dragged on the cigarette—she didn't particularly like smoking but she liked the way she *looked* while smoking—and continued to survey the crowd at the Whisky.

"Who's the singer?" She turned to Jack. Jack Daniels—she stifled a giggle by sipping her drink, her usual mai tai. She didn't even have to ask for it anymore; someone always brought it to her as soon as she entered.

"Some hippie chick, Janis somebody."

"She looks like she needs a bath." Mindy rolled her eyes as the girl onstage tore into a song with a surprisingly raspy voice, full of soul. She wore frayed bell-bottoms and a fringed vest—that typical San Francisco look that was so out of place in L.A. Her long curly hair was tangled in a way that reminded Mindy of her sister.

But the girl could sing; Mindy couldn't deny it.

She'd seen a few bands start out here at the Whisky and then explode into fame—she remembered when the Doors were the house band, already known for missing gigs because Jim Morrison was stoned out of his head. She'd seen Jefferson Airplane before Grace Slick, before "White Rabbit" and "Somebody to Love," when they were just another San Francisco band and everyone knew that the music scene was here in L.A., not up north.

The Whisky was where it was at, and she couldn't help herself from casually dropping information like that—that she knew Jefferson Airplane before Jefferson Airplane was cool. But if Mindy were being honest, she would have admitted that she liked the music at the Troubadour, a few blocks south on Santa Monica Boulevard, better. The Troubadour was where the folkies performed, but some of the folkies were kind of morphing into more of an electric sound. She'd seen Dylan there last year, and his music filled her head for days, grabbing hold of her brain, reverberating down to her heart.

How had she never heard of Bob Dylan before? It was tragic, that's what it was—how much she'd missed, before. Music. Poetry, too— one of the vacant actors she dated gave her a copy of Jack Kerouac's *Mexico City Blues*. He said his agent recommended he be seen reading it, but he couldn't understand it.

Mindy didn't really understand it either, but it prompted her to seek out other poets, and when she read Emily Dickinson she felt, for

the first time, that sanctity when you recognize yourself in the words
of another and know that you've been seen:

> Pain—has an Element of Blank—
> It cannot recollect
> When it begun—or if there were
> A time when it was not—

How empty she'd been, all those years. How lonely. Even with
Ginger holding on to her, preventing her from ever having the time
to learn, to experience—

Life.

The Troubadour wasn't as sleek and shiny as the Whisky. It was
more about the music, so older celebrities didn't go there much—
there was no way you'd see a perspiring Sammy Davis, Jr., doing the
Hully-Gully. It was like taking a day off from work, in a way, to relax
at the Troubadour; she didn't doll herself up as much, she went with
people she liked, not people she should be seen with, and she drank
warm beer, which was practically the house drink, and it brought
back memories, but not so many they overwhelmed her, only sweet
reminiscences of something lost but still within reach should she ever
care to go looking for it.

But she wasn't going back. Not even after what happened to
Mom. Ginger, though . . .

Mindy sighed, remembering the night that Tom Riley had come
stumbling into the Whisky. She had no idea how he got in; usually
the bouncer blocked people who were that strung out. The parking
lot around back was for them, a murky place full of dealers and kids
with matted hair and dirty clothes.

But there Tom was, swaying in front of her table. He had cleaned
himself up; he was wearing a shiny shirt with a collar and sported his

hair slicked back, and he was walking, comically, almost like Charlie Chaplin, in stiff black loafers. She had never seen him wearing anything other than sandals before.

"So there she is, the supreme traitor of all time. Benedict Arnold in a slutty dress."

"Hey." Mindy's date that night—she forgot his name, he was a singer and had had one song chart—started to rise, but Mindy tugged him back down.

"I can deal with this," she assured him as he glared at the Surf God. "Hello, Tom," she said coolly, eying him as brazenly as he was eying her—but there was no gleam of lust in *her* eyes. He was ridiculous in these clothes. He was a surfer who should remain a surfer primarily because he looked good in board shorts and nothing else. Clothes diminished him. She couldn't imagine what she'd ever seen in him, back when she had that schoolgirl crush.

"I've come to save you," Tom intoned. He was sweaty; he kept tugging at his collar. But suddenly he focused his gaze on her in that intense—comically intense, she thought now—way, and he lowered his voice to that smooth croon. "I've come to save you, to show you the way back. I'll take you back, I want you to know that. You are among the chosen. You always were, but you wouldn't see it."

"Back to what?" Mindy gave an exaggerated yawn, knowing it would infuriate him. He swallowed hard; his Adam's apple almost sliced through his tanned skin.

"Back to the purity of our way of life. The life you were born into, the life your mother made possible. The true religion, the sand and the surf, nothing else. Mother Sun, our Mother Sun—I am the light and the way, and I choose you."

Her date—Johnny something—laughed. Tom's fists balled up.

"Go away, little boy," she told Tom, and suddenly he sprang on them, lurching across the wobbly table, spilling drinks. Johnny rose and decked him with a swift, sure right, and then Tom was splayed on his back, his face mottled and spittle foaming at his mouth.

"You bitch! You superficial bitch!" he screamed as he lay on his back like a helpless crab.

Someone hauled him up—no one was too alarmed, fights broke out here all the time—and he shrugged off any help. Mumbling, weaving, he started to head for the exit.

"Wait!" Mindy couldn't stop herself; she ran after him, grabbing his arm. "How's Ginger? Is she all right?"

"Don't worry about your sister. She's in a far better place than you are, with your gooey face and sickening clothes. You should see yourself. You were a goddess once—God, to watch you out there, it was like looking at the Venus de Milo. Now you're nothing but tinsel. Flimsy tinsel, here one day, in the garbage can the next."

These words pierced her as had nothing else he'd said. He was suddenly clear-eyed; he spoke reasonably, without any of his usual bullshit. But he was also wrong, so wrong. She'd been a wild thing then, one of an untamed bunch of outsiders.

Now she belonged. People wanted her. Even better—

People wanted to *be* her. Tinsel and all.

"Tell Ginger—tell her—"

But Tom was gone, the liquor on the floor wiped up. Her date was already out on the dance floor, beckoning to her, and she moved, her hips leading, feet following. Soon she was swallowed up in the crowd and when they left, five teenyboppers asked for her autograph and she signed it as she always did:

Hang Ten! Love, the Girl in the Curl.

. . .

"Penny for your thoughts."

Mindy rolled her eyes. This idiot—Jack Daniels—was pretty in that vapid blue-eyed-blond-with-nothing-going-on-upstairs way. She'd never been attracted to blond men. Always brunets, like Tom with his light brown hair or Jimmy Cho.

"Let's get out of here." Suddenly the Whisky was too loud, too hot, too smoky; she'd put her own cigarette out but it didn't matter, her hair and clothes would reek of smoke anyway. Desperate for fresh air, she rose and pushed her way out of the club, not even looking to see if her date was following her.

Outside, she inhaled, but it wasn't fresh at all; the skunky smell of pot fermented the air. The street was packed; kids—some bright and shiny but others with stringy hair and tattered clothes, obviously strung out—were milling about on the sidewalk like a bunch of zombies. On Sunset, a parade of cars, mostly convertibles, rolled so slowly by—the lanes were jam-packed—she could walk faster than they drove. The night rang with the cacophony of car horns, music blasting from radios, catcalls, hoots, laughter. It was almost louder outside than in.

Lowering her head, she battled her way past the line of people waiting to get into the Whisky; she was a salmon swimming upstream, but she didn't care. She didn't know where she was going—her date had driven her here—but she wasn't that far from the Troubadour. It would be a hike, especially in her sparkly silver Mary Janes with the slippery soles, and parts of the route were sketchy, but she couldn't think of anywhere else to go.

"Hey, watch it, blondie," someone called out as she clipped an outstretched hand.

"Sorry," she mumbled, but then she heard her name—

"Mindy? Mindy Donnelly?"

She stopped. When people called out to her on the street it was always "Aren't you the Girl in the Curl?"

"Mindy? Hey! It's Jimmy. Jimmy Cho."

"Jimmy?" Mindy stopped, looked up. His eyes—dark brown, the kind of eyes you could get lost in if you didn't have a map—were the same. But he was a man now, not a skinny teenager. Taller than her, but not too tall; he was wearing a striped short-sleeve button-down, with the buttons undone to show off his smooth, muscled chest. His hair was jet-black and the bangs swooped down into his eyes. His jaw was heavier, more determined, and he smiled more easily than she remembered.

"Wow," she said, feeling a blush steal her cool, wondering if it showed beneath her makeup. "You're grown-up."

"So are you." He smiled approvingly. "The Curl Girl, right?"

"The Girl in the Curl." She shrugged, suddenly aware of how silly it sounded. "It's something they came up with for those movies. It's kind of dopey."

"Nah, you could never be dopey. Remember, guys?" He turned to his friends. Mindy didn't recognize most of them, although one was vaguely familiar, a smaller young man with high cheekbones and the thickest hair Mindy had ever seen. "This chick won Makaha, what was it . . . ?"

"Nineteen sixty-two," Mindy supplied. Five years ago, almost.

"Yeah, you were good."

"So were you. You should have won."

"Yeah, well, same old story. California dudes invented surfing, right? And California Girls, too?"

Mindy studied the pavement; someone's spilled beer—she fervently hoped that was what it was, anyway—was trickling down a crack and pooling at her feet; she stepped away from it so her shoes wouldn't get soiled. She was ashamed, all of a sudden; her win at Makaha had been a catalyst for a lot of things, some she didn't feel like contemplating because they were wrapped up in Mom and Ginger and the end of the Plan and her abandoning them. But it was also a catalyst for this life she was leading now—this *tinsel* life, if she believed Tom Riley, but it was certainly an enviable life. *Anyone* would say it was more enviable than the life Jimmy Cho was probably leading. So why did she feel so off balance?

Jack Daniels came panting up, escalating her embarrassment.

"Hey, Mindy, why'd you take off like that? Are these guys bothering you?" He frowned suspiciously at Jimmy and his friends, who grinned insolently back at him.

"No, nothing like that." Mindy sighed in exasperation. "Jimmy Cho, this is Jack Daniels," she said, and steeled herself for the laughter.

"Oh, hey—you're that guy on TV!" Jimmy said, and his smile seemed genuine, anyway.

"Thank you," Jack said, and Mindy wanted to hit him with her purse. "Would you like an autograph?"

"Nah, man, that's OK. Nice to meet you, though."

Jack's blandly handsome face scrunched up in confusion, and Mindy had to stifle a giggle; Jimmy caught her eye and she knew that in a minute she would be guffawing, so she quickly turned Jack around and pointed him back toward the Whisky.

"You go back. I'm OK, I just wanted a change of scene. You know how it is. I'll see you later, OK? At that party up in the Hills tomorrow?"

"You sure?"

"Yes." And Jack didn't hide his eagerness to get back to the beautiful people, away from the riffraff that was Jimmy Cho and his friends standing around on a sidewalk with no one taking their pictures; he gave Mindy a cursory peck on the cheek and left with one last benevolent wave to the little people.

"He's an idiot," she explained to Jimmy and his friends, and they all hooted with laughter.

"I didn't want to say anything." Jimmy winked at her, and suddenly, Mindy didn't want to be anywhere else; any impulse to be alone vanished.

"So what are you doing in California?"

"You say it like it's a surprise. Breaking news: Hawaiians invade the mainland."

"No, I—I didn't mean it that way," Mindy stammered, but then she saw a devilish twinkle in his eyes and she knew he was teasing her. "Jerk," she said, playfully swatting him with her purse.

"Sorry. We're gonna watch the Malibu Invitational next weekend—we weren't invited, big surprise. But we're here to support Dave. He's gonna rock it, gonna take home the big prize, aren't you, man?" Jimmy slapped the familiar-looking guy on the back.

"Oh, that's why I know you! You're David Nuuhiwa." Mindy had seen his photo in some surfing magazine; he was a Californian who'd done well at the Worlds in San Diego last year. Why had she assumed he wasn't from around here, just because he looked like Jimmy?

"That's what they tell me," Dave said coolly.

"You going to compete?" Jimmy asked Mindy.

"Of course!" She could have bitten her tongue off; she sounded so insufferable.

"Of course. I bet they sent you an invitation on a white horse, surf princess."

"Stop it." His teasing was getting a little annoying. She didn't have anything to be ashamed of. She was good, dammit. Or at least, she had been and could still be, when she concentrated on it. And what was wrong with having some fun, making a little money, and enjoying a little fame? She wondered if Jimmy would be so patronizing if she were a guy.

"Where were you going? Was your date getting too handsy?"

"No, he's—my agent set it up, he represents us both. You know, it's good for business, all that. Being seen, I mean."

"Being seen with a cool white guy. Yeah, I get it." Jimmy didn't smile when he said that.

"Being seen with a TV star."

"So why don't you want to be seen with him now?"

"I don't know, it felt—" Mindy shook her head, then peered up at Jimmy. Staring into his brown eyes, she was astonished by a desire to throw away every map she possessed—her map to fame—and get lost with him, go somewhere quiet and dark with ocean breezes, the surf insistently licking their bare feet with its cool, foamy tongue.

A horn blared, brakes squealed as a crowd of kids thronged into the street, and suddenly she was back on the Sunset Strip on a Friday night. Back in her sparkly Mary Janes, her white stockings like paint, suffocating her skin. Her fake eyelashes so heavy, it was an effort to keep her eyes wide open.

"I don't know," she finished lamely.

"Look, do you want to go somewhere to have a drink? Or a cup of coffee? I can ditch these guys, right?" His friends grinned and made wolf whistles, but Jimmy looked earnest—his face was honest. The kind of face that couldn't pretend. He would have been an awful actor. But he was probably a nice guy—she didn't really know.

All of a sudden, she wanted to find out.

Curiosity—it was a surprising emotion, one she'd forgotten. Curiosity about another human being, anyway. None of the people in this new world of hers inspired that—ambition was the trait they all shared and all they could talk about. She knew them because she knew herself.

She knew nothing about Jimmy Cho other than the fact that she wanted to know *everything* about Jimmy Cho.

"Sure. We can catch up. I know a place, up a bit closer to the Playboy Club. You ever been there?"

"To the Playboy Club? Girl, are you stoned? How could someone like me get into a place like that?"

"I—sorry." She was an idiot. Of course he'd never been there. She was one of the beautiful people, and he—

Was not.

But right now, he was the one she wanted to be with, so she took his hand—it was so warm and strong—and pulled him through the hordes of kids blocking the sidewalks, not moving. Standing in line to get into clubs like the Whisky or the London Fog. There used to be another, Pandora's Box, but it was demolished last year after the riots.

Last year, the city, prompted by local businesses, had grown uneasy about all the drugs and doped-up kids strangling the area and tried to instill a curfew, but that only made it worse. Riots broke out—even Peter Fonda and Jack Nicholson demonstrated and were arrested. Things were pretty much back to normal now, except that there were more hippies than before. Older movie stars didn't come to the Whisky as much. They holed up in their mansions in the hills, afraid to dip their toes in the dirty, swirling miasma of the Strip.

Still hanging on to Jimmy, she expertly steered them east up Sunset. Jimmy kept exclaiming at the crowds, the incessant honking, the ineffective police presence; groups of kids would roll into the street, willy-nilly, not caring about the parking lot of cars. It used to be that the Strip was known for cruising, but it took hours to get from one end of it to the other these days.

"Why do they all come here? Isn't there anywhere else in L.A. for them to go?" Jimmy shouted as they inched their way toward Ben Frank's.

"Music. It's the music. There's no place like it on earth—you know that TV show *The Monkees*? It was practically born at this place."

"What do you mean?"

"I saw the audition notices—they were looking for Ben Frank's types."

"What does that mean?"

"You'll see."

Finally they reached Ben Frank's, a place right out of a science fiction movie. A building with an eerie orange roof, sharply pitched, and a futuristic needle planted outside the door with signs reading *Ben Frank's* and *24 Hour Dining*. It was crowded, but not nearly as packed as it would be later when the clubs let out.

Mindy and Jimmy pushed their way through the waiting area, where the benches were full of hungry kids. "Look, there's two spots at the counter!" She spotted the holy land, left Jimmy behind, and ran to grab the stools before a middle-aged man in a baggy suit and tie, accompanied by a woman with a Lady Bird Johnson hairstyle, could; she neatly slid onto one seat just as the man put his hands on the back of it.

"Oops," she said, fluttering those heavy eyelashes right up at him. "Looks like I got here first!"

The man smiled uncertainly, but as soon as Jimmy joined her, his putty-like features formed a disapproving scowl.

"You'd better watch yourself, young lady," he scolded, nodding toward Jimmy. "You look like a nice girl. Do your parents know who you're with?"

"Listen, mister, you'd better shut your damn mouth—"

"Ooh, it's too bad I'm an orphan," Mindy said with a woeful pout, as she grabbed Jimmy's iron-like arm, preventing him from taking a swing. His every muscle was straining.

"Young lady," the man sputtered, taking several steps back away from Jimmy. Then he grabbed his wife's arm.

"Oh, and go fuck yourself," Mindy called after them. She started to laugh at the sight of the pair as they scurried away like bugs. She quickly gestured to one of the waitresses behind the counter for menus, and the moment was over.

But not forgotten.

"That son of a bitch," Jimmy snarled, plopping down on the stool next to her. "And you didn't need to fight my battle for me, you know. I'm perfectly capable. I do it all the time."

"Sorry," she said with a shrug. "It just seemed the thing to do. This isn't usually that kind of place."

"What kind of place?"

"You know, where people judge, get uptight."

"You mean show their racist asses?"

"Yeah. This isn't Alabama, this is California. And Ben Frank's is usually pretty laid-back."

"If you say so." He pushed his menu away, asked for coffee, and Mindy did the same while she searched her mind for a way to ease the tension. All around them people were talking, laughing—over in one booth there must have been fifteen people all squished together, and one of them had a pair of drumsticks he was drumming on the table, keeping up a lively staccato beat to the conversation. There were girls as glammed up as she was, but also girls who looked like they'd driven straight down from San Francisco without stopping to freshen up—long straight hair parted in the middle, peasant blouses, jeans. Boys with hair almost as long, too. You could certainly spot a San Francisco hippie, she thought.

But most of the kids were younger than she was, striking a middle note in attire—boys in paisley shirts, their hair like the Beatles', long but only to the collar. Teenage girls in short skirts and shiny boots. Pairing up for a Friday night on the Strip.

"Most of the musicians come here after the clubs close. I saw Nancy Sinatra once. And Sonny and Cher—he really is that short," she said to Jimmy. Then she realized how schoolgirl—how *starstruck*—she sounded and wished she hadn't.

"Cool."

"So, where are you staying while you're here?"

"With my friend Howie and his girl, Jen. They're great."

"Nice."

The coffee came; she stirred hers to cool it, but Jimmy started drinking his piping hot. He kept staring moodily across the counter; his dark brows were knit together. No longer was he the confident, teasing hunk she'd bumped into on the street; now he was a coiled, seething—wounded—young man. Just because of what that idiot geezer had said. How stupid, how ignorant, people were.

"Look, I—you don't—try to forget that asshole," she said.

"Forget? You know how many times a day people say stupid shit like that to me over here? They either ask me if my folks run a laundry, or they wonder if I know Don Ho. And the surfing—forget it."

"What do you mean?"

"We aren't welcome, that's what I mean. You know, haoles have been surfing our beaches for years—your mom was one of the first. What did we do other than welcome them with open arms, because we always welcome white people with open arms, because we are stupid, pathetic *Hawaiians*? It's like we forgot what happened when the missionaries came. White people mean money, money we can't seem to find a way to make on our own. So we swim out to their ships, we make our sisters dress up in hula skirts and throw leis around them when they get off the planes. We brothers become beach boys; we take uptight white ladies out on surfboards, paddle them around, rub up against them so they'll get horny and want to lay us and give us big fistfuls of dollars as thanks and also to keep quiet so their husbands don't know. That's about the best we can do, if we stay. But where the hell are we supposed to go? Not here. Here, we're told to go back home where we belong. By skinny white boys who act like they invented surfing, who'd still be splashing around in kiddie pools if it wasn't for us."

"Not everyone is like that, Jimmy. I'm not."

"Just because you told those geezers to fuck off doesn't mean you don't think like everybody else."

"Let me speak for myself, OK? Don't put thoughts in my brain or words in my mouth. We just met, really. Before, we were kids. You don't know anything about me. Jesus." Mindy sipped her coffee. It tasted bitter; she realized she'd forgotten to put sugar in it but she didn't want to in front of Jimmy. Which was ridiculous. Why did she care so much about what he thought?

"OK, so tell me about you. Who are you? *What* are you? Look, it was admirable that you told those geezers off, but I could have done it myself, I don't need the Curl Girl to do that—"

"The Girl in the Curl," Mindy said sharply.

"Whatever. It was nice, OK? I hope you feel good about it. I hope it helps you sleep at night. I—I don't know, I guess I overreacted. I should be used to it by now." Jimmy exhaled loudly. He swiveled on his counter stool, turning to face her. "So tell me. Let's start again. Who are you, Mindy Donnelly?"

"I'm a surfer. Like you."

"Nah, not like me." He didn't sound superior or smug, simply matter-of-fact. "Not anymore, anyway. Maybe you could have been, once. Look at you now—you're gorgeous, of course. But I didn't recognize you—I wasn't sure it was you until one of the guys said it was, and it was only because he remembered you from those idiotic movies."

"I'm glad you did recognize me. I'm really glad."

"Yeah?" Suddenly Jimmy's face cleared; he broke into that charismatic smile that made his eyes crinkle up. "Well, I am, too."

They didn't say anything for a few minutes but it wasn't an uneasy silence anymore. It was the silence between two people who aren't in a hurry, because they know where they're going. Somewhere that will wait for them for as long as necessary.

"You said you're competing at Malibu?" he asked.

"Yeah. I need to get out on the water this week, though. It's been about a month since I have. Too busy."

"Too busy being the Curl—I mean, the *Girl* in the Curl. What's that like? I mean it—I'm not teasing now," he said, and she was relieved that he knew he'd been hard on her earlier. It meant that he really was the same Jimmy she'd met the night she'd won Makaha. Maybe more brittle because of necessity, but still kind. Still understanding. Still someone she wanted to know better.

"Oh, it's—well, it's thrilling, that's what it is," she said, laughing, and to her relief, he laughed, too. "I mean it—it's fun! Oh, Jimmy, I get to meet so many people—I taught Elvis how to surf, can you believe it?"

"What's he like?"

"Shy, kind of sweet. He asked me out, to this crummy little fried chicken place in Ventura. He said he hated L.A. nightlife. He was cute, like a little boy—he held my hand the whole night—but he didn't ask me out again."

"Ooh, cold. Ditched by Elvis!"

"He couldn't surf at all, so it wouldn't have worked out."

"Is that a requirement, then? Does Mindy Donnelly only get serious about guys who can surf?"

"Maybe."

"Good." Jimmy nodded, smiling softly to himself, and Mindy felt her stomach flutter, her skin warm. She hadn't been attracted to a man in so long. Not since Tom Riley, actually. All the dates she'd gone on with famous and fame-adjacent guys had been fun—what girl wouldn't enjoy being seen with the dreamy oldest son from *My Three Sons*? But the fun in dating like that was mostly in the preparation—choosing the right dress, the makeup, the hair, the excitement of knowing she'd be photographed, the fun of looking through the papers the next day to see if she was mentioned. The men were all unfailingly polite but also unfailingly as interested in her as she was in them, sexually—mainly, not very. A few dates ended in the bedroom but usually it seemed expected, as if to put an exclamation point on the entire evening: *We're young and having fun and our parents can go to hell!* But she'd never felt physical attraction toward any of them like she was feeling now.

Sitting next to Jimmy, her body leaning toward him as if he were a magnet, she was helpless to break away. And she knew that this time, the anticipation wouldn't be nearly as enjoyable as the resolution. Everything about being with him felt different—she was relaxed and ticklish at the same time, her body happily anticipating something more while her usually feverish mind slowed down a tick or two. She wasn't constantly surveying the room to see who was watching her; she wasn't checking her reflection in a window or adjusting the hem of her skirt or reapplying her frosted lipstick or laughing too loudly or dancing too wildly or indulging in any of the little habits meant to attract attention, to further her career, that she'd fallen into lately. Right now, she was merely herself. Mindy.

Not the Girl in the Curl.

It felt like home. A home she'd never known, but a home whose every inch she was aching to explore. A place where someone would look out for her, instead of the other way around.

She sighed deeply—and then blushed, because Jimmy turned to her with such a quizzical expression on his face.

"What? Is something wrong?"

She shook her head. She found she didn't possess the words that could explain to him just how right everything was.

Someone had put a nickel in the jukebox; the mellow, close harmonies of "California Dreamin'" started to play, weaving in and out of the noisy diner chatter like wisps of gossamer. Soothing.

Seductive.

7

"And the champion in the women's division is . . . Mindy Donnelly! The Girl in the Curl!"

She grinned, ran up to the rickety podium, took the plaque from the requisite bikini-clad Miss Malibu. Mindy was also in a bikini; she'd taken off the competition T-shirt with her number on it to reveal the newest bikini from Jantzen, one of her sponsors. It was a cute yellow and green floral, and she knew she looked great in it with her tanned skin and daffodil-colored hair.

Back from the podium, standing on the beach, she was surrounded by photographers, courtesy of her publicist. Holding the plaque up—so it wouldn't cover the bikini—she beamed, turning now this way, now that way. But her eyes were searching the crowd, looking for Jimmy.

He was the reason she'd won today. He'd gotten her out on the water each day this past week, pushing her, challenging her. Riding alongside her, so she was forced to keep up with him. Bobbing up and down on his own board in the shallows, surveying her rides with a critical eye.

"You look great. Like a statue out there. But that's not surfing," he told her once. "Girl, it's changed. You've got to do more than ride cleanly. You've got to take more chances, make the board move, cut left, cut right."

"Malibu doesn't have the right kind of waves for that," she'd protested. They hadn't practiced in Malibu—not at Surfrider, anyway;
they were farther up the coast at a break called Zuma. It was less
crowded than Surfrider, but with the same kind of long, consistent
ride.

"Yeah. I think you're more of a big-wave surfer, to be honest. Like
at Makaha."

"I don't know about that," she'd said modestly, but her pulse
quickened, remembering her win there in the big surf.

They were sitting on the beach, cross-legged, taking a break; their
surfboards were planted in the sand, shading them from the sun.
Gulls cried, and the incessant waves washed over the rocks with the
comforting regularity that felt like being back in the womb—like a
mother's heartbeat. Her mother's heartbeat, the pounding of the
waves—they were once one and the same to Mindy. Her own heartbeat slowed down, keeping time with the waves. She realized she'd
been tense for years, probably. Her body so tightly coiled, an engine
striving for ever more fame, acclaim, photos. Admiration.

These long days spent in the surf had stirred up so many emotions
and memories. The memories of the guilt she felt when cutting
school as a girl to be with her mother, Ginger always tagging along,
not able to keep up, a constant worry for Mindy. The first days they
learned to surf, the most time they'd ever spent with Carol. The tension in her stomach, wondering if it would last, if the Plan would
work. Would her mother get annoyed or bored and leave again?

Mostly, however, she was content that week. Blissful, even. Because she was with Jimmy rather than her pathetic excuse for a
mother. Jimmy was a god on the water—she loved to watch him, he
was so beautiful, so powerful and graceful but in a casual way, as if
he simply couldn't help himself. He rose in such a fluid manner, and

he leaned so far on the rails he could drag his hand through the white foam. He cut and turned with such ease, he looked like a water creature out there and not just a guy on a surfboard.

But even better than watching him in the water was sitting with him like this, sheltered from the sun, neither of them speaking. It was the silences she cherished most, because she realized all she did was talk, chatter, natter, all day long—with Paula in the apartment, at her agent's, her publicist's, on commercial shoots, shouting on the dance floor at the Whisky. She talked and talked and didn't say a thing worth listening to. Nobody did. For her, and the others like her, the music they listened to was their deep thinking, their commentary on the world—*We Can Work It Out with the Sound of Silence on the Sloop John B this Monday Monday while we Paint It Black during Summer in the City in our Yellow Submarine.*

But with Jimmy, such inane chatter would spoil everything. Their silences were too comfortable to ruin with words. Their language was the language of youthful bodies pushing themselves to the max, of seagulls crying and sandpipers running on their alien legs, of water glistening like the glass shards of broken dreams, the broken dreams of those who'd tried to fly too high. *Their* dreams would never be broken, because with Jimmy, Mindy knew where she belonged. She belonged on the water, the mermaid instead of the sun goddess. With Jimmy, somehow it wasn't shameful. With Jimmy, it was perfect.

They never even kissed, those long, golden days. They sat so close together she could feel the sun radiating off his skin, their sand-covered toes playfully tickling each other. Sometimes they fell asleep with the sun as their blanket. Jimmy snored, softly, and she wondered if she did, too.

But he never made a move. She was glad about that. Because that would have been too clumsy and expected. Not that she didn't long to kiss him, to touch him, to be covered by him and not the sun. But somehow, during those days in the water and on the beach, she rediscovered her truest talent—"You were born to be a surfer," he told her, and it wasn't anything she didn't already know, only something she'd tried to run away from, but Jimmy called her back; she ran toward it, and him. And in doing so, she discovered her true love. It would have been one beautiful thing too many if they'd given in to their desires then.

She knew he felt the same way. He would look at her with eyes so full of wonder while she lay beside him, eyes full of lust. But he would only reach out to brush some sand off her shoulder, perhaps as if that was all he could trust himself to do.

She'd never known what a gentleman was, until she knew Jimmy Cho.

As her name was being called, over and over, she listened for his voice above all others, and finally she heard it.

"Mindy! You did it!"

"*We* did it," she shouted, spotting him over the shoulder of one of the photographers. Pushing her way through the crowd, she let him lift her up in a triumphant hug, and it was the first time she felt his warm skin against hers, and it triggered something inside her— usually she enjoyed this part, the photographs and the interviews and her sponsors making her pose with their products, signing autographs.

Today she was impatient to run away with Jimmy somewhere private and let that one last, beautiful moment complete the tapestry they'd woven together this week.

"I'm so proud of you," he exclaimed, setting her down. "You were great out there. Really great."

"I wish—"

But before she could say what she wished for, she was being tugged toward a VW bug that was parked on a platform on the sand. The Malibu VW dealership wanted her to pose with the car; the suited, perspiring dealership owner was dangling keys in front of her like they were diamonds, telling her something about coming in on Monday to see about taking one of these babies home, at cost.

She glanced back at Jimmy, who was laughing, waving his hands to indicate it was all right, he'd wait.

Mindy smiled her expert smile, sucking in her stomach, squaring her shoulders, still holding the plaque.

"You look just like Mom," a familiar voice called out, and after the camera clicked, Mindy raised her hand to shield her eyes, searching for her sister.

"Ginger!"

Ignoring the photographer, who pleaded for one more, Mindy ran through the sand toward Ginger. Her baby sister, with that tangle of curls hanging over her face, although the curls were tangled more from lack of shampoo than from salt water and humidity, was grinning at her. Ginger was wearing an old bikini, so worn it was almost see-through, and Mindy wished she had a sweater or a shirt with her so she could cover her sister up.

Hide her. Keep her safe. Keep her from other people's eyes.

Because Ginger was a mess. Not only the once-white suit that was now a grayish beige. Not merely the dirty hair. But her curves were less ample; she'd lost weight. Her pelvic bones rose in sharp relief over the top of her bikini bottom. Her nails were short, bitten off. There were bruises on her arms, yellowed splotches dotting her tanned skin.

"Ginger, my God."

There was no use hiding her shock, and Ginger didn't seem surprised by it. She crossed her arms over her chest, nodding. Waiting, as if she expected something more.

"How—how are you?"

"I'm OK," Ginger replied. "We're OK."

"We're—you mean Tom." It wasn't a question but an accusation.

"Yes, of course. What did you think I meant?"

"Where is he?"

"He's—he's—" Ginger couldn't, or wouldn't, complete the sentence. But her big blue eyes filled with tears, and she glanced away, toward the ocean, wiping them with her index finger. "He had to go away for a couple of days. I would have gone with him, but— I wanted to see you. He was mad about that, but he had to go, so— here I am."

"I'm glad, Ginger. Truly glad."

"You looked great out there. I knew you'd win."

"Thanks, I did—I felt good. *It* felt good. It's been a while since I took a competition seriously. It's mostly been for fun, for publicity— you know how it is."

Ginger's eyes widened as she took in the VW behind Mindy, the plaque in her hands, the photographer still calling her name. Then she grinned.

"No, I have no idea how it is, but I think it's cool. I really do—all your success. Tom thinks it's putrid, that you've sold out and are dangerous. I hate that he thinks that, but I do get where he's coming from."

"He's jealous," Mindy said as she realized it for the first time.

"No, no." Ginger shook her head violently. "It's just that he thinks—and I do, too, of course, except for you—that commercialism is the end of surfing, of what surfing should be. That these competitions and the movies and the clubs like Windansea, they're polluting the beaches, the water—look at it out there!"

Mindy gazed out at the surf; yes, it was brimming with tanned bodies on boards, some splashing around and laughing, others paddling out, but the lineup was so crowded it wasn't defined at all. The surf broke with its Malibu regularity, neat, clean sets, but the water was so crowded it was impossible for anyone to ride all the way in. The beach, too, was a maze of towels, bright Styrofoam coolers, Coke bottles, transistor radios all blaring different stations, kids making sandcastles and teenagers having picnics. It was a far cry from the first time she'd seen Malibu.

"It's just today," she told Ginger, even as she knew that wasn't exactly true; Malibu was like this all the time now. "They said there were a thousand people out this weekend to watch the tournament."

"Anyway." Ginger sighed, as if the conversation was too much for her without Tom to feed her his words. "How's Mom?"

"I have no idea." Mindy plopped down on the sand, and Ginger followed suit. Mindy felt like a little girl, suddenly; she dug in the sand with a stick, making letters and silly shapes. She drew a grid for tic-tac-toe, grinned at Ginger, and they began to play; when one game was done she would smooth the sand and they would start another. Most of the time, she let Ginger win.

"I figured you would have checked in with her."

"Why? Because I'm the responsible one?"

"Well—yes."

"Not anymore. Carol Donnelly can go—never mind." Mindy hated that she felt so gutted, still. Some wounds time can't heal.

"Mindy, what happened between you two?"

"Never mind—it doesn't concern you." Although it did, of course. But Mindy couldn't stop trying to protect her sister, even now. "I'm sure she's fine, she has that friend who checks in on her, and DeeDee. Besides, the accident was a couple of years ago. I am surprised she isn't here today." And suddenly she was. She hadn't even registered the fact that her mother was not in one of the judges' chairs.

It was the only time they saw each other—at surfing competitions. They were always polite. Like cordial neighbors occasionally encountering each other at the park. But Mindy was always surrounded by other people now, begging for her attention or telling her to go pose for a photo. She didn't have to see her mother for very long, thank God.

"One of the guys said he saw her at Brooks Street, but she wasn't surfing. She was just sitting on the sand, watching," Ginger offered.

"That doesn't sound like her."

"No, it doesn't."

"It was so stupid of her," she burst out. "It was all her fault. Surfing at night, by herself. She of all people should have known better. Why should we worry about her? She never worried a bit about us. She never gave a damn."

"I guess."

"I send her money," Mindy reminded Ginger defensively. "It's more than she deserves."

"Mom would never ask us for help, even if she needed it," Ginger replied reasonably.

"I don't want to talk about Mom today, OK? I want to talk about you. Where are you staying? Still in that shack up the road? Are you eating enough? Do you need money?"

"We're fine," Ginger said, just as defensive. As if she couldn't see herself—and probably, she couldn't. Mindy didn't imagine there was a mirror in that shack. She shuddered to think of the bathing and toilet options. "We have enough to live the way we want—that's all that's important."

"How do you manage it? Is Tom working?"

"We manage it," Ginger said, a bit more testily.

"I can give you some—I don't have my purse with me but I can stop by and—"

"Don't," Ginger said sharply.

"So, I guess you guys have surfed some pretty cool spots, then. Have you gone up to Santa Barbara? Or down to La Jolla? I guess that's what Tom wants, right—to follow the waves? That's his ideal."

"We do," Ginger said, nodding. "You know I'm not like you out there. I can't keep up with Tom. Some of the other guys, from the old gang, they've moved on now. A lot of people have from those days. I hear Gidget even went to college!"

"Yeah." Mindy grinned. Kathy Kohner, the original Gidget, was married now.

"Do you wish you'd gone to college?" Ginger asked. "I think you could have. Not me. But you're smart enough."

"I would have had to graduate high school first," Mindy said sourly. Mom hadn't exactly encouraged her to drop out, back when she was really starting to surf competitively. But she hadn't discouraged her, either. One more thing to blame her for. "I wish a lot of things. I wish we'd had a different childhood. I wish Dad remembered that we're alive."

They hadn't seen their father in a couple of years; he was remarried, with two toddlers. She assumed he paid Mom something in alimony. How else could she afford that apartment?

Not that it was any of Mindy's concern.

"I wish you would come live with me and forget about Tom Riley." Mindy blurted it out, surprising herself even more. "My life, it's so different now from when we were growing up, so fun—and you'd be a natural in front of the camera, my agent could get you some modeling gigs, I'm sure of it. There's room for you in my apartment, Paula wouldn't mind. Only come home with me today, OK? I miss you." Mindy could put Ginger out of her mind when she was being swept up in the current of minor celebrity. But seeing her here, touching her but knowing that she was somehow out of reach—

Now she missed her with an ache that invaded her very bones.

"I miss you, too." Ginger's hand reached toward hers, and Mindy clasped it. Just like when they were small, and waiting, shivering, for their mother to remember to pick them up from swimming lessons. She'd always felt so sure of herself, of her ability to steer herself and her sister through the shoals of childhood. She'd come up with the Plan, hadn't she? And it had worked, for a long while.

But the Plan had only been to get through childhood without being taken in by the authorities. She'd thought that once they became adults, life would be easier, that they'd be safe. Sitting next to her sister, though—smelling her body odor; taking in the bruises, suspiciously like fingerprints, on Ginger's arm—she realized she'd been a fool. Her sister needed caring for *now* more than ever. And in Mindy's absence, she'd turned to the exact wrong person.

"What do you say? Come home with me. We'll get all dolled up, we'll go out for dinner. My treat. Then we'll stay up all night talking and planning."

"No," Ginger whispered. She gazed out at the ocean. "I can't. Tom needs me."

"No, he doesn't."

"Yes, he does! He needs me more than I need him, only he doesn't realize it. And that's wonderful—remember what Dad said, that one time? 'Never fall in love with someone who doesn't need you'? Well, Tom needs me. He needs me to feed him, to comfort him, to keep him balanced. He needs me to be there for him when he comes home. He needs me for—"

"What does he do for you?" Mindy wanted to shake her sister until her teeth chattered. She knew Ginger was a weaker person than she was—hadn't she always known that? And hadn't Mindy always delighted in it, too, because that meant that she would always be the one who came in first, who was in charge, who was strong, stronger than Ginger, stronger than their mother? And maybe she'd done nothing to help her sister grow a spine, get some self-esteem. OK, sure—she hadn't.

But it wasn't too late. It couldn't be too late.

"Tom loves me," Ginger said stubbornly. "He can't live without me."

"And how does he show it? By hitting you? By leaving you?"

"He doesn't hit me," Ginger said. But she said it very quietly. "Not really. And he always comes back. And that's why I can't leave him. Because if he came back and I wasn't there, I don't know what would happen to him or if I'd ever see him again."

"And what would be wrong with that?"

"He needs me," Ginger repeated. Firmly. "Mindy, you never did need me. You don't need anybody."

It was like being kicked in the shins by her board, an unexpected blow that made her knees weak. Was it true? Did she not need *anyone*? And if so, was that necessarily a bad thing, the way the world was? If she didn't need anyone, she would never be hurt. Or be abandoned. Never again.

She'd been so selfish, these past few years. With reason—or so she'd told herself. For the first time in her life she'd put herself first, dared to reach for things she alone wanted, not her sister, not her mother. And while she'd cherished her independence, now she realized that maybe, just maybe, it diminished her. That perhaps she was less, somehow, without someone else to care for.

"I'm serious." She lowered her voice to a gentle coaxing. "You need help, Ginger. If you could only see yourself—you're not eating enough. Let me take care of you again. Let me come up with another plan."

"I need to get back." There was panic in Ginger's voice, and she jumped up, brushing the sand off her legs. Mindy scrambled up beside her.

"No, Ginger. Please. Please, for me—stay here. Stay with me."

"I can't." Ginger smiled sadly, and suddenly she seemed years older than Mindy—wiser, more patient. Her eyes, still wide and fringed by long lashes, looked as if they'd seen things Mindy had never known existed.

"Hey!" Jimmy ran up. "What took you so long?"

"Hi, Jimmy," Ginger said with her shy smile.

"Jimmy, you remember my sister, Ginger?"

"Yes, I think the last time we met you were throwing up on my sandals."

Ginger hung her head, but Jimmy laughed.

"I—I'm sorry," Ginger stammered.

"Forget about it. Hey, what about your sister? Wasn't she terrific today?"

"Yes." Ginger raised her head and smiled at Mindy. "Yes. She's terrific."

"I was asking Ginger if she'd like to go out to dinner with us. Wouldn't that be fun?" Desperate to keep her sister with her, she hoped Jimmy's presence would magically change Ginger's mind. "My treat!"

"I'm sorry, I can't." Ginger smiled that wise, sad smile again. "But it was nice to see you, Jimmy. And, Mindy—"

Ginger threw herself into her sister's arms, nearly knocking the wind out of her. Mindy wrapped herself around her baby sister, ignoring the body odor, the greasy hair. Remembering instead the little

girl with whom she'd shared a bath, a bed, makeshift meals at the
dinette table in the kitchen back in Van Nuys. The little girl who
loved new clothes, who was disappointed on her birthdays when her
mother forgot to get her a frilly dress or a matching shorts-and-
blouse set. One time, Mindy had taken some money from Mom's
drawer—the girls never did get an allowance; her mother didn't
know how to do basic parenting things like that—and she'd gone to
the Broadway store and bought Ginger a lacy blouse with puffy
sleeves. Frivolous, girlish. Ginger loved it so much, she would have
worn it to school every day if she hadn't known that that would set
off alarm bells among the adults who could have taken them away.

Sad, wasn't it? Mindy's shoulders drooped, memories of her childhood clouding the sun. Sad that two little girls had known those
things. That they had understood the need to be not quite invisible,
but certainly not exceptional, in order not to attract scrutiny. That
they had known that if any responsible adult knew too much about
them, they'd be separated. And look at them now. One sister lassoing
the sun, the moon, all the glittering stars, to be noticed, finally—to
be exceptional. And the other, now disappearing—literally, the sharp
outline of Ginger's ribs pressing into her—to the point of invisibility.

"Please let me drop by and give you some money, at least," Mindy
whispered in her sister's ear. Ginger was the only other person in the
world who knew what it had been like, growing up the daughter of
Carol Donnelly. Maybe she couldn't kidnap Ginger from Tom Riley.
But she could at least buy her a decent dress and a couple of bags of
groceries and establish some kind of regular contact.

"No, really. We're fine." With surprising firmness, Ginger pushed
herself away. Then before Mindy could say another word, Ginger
started trudging through the sand, up the stairs to the Coast Highway.

Jimmy took Mindy's hand, squeezed it.

"She'll be fine," he told her, but he didn't sound sure. "She's still with that Riley guy?"

Mindy nodded.

"Huh. Listen, I don't want to worry you, but he's into some stuff, I hear. Some crazy stuff."

"What stuff?" Mindy turned toward Jimmy, who shook his head.

"I think we need a drink" was all he said. And she let him pick up her board and lead her back to her car. When they got to the highway, she searched for Ginger among all the others lugging surfboards and beach chairs, trying to cross the busy road while traffic zoomed up and down, heedless of the crowds spilling up from the beach like ants from an anthill. But she didn't see her sister. It was as if she'd vanished into thin air.

It was after that drink—at the apartment where he was crashing, a couple of shots of tequila, not what she'd had in mind at all; she'd assumed she would go back home and shower the sand and sweat off, tease her hair a bit, put on a cool shift, and take Jimmy out to Trader Vic's—that he told her what Tom Riley was up to.

It was after he told her that they finally made love, her confusion, anger, and fear stirring inside her, mixing with the desire she'd been feeling for Jimmy all week. All it took was his sympathetic look, his hand on her arm, his nuzzling her neck as she sat there in disbelief, to ignite the flame. Her skin was dry kindling, her blood gasoline; she found his lips, she kissed him, bit his lip, took his hands and placed them on her burning breasts, explored his muscled chest as if she were blindly seeking treasure. And she discovered it when she reached inside his shorts and took his ready penis into her hands.

It was after she'd enjoyed her second orgasm, and she'd lifted his head up from between her legs, cradled it wonderingly, smiled into those kind eyes, that she fell asleep with Jimmy sprawled, naked, atop her own naked, sated flesh.

It was after she awoke in the morning, stiff from the couch and what Jimmy and she had accomplished together, sticky with residue, heavy with satisfaction, that she kissed him and said she should go home to shower, but she'd call him in the afternoon. Would he go with her to see Ginger and convince her to come home with them?

It was after he agreed, brushing sleep out of his drowsy eyes, his hair tousled like a little boy's, that she went home.

And picked up the newspaper outside her apartment door. Saw the words *N— Lover* scrawled in thick red ink, so recently written she still smelled the marker. Recognized the photo that was also circled in red.

A photo of her and Jimmy on the beach—"The Girl in the Curl wins Malibu Invitational," the caption read. Her face was captured as she hugged him, so you could only see his muscled back, his black hair. But the photo was altered so that Jimmy's skin appeared dark, so much darker than it actually was.

The phone began to ring inside the apartment; her hand shook as she fumbled the key into the lock and ran inside to answer it, as if it could save her from the tsunami she already knew was coming toward her. The paper and any thought of her sister were left to their own devices outside on the stoop.

Where, as the minutes, then hours, ticked away, both began to fade in the California sun.

8

Ginger—her feet crusted with dirt but the skin so hardened from her going barefoot for months, she didn't register the little pebbles and flecks of asphalt that stuck to them—crossed the highway after she left Mindy, just one of many weary revelers fleeing the beach at the end of a typically sunny day. She walked along the narrow sidewalk, heading north; she trudged through parking lots and hamburger stands, a car dealership, before she reached the empty lot. Picking her way through the piles of trash, she climbed up the worn path to the shack.

There was something stuck on the makeshift door, a faded shutter leaned against an opening. She plucked the flyer off, the tape sticking to her fingers.

> Condemned—by order of the county of
> Los Angeles, California. This lot to be developed.
> Vagrants must vacate the premises.

Her fingers shook; her empty stomach tightened. She fought off the rising nausea. She wasn't sure which was more upsetting, the news that they had to leave or the word *vagrant*.

Which was pretty much the same as *homeless*, wasn't it?

She slid through the opening between the shutter and the rusty metal wall—if you could call some old sheet metal stuck in the ground a wall. The shack was empty. Tom and the others weren't back yet. She knew they wouldn't be, of course. They'd only left for Mexico this morning; they wouldn't be back until tomorrow at the earliest. She was supposed to go, but she had stood firm, for once. She'd wanted to see her sister.

"So you're choosing her over me?" Tom had said, and Ginger had suppressed a sigh. Sometimes the Surf God was just a predictable man.

"No, of course not. I haven't seen her in a while, that's all. And now that you know to pay the police, you don't need me at the crossing anymore."

"The ways I need you, you will never understand," he had crooned, pulling her close, pressing his hand between her legs, and for a moment she wavered. But she'd held her ground, and instead of punishing her for it—she'd taken a step back, her arm protecting her face—he only shrugged and said he'd see her when they got back in two days. Sometimes, he wasn't so predictable.

The first time Tom had left her for more than a night, it had been for Mexico.

The second time he left, he took her along.

"You're eye candy," he told her. "A pretty blond chickie like you, nobody's gonna even look in your surfboard for the stash."

She was so naïve. She'd laughed, asked him what on earth he was talking about.

He'd stared at her without even a glint of fondness, as if she were a stray dog.

"Jesus Christ, sometimes you are so stupid" was all he said before storming out with his surfboard to get in some time on the beach.

The next morning, before dawn, they piled into a borrowed van that reeked of skunky weed; there were no seats in the back, so Ginger and most of the guys rattled around on the floor while Tom drove and his lieutenant sat next to him—a guy named Switchblade. He'd recently started hanging out with them, showing up out of nowhere one day with bags of weed; they'd had quite a party that night.

The boards were strapped to the top of the van, all newly hollowed out; Tom and Switchblade had spent hours cutting out precise rectangles, just big enough for the bags of pot, then fitting the pieces back in like a jigsaw puzzle, then waxing it over. They were still OK in the surf, he'd told her; they had to be. They had to do some surfing while they were there and the waves were pretty rad at Baja; it would be a shame not to sample them. And it would throw off the authorities, maybe. If they even cared to sniff around.

But it was Mexico, and nobody cared that much, at least not at the crossing south. The border patrol guy waved them over with a yawn; they were only another carload of kids partying down in the land of plenty where everything was so much cheaper than in California: Beer, food, women. Drugs.

They drove for about an hour down the coast, which looked like the coast back north—rocky, with a few great breaks. But it wasn't nearly as crowded, and when they got out of the van and Ginger felt the cool, smooth sand between her toes, no discarded cigarettes or bottle caps to worry about, she was happy. Like she was on vacation—if only Switchblade and the other guys had been left behind, it would have been her and Tom, together in paradise. She was so starved for something new it startled her, made her giddy.

"Let's stay a few days," she'd blurted out, running to throw her arms around Tom.

"You are ridiculous," he'd said, but he laughed. She knew she was pretty when she smiled; wasn't he always telling her that? So she smiled up into his face, and his dark brows, like thunderclouds, unknit and his eyes sparkled and he grinned down at her; she felt his benediction wash over her. She sighed. If only it could be like this all the time.

But Switchblade cleared his throat, and Tom pushed her away. "Let's hit the water first."

Grabbing their boards, they didn't pause to study the other surfers in the water, because there weren't that many. But this break looked easy, like Malibu, with a long, parallel ride from not that far out. Ginger paddled out with them, the last one as usual. Tom never watched out for her in the water like Mindy used to. He did shout something about keeping an eye out for sharks, which made Ginger keep her feet out of the water as she paddled, searching the waves for that treacherous dorsal fin. But she didn't see anything, although who knew what lurked beneath the surface?

The ocean is the same everywhere, she lectured herself. The sun was the same—the bleached-yellow ball that made her squint, that baked her skin brown, her hair brittle. The salt water was the same, coating her skin, drying it out. The gulls sounded the same with their cries— she giggled, imagining their speaking in Spanish, crying "Olé!" instead—and the waves formed and broke with the usual jarring rhythm. It was always there, that nerve-jangling percussion. She wished she could sleep just once somewhere it wouldn't puncture her dreams.

They surfed awhile—she wiped out a couple of times but mostly rode cleanly, if not adventurously. Not like Tom, who walked up and down his board like a graceful animal, a cat on a window ledge. He even turned around and rode in backward, grinning at her, and she waved at him, timidly, so she wouldn't lose her balance. They surfed for a couple of hours, until the sun was about three-quarters of the way to the horizon. Then Tom barked, "That's a wrap," and they all dragged their boards back to the van.

Switchblade hadn't surfed at all; he'd sat in the sand in his tattered jeans and leather belt, shirtless, as the others frolicked in the water. He wasn't really one of them, but Tom liked him, which was odd. He never liked civilians. Switchblade was the lone exception.

"About time," he muttered as they all dragged their boards to the van, where the guys lashed them to the roof.

"I told you, it's all part of the game," Tom said.

"I'm hungry," Ginger said, her stomach making alarming noises. She'd only eaten a couple of bananas hours earlier. "Can we find something to eat?"

"Sure, that's the plan," Tom said. So Ginger tried to relax in the back as Tom drove the van out of the parking lot. She had no idea where they were going—she couldn't see out the front window—but she hoped it was a taqueria or something. Tom carried all the money, of course—he always did. She didn't know how much, but hopefully enough for a real meal, a burrito and beans and rice and chips and salsa, the whole works. She couldn't remember the last time her belly was full of warm, comforting food.

When the van stopped, the gears grinding with little shrieks of protest, and Ginger began to stir, Tom turned to her.

"Stay inside. I'll bring something back."

"But, Tom, I have to pee!"

"Here's a can." He flung an old coffee can at her. "Just don't go outside."

"Tom!"

But he was gone. The other guys went with him—including Switchblade. Ginger shivered a little. She had been afraid he'd be left with her.

She peed—hovering over the can, splashing on her fingers, wincing at the warm liquid. She wanted to throw the can outside—how could she sit inside that dark van with a can full of her own urine? But she did.

Tom had told her to.

She had no idea how long she waited with that can in her hands; she felt too stupid, too frozen, to put it somewhere else. She was famished, she was holding her own urine, she had no idea where she was, and if something happened to her, who would know? How would Mindy, how would Mom, ever find out?

But Tom had told her to wait. And he would be back, of course he would. She needed to stop being such a baby.

Tears escaped her eyes—which were shut tight so she couldn't see the coffee can. And she remembered all the times that Mom had forgotten her and Mindy when they were little and they waited forever for her after swim lessons or after school. The time Mom went to Hawaii. The time Dad left with only a note.

What did she have to do to get someone not to leave her? What was wrong with her that everybody did? Even Mindy had, that day on the movie set. No matter that Ginger had chosen to follow Tom— Tom, who knew her better than her sister; Tom, who had *seen* her that night at Makaha. If Mindy loved her, truly loved her, she would have fought for her. She would have come to the shack and thrown her in a car and driven away with her. She wouldn't have forgotten all about her.

And where *was* Tom, anyway? Why didn't he come?

A sob escaped, she shuddered, and she felt she might go mad if she had to sit there with her pee one minute more.

Then the van doors opened, and Tom and the guys—and Switchblade—poured in. They carried bags of food—smelling onions, garlic, seasoned meat, she had to stop herself from tearing the bags out of their hands. She quickly darted over to the door and set the can outside, took a deep breath, filling her lungs with air that wasn't stale with fear.

Tom placed a bag—one that didn't smell of food—beneath the

driver's seat. Then he joined her in the back of the van. Someone lit a candle that she hadn't noticed before, and they sat there, stuffing their faces with tacos and burritos. Someone else made a crack about the beans and the long drive home. Ginger was too tired to laugh. She leaned into Tom, and he put an arm around her, grinning with his mouth full; after he swallowed, he kissed the top of her head.

"You did good. We got what we came for. Now, when we drive over the border, I need you to sit up front with me. Smile your prettiest smile—you're a knockout. I'm the luckiest son of a bitch alive."

And the time spent waiting for him, holding that disgusting can, was forgotten. After they ate and stashed the hash in the surfboards, meticulously cutting into the wax with penknives to remove the pieces, stuffing the hash inside, sealing them all up again, she sat next to Tom up front. When they reached the border crossing with its harsh lights, she leaned across Tom so that the guard could see her breasts as he shone a flashlight into the van. She smiled, shook her hair, asked him how his day had been, told him this was her first time coming to Mexico and they'd had such a great day surfing, she couldn't wait to come back!

She'd never felt so brave. And it was because Tom was right there, stroking the back of her neck, smiling proudly.

They were waved on without any questions, and as soon as they were over the border, the guys cheered and told her she was the best bitch they knew.

Switchblade—forced to sit in the back with the foot soldiers, as he called them—was the only one who didn't say a word. She felt his sullen stare on the back of her head the rest of the drive, but she didn't care. She held Tom's hand the whole way, and he didn't shake her off once.

. . .

That had been the first of many trips south. Tom and the others were dealing, of course—she knew that now. It was what kept some food in their bellies, it was what let them buy the old van outright. But she thought there should be more money—after all, Tom told her how cheap pot was in Mexico and how eager all the surf bums were to buy it. They went to competitions now solely to deal, not to convert the masses. They never came home with any weed left over.

Once she asked Tom about the money. He kept it hidden somewhere even Ginger couldn't find. He doled it out sullenly, when necessary; mostly he was the one who bought the groceries, paid for the gas, handed out a few dollars if someone needed to replace a shirt or a pair of pants that were shredded beyond what Ginger could clumsily repair with a needle and thread.

"Tom, how much money do we have now?"

"Why do you want to know?"

"I thought that maybe we had some saved up. Do we?"

That was the only time he was really rough with her, beyond the usual shove if she got in his way on a wave or the cruel jokes he liked to play, not only on her but on the other guys, too; he delighted in tripping them unawares if their arms were full of driftwood for a bonfire. Or kicking sand in their faces to wake them up in the morning. Or taking off in the van and leaving her behind at the grocery store, laughing at her bewildered face as he tore out of the parking lot, making fun of her tears when she finally got back to the shack, her feet sore, her arms aching from carrying the bags of groceries.

Now he grabbed her arm so tight, he left bruises.

"Don't you trust me?" he snarled. "Stupid bitch, you're just like my mother, always nagging my father about money. We had tons of it, you know. Growing up. I'm a rich kid. One of the richest. And my mother was stinking with jewelry and furs but it was never enough. Drove my old man crazy, drove him to an early grave. She didn't care.

She's richer than before. Such a stuck-up bitch. I thought you were different." He dropped her arm and pushed her so hard she fell down, scraping her back on one of the exposed legs of the cot.

"I am, Tom! I am different!"

She never asked about the money again.

But now—with the *Condemned* sign in her hand—she couldn't help but wonder. Where would they go? Surely they had enough for a little apartment now, just the two of them? Ginger would keep it so clean; she'd make curtains for the windows. She'd go to a thrift store and buy decent clothes and go grocery shopping, but she'd be so careful, the opposite of his mother. She would cut coupons. They could live on so little. All they needed was each other, and the ocean, and their boards.

The others—including Switchblade—could go their own way. They could still do business together, but they didn't all have to live together anymore. It was time they—well, it was time they grew up. A little. They could still surf all day. But they could also have a roof over their heads and a bathroom. And maybe . . .

Maybe even a baby. Someday.

Ginger pulled on a threadbare T-shirt that advertised suntan lotion, one she'd worn a couple of years ago while she handed out samples at one of the competitions, earning a few bucks and a lot of unwanted gropes in the process, but it was for Tom, it was all for Tom, so she didn't mind. Sitting down on an old orange crate, she hugged her knees to her chest. She hated it when Tom was away. She didn't know what to do—she felt like one of the planets she saw when they tripped at night, dancing with no direction across the sky, left out from the other planets, who turned their backs on it. She loved those trips, taken with Tom; they had become so close, he told her, that they saw the same things, experienced the same enlightenment, when they tripped together. He saw the planets, too, and he

told them to behave—she saw him do it, his head huge, lit from behind by the moon, high up in the velvet canvas of sky, talking in his
musical voice to the other planets, murmuring to her, crooning the
secrets of the universe. God was nothing, a sham. They were their
own gods and goddesses, no one could touch them, they had achieved
a spiritual unity that she could never know on her own.

But then sometimes he abandoned her, like today—and she'd get
confused. Lost. If she stayed here and waited, she'd go hungry, and
she was already famished. She might get arrested—who knows, whoever taped the notice on the door of the shack might have found
some of the unsold pot still in bricks, hidden between the springs
and the thin, rank mattress of the one twin bed, which Tom slept in.
Everyone else—including Ginger, when Tom was mad at her—slept
in sleeping bags on the floor.

She should go to that market down the highway, shoplift a packet
of bologna; she was a little light-headed, to tell the truth. Probably
from the sun today. But maybe because she hadn't eaten breakfast;
Tom had taken all the food with him when he'd left this morning.
He'd never done that before, and she'd been too stupid to wonder
about it, until now.

God, she was *so* stupid. She should have accepted Mindy's offer,
just taken a meal and a few bucks, and then she could have come
back and waited for Tom. But in the moment, she'd heard Tom's seductive voice crooning in her ear—"Your sister is the worst of the
sellouts. You're better than she is. You don't need anything she can
give you."

But sitting in the condemned shack with no food and no money,
she saw herself for the dummy she was when Tom wasn't there to
think for her.

The shack, despite all the cracks and holes, suddenly seemed air-
less; it always stank of unwashed bodies and weed. She needed to get

outside, breathe something less rancid; she squeezed herself between the shutter and the wall again. She sat down on the sand; at least this way she could see who might be coming to make her vacate the premises. Or be ready to greet Tom as soon as he and the others came back from Mexico, and warn them.

She heard the ocean from across the highway—she couldn't see it, a beach house blocked her view, but she couldn't escape the incessant pounding of the waves. Each one was always like a little electric shock to her brain, only today each shock shook her entire body; they were lightning bolts. How would she ever get to sleep tonight?

Yet her eyes started to feel heavy—heavy enough to blot out the hunger pangs, the confusion, the fear. As the sun fell behind the house, and the sky deepened from pale blue to pale pink, then purple, then finally the indigo of night, Ginger slept.

9

"Well, it's a shame. A damn shame."

Fred Nelson, Mindy's agent, let the newspaper fall to his desk. Lighting a cigarette, he swiveled in his chair, away from her.

Mindy sat in her most attractive Gucci print shift, her legs crossed ladylike at her ankles. She wore her thickest eyelashes, her hair teased and coaxed into a perfect Julie Christie bob. Fred had summoned her here, the Monday after she found the newspaper on her front stoop; it was he who had been on the other end of the ringing phone when she came home from being with Jimmy.

"You sure he isn't a Negro?" He swiveled back around. His hair was black with a little wave off his forehead, and he wore a pin-striped suit. She'd never seen him not in a pin-striped suit. He looked like Rock Hudson with a slightly receding hairline.

His secretary, his receptionist, even the valet parking attendants in this building—they were all gorgeous, all marking time until they were discovered, like everyone else in L.A. The women were all taller than Mindy, bigger breasted. She always felt like a flat-chested shrimp when she visited the office.

"No, he's Hawaiian," she repeated. "A friend. He's a great surfer, he helped me get ready for the invitational. Which I won, by the way. That was also in the newspaper."

"Doesn't matter. He sure photographs like a Negro." Fred sighed.

He massaged his temple with one manicured finger. "This reminds me of that photo of Johnny Cash and his wife. A couple of years ago, I think it was. Remember it?"

She shook her head.

"He was busted for drugs coming back from Mexico. His wife appeared with him in court and the photo at the courthouse made her look as Black as Cleopatra. Did you know that? That Cleopatra was Black as spades? Egyptian, you know. And Liz Taylor played her—I wanted Eartha Kitt, she's a client. But of course not, they had to have Liz. Anyway, that Cash thing—it was a mess for a while."

"But he—he's still famous. It didn't hurt his career," Mindy said hopefully.

"He's Johnny Cash," Fred said simply. "You're not. And don't even mention Sammy Davis, Jr., and his wife."

Mindy didn't know what to say; she could only stare helplessly at Fred, who swiveled away again so his back was to her.

"I mean—" she said, desperate to fill the silence. "I mean, it was just in the one paper."

"American International called this morning," the voice behind the chair said. "They dropped you. They said it's because the beach party movie is dead—and the last one laid an egg, that's true. They said they had no use for a surfing girl now."

"But what about *Endless Summer*?"

"It's a documentary. Also, were there any chicks in that?"

"No."

"Point made. Wait a minute!" He swiveled around again, leaned across his desk. "Nobody really knows your name outside of the surfing world. Maybe we can salvage something. Can you sing?"

"What?"

"Sing! La la la la la—Jesus Christ! Sing!"

"No!"

"You sure? Everybody's singing these days. That friend of yours, Paula—she had that nice little hit. Patty Duke has an album. We grow your hair out some, put you in real clothes, not a bikini. Voilà! You have a new career."

"I don't want a new career!" Mindy's hands clenched on her knees. "I want—I want—"

"If you want a career at all," Fred said icily, "you'll take my advice. Otherwise, good luck, I'll see you never."

Mindy clutched the hem of her skirt, her knuckles turning white. She took deep breaths. How was this happening to her? She'd only just arrived! Discovered on the beach like in a classic Hollywood fairy tale—no, that wasn't true; she was mixing up her official bio with the actual facts. She had made this happen herself that day when she followed Paula. Maybe what happened after that was luck, that kind of California luck that smiled on all sorts of peppy teenagers in the right place at the right time ever since Lana Turner showed up at Schwab's in a tight sweater. But Mindy deserved for it to last a little longer, didn't she? To make up for her crummy childhood?

The bottom line was she had no idea where to go, what to do, if she wasn't the Girl in the Curl, the face in the magazine. The surfer girl with endorsements that paid for her transportation, her rent, her clothes. She couldn't go back to where she'd come from—or to where Ginger seemed to be headed. However she'd felt that last week with Jimmy at the beach—that feeling of coming home, of being where she belonged, a sea creature once more—vanished the instant she saw that newspaper on her porch. All she wanted now—more than she ever had before—was the one thing she was on the verge of losing.

She needed a plan. A new plan to take the place of the Plan. She'd done it before, when she was a child. Surely she could do it again.

"I'll give it a try," she said meekly, smiling gamely up at Fred.

"I'm not sure I heard you," he said flatly.

"I mean, of course I can sing—I can't wait to go in this new direction!"

"That's what I thought you said. OK, stay home by the phone, I'll set something up. It might not happen right away, I'm warning you. Meanwhile I'll see if I can get you some modeling jobs for print, something as far away from surfing as possible—and if I were you, I wouldn't enter any more tournaments. We need to pivot. You OK for money?"

She gaped at him; she hadn't taken him for a kind man willing to help out a broke starlet. Not without strings, anyway, but in all their dealings Fred had never crossed that line, not the way Paula said her agent had done when he first signed her. Before Mindy could thank Fred, he continued.

"I could get you a gig up at the Playboy Club. It's not exactly fun, of course—they expect you to keep their clients happy, in every sense of the word. You wouldn't quite be a Bunny, but something a little more. Like a call girl, I suppose, mingling with the male guests. But there's money in it; those players know how to tip."

She pressed her lips together; even coated in frosted lipstick, they were suddenly dry. So was her mouth, she longed for a glass of water.

"I'm—" She hated herself for letting her voice shake; she took a breath, tried again. "I'm OK. Thanks. I'll let you know if—if that becomes necessary."

"Smart girl. You'll be all right, as long as you stay away from whoever that was in the picture. And don't make a mistake like this again, for God's sake."

"I told you, he isn't a Negro. He's Hawaiian."

"I don't care if he's Don Ho himself. You're white. He's not. The end. Little girls like you don't get two strikes in this business, because there's an endless supply. You're all interchangeable. But I like ya, kid. So I'll see what I can do." And with that, Fred dismissed her with a wave of his hand. Pressing his intercom button, he barked at his receptionist—who vaguely resembled Marlo Thomas from *That Girl*—to let in the next client. Mindy rose, left the office, nearly bumping into the client—a tall cowboy type with long sideburns, probably a singer—and stumbled to the elevator. Once on the ground floor, she pushed through the revolving door into the fresh air. Her knees wobbled, so she pressed herself against the side of the building and stared out at Wilshire Boulevard. The palm trees were taller than the streetlights, and the buildings were a mix of two-story Spanish-style offices, some new skyscrapers, with the Art Deco Saks Fifth Avenue mansion standing out like a sore thumb.

She reached into her purse for her valet ticket, waved it at the attendant—who resembled Troy Donahue; she wondered if the agency only hired people who looked like movie stars—and waited for her car. Soon her powder-blue Ford Mustang was idling in front of her. She tipped the attendant, got in, and wrapped a scarf around her hair. Putting the car in gear, she nosed out into traffic, threading her way skillfully through the congested streets, heading back home, because she didn't know where else to go.

She pulled up in front of the bungalow, and her heart sank. Because there, sitting on the stoop, was Jimmy. He raised his head when he heard her drive up; his grin pierced the fog of her chaotic thoughts. She was still numb from the meeting with Fred, still trying to sort it all out—she knew she should be outraged, of course, on Jimmy's behalf. On behalf of Negroes everywhere—for God's sake, hadn't she once told the lead singer of the Temptations that he was the sexiest man she'd ever seen?

She was no bigot, no J. Edgar Hoover or George Wallace. She'd given money to the NAACP, even!

But she didn't feel outraged. She felt only terror. Personal, small, selfish terror.

And then she saw Jimmy smile. But the terror didn't leave; it sat squarely in her belly, pitching a tent, planting a flag. Her stomach quivered as she walked toward him, but this time it wasn't from lust.

"Where have you been? You said you'd call me yesterday, but you didn't. Your roommate wouldn't let me inside—who is that chick, anyway? Kind of a bitch." Jimmy smiled, shaking his head.

"I'm sorry, I'll talk to her. Won't you come in?" She hated herself for sounding so stiff and polite. She ushered him into her apartment like she was a stewardess welcoming him aboard a plane.

"So," Jimmy said once they got inside the front door; he didn't even wait until they'd gotten to her bedroom. His arms were around her, pulling her to him with such confidence. He fingered her stiff hair, laughing. Then he began to nuzzle her neck.

"Jimmy," she protested, fighting the urge to give in, let him do to her whatever he wanted. One last fuck for the road—what would be wrong with that?

Only everything.

"Jimmy, don't—stop."

"You liked this the other night," he murmured, and she realized that his voice was always like this when he was with her—filled with teasing laughter. Jimmy was sunshine, was music, was happiness, was—easy. Yes, easy. It would be easy to be with a man like this all the time. She'd never thought it would be easy to be with any man before.

You don't get two strikes in this business.

"Stop, I said!" She pushed him away, straightening her dress.

Sunshine was hidden by clouds; the music ended. Jimmy's eyes hardened—the way they had in the diner that night. When the bigoted couple tried to shame them.

"What happened?" he asked, his voice flat.

"Nothing." She moved toward her bedroom, so he would follow. So she could shut the door since Paula was around. Shamefully, she even began to close the blinds—*No one must see me with him,* she thought wildly—before she stopped herself.

"Something happened," Jimmy insisted. He stood inside the room so she could close the door, but he wouldn't come near her now.

"Did you see the paper?"

"Nah, what do you mean?"

"Here." She opened the top drawer of her bureau, pulled out the offending newspaper with the hateful words scrawled across it. She threw it down on her bed. Jimmy picked it up and studied it.

"So?" He peered up at her, and his tension was gone; he looked relieved. He smiled again. "That's stupid. I'm not Black. This is just some cracker being ignorant."

"No, it's not. Jimmy, the producers of those films dropped me today. My agent called me on the carpet. This kind of thing—it can ruin a career."

"I don't understand. All you have to do is explain that they're wrong, that I'm Hawaiian."

"It's not enough. And, well—my agent said it doesn't matter. Even though you're Hawaiian—he said people would still—it's—it's—"

"I see," Jimmy said, turning into someone else as he slammed the paper down on her bed. He was no longer the man who had held her in his arms the other night. His face was closed off; his heart was, too, she knew it by the way he folded his arms across his chest, as if to protect himself. From her. "I'm wrong, is what you're saying. You and me. We're wrong, it's wrong, it's always wrong!" He balled his hands into fists and punched the air in front of him, just once, before shoving his fists into his pockets. "Heaven forbid I look at a white woman here in California." His lips were pale with anger.

"No! *I* don't think that—you know I don't!"

"Oh, for God's sake, Mindy! Yes, you do, or you wouldn't be doing this!"

"It's not about us, it's nothing to do with us—"

"OK, then. So tell me. Tell me that it'll be the way it was, that we're going out tonight, that I'm making love to you after, that we'll be walking hand in hand down Sunset for all the world to see. Tell me that."

She hung her head.

"Because," he continued, his voice shaking with anger—or hurt. "Because that's what *I* want. And it's what I thought *you* wanted. I want to be with you every day. Every night. I want to take you home to meet my mother. I want to go see yours. I want you to know my world, to know what it's like to live among the gods. And—Jesus Christ, I don't know why, but I do—I want to know *your* world. I want you to introduce me to—to—hep cats and movie stars and whoever it is you're so impressed by. I want to watch you get your photograph taken, and I want you to want me to have mine taken with you. That's what I want. So tell me. Tell me that you do, too. Tell me the hell with these idiots, and we'll be happy together, and it won't matter because, because—because we'll be happy," he finished, his voice raspy. Begging.

But not bargaining.

"I'm sorry, Jimmy," Mindy whispered, hating herself, hating her stiff hair and false eyelashes and the invitations to premieres and parties pinned to her bulletin board—as if she were a schoolgirl, pinning up invitations to the prom! Invitations she'd never received, so she'd been making up for it these past few years, filling her life with dresses and shoes and newspaper clippings, the popular girl, finally. And she hated Paula, probably listening with her ear at the door, for tempting her in the first place, for opening Pandora's box.

"Tell them all to go to hell, and come with me to Hawaii," Jimmy whispered. "Live with me there, on the beach. Forget all this. We were happy this past week, weren't we? I know we were! You were more relaxed, more yourself—the first time I saw you again, outside that club, you were wound so tight I thought you would snap. But when you're at the beach—when you're on a board—man, you are a goddess. That's where you belong."

"No!" She closed her mind to the memory of that perfect week. It was perfect because it was finite; she had still gone home to her apartment like a normal person, slept in a real bed. She still had decent meals on a kitchen table. Her agent had still returned her calls, made plans for her, big plans. "You want me to live like my *mother*? I can't do that—I won't do that. Not in a million years."

"What's so wrong with following your passion? Because *surfing* is your passion—I've seen it. I see how different you are out there, away from all—this." Jimmy threw open the closet door, revealing her racks of clothes—miniskirts and gowns, bikinis made of tissue-like fabric that would shred out on a board. "What is so special about this? You saw how quickly it can turn on you."

"Because I deserve it! Because it's better! I'm going to have a house someday, a real house like we used to have in Van Nuys, maybe bigger. With a swimming pool. I drive a real car, not an old station wagon with a surfboard tied to the top. I meet people, artists, musicians—people who have more to talk about than clean sets and surfboard wax. It's *legitimate,* my world. And I'm a responsible person here, not someone who would run off and leave her children. And I want children, someday. I want them to go to school, graduate from high school—have choices I didn't have. It's only *now* that I have them—it's only now that I'm *real.*"

"What do you mean, 'real'?"

"That I'm someone people look up to. I can tell people what I do, Jimmy, how I spend my days, and they won't turn up their noses. They won't feel sorry for me, they envy me! They don't think I'm just the kid with a mother who's a bum. Or that I'm a bum, too."

"So that's what you think of me?"

"No, not you, but—" She looked down at the carpet so she couldn't see him standing there so quietly, judging her.

"Right." He closed her closet door with a sigh. "So what's the Girl in the Curl going to do now? To keep her clothes and her car and her *respectability.*"

"Sing." She shut her eyes, wished she could clap her hands over her ears. It sounded so absurd, away from Fred and his celebrity look-alikes in his glass-walled tower overlooking Wilshire.

"You've got to be kidding me."

"No, Fred—my agent—said that's the best way forward for me. He said that surfing movies are dead, anyway. So he's going to try to set me up as a singer."

"Mindy, look at me."

Too weary to remain standing, she plopped down on her bed, fingered the white fake-fur bedspread. She raised her head.

Jimmy wasn't angry now. His brows had unknit; his voice was reasonable, patient. As if she were a stupid child.

"This isn't who you are," he said, sitting down next to her on the bed but not reaching for her. He kept two feet between them. "I'm no wizard, hell, I'm just a surf bum, apparently. But even I can tell that you aren't the girl I first saw on Makaha. I get it, it's fun and all—hell, I'd like it, too. For a little while. But soon enough I'd have to go home. I'd have to return to what made me who I am. I'd have to be *authentic*. That's all a person can be—true to himself. Whatever you do next, singing or juggling or dancing on some TV show—no matter how much you say you want respectability, or legitimacy, or whatever it is, you'll be a fake. And how long can you live that way? Pretending to be someone you're not?"

"As long as necessary," she replied. "I *want* this. And I don't have a home to go back to like you. Mom—my childhood—Jimmy, you just don't know."

"Then *tell* me."

"It's too late now, Jimmy. This week, we've—well, it's been wonderful." Now she really couldn't look at him, because if she did, she'd waver. She wasn't strong enough to stand firm before the onslaught of his reasonableness. His wisdom, whether or not he was a wizard. "But it's too late for confidences. This last week was perfect; we didn't have to spoil it with words. Let's keep it that way. It was a great week, we had fun, let's not ruin it now."

"Right," Jimmy said, his voice tight. "I wouldn't want to ruin anything more for you. I guess I already have."

The newspaper lay before her on the bed; Mindy stared at it, at the blurry picture that had angered so many, destroying everything. Only a grainy photo.

Black and white.

There was no sound except for a lawn mower outside, a lawn crew clipping hedges—the background music of L.A. She'd traded the soothing cadence of waves for something more nerve jangling, she realized in that moment.

But it was what *she* had chosen.

"What will you do now?" Mindy massaged her temple; her head was pounding, and she pushed away the notion of going to the beach for one last ride with Jimmy, even though it was the very thing that would cure her headache. Fresh air, the ocean breeze, water to wash away her sins—she knew why her mother always fled to the sea. The ocean cleansed you of all your transgressions, like leaving your children.

Like breaking a good man's heart.

"I know you didn't come over to the mainland just to see me," she continued. "You must have had plans of your own, right? So now what?" Stroking her shiny shift dress, its threads of silk woven in a bright geometric pattern of orange and green and navy, she retreated into her armor, breathing deeply, calming herself. Protecting herself from this man who was the one—the only one, even more than her sister—who could drag her back down. Mobility, forward motion, what are you doing next? That was what it was all about, darling.

"You know, you made me forget why I came here in the first place." Jimmy shook his head. "I did have plans. To surf California and see for myself what passes for surf culture over here. To maybe take some ideas back home—I'd like to have my own business someday, taking tourists out on real longboards, like Hawaiians first used. It's just a crazy thought, and you pretty much drove it out of my head, this past week. But now, well—but then there's the draft. Maybe I'll get lucky and my number will come up," Jimmy said with a dry cackle. All of a sudden the world intruded—the world she'd been too busy, too shining, too dazzling, to notice much. A war—no, a *military action*—in Vietnam that was escalating daily but that she was aware of only because of the background hum of her television. Her world seemed insulated from that, too. She didn't know anyone who had been drafted once they appeared before the board. All these bright young things, sons of politicians and executives and actors, possessed the golden ticket.

Guys like Jimmy didn't. Had any of the guys from Malibu been drafted? She didn't think so. She knew those guys. If they'd been summoned, they'd probably lit the notice on fire or thrown it in the sea and kept surfing, kept moving, up and down the coast, maybe out of the country, to evade the authorities.

But Jimmy wasn't like that.

"Don't say that," she warned, her stomach tightening. "Don't even joke about it."

"Maybe I'm not joking," Jimmy said. "What else is a *bum* like me going to do, Miss Girl in the Curl?"

Mindy flinched, her own word thrown back at her like a poison-dipped dart. Her silk armor couldn't protect her from that.

"You're not a bum. You're the opposite of a bum, whatever that is."

"And you're still going to cut me out of your life like you did your mother. And your sister."

He made her sound so ruthless—but she wasn't! She wasn't that cold and calculating. All she wanted was a *nice* life.

All she wanted was everything she'd never had.

"What's wrong with wanting something more for myself?" She jumped off the bed, pushed him off it, too, furiously smoothed the bedspread where it was ruffled. "What's wrong with being ambitious? Is it because I'm a woman? You think I'm a bitch for wanting to get ahead—sure, maybe even be famous, more famous than I am now? If I were a guy, what would you think of me? You'd think I was smart, that I was focused."

"So focused that you'd turn your back on someone because of the color of his skin," Jimmy replied coolly. "Yeah, and I'd still think you were a bigot and a fraud. Being a chick has nothing to do with it."

"You'd better go," Mindy said, unable to look at him. To look in his eyes was like gazing in a spectral mirror, her soul reflected up to her instead of her reassuring physical appearance. She couldn't afford that kind of soul searching now; she couldn't stop to think about how right he was, how wrong she was. Because she had things to do. People to call, to placate, to reassure that—that—

That Jimmy wasn't a Negro and that she wasn't that kind of girl, whatever that meant. But she would say it, say whatever she needed to in order to keep her car, her motorcycle, her apartment, her table at the Whisky, her face in the magazines, her invitations to premieres, her tiny fan club. Anything to keep her from being her mother, and her sister.

All of a sudden, Mindy was starving. She hadn't eaten all day; she could devour an entire pizza right now.

And even with her belly stuffed, she would still be ravenous. For *more*—more lights, camera, action, look this way, baby, smile, chickie, smile, will you sign your autograph, would you like your regular table, will madam be having her usual, I'll pick you up at eight and look your best because there'll be paparazzi, what's your favorite color because our readers want to know, how do you do your hair that way, all the girls want to copy it, stay awake, stay pretty, stay fabulous, stay away from the orphanage, stay away from the riffraff, stay young.

Forever and ever and ever, amen.

"Yeah, I'm going. You don't have to tell me. I really can't stand to look at you right now. Bye, Mindy. I hope you get everything you deserve."

"Jimmy—"

But he was gone, the front door slamming like a thunderclap.

There was a soft knock on her bedroom doorframe. Paula peeked inside, eyes wide and hair redder than ever; she must have been to the salon that morning.

"Everything OK, hon?"

"Yeah, sure. You know how it is—I had to let him down, we had a fun time but he wanted more. *You* know." Mindy made a face, and Paula rolled her eyes in sympathy.

"Now." Mindy turned to survey herself in the mirror. Hair and makeup were still intact. She'd firmed up a little this past week; her arms looked great, barely sculpted, not an ounce of flab on them. She was model-slim; she could picture herself on an album cover. "I look good, you look good, let's go out for dinner. Somewhere *fabulous*."

"Trader Vic's?" Paula gave a little squeal and clapped her hands. "Mai tais?"

"I can't think of anything I'd like better," Mindy answered with an expert smile, the smile she bestowed upon the public. But the muscles around her mouth felt a little stiff, and she realized she hadn't smiled that particular smile all week. Not with Jimmy. With Jimmy, she wore a different kind of happiness. She wished she knew what it looked like.

As she made sure her fake eyelashes were still firmly glued in place, sprayed herself with Tabu, and touched up her lipstick, her hand faltered; she had to wipe off the lipstick and reapply it.

"Let's go. We'll pick up some guys at the bar and go dancing later, OK?" She dropped her lipstick in her purse, snapped it shut, turned off the bedroom light, and shut the door.

Ten minutes later they were cruising up Wilshire just as the streetlights were coming on, the ocean swallowing up the sun at their backs.

10

Ginger was getting desperate.

It was Tuesday and Tom and the gang still weren't back from Mexico. She couldn't think what had happened to them—

Except of course she knew what had happened to them. They'd probably been busted, but where? At the border? Were they in a California jail? Or worse, a Mexican one?

And that was the more pleasant of the two scenarios that zoomed through her mind like two race cars chasing each other. The other was that he had left her. That he had forgotten all about her; that he had never needed her at all. Just like Mindy said.

Just like what happened to Dad.

Ginger had spent the last three nights outside the hut; she was stiff, cramped, and weary. It wasn't what you could call sleep, even though she'd dragged a sleeping bag outdoors so she had something a little soft to lie down on. But she was so exposed and vulnerable. She heard coyotes up in the hills behind her, the rush of traffic on the highway. One night it had rained, a lukewarm, dismal drizzle that gradually invaded her bones, even after she found a sweatshirt and a plastic trash bag to protect herself. Still, she didn't go inside; her damp misery numbed her beyond reason.

Each little noise—the clang of a metal lid being clamped down on a trash can from one of the businesses nearby, a rustle of paper being blown across the lot—woke her up, heart in her throat, when she did manage to sleep.

But she had to remain outside. She had to watch out for whatever, whoever, was going to come and kick her out and demolish the shack. She had to protect it, for Tom. He would be so proud of her when he found out what she'd done! He'd tell her she'd done good, that she'd saved everything.

That he couldn't live without her.

She was hungry, though. Even though Tom had taken most of the food with him, she found a nearly empty jar of grape jelly and half a sleeve of stale saltines in a knapsack. She'd scraped up the last of the jelly with her fingers, and she'd eaten the last of the crackers yesterday. And drunk the one bottle of Coke. Her stomach had ceased growling, but she felt light-headed when she stood up too quickly. And she was smelly—grimacing, she sniffed her armpit. She needed to go for a quick dip in the ocean. She for sure needed food.

But she didn't have any money.

Ginger wasn't afraid of shoplifting a little. However, she needed to be more presentable than she currently was. There was no choice but to grab a pair of cut-off shorts, slip into a pair of rubber thong sandals, and leave the shack unprotected. She took one last look at it—there was nothing more she could do, no lock to fasten, no window to shut. A kid could have built a more substantial dwelling with Tinkertoys; it had never appeared as rickety as it did at this moment, leaning ominously to one side. But she had to leave it. Picking her way through the trash and rubble of the lot, crossing the highway, she walked up a block, then down the steps that led to the beach. She kept her head lowered, her hair shielding her face; she didn't want anyone to recognize her.

Tearing off the T-shirt, leaving it in a heap with the shorts and sandals, she stepped into the swirling water. It was cool but not cold;

it was only, what? September? She couldn't remember. They didn't have a calendar anymore—there was no need for one, Tom said. Only drones, worker bees, kept track of such ridiculous constraints as time and days of the week. She only knew it was Tuesday because the competition had been on Saturday.

Walking out to where she could crouch beneath the waves, she gave herself a good bath of a sort—of course, they didn't have any soap, but water was enough. That was what Tom said. It was good enough for the fish and fowl; it was good enough for them. She held her nose, kept bobbing her head down, running her other hand over her scalp, picking at the tangles, the knots, the bits of dried skin. She remembered bath time when she was little, how Mindy always dumped too much shampoo—Johnson's Baby Shampoo with its fruity scent—and the shampoo would run into her eyes and she almost always cried. Mindy scolded her—"Stop being such a baby! It says it right here on the bottle, *no more tears!*" But still she scrubbed, still she made sure that Ginger was as clean as possible.

"We have to keep up appearances," Mindy always said. "If not, they might take us away."

Where was Mom, those nights? In her room, Ginger guessed. She didn't really remember anymore.

Still beneath the surface, she heard the concussive sound of a wave breaking over her, but it wasn't frightening because she was so close to shore. There were long tendrils of kelp floating around, but she didn't see any fish. It was a fight to stay out where it was deep enough to remain submerged because the waves kept wanting to push her up on shore. But she wanted to stay out a bit longer; the water soothed her skin, which was so dry from the sun.

The waves were sloppy, losing formation almost as soon as they broke, so it wouldn't have been a good day to surf. But even if it had been, she hadn't brought her board. She never brought her board unless she was with Tom, or before him, Mindy. On her own, she didn't need to surf. She really only liked the ocean when she was sitting on the beach watching it. On the water it was something else; it was bigger than you, more powerful, overwhelming. And too much of life was overwhelming. She didn't need to constantly seek more of it, like Tom did.

Like Mindy did.

Ginger ducked her head back under one more time, raking her fingers through her hair. She didn't even own a comb anymore. How was that possible? It had gotten broken, someone had taken it—she had no idea. But she didn't possess a comb or a mirror or a razor to shave her legs and pits, she didn't even have tampons—she was forced to beg Tom to give her money for pads. Just when had she started to let go of all the things she'd so desperately wanted when she was a girl? She remembered dreaming of pretty clothes, makeup, a white vanity table from Sears that she once saw in a friend's bedroom, a shiny black patent-leather purse with a clasp that made a reassuring sound, like money dropping into a piggy bank, when it shut. They still were as out of reach to her as they'd been when she was a child, so she'd stopped dreaming of them, stopped believing they could be hers.

Popping up to the surface once more, Ginger blew salty water out of her nose, tilting her head so it would run from her ears. She tried to smooth her hair but knew that it would soon be crazy, tangled curls. Grabbing a handful of wet hair, she studied the ends; they were ragged, split. Her hair hadn't been cut in over a year.

She rose, the waves trying to push her off balance like eager little puppies nipping at her heels. Carefully she stepped up to the beach, water swirling about her knees, then her shins, then her ankles. A towel would have been nice, but that was another thing, along with her girlhood dreams, that she had lost along the way.

Sitting on the beach, trying to keep her wet legs from getting coated in sand, Ginger let out a deep sigh, one so loud it almost overpowered the waves. She was cold, wet, hungry—and sad. She couldn't remember the last time she'd felt anything close to happiness, felt anything other than tired and heavy-limbed, her head clouded with doubts and worry, her stomach always empty, demanding to know why.

Mindy had looked so happy! So peppy, so pretty, and evidently she was with Jimmy Cho now; Ginger remembered the way they had gazed at each other, as if they'd each been given an unopened gift. Jimmy was hot—she grinned, thinking of him, thinking of her sister's good fortune.

But Tom would have something to say about the match, for sure. He still felt it was his responsibility to keep the beach for just them, the locals, the purists. But he had a look to him when he did this; his eyes gleamed, and his mouth opened in a snarled smile as if he were the Big Bad Wolf and everyone else were Little Red Riding Hood. It made her shiver, to see him like that.

She was shivering now, her arms crossed in front of her chest, the swimsuit top still damp. But she needed to get going; she pulled the T-shirt over her head, shrugged into the pair of shorts. Brushing the sand off her legs, she rose, stumbled a little—there were bees buzzing around inside her brain, making her dizzy. Taking deep breaths, she waited for them to stop, and finally they did.

The sun was about two-thirds of the way to the horizon, and she panicked. How long had she been here? What if Tom had come home? What if something had happened to the shack? She fought the urge to run back, because first she needed food. Her hunger was so overwhelming, she couldn't stop herself from shaking. She'd be no good to anyone if she fainted dead away.

Walking tentatively, slowly—too slowly; when would she ever get back to the shack?—Ginger made her way through the sand, which was so heavy now, she fought the sensation of being pulled down into it, never to be seen again. Grasping a rusty rail, she trudged up the pitted concrete stairs, which seemed to grow steeper with each step. Finally she was level with the Coast Highway; shuffling carefully across, she spied a small grocery store across the four lanes, which loomed as wide as a football field. Someone whooshed past her on a skateboard, almost knocking her down. She was too tired to protest as she kept trudging, her sandals making slapping sounds against her feet.

Once she got to the door of the store, the lights shining so brightly inside the windows they hurt her eyes, she held on to the handle for support. As she struggled to open the door, she heard someone call her name.

"Ginger?"

Her heart leapt; her head spun from both the bees and an explosion of relief—she turned around, one arm reaching out toward—

But it wasn't Tom. It was Jimmy Cho. Dizziness encircled her; she was inside a tornado of dashed hopes and fear. Was Mindy here? She didn't want her sister to see her, she couldn't shoplift if Mindy was around. But Mindy might buy her something, an orange, a piece of bologna, a slice of bread—

She fell sideways but didn't crash to the ground. Jimmy's arms were around her and he was saying something; she was smiling up at him and nodding, even though she couldn't understand him because of the bees. Her head was enormous, a hive, they must have been coming in and out through her ears. She raised her hand to swat them away, then she saw black spots in front of her eyes—the bees were trying to get in through her eyes! She shut them, shut her mouth tight, and then—

She didn't know anything anymore.

11

Ginger blinked. Her head throbbed and it took her a few seconds to realize she was flat on her back. Blinking again, trying to focus, she looked up into brown eyes, eyes wide with alarm.

"Ginger? Ginger? Are you awake?"

Jimmy Cho was hovering over her. She turned her head and realized she was still outside the grocery store, sprawled out on a narrow, splintery bench. Jimmy held a bag of pretzels and was trying to shove them, one at a time, into her mouth. She sat up—too quickly; the bees threatened to return—grabbed the pretzels, and began to wolf them down, forcing herself to slow up as her cavernous stomach started to clench, threatening to bring them back up again.

"Water," she croaked, and Jimmy handed her a bottle of Coke, already opened. She gulped some down, ate a few more pretzels. She was panting like a dog—a starved dog, the effort of eating almost too much for her in her weakened state. She leaned back and closed her eyes, taking deep breaths.

"Jesus Christ" was all Jimmy could say. She opened her eyes, tried to smile up at him as he stood there, rumpling his hair, looking like he had no idea what to do.

"It's OK," she said, her voice stronger. "I'm just hungry."

"You passed the fuck out from hunger, Ginger. What the hell?"

"I was on my way inside to buy some groceries."

"Really?" Now he looked suspicious. "With what? Your good looks?"

She gazed down at her hands, still trembling as she plucked another pretzel out of the bag and shoved it into her mouth. She concentrated on the taste, now that her belly had something in it; the crunchy, slightly burned outside, the crystals of salt, the dryness. Downing more Coke, she let out a satisfying burp.

She was too weary to pretend to be embarrassed by it.

"OK. I was going to shoplift. Fine. You caught me. Go tell Mindy, then. I don't care." Tears sprang to her eyes, running down her burning cheeks. She didn't care. All she cared about was more food.

"Let me go in and get you something else. What? I'm not made of money, though." He laughed teasingly; she smiled, too. It was the least she could do.

"Ha ha. Some bread, some lunch meat, maybe some cheese? And some more Coke," she said. "Is that too much?"

He shook his head, went inside the door, which rang a little bell when he opened it. She could tell there was a transistor radio inside the store because as the door opened, she caught a snippet of "We Gotta Get Out of This Place," and chuckled. Was it some kind of sign?

Still clumsy with exhaustion and stuffing her mouth with dry, salty pretzels, she waited patiently. The pretzels were gone in an instant, so she licked the crumbs off her fingers and let out another huge sigh. Thank God for Jimmy.

But Tom. What if Tom saw her with him? And where *was* Tom, anyway?

Too much, it was all too much—the shack, Tom, the shame of passing out and being found by Jimmy, the hunger, always the hunger. Just look at her nails! They were an embarrassment, dirty, ragged. She wanted a nail file. She wanted nail clippers. She wanted soap.

She wanted perfume, powder, lotion to make her crusty skin smooth again. She wanted decent clothes. More than anything, she wanted to go into a restaurant and sit at a table and be brought food, whatever she wanted—ice cream and fried clams and onion rings and hamburgers and pieces of pie. To eat from real dishes, with cool, heavy silverware. To drink milk—oh, milk! She hadn't drunk milk in so long! Cold, frothy milk out of a glass—

More tears ran down her cheeks. All because of milk! What was wrong with her?

Jimmy came out with a paper bag, and it took all her self-control not to snatch it out of his arms and tear everything open right there and then. But the food was for Tom, too. And the others. She could make it home now, probably. Get back to the shack, make herself a sandwich—only one—and then she'd be able to show the others the bounty. When they got back.

Only one thing was wrong.

"I—I can't pay you," she told Jimmy, deciding that honesty was the only thing she could give him. "I'm broke. There's no money, not until Tom comes back."

"Where is he?"

Honesty, she reminded herself. She squared her shoulders, looked into his eyes.

"I don't know. Probably Mexico. He goes—we go—to score pot and sell it here. That's where he said he was going but it's been a few days and he should be back by now. Don't tell Mindy, whatever you do."

"Don't worry about that," Jimmy said with a scowl.

"What do you mean?"

"I mean your sister dumped me."

"No! Not—I saw you two! She's crazy about you!"

"She's crazy about her career and someone like—me—is—can

only be—can only get in her way. She made that very—she made a decision. She doesn't need me."

"That doesn't sound like her," Ginger began, but then stopped. Mindy was so single-minded. The architect of the Plan. It sounded *exactly* like her.

"Never mind me, I'll get over it." But there was a catch to his voice, and he looked away for a minute, cleared his throat. "What about you? Let me walk you back home, anyway. You shouldn't be alone, you might faint again."

"No, I'll be fine."

"Tough. I'm coming."

Jimmy shifted the groceries and waited for her to rise shakily from the bench. She held on to his steady arm and started leading him back to the lot.

They didn't talk; she couldn't think of anything to say and he seemed lost in his own thoughts, probably about Mindy. Her stupid, selfish sister who didn't have any idea how lucky she was. But when they finally got to the lot, Ginger cried out in despair.

Because the shack wasn't there. It had vanished. How long was she gone?

"No, this can't be happening," she mumbled, running toward the ruins of her life. There were tire tracks in the lot, big wide ones, probably from a truck. The shack wasn't entirely demolished, as she'd first thought; there were some remnants left. The walls and roof were gone but the sleeping bags were still there, the overturned garbage can they used as a table. Some clothes were on the ground—some of Tom's T-shirts, board shorts, one of her bathing suits, an old charm bracelet; she rushed to them, gathering them up desperately along with some magazines that Mindy had been featured in, which she'd hidden from Tom.

Everything else was gone. Even the weed. Thank God Tom had taken the money with him, after all.

"What? What's happened?" Jimmy was staring at her as she crawled through the rubble, snatching at things—there was a spoon, surely she would need a spoon! And a coffee can, still a third full. A coffee cup she'd lifted from a diner—it was chipped, not cracked.

"They—they took it down! Our home—it's gone. It used to be here and it's not. Oh, what will Tom think? I let it happen, I did! I should never have left! It's all my fault and he'll, he'll—" Waves of sobs rattled her body; she was crying so hard she felt like she was vomiting. "He'll never forgive me. He'll leave me. If he hasn't already. Oh, what do I do now? What will happen to me?"

"Try to calm down," Jimmy said, dropping the grocery bag. He stepped over a broken plate, put his arm around her. "Jesus, Ginger. It's only a dump."

"It's my *life*," she snarled, throwing off his arm. "It's my whole life. And it's gone. Everything's gone—everyone always leaves me!"

Jimmy looked so bewildered, his eyes wide, his mouth half-open. She took some ragged breaths, trying to calm down. It wasn't his fault, he was being kind. But he wasn't the person she needed right now. *Tom* would tell her how it would work out. *Tom* would have some kind of plan in his back pocket.

"It's all gone," she repeated, deflated. "This is where I lived. With Tom, and some other guys, and when they come back and the shack's gone, what will they say?"

"But they're not here now. You are. You can't sleep here tonight, not in the open."

"I have before."

"I'm not going to let you do that. You're coming back with me— I'm staying with this friend of mine, Howie, and his girlfriend. I've been crashing on their couch. You can stay there tonight. You have to, Ginger."

"But—Tom—if he comes back, how will he know where I am?"

"Leave a note. Here." Jimmy tore off a flap of the grocery bag and pointed at a pencil on the ground. "Write him a note. It's up on Palisades, I'll write the address. Tell him you'll be back tomorrow."

"OK." Ginger obediently wrote the note and pinned it beneath a brick, where the door used to be. "I hope he'll see it."

"C'mon. I borrowed Howie's car—I was going to surf today but the waves were shit. That's why I was at the grocery store, to pick up some grub to bring home. Good thing I was."

"I guess."

"Let's go. You'll spend the night, I'll bring you back tomorrow. Unless—do you want me to take you to Mindy?"

"No!" The idea was jolting. It was bad enough that Jimmy had to witness this. She couldn't bear it if Mindy knew the truth about her circumstances. "You sure it's OK with your friend?"

"Sure. Howie and Jen are cool. They've been putting up with me. Although I'm going back home now. I've—well, I guess I've done enough here. The California dream isn't what it's cracked up to be, at least not for me."

Jimmy sounded as if he wouldn't mind sharing more, but Ginger was too tired to encourage it. Mindy had dumped him, he was sad. But she had her own problems.

They rode in silence, and when they entered the apartment, Ginger was so overwhelmed, so crippled with shyness, she wanted to run away. She was a feral creature, she realized. Not used to society. Not used to *kindness*. Jen—a stunningly tall woman with long brown hair that hung straight and shining, ends trimmed neatly, down her back—clucked over her as soon as Jimmy explained she needed a place to stay the night. Howie sported a neatly trimmed beard, like a professor, although he was lounging in a beanbag chair smoking a joint.

"Could I—could I take a shower?" Ginger stammered, because Jen looked so understanding.

The other woman smiled broadly, showed her the shower, went to her closet, and grabbed a sundress that was so pretty, with red poppies on a cream background, Ginger nearly burst into tears.

"Take this. It's too dainty for the likes of me, but it'll look gorgeous on you. Please. I insist."

Ginger nodded. Her face burned with shame, but the dress was so beautiful, she couldn't help but want it. She went in the bathroom, wiggled out of her threadbare clothes, turned on the shower. There was a bottle of shampoo, a creamy bar of soap. Even a slender Gillette women's razor—the pot of gold at the end of the rainbow. She stepped beneath the warm water—ohhhh! It had been so long since she'd felt anything this good, the soft, warm water that didn't make her flinch, the papaya smell of the shampoo, the luxury of soap suds, the satisfaction of scraping away her fair leg hair, exposing smooth, clean tanned skin. She could have stayed in the shower forever, but she was a guest, she should leave some hot water for others.

Then the bliss of pulling on that adorable sundress—no panties, but that was OK. She might ask Jen later if she could have a pair or two. Jen seemed like the kind of woman who enjoyed taking care of others. Ginger borrowed a comb from the medicine cabinet and pulled it through her hair, even dared a side part. Maybe, with real shampoo and away from the salty, humid ocean air, her curls would behave themselves.

Shyly, she stepped out of the bathroom, releasing a cloud of papaya-scented steam; she asked Jen if she could throw her old clothes in the trash.

"Oh, honey, by all means," the older woman said. "Look, I have a pile of things I never wear all ready for you, in this bag. You don't mind, do you?" Jen looked anxious, as if Ginger would be offended.

But it was only gratitude that flooded over her; she shook her head, afraid to trust her voice.

They ate a hearty meal, a stew of some kind that had been simmering on the stove, smelling of spices and browned meat. And there was crusty bread with real butter, and a salad with creamy dressing. Ginger's hand shook as she tried to eat daintily; on her own, she would have wolfed it all down with her hands, drunk the stew right out of the bowl. The others pretended not to notice that she greedily took seconds.

"Kids, we're going out to a movie. You want to come?" Howie glanced at Jimmy and Ginger. Jimmy had been silent all evening, morosely eating his food, although he had whistled when Ginger first stepped out in the new dress.

Now he turned to Ginger, cocking an eyebrow.

"No, thank you," she said politely. She was so tired now, her belly full. That people lived like this—generous, civilized, their refrigerator full of food and their closets of clothes they didn't wear—was so overwhelming. As the entire day had been. Her home was gone. Tom was missing. She'd fainted, and Jimmy Cho had rescued her. And now she was here, under a real roof, protected from—well, everything awful. It was too much; her eyes were already half-closed with exhaustion.

"I'll stay in, too," Jimmy said, as if Ginger were a child who needed a babysitter. But he flashed her a grateful look; she knew he was happy for the excuse. He hadn't mentioned Mindy to Howie and Jen, and she wondered if they even knew about Jimmy and her sister. "We'll do the dishes. You two go have fun."

"Thanks." And Jen and Howie were soon out the door, while

Mindy found herself at the kitchen sink drying as Jimmy washed up. How cozy and domestic it seemed! Last night she'd slept outside a shack in a sleeping bag, swatting at sandflies, shuddering at howling coyotes. Now she was wearing a dress while drying dishes. It was like they were playing house, she and Jimmy. She started to giggle.

"What's so funny?" Jimmy asked as he handed her a plate. He was surprisingly easy to be with, calm and collected although obviously thinking of Mindy. He didn't talk much, but his silence wasn't full of unexpressed emotions, either—not like Tom's silences were. Tom could glare, be aloof, or shun, depending on his mood. His silences were as confusing and entangling as his words were. There was nothing easy about Tom, she was forced to admit.

But she missed him now like she would have missed a leg or an arm. She felt rudderless, too overwhelmed by decisions. Jimmy had told her to come here tonight. But who would tell her what to do tomorrow?

"I just—it seemed funny, all of a sudden. Playing house like this. I haven't stood at a kitchen sink in so long. I haven't eaten from real plates, with real utensils. It's like I'm in a commercial or something."

"Honey, look at how clean these dishes are—why, it's a miracle!" Jimmy grinned, getting into the mood. His voice was deep, like an actor's. "I can see myself in this plate!"

"And no dishpan hands, either!" Mindy held up a hand, like she was a model. Then they both cracked up.

And fell silent again. She could only guess at Jimmy's tangled thoughts. Her own were all of Tom, and tomorrow, and the shack, and how she'd get money if Tom didn't come back. She'd have to get a job. She could probably waitress or something. She might ask Mindy about that modeling job she'd mentioned, although as much as she sometimes missed her sister she really didn't want to be around her right now. She didn't want to hear "I told you so." She didn't want Mindy bossing her around, even though that was exactly what she needed from Tom.

It was Tom, all Tom—how could he have left her for so long? Wasn't she his girl? He'd told her that so many times—even when she knew he was coming back after being with someone else. She could always smell it on him even if there wasn't any obvious perfume. She'd tried pouting, tried throwing things, tried begging. Nothing worked. Yet he always did come home to her—and wasn't that enough?

He told her it should be. That she would never have another man like him, that she was the special one. Those other girls would have other men. Ginger, he explained, never would; she was his vessel. His alone.

"Done," Jimmy said, flipping the sponge into a little dish next to the faucet. "Thanks for helping."

"I should have done them all, to repay you—to repay Howie and Jen," Ginger said, her face burning. Why hadn't she offered? She didn't know how to behave around other people anymore. While Tom thought that admirable, right now Ginger was ashamed.

"I didn't have anything else to do, and I didn't want to go to that movie."

"I'm sorry about Mindy," Ginger said as they moved into the tiny living room. The apartment wasn't big, a pocket-sized kitchen, living room, and bedroom. There were surfboards leaning against a wall in the living room; a surprisingly large TV; a comfortable, saggy blue couch; a coffee table piled with candles, *TV Guides*, roach rings, and rolling papers. She sat down next to Jimmy on the couch. He turned on the TV with a clicker, the sound off. The news was on; she recognized Walter Cronkite although she couldn't remember the last time she had watched TV.

"It's not your fault. You're not your sister's keeper."

"I thought she was—well, she really liked you. Although I've never seen her with a guy before. She never dated in high school. Neither of us did."

"The Fabulous Donnelly Girls never dated? That's crazy. You guys, with your mom—wow. When the three of you showed up at Makaha that time, I couldn't believe it. Three golden goddesses who could actually surf."

"They could. Mindy and Mom. I never could keep up with them. It was hard, you know, being the other one. A lot to live up to. Tom helped me realize it wasn't shameful if I didn't place in a competition. If I couldn't keep up with them."

"Yeah, you have to find your own path. You don't need someone to tell you what it is," Jimmy said agreeably, but she sensed he meant something more. Crossing her arms over her chest, she realized he meant Tom, and her skin felt prickly.

But Jimmy didn't say anything else; he pointed the clicker again and turned up the TV volume. "Five thousand more troops were sent to Vietnam this week," Walter Cronkite intoned in that rich, soothing voice. Jimmy quickly changed the channel, to some old black and white movie.

They sat there, the glow of the television casting ghostly light upon them. Ginger's eyes drooped; she yawned. Grabbing a throw pillow, Jimmy plumped it up and placed it on his lap.

"Here," he said, patting the pillow. Ginger stretched out, her head in his lap; his arm fell across her stomach, a warm, anchoring weight. Turning her head toward the television, she recognized the movie, something with Humphrey Bogart and a bird. A falcon, she remembered—had she maybe watched this with Dad, before he left? Sometimes when he still lived with them, she got out of bed at night if she heard the TV on. Mindy always slept so soundly an earthquake wouldn't have bothered her, but Ginger was prone to dreams that woke her up. And she would go to the living room, where Dad often was sitting up late watching an old movie on TV. That was their special time together, hers and Dad's. She'd crawl into his lap and he'd hold her tight, and sometimes she fell asleep there and woke up in the morning back in her own bed. When she fell asleep on Dad's lap, she never had those wild dreams.

Her eyes felt heavy again; the TV screen grew dark, then light, as she struggled to keep her eyes open. But it was so nice, lying here with Jimmy. Jimmy Cho. He was cute, he really was. And hot—his muscles were bigger than Tom's, he wasn't as stringy. He was, well, he was hot, that's what he—

His fingers were stroking the fabric of her dress, sending electrifying darts of pleasure up and down her legs. She squeezed her thighs together, trying to suppress the flame of desire that suddenly roared into being. But pressing her legs together only made it more insistent, and she squirmed.

"Nice," Jimmy murmured. His fingers began to gather the hem of the dress, raising it up, exposing her knee, her thighs. She wasn't wearing panties, she remembered. She was glad.

"Ginger," Jimmy said throatily, shifting so she felt him straining through the thin fabric of his shorts. She groaned, clasping his hand down between her thighs, keeping it there, urging him on.

She didn't say his name.

12

1968

"Ya sank quicker than the *Titanic,* kid."

Summoned once more to Fred's glass-walled office, Mindy sat meekly in front of his desk and nodded miserably. His secretary du jour—who could have been Cher's twin, with long black hair parted in the middle, her abdomen framed by a suede halter top and low-slung bell-bottoms—brought her a sympathy cup of coffee. Fred himself had morphed from Rock Hudson to Peter Fonda. Gone was the tailored suit and Brylcreem; now his hair reached to his chin. He wore yellow-tinted granny glasses and his silk shirt was open to his chest, accented with a denim scarf knotted sideways at his neck.

Mindy still clung to her Pucci print dresses and opaque white hose, frosted hair and Mary Jane heels. And that was the problem, according to Fred.

"We misjudged the temperature of the room; we packaged you wrong. Everything changed while you were in the studio recording that thing. Which, by the way—yowie. Good thing you had a genius engineer who knew how to layer on some tracks, because you're not a natural, honey."

"I never said I was," Mindy protested.

"Anyway, it was all wrong. Two years ago I could have put you on

Hullabaloo or *Shindig!* and we'd have made a fortune. You're cute, you're peppy, you move OK. But it's all about authenticity right now. Cass Elliot, Michelle Phillips, this new girl Janis Ian. You're too square, kid. And you can't write your own songs or play the guitar."

Mindy nodded. There was no use arguing against any of this. She'd hated the whole thing, from start to finish. The humiliating studio session when everyone discovered she couldn't sing, and the hushed conference—which she was not invited to participate in—that resulted. She was given some quick breathing lessons, placed in front of a microphone, backed up by about twenty female singers, and told to whisper-sing, which made no sense but she tried her best.

Nobody could ever say she wasn't game. She tried, oh, she tried to infuse some life into "Just Me and You!" It was a silly novelty song, written by someone she'd never heard of:

> We can shimmy and slide *(dance break)*
> We can groove and glide *(dance break)*
> But the best is when
> We come home again
> And we make our own song
> Dancing along
> To a tune that's new
> Just me and you!
> *(Extended dance break, then repeat)*

It wasn't exactly "Blowin' in the Wind."

She'd recorded a B side that was even worse, a cover of "Puff, the Magic Dragon." Then Fred made her pose for the cover of the forty-five—he dropped the idea of an entire album. He sent her out to radio stations up and down the California coast. She wore white go-go boots and her tailored dresses, always the best-dressed person in the studio. Especially in San Francisco, where she encountered more and more people wearing fringe vests, blue jeans, sandals, beads in their uncombed hair. What she and her friends used to make fun of a couple of years ago was suddenly cool, and she felt ridiculous. As out of touch as Pat Nixon, almost—too perfect. Too coifed.

And the damn thing was, she knew she'd look terrific in a bare midriff; all those years of surfing had sculpted her abdomen. She could grow her hair; its natural color was almost a pure blond, and she'd probably look exactly like Michelle Phillips, maybe even better. But something prevented her from loosening up; her precious wardrobe—those first respectable, grown-up clothes she'd bought the moment she could afford them—had become armor. She relied on her Girl in the Curl image more than she relied on talent because she knew she really didn't have any. Except a talent for being slightly well-known for nothing at all, a girl whose face you'd recognize but not remember where you'd seen it.

The single fizzled out, despite the hours she spent schmoozing with disc jockeys, giggling, letting them put their arms around her, their arms brushing against her breasts, their hands pinching her pert ass.

"What a cutie! Isn't she a cutie? Look who stopped by to visit—Little Mindy D!" they'd gush into the mike while she sat next to them within hands' reach, a huge pair of headphones on her head—she always felt like someone from mission control—and she giggled nonsense and tried not to throw up when they played the song.

But no listener ever called in to ask for it to be played again.

Now she was in Fred's office for the postmortem, and she knew he was going to drop her. Her armpits were clammy; her nose and forehead were probably so shiny they could be seen from space.

"I'm going to drop you," he announced, with the exact right touch of regret in his voice. He was good at this; she was probably the third person he'd dropped that day. "I've tried, sweetheart. We all have. Your kind of pretty went the way of Annette Funicello and Shelley Fabares. It's a whole new world out there."

"I'm not surprised," Mindy said evenly, and it was a relief, in a way. The thought of having to keep pushing that horrible song, or worse yet, recording another, made her want to dig a hole in the sand and disappear into it. All the glittering glory she'd so briefly experienced before the colossal joke that was Little Mindy D seemed like a lifetime ago.

But it was only about nine months. Nine months since she'd picked up that newspaper from her porch. Nine months since she'd seen Jimmy Cho.

"I do thank you for trying," she continued, an odd catch in her voice; she paused and cleared her throat before continuing. "Can I ask one last favor?"

"Sure, kiddo."

"Can you get me on the Bob Hope USO tour? To Vietnam?" Bob Hope was the only celebrity she knew who had a USO show. She figured it would be one last hurrah for her pathetic fame and be a positive thing to do, at that.

The war wasn't popular anywhere—there were big bonfires of burning draft cards almost every night on Sunset. Some of the guys she still knew from the old beach days had gotten out of the draft by doing so much acid the night before they were scheduled to show up to the draft board, they were certifiably insane—at least temporarily—and declared mentally unfit.

But Mindy remembered her father talking about the USO shows when he was in World War II, overseas. Bob Hope and Frances Langford and Jerry Colonna had entertained the troops at a base in Guam. Dad had loved it; he'd talked about it a lot. And while Mindy didn't usually think much about patriotism and love of her country, she felt this was her last chance to do something exciting and glamorous, as well as patriotic. While she was on tour, she'd still be "Little Mindy D."

When she came home, she'd be a has-been. At the age of twenty-three.

"Bob Hope?" Fred exploded with laughter. "You, with Bob Hope? Sweetie, no. Do you have any idea how many legitimate stars want to go on tour with him, just to prove they're brave, and also, by the way, to be featured on his annual television special? Ann-Margret's going this year. Raquel Welch went last year. And, honey, no offense, but you're no Ann-Margret or Raquel Welch."

"Oh." Why had she thought it would be easy? She was still so naïve.

"However," Fred said, thumbing through his Rolodex, "I could maybe get you on Johnny Grant's tour. You know the guy—he's the honorary mayor of Hollywood or some kind of bullshit, but he emcees all the premieres. His tour is nothing compared to Hope's, you won't get much press coverage, but if you really want to go over there—and I'll tell you right now, I think you're a lunatic—I can hook you up with Johnny. You can sing your song—those soldiers won't give a shit that you can't sing, all you have to do is dance around and wiggle your ass. You'll get all the do gooder points, let me tell you. It won't be easy, and it's not at all glamorous. But sure, it'll give you a couple more months, and you never know what might happen in the meantime while you're there. Maybe all the hippies and druggies will vanish and the world will be sane again." Fred gave a wistful sigh, which touched Mindy. She realized he was uncomfortable with the granny glasses and long hair, with his looser "threads," as he called them. He wanted his suit back, his secretaries dressed in tight skirts and sweaters. He suddenly seemed lost, as lost as she was in this new, messier reality of California in the late sixties.

"Great, I really appreciate it."

"And I'll take five percent of your pay, instead of the usual ten. Only 'cause I like ya, kid."

"Thanks, Fred."

When Mindy walked outside and handed her ticket to the valet, she couldn't help but notice the young man looked like Steve McQueen.

She didn't have much time before Johnny Grant's next tour left, so she was told to get herself down to USO headquarters immediately, where her arm became an achy pincushion after a series of vaccinations for mysterious diseases like yellow fever. Then she was issued a helmet and a flak jacket and given some basic first aid training "just in case." She was told to provide her blood type for her dog tags and was given a bottle of antimalarial pills that she was instructed to take daily "or else."

"Oh," the humorless nurse said as Mindy tucked the pills into her purse. "Write a will before you go, honey. They always forget to tell you girls that."

"A will?" Mindy squeaked, and the nurse glared at her over her glasses.

"All you pretty young things react the same way. Yes, a will. You're going to war, not a high school dance. Now, who's your next of kin?"

Mindy's mind went blank, at first refusing to understand the implications of the question. The nurse began to sigh heavily and reorganize a medicine cabinet while she waited for Mindy to make up her mind.

Finally, only because she had no idea where Ginger was, Mindy picked up the clipboard and listed Mom's address, which conjured up too many emotions. Rage, hurt. Lately, guilt. She hadn't seen her mother in too long. She hadn't intended to let Carol know where she was going.

She still needed to punish her mother. Although she had no way of knowing if Carol even thought of her at all, of course. Remembering that night on Makaha, Mindy doubted that she did. But one thing she did not doubt was the fact that none of this—shots, pills, flak jacket, and unwanted guilt—was what Mindy thought she'd signed up for.

It only got worse from there.

"They have to see you in the last row. There'll be soldiers hanging from trees to get a look at you girls. You gotta dazzle, honeybunches," Johnny Grant told them on the cold, noisy transport plane from Los Angeles. Besides Mindy, there was a flamenco guitar player, the current Miss Santa Monica, and a sister folk act.

It was these last two that he trained his bright baby-blue eyes on. "And no hippie-dippie shit. I don't care if you're singing about Tom Dooley about to die, you wear short skirts, lots of big hair and eyelashes, and show your boobs. That's what these boys want, trust me. This is my fourth trip. They don't want to see me—they want girls. Girls with a capital G. Got it?"

They all nodded, although one of the folk singers, fingering her long, straight hair, stifled a sob and was comforted by her sister. Mindy watched them with a twang in her heart; she couldn't help it. How different life would have been if she and Ginger had been singers, or dancers, or simply sisters who followed each other to college! Anything, anyone, instead of the daughters of a surf bum. Maybe she wouldn't have been on this plane to Vietnam. Or maybe Ginger would have been with her, the two of them facing this gaping maw of uncertainty together. Mindy had always felt stronger with Ginger. The big sister in charge. Being brave for her sister, and so then, brave for herself.

She could have used some courage as they winged ever nearer to Saigon.

"I can lend you two some of my wigs," Miss Santa Monica assured the bewildered girls with a sunny smile. "And all it takes is a pair of scissors to make anything a miniskirt. I majored in home ec!"

While Johnny went on to tell them about how important it was to always wear their helmets except onstage, and to always obey the military escorts whose jobs it would be to keep them alive, and to try not to vomit the first time they saw a burn victim, Mindy felt herself begin to shut down and finally fall asleep for a few hours. She didn't register anything else until they neared Saigon. Suddenly escort helicopters were flying dangerously close to the wings; gunners were hanging outside the copters, cigarettes dangling out of their mouths like they were at a picnic. As the plane descended through the clouds, Debbie, one of the folk singers, pointed out the window to a faraway gray puff of cloud that had burst up from the canopy of palm trees blanketing the entire landscape outside of the city.

"Is that enemy fire?" she asked. No one could answer her, but Mindy's stomach liquefied.

"I want to go home," Debbie's sister, Sally, wailed, and while the rest of them glanced away, embarrassed for her, Mindy knew they all felt the same.

In the weeks after that memorable arrival, Mindy's vocabulary expanded. Now she knew that *Charlie* meant the enemy, the Vietcong; a *boondoggle* was a mess of a military operation that usually turned into a situation that was FUBAR—a total disaster, from the soldiers' point of view anyway. *Boondocks* meant deep in the jungle, and sometimes they did venture there, to tiny little makeshift bases surrounded by Charlie, the most dangerous places of all, where they often heard the muffled, but still terrifying, din of firefights not far from camp, and where they had to sleep with their helmets on. And perform with them on, too, to the disappointment of the soldiers.

Bugs—cockroaches the size of small dogs, centipedes the size of hands—snakes, mosquitoes, more mosquitoes, more cockroaches, hairy spiders, more snakes. She was terrified to go to the john when they were in the boonies; the soldiers teased them about the vipers that hung out in the latrines. The teasing always ended in a very serious, "No, really, they'll kill you." Mindy learned to pee in a Coke bottle and do worse in an old helmet the girls washed daily, passing it around like, well—like a hat you were forced to shit in. But at least if there were snakes around, the rat population wasn't as bold. At night, deep in the jungle, which was so turbulent with the chatter of birds and monkeys and frogs, a cacophony that never ceased, the girls slept in mosquito-netted cots only a few inches off the ground. Sally swore that one night, a rat nibbled the ends of her hair. So they pushed their cots all together, a little island of terrified women clutching their shoes so they wouldn't wake up to find a scorpion in them, curlers in their hair—they needed to look fabulous in the morning!—and holding hands. As if this would scare off the rats and snakes—but sometimes, it did seem to work.

As wretched, as primitive, and as dangerous as those tiny camps were, Mindy sometimes preferred them to the larger, relatively safer bases. Because at the bases, they had to visit the military hospitals.

The first time they approached a hospital, she'd clutched Miss Santa Monica's hand tightly. Her real name was Sherry Jones, but for some reason Mindy always thought of her as her title. Miss Santa Monica clutched Mindy's hand just as tightly. Sherry was trembling, although Mindy willed her surfer's legs to stay strong. Her stomach somersaulted, as if a rogue wave were about to wipe her out.

Rows and rows of cots, separated by spectral white curtains. Far off in the corner, unearthly shrieks, cries of "Incoming, incoming!" that made her heart leap out of her chest until a nurse—a girl as young as she was but whose eyes appeared decades older—explained that it was shell shock, the head cases.

"They still think they're in the jungle," she said. "Try not to let it get to you."

Sally, the weepier of the folk singing sisters, turned around as if she was about to flee, but Johnny—wearing his khaki uniform, like the soldiers—prevented her.

"You can't," he said firmly but kindly; his eyes glistened softly, but he blocked Sally's exit. "This is what you signed up for. They can't leave, so neither can you. You have to keep going, talk to them, write letters for them, anything they want. You can't let them see you cry or faint—afterward, you can scream all you want, sweetie, and I'll scream right along with you. But not now. Not here."

They remained in their little huddle, uncertain what to do next, until Johnny pulled them apart, forcing each girl to take a different ward. Miss Santa Monica volunteered for the burn unit, which earned her a special grin from Johnny, a hearty "Attagirl!"

Mindy was ushered down a row of beds, handed some paper and a pen, and told to offer to write letters home. "Don't let them harass you," the young but worldly nurse told her. The nurse was in khaki combat fatigues like all the other soldiers; the only thing that made her look different was that her hair was long, in pigtails, and she wore a stethoscope around her neck. "They'll try, some of them. Even on their deathbeds, some of them try."

"OK," Mindy said with a gulp. Then the nurse left—and she was standing alone in an aisle lined on all sides with men in beds. Plastering on that fake Donnelly smile, she pulled a curtain aside and sang out, "Hello, I'm Little Mindy D!"

She'd visited many hospitals since then; she'd taken her turn with the burn victims with flesh unrecognizable as human. Her nostrils were singed with the smells, her ears rang with the cries for morphine. She'd seen soldiers with heads half blown off, but thankfully they were bandaged, so the worst was left to the imagination. She'd seen amputees, held soldiers' hands while their death rattle commenced, a sound she would never forget—like snoring, only not; a saber battle between this life and the next taking place in the lungs. She'd slapped away hands from her breasts, her skirt, her ass. She'd refused impulsive proposals and then sat down to write letters home to the girls they'd left behind. Struggling not to cry, Mindy had held the tape recorder while soldiers awkwardly tried to find the right words—not too chipper, not too terrified, usually nakedly sentimental—to say to their mothers and fathers. Once a man had vomited up yellow liquid on her shoes and sobbed with embarrassment while she tried to turn it into a joke.

The worst were the ones who didn't say anything at all, the ones who seemed locked into a nightmare, unable to escape.

Over those endless weeks, Mindy and the others toughened up. No longer did knees shake, and the impulse to turn around and flee was squelched. That iciness she'd first felt on the plane—that opaque curtain that had fallen between her and reality—took over. When they'd first landed in Saigon and encountered a long line of soldiers waiting to board a transport plane home, she'd been struck by how joyless they were at the prospect. Shouldn't they have been jumping up and down with relief? Falling to their knees in thankful prayer?

But no. There was no chatter, no horseplay. No emotion at all—their eyes had the same dazed expression, blank, seemingly unable to register either happiness or fear.

Now sometimes after a rough hospital visit, Mindy recognized that look in her small compact mirror. It wasn't as pronounced as the soldiers', of course. She hadn't had to scoop out her buddy's guts from a helmet or seen a head explode next to her. But she'd seen enough.

The terror of performing that she'd experienced back home had been replaced by relief. Parading about the stage, shaking her ass, bopping her head as she butchered that terrible song, then joining the other girls in the big finale (a medley of "California Dreamin'," "Happy Together," "I'm a Believer," always ending with "Blowin' in the Wind," which made even tough soldiers wipe their eyes)—this was easy now. She still felt like a fool, like an alien, onstage. But compared to the terrors of open-sided helicopters, snakes in johns, men missing limbs and reason, she'd take it. She never thought of her tattered joke of a career; that was so far away, so ridiculous as to be a little girl's fantasy.

In the jungle, perched on the edge of a blood-soaked hospital cot, she only thought of the here and now, not the past or the future.

"And now, gentlemen, I'd like to introduce you to a real California Girl, right here in Vietnam. Let's welcome Little Mindy D, who's going to sing her hit song, 'Just Me and You!'" Johnny Grant waved at her in the wings. As the jaunty opening notes of her background music teed up through the staticky loudspeakers, Mindy stared out at the sea of khaki before her.

They were in Dong Ha, in the central part of Vietnam.

This was the twentieth show they'd performed since they landed two months ago. Mindy took a breath; the humidity was so heavy, it was an effort to get enough air in her lungs. Even after all this time, she still wasn't used to it. But she smiled wide and trotted out onstage in her gold-spangled minidress and white go-go boots, waving her arms as she was greeted by wolf whistles and thunderclaps of applause. Then she launched into the dreadful song, really going at it during the long dance break, when she reached down into the front row and pulled some lucky soldier up onstage to dance with her. That cat could really groove! He just about stole the whole show, and as she took her bow alongside him, her sides heaving, trying to catch her breath, they were showered with hoots and hollers and whistles, the guys clapping their hands until she thought they'd come off.

By now, though, she knew they weren't clapping for her, Little Mindy D. Or even for the soldier, one of their own.

They were applauding the fact that for this moment, they were alive, despite the bombs and firefights and land mines and pits full of deadly snakes in the jungle, booby traps courtesy of Charlie. Right now, this breath, this smile, this blink of an eye, there were pretty girls and loud music and corny jokes. There was laughter.

In five hours, or ten, or twenty-four, they'd have to go back out in the jungle with their heavy packs, drenched in sweat, creeping through choking foliage, listening for that giveaway snap of a twig or rustle of leaves and falling on their bellies, or taking cover or returning fire or praying to God or thinking of Mom or whispering the name of a sweetheart or crying out the name of their best friend on the right who'd just taken a hit.

Mindy knew, because she'd asked, that of an audience of a hundred soldiers—boyfriends, sons, husbands, fathers, best buddies, the guy who lived around the corner who once got your mail by mistake and returned it with a shy knock at the door, that frat boy who once bought you a milkshake at the student union—

A quarter of them would never make it home alive.

China Beach, Da Nang, on the South China Sea.

"Last stop before home," Johnny announced as they clustered on the tarmac, having just disembarked from the transport plane. Both the folk sisters cried. "You've done good, girls. I hope you'll consider coming back on my next tour."

None of them could meet his gaze, and he sighed resignedly.

"So we'll do a couple of shows but the rest of the time we get R & R at the beach. You'll still have to tour the hospital there and be peppy and pretty and nice to the guys on leave. But you can get some sun on the beach, go swimming if you want. They surf there, the guys. It's a kick to see them out there—they have a surf club, if you like to watch that kind of thing. Some of those guys are pretty good."

"So am I!" Mindy couldn't believe how quickly it popped out of her mouth. Or how intense was her desire, right then, to paddle out on her board, to feel the cool water wash over her, marvel at the way the sunlight glistened on the water, blinding at first until you got used to it. Feel that same healing sun baking her salt-coated skin. Her hair loose and natural, wet, then halfway dry, then wet again as she caught wave after wave. The power beneath her feet, the confidence that she could harness it, use it to hit high after exhilarating high, the shore rushing up, the roar of the waves at her back.

She hadn't surfed since that day at Malibu. The day she won. The day she slept with Jimmy.

At every base, at every small outpost, she'd wondered if she would see him. He'd threatened to enlist, and she had no idea if he had. But it seemed likely, because Jimmy didn't make idle threats. He didn't have a grand plan for living—no goals, no checklist of things he wanted to do before he was thirty, that kind of thing. But if he said he was going to do something, he did it.

Like loving her—that hadn't been an empty declaration, not at all. When he'd told her, that awful afternoon, that all he wanted was to be with her, nothing else, she knew he meant it. He wasn't saying it to seduce her. He wasn't saying it to stop her from dumping her. He said it because it was all he wanted in that moment.

But she'd hurt him, so much she couldn't think about it anymore—
she'd spent too many sleepless nights recalling her words, the look in
his eyes: disbelief followed by pride and anger and finally, total disdain.
So she'd stopped thinking about it, forced herself to block the memories. She'd concentrated on her career, that colossal joke. Once again
using it as an excuse to run away from commitment, and yes, she was
like her mother, and no, she didn't care to think too much about that.

Then she ran away even farther, to Vietnam.

Where she did think of him, more than ever. She couldn't help
it—every time she saw a muscular soldier with thick black hair and
laughing brown eyes, she thought of him. And she questioned her
decision to come here, after all. Had she been so desperate to join a
USO tour because she wanted to find Jimmy, not her career?

What an imbecile she was. To think that she'd find one soldier
among thousands, in the jungles of Vietnam.

"Remember, show's tonight at eight. But you have the rest of the day
off. Enjoy, don't leave base, and I'll see you at the bar." Johnny Grant
wiped his glistening bald head with a handkerchief as they stood surrounded by their luggage. He seemed happy—happier than Mindy
had seen him so far. The end of another tour and no casualties.

They'd been shelled at a base only once, right in the middle of the
show. She was standing next to the rickety stage, watching the sisters
strum the first few chords of their act, when she heard whistles, not
the usual wolf whistles but something louder, growing in intensity.
Then she was flat on the ground, dirt in her mouth and nose, a soldier pinned on top of her hissing, "Stay down, stay down." As if she
needed to be told! Guns from the base started firing back, deep
booming percussions; she clamped her hands over her ears, shut her
eyes, and prayed to a God she'd never really had much use for before.

She regretted neglecting Him now, but she prayed anyway, over and over—"Dear God, don't let me die. Dear God, don't let me die. Dear God, don't let me die."

Before she could say it again, the shelling had stopped; she opened her eyes, stared at the loamy dirt, and spit some of it out of her mouth. The soldier was pulling her up; he was laughing.

Laughing!

"They like to do that just to keep us on our toes," he explained as he helped her brush the dirt off her minidress. Around her, the other girls were brushing off their dresses, too, and Johnny Grant was reaching for a flask he always carried in his back pocket. Miss Santa Monica was sobbing; the soldier who had shielded her was patting her on the back.

"Charlie's too cowardly to show his face," Mindy's soldier—forever he would be that, *her* soldier, the one who would have taken the incoming shells for her—continued as his eyes scanned the perimeter of the makeshift stage they'd set up; the jungle was right there, it always was, full of trees and fronds and foliage you needed a machete to cut through. Mindy shivered, wondering how close the Vietcong—Charlie—had gotten to them.

"Thank you," she remembered to say as her soldier walked away, joining a patrol that was forming.

More inadequate words had never been spoken. The show was canceled, of course; they spent the night huddled together, unable to sleep, counting the hours on Miss Santa Monica's Timex wristwatch until they could be helicptered out.

Now it was over. All over. No more snakes in latrines. They could be shelled here, she supposed—Johnny said it had happened before—but it didn't feel like being at war, not at all. Not at China Beach. And then, after two more shows here—

Home. What she'd do once she was there, Mindy didn't care. Not right now. She only wanted to be safe. To be able to go to the john and not worry about snakes sticking their diamond-shaped heads out of the toilet.

They had been waved onto the base by the armed guard, the jeeps passing under a big, arched sign that proclaimed *China Beach*. A few hundred yards away was a red and white water tower. The usual barbed wire lined the perimeter, including the beach. But there were also picnic tables and barbecues in shady groves of mangrove trees, tiki huts among the usual Quonset huts. Women—nurses on leave— and soldiers were strolling around in vacation clothing—most of the guys shirtless, their dog tags gleaming in the sun, the women in shorts and sleeveless blouses. Everyone was in sandals or barefoot, not a combat boot in sight. Sniffing the air, she inhaled the scent of coconut oil. With that one whiff, she was back in California.

And the ocean—it reminded her of California, too, although the waves were mushy today. Still, there were guys out there on boards, obviously beginners. Getting a surf lesson or two on leave.

A lifeguard in his stately tower surveyed his kingdom, binoculars in hand.

Suddenly Mindy couldn't wait; she needed to get into her suit right now, find that surf club Johnny mentioned, and beg, borrow, or steal a board. It was as vital as breathing, as comforting as home. And she *was* homesick, she realized—not for a house or a piece of furniture or any kind of possession, or even for a particular person, but for familiar *sensations:* the sound of the pounding surf, the smell of salt water and seaweed, the joyful screeches of people splashing in water. *This* was home—water, sun, surf.

Why had she been running away from it in heels these last few years? Betraying her truest self, Benedict Arnold in a Pucci print?

Jogging with the other girls to their barracks, joining in their girlish shrieks of laughter, she felt ten years younger.

She felt like herself.

Mindy Donnelly.

In her bright pink bikini, she strolled over to the colorful collection of materials that composed the China Beach Surf Shop—the siding was made of different types of lumber, painted in vibrant colors; the roof was corrugated tin, held down against tropical winds by huge rocks. There were surfboards stacked up, and the usual collection of guys in board shorts lounging in beach chairs. She didn't see any women.

There was a sign hanging next to a half window cut out of one of the walls: *China Beach Surf Shop, Boards to Members Only.*

"How do I become a member?" Mindy called out, startling the drowsy bunch drinking beer. Washboard abs, rounded biceps on otherwise lean arms—they looked like they belonged in Malibu, not Vietnam. Only the buzz cuts and dog tags nestled in chest hair labeled them military.

"No girls allowed," one of the guys shouted back.

"Stop with the clubhouse stuff. Seriously. I want to surf."

"Only experienced surfers allowed here, girlie. But nice bikini!" Wolf whistles pierced the air, drowning out a record playing on a wobbly turntable—Jefferson Airplane's "Somebody to Love." For a minute Mindy was back at the Whisky, watching the new band from San Francisco take the stage. That was before Grace Slick and their meteoric success, of course. The smoke-filled room, the girls dancing above the crowd, the movie stars, the cigarette holder she used to use—worlds, a universe or two, away. She hadn't smoked a cigarette since joining the USO.

"We could use a mascot, though, right, guys? Gidget, you can be our mascot. Bring me a beer," one of the soldiers—a blond with wavy hair—proclaimed, pulling her back to reality.

"I'm no Gidget. I can surf rings around Gidget and around most of you, I'm guessing."

"Sure," someone scoffed—a guy with a surprisingly substantial beer gut hanging over his shorts, but otherwise his arms and legs were lean. You didn't see many guys with extra flesh over here. He must have been drinking beer nonstop since beginning his R & R.

"Try me," Mindy retorted. "Give me a board and see."

"What do you say, guys? Let Gidget here show us how it's done?" The beer-gut guy laughed.

"She'll look even better wet," the blond said with a shrug. "OK, Gidget, here's a board. C'mon, guys."

He chose a yellow board with a striped fin and a surprising kick to the nose; Mindy ran her hand over it and laughed at the sensation, the smooth waxed surface, warm from the sun, with a nice bit of grit on top.

"Excellent," she said, lifting it up, holding it over her head so that it shaded the sun. "Not too heavy. You shape them here?"

"Yeah," the blond said, looking at her with new interest. "I do. I'm one of the lifeguards."

"They have lifeguards? Like, this is your regular job, you don't go on patrol at all?"

"No," the guy said, looking defensive. "You have no idea how many idiots almost drown out there. And I don't know if you've heard, but we need bodies. Living, breathing bodies to fight Charlie. It's my job to keep them alive so they can go back."

"OK, no judgment. I'm just surprised." And Mindy hoisted the board beneath her arm and started off toward the surf. She glanced back; a trail of bemused soldiers followed behind like ducklings.

"Aren't you afraid of snakes?" one of them sneered, and she stopped.

"Snakes?"

"Water serpents, the ocean's full of 'em."

"Stop it, Conrad," the blond said. "Don't mind him," he told Mindy. "Yeah, there are snakes, but the lifeguard on duty would have a flag up if there were a lot of them today. They come and go."

"OK." Mindy squinted up at the lifeguard on duty, who now noticed the odd-looking group trudging through the sand; he'd turned and trained his binoculars on them. But she didn't see any flag, so she kept going.

She maneuvered her way through men and women on beach blankets, trying not to step on any cans or bottle tops—this beach hadn't been raked in a very long time. The guys behind her kept up a steady stream of adolescent jokes and chortles, and she felt like a schoolteacher with a class of naughty boys. She grinned, anticipating their surprise when they saw her out there. She couldn't wait, she was almost to the water—there were a few guys on boards paddling around. The waves weren't great, though—not sharp and defined; only occasionally was there anything that appeared rideable. But she didn't care, she was dying to be on a board in the ocean—

"Mindy? Mindy Donnelly?" The lifeguard held up his bullhorn and her name rang out, far too loud and piercing and filled with static. She stopped, felt her cheeks blossom with embarrassment. Shading her eyes with her hand, she turned toward the lifeguard, about thirty yards away and still on his perch. The sun was behind him, so she couldn't make out any features.

"Yes?" she shouted, and now everyone on the beach was looking at her, and the guys behind her started making *tsk tsk* sounds.

"I bet Ol' Granny Pants won't let her out," one of them said.

"He's such a killjoy," another agreed. "Just because he's from Hawaii and thinks he invented surfing—"

"From Hawaii?" Mindy spun around, whacking one of the guys with her board. "The lifeguard? What's his name?"

"I don't know, he's some guy who's stationed here and won't let people out unless they know their stuff. He's like a drill sergeant, if you ask me."

"Worse than," one other guy piped up.

"But what's his name?" Mindy repeated, exasperated.

"Cho," the blond supplied. "Jimmy Cho."

"Oh, fuck," Mindy said, dropping the board. "I mean, I—oh, fuck. I don't know what I mean."

Jimmy was signaling to someone else to take his place; the blond ran toward him, grumbling. She had no choice but to stand there, her heart trying to run away, beating at her chest for release, while her legs were like cement blocks, until Jimmy climbed down the ladder and handed the binoculars and bullhorn to the other guy. It seemed like an eternity. Because Jimmy was clearly taking his time, enjoying making her wait. He said something to the blond as he pointed to a few surfers paddling near the shore. They shared a knowing nod, a laugh, and finally—*finally*—Jimmy was walking toward her. With each step, his face became more readable. And it wasn't a smiling face. His mouth was set in a straight line. His dark eyebrows were knitted together in that thundercloud. His brown eyes held no warmth or laughter.

"Well," he said when he finally reached her.

"Well," she replied, her throat dry, her voice choked. She wished she had a Coke. She wished her legs would stop trembling, which they'd started to do once he was about five feet away. She wished her heart would stop its frenzied fight to escape. She wished *she* could, though. Escape. Fly away. Run away. Run into the ocean.

Run into his arms. Because *that* was home—she knew it as soon as he stopped in front of her. Jimmy was home. More than the sun, the beach, the water, the taunting cries of the seagulls, the comical gait of the sandpipers. She had never felt more at home than she had when she'd been with him on the water, with him on the beach. With him on that couch of his friends'.

"Little Mindy D in the flesh," he said tauntingly, piercing her ballooning fantasies. "What a privilege, to have you on my beach. Let me roll out the red carpet."

"Oh, stop it," she snapped, that idiotic name weighted with all her stupidity, her ignorance, her careless treatment of this good man. What a child she had been, chasing a fool's dream of a life. Only a child ran away from something—from *someone*—as good as Jimmy Cho. At least the Jimmy Cho she'd thought she knew, in California.

She wasn't sure about the Jimmy Cho she was meeting in Vietnam.

"I heard there was a USO show coming. I never thought you'd be in it, *princess,*" Jimmy continued in that flinty—utterly unrecognizable—tone. He folded his arms across his muscled chest, and when he did Mindy heard a woman nearby sigh.

"Can we go somewhere?" She leaned toward him, lowering her voice; Jimmy took a step back. "Somewhere we can talk? I want to try to explain—things."

"Oh. *Things.* No, I think we can carry on a perfectly civilized conversation right here."

It was the word *civilized* that made her flinch.

"Oh, well, fine, then, OK." She couldn't stop herself from stammering, but she was on his turf. And he looked so forbidding, so unlike the Jimmy she had thrown away.

"What would you like to talk about?" His voice was as disdainful as his gaze as it swept over her.

"I, I'm—it's a lot. Seeing you here. A lot. I didn't expect it but I also hoped I would see you. Here. In Vietnam," she finished lamely.

"I didn't expect to see you, either. I didn't expect to see you again, ever. You made that very clear. Sorry I had to ruin things for you. Again."

If only he would move—shift his legs, unfold his arms, cock his head. But he was a monolith, planted in the sand thousands of years ago. She thought that if she scratched him, he wouldn't even bleed. And she'd done this, hadn't she? Turned a lovely, warm, kind man into stone.

Suddenly she was aware of all the faces turned their way, all the ears listening in, and she lowered her voice and asked him again, "Please. Can't we go somewhere else?"

"If you want to talk to me, do it now. Here. But make it quick. I don't have all day. I actually have to work. Some people do, you know."

"Oh, Jimmy, don't. Don't be like this!"

"Like what?" If only he'd blink, if only he'd shade his eyes from the sun—move, twitch, anything! Anything but standing so still, judging. Mocking.

"Like someone I don't even recognize!"

"It hurts, doesn't it? To see someone you thought you knew turn into a monster."

"Jimmy!" She wouldn't cry, she wouldn't. But she also wouldn't let him get away without trying to explain. She wouldn't ask for forgiveness, no; she didn't deserve that. And he didn't owe her anything, she knew. Still, she had to try to reach him, crack open his façade.

"Look, I really do have to get back—"

"No—I wish—I wish I could take it all back. Everything I said that day. Everything I did. I hurt you, and now I don't even know why. It was a reflex, I guess. Self-preservation—it made me say and do terrible things. It's not an excuse, I know. And I know you hate me and I deserve it. I think about what I did to you every day and every night and I know I'm no better than that racist couple at Ben Frank's that night. Remember them?" Was there a slight relaxing of his stance?

"Go on" was all he said, but it was more than she had hoped for.

"At the time, I thought I had lots of reasons that justified my behavior. Now I know there was no reason, there couldn't be. But still, you wanted to know what they were and I wouldn't—I couldn't— tell you then. I don't even know why." Her voice dropped as she studied the sand; she was explaining this almost as much to herself as to him. Then she raised her head again, searching his face for a sign of the man he'd been before she wounded him so. "But now—I *want* to tell you. I want to tell you *everything*. I want to deserve you. I want us to be the way we were before—before I ruined it all. Isn't this *insane*? That we found each other again, here of all places? Doesn't that mean anything to you?"

Jimmy swallowed, looked out at the water. He let out a small hiss of air, like the steam from a radiator, then he shook his head. Turning back to her, he pointed to the surfboard she'd dropped.

"I thought you wanted to surf."

"Well, yeah, but—"

"Let's go, then. Hold on a minute." And he marched off toward the surf club, where he quickly selected a white board with a red fin. When he headed back, he passed her by—she was still rooted in the sand, her legs no longer wobbly but seemingly incapable of movement—and then launched himself and his board into the surf in one fluid, graceful movement. A movement she remembered so well, from before.

Then she was doing the same thing; she didn't remember picking up the board or running through the sand. She only came awake once she was paddling in the water beside him, both of them aiming for the break, arms slicing through the murky water.

"Are there really sea snakes?" she shouted over the pulsating surf.

"Guess you'll find out," he shouted back, still paddling fiercely, not turning to look at her. "I'd try not to wipe out if I were you. If that's possible."

Did she hear a thawing of his voice? Or was he luring her out to the ocean only to let her be devoured by snakes, his ultimate revenge?

"I won't wipe out, don't worry," she shouted back, although her voice did quaver. "I'm not so sure about you, though." Sass—her old, reliable friend—rescued her just in time.

Then they were off, and even though Jimmy still wore that grim look on his face, Mindy felt only joy in the surf spray, a loosening in her chest, power in her limbs as she tried to outpace him toward the break. He didn't give her an inch, although he did turn back once with a slight grin, which made her heart soar. Then he was turning his board as a wave approached; she paddled into line behind him and did the same.

She popped up right after he did; it was as easy as she remembered, that feeling of being one with the board and the water. She found her balance quickly, her left leg planted in front, toes gripping the wax, calves straining, but she welcomed the burn. She was more attuned to her body—every muscle, every nerve—than she'd been in years. Little Mindy D—aka the Girl in the Curl—had covered her body, adorned it with perfume, dresses, and jewelry. She'd used it as advertising, as a front—her mind and her heart retreating behind it, the three never fully in sync.

Not now. *I'm an athlete,* she realized with a shock. *I'm a surfer. I'm like Mom.*

For once, she didn't immediately reject the thought—she remembered her mother's swimming medals, the photos of her standing proudly, shoulders back, stomach flat, in her competition swimwear. In running away from everything her mother stood for, Mindy had been running away from the truest part of herself.

She'd also been running away from joy. From Jimmy, who whooped as he cut in, coming close to her, so close she saw his eyes, softer now than they'd been on the beach. So close she wanted to reach out and touch him, but now he cut away with another whoop and she dug into her board, crouched down and leaned as the ocean spray coated her, heading toward him. The wave wasn't huge, it wasn't fast, but the two of them rode it with such furious expertise, such palpable delight, that people on the beach stood up, pointing.

She was losing speed now, the wave giving out with a whimper, not a roar; she fell to her knees, paddling over to where Jimmy was also kneeling on his board, bobbing up and down in the surf.

After a long moment, too long—she was about to turn and paddle back in alone—he suddenly reached out and pulled her board toward his. Tears filled her eyes.

And then she waited, catching her breath because she was out of shape, after all. Her calves burned, her toes cramped, her thighs felt shaky from the effort. Even after she was breathing normally, he didn't speak. That was OK. She knew she would wait five minutes, an hour, a day—whatever it took. Whatever she could give him, to bring him back to her, she would.

"So," Jimmy finally said. He wouldn't look at her; his eyes were scanning the water. Looking for snakes, she hoped.

"I haven't done that in a long time—surf, I mean." She shook out a cramping leg, then tucked it back under her. She didn't want to dangle her legs in the surf.

"Since when?"

"Since Malibu. The invitational." Splashing some water on her face, she studied the beach. Her regiment of boy surfers were point-ing at her, hooting and hollering in admiration. Jimmy glanced over his shoulder at them.

"I see you have some fans."

"They didn't want to let me in their club. I'm a girl, you know."

"I think I remember." He blessed her with a very sly—and very sexy—smile.

Now her heart was beating rapidly for an entirely different reason; the memory of that night, of his lips on her thighs, her stomach, her hand on his hard chest, the way they'd come together—she was sud-denly wet with desire.

But there were still things she needed to say.

"Jimmy, I have no explanation, other than fear, for what I did to you. That photo in the paper—it shouldn't have meant anything to me—to *us*. I should have been able to be with you no matter what anyone said or felt, because the only thing that really mattered was how you and I felt—I know that now. All I can say is that I was—smaller then. I mean, more selfish? I didn't feel like I was strong enough for whatever might happen if we kept seeing each other. I wasn't—well, as Fred said, I was no Johnny Cash."

"What?" Jimmy looked perplexed, as well he should have. She shook her head.

"I mean—I wasn't a big enough star. Now I know I should have fought more, told Fred and the world to go to hell. But I was so afraid I'd lose everything. I couldn't go back to how my childhood was. I didn't want to be my mother, oh God, I *never* wanted to be my mother! You don't know—but I'll tell you, I will, I promise. And even after this singing thing, I'm a failure, anyway. Isn't that rich? I'm a total bust—my agent dropped me. This USO tour was my last gasp. Farewell, Little Mindy D. Farewell, the Girl in the Curl." She couldn't help herself; she sighed. As much as she hated singing, she still mourned the end of her career. She had a right to do that. No matter what Jimmy might say next.

She gazed at his profile, outlined against the blue sky and paler blue water, the sun's rays bathing him in an almost otherworldly glow. For the first time, she realized he had a little gray in his hair, threads of tinsel. Hardly noticeable, except for the way those threads caught the sunshine. He looked harder, in a way—his body leaner, his jaw set. He'd always been part little boy, part man—an easy grin but eyes that could pierce you with barely sheathed anger. Anger he directed at the bigots of the world, like the couple at the diner—

Like her. Now Jimmy seemed to have lost any semblance of the little boy. His grin, while still as miraculous as the sun coming up after a stormy night, was a man's grin, not so freely given. She had to imagine his heart would be the same.

"I sometimes forget how young you are," Jimmy said after a moment. The water gently sloshed around them, lapping the sides of their boards. They were a little apart from the others splashing in the water.

"I'm not that much younger than you!"

"Nah, but—a guy like me, I'm just older. I am. I can't explain it. But it's no excuse, either—your youth. You knew what you were doing. I'm not going to sugarcoat it, Mindy. You hurt me. Stabbed me right in the back, it felt like. Kicked me in the nuts. I hated you, you know. Missed you and hated you at the same time—I never knew that was possible. But it was."

Mindy winced.

"Because I thought you and I—I thought we belonged together. That week, when we surfed and got you ready for the invitational, I felt that this was it. Yeah, I'd come over to the mainland for other reasons but that week, it seemed to me that it was really to find you.

And I thought you felt the same way. But then you made it clear that I wasn't the most important thing to you. Very clear. So I wanted to hurt you, too."

"I deserved it."

"Yeah, you did. But I—" Jimmy frowned at the water, plucked at some seaweed that had clung to his board. Then he let out a weary sigh. "That was a long time ago. Things happened. To us both."

"When did you come over here?"

"I enlisted a month after you dumped me."

"Ouch."

"The truth is harsh, isn't it?" Once again he looked as he had on the beach, and she longed to touch him, to reassure herself that his skin was warm, not cold as marble. But of course, she couldn't. She didn't have the right.

"Anyway," he continued, "yeah, I joined up. But don't look like that. I probably would have enlisted anyway, because all this with you got me thinking about my family back home. I went to the mainland to learn more about being Hawaiian, I see that now. To see with my own eyes how the thing we invented was being used by white people. I wanted to reclaim it, to take what I learned and go back home and find a way to make money with it. And being from Hawaii—well, we saw the last world war start there, of course. In our own backyards. My dad, he was military. He was a navy corpsman stationed on the *Nevada*. The one ship that got away from Pearl Harbor. I thought of him, and all the other Hawaiians who served in that war, though Hawaii wasn't even a state then. Even though a lot of them—the Japanese families—got locked up. I like to think he—and they—would have approved of me enlisting."

"So you didn't enlist because of me?"

"Jesus, what an ego! No, Little Mindy D. I did not enlist because of you."

"I'm sorry." Mindy felt her face burn. He was right. How stupendously egotistic of her to think that in losing her, he had lost the purpose of his life. When really, it was the other way around, wasn't it? Without him, she'd lost everything.

"How'd you get this assignment, Jimmy? Lifeguarding? Did you see any action?"

"Only the first few days I was here. Nothing terrible, not like a firefight or anything. A simple patrol. It was weird, though, because I swore I felt their eyes on me, Charlie's. We all did, it was like they were hiding in the jungle. Watching. But when we returned to base, a sergeant had just gotten back from leave here and was talking about the surfing, and I couldn't stop myself from boasting about how wonderful I am." He grinned, shaking his head at his own bravado. "The dude was interested, said that they needed a real lifeguard, a waterman, and of course being Hawaiian all I had to do was flex my muscles—like the Duke—and bam. I was transferred here. It's not all fun and games—we get shelled, they're always trying—and yeah, there are sea snakes and idiots who panic in the water and could drag me under, these big dogs. But I'm not complaining. I know I'm goddamned lucky, compared to the rest of the guys I went through boot camp with."

His face darkened, and Mindy knew enough not to push for more.

"I think it was brave of you to enlist. It's weird at home, though—burning draft cards, guys taking off for Canada. Guys in uniform are treated like shit; sometimes people call them baby killers. People are just so angry because of all the lies. I mean, what *are* we doing here? But it's not the soldiers' fault. I don't know whose fault it is."

"You enlisted, in a way. It's dangerous, doing a USO tour."

"I never felt brave, let me tell you. Just so desperate to hold on to something that isn't right for me that I'd go to a war zone to do it, and now I know what a fool I've been all along. Seeing you—being here—now I know. You once told me I wasn't being authentic. Remember? That's funny, because my agent said the same thing." Mindy frowned, remembering what Fred had said in their last meeting: *It's all about authenticity right now.* Meaning music. "Anyway, I'm through. When I get back, I don't know what I'm going to do."

"Have you—how's Ginger?"

"Ginger?" Mindy cocked her head, surprised he'd asked about her sister.

Ginger.

How *was* Ginger?

She had no idea.

Before she'd come over here, she'd gone looking for her sister at that beach shack. But the shack was long gone, the empty lot now a Chinese restaurant. Of course nobody at the restaurant knew anything about Ginger, although she'd asked. Then she went to the beach, to Surfside, but neither Ginger nor Tom was there, and there were few familiar faces. She asked around, but nobody knew where they'd gone, except for one guy from the old days, Danny the Klutz.

"I heard they joined some kind of cult," Danny the Klutz had said. "Or commune. I'm not sure which. Maybe the Brotherhood."

"The *what*?"

"The Brotherhood of Eternal Love. That drug-running hippie commune down in Laguna. You ever dropped acid?"

She nodded; who hadn't? But she hadn't liked it; she hadn't felt in control of anything—her thoughts, her motions, not even her breathing. It was like some demon had tried to possess her, so unlike all the tales of cosmic understanding she'd heard about from others.

"Likely it came from the Brotherhood."

"You think Ginger's there?"

"Maybe." Danny shrugged, grabbed a board, headed out.

She hadn't had time to go looking for whatever the Brotherhood was; she had to get on the plane to Vietnam the next day. And her mind rejected any notion that Ginger might be in some druggie commune—not her sister! Her sister, who had wanted the pretty things in life—dolls and dresses and ballet shoes—far more than Mindy had. Sure, she'd looked like hell the last time Mindy saw her, but to go to such an extreme—

Although, Mindy's mind could too readily accept that Tom would be in a cult. And where Tom went . . .

"I heard she and Tom might be in some kind of commune," she admitted to Jimmy now. She supposed it probably was true. "Brotherhood of something—ever heard of it?"

Jimmy gave a little start. He ran his hand through his short, thick hair. "Really? So she's still with him?"

"I don't know for sure. I didn't have time to look. I will, though, when I get home. I need to. I miss her so much." The way her heart twisted up—oh, how she did miss her little sister! She'd failed her, Mindy had; she'd failed to keep her safe. To stick to the Plan, the two of them together no matter what. If anything happened to her, it would be all Mindy's fault.

But she couldn't think about that right now. One thing at a time; she was in Vietnam, after all. In Vietnam, with Jimmy Cho—that he was here on this beach at this moment was nothing short of a miracle. A second chance. She wasn't going to blow it again.

"Well, if you see her," Jimmy said slowly, obviously choosing his words carefully, "tell her—tell her—oh, hell. Tell her I'm sorry."

"For what?" Now it was Mindy's turn to look startled. Jimmy wouldn't meet her gaze as he chewed his bottom lip. "When did *you* see Ginger?"

It took a moment—a long moment, and she started to shiver from the clamminess of her wet bikini while the sun hid behind some clouds—before he answered.

"At a store, once. Before I enlisted."

"And she was OK? She seemed OK?"

"It was right after the invitational, when you saw her. A long time ago. I'm not perfect, you know—I . . . never mind, it's nothing. Not important right now."

Then he grinned at the same time the sun decided to make a very showy reappearance; her flesh warmed. So did her heart, because Jimmy pulled her board closer again—she'd drifted a bit away—and leaned toward her.

She inhaled him—masculine, strong, like ripe fruit. Ready to be devoured. Reaching over, tilting her chin, he kissed her. Very gently, almost as if he was afraid.

She tasted the salt water on his lips, opened her own, let him probe her with his tongue, so delicately it made her squirm. They kissed like this for a long time—lightly, tenderly, belying the growing desire in her very core. She felt that desire gushing out of her, her need for him to take her somewhere and cover her with his body, claim her with his hands and this tongue that was still so gentle, playing with her own tongue in a way that brought to mind a memory so exquisitely sweet, she almost cried out.

Finally, he released her, his eyes stunningly brown and full of warmth now, of a softness that might be called love, if she so dared to; they quickly paddled in and dragged the boards up to the shack, ignoring the catcalls from those idiots who seemed like kindergartners next to the man that was Jimmy Cho.

They said nothing as she held his hand and let him lead her to his barracks, past all the beds to a kind of community room in the back, a room with a cot and lots of half-burned candles, and she didn't care how many people had been there before them.

All she cared about was that she was here now.

With Jimmy.

.   .   .

"When do you get back?" Jimmy asked as she packed her few belongings. It was the morning after the last show.

How idiotic she'd felt onstage last night, knowing he was in the audience! The natural radiance she'd felt on the beach, winking at her Sister Sun, drained away, and she felt as clumsy as a turkey. A costumed, cartoon turkey gobbling away. She'd made him stand in the back of the PX, behind the audience of wolf-whistling soldiers, so she couldn't see him beyond the lights. But she felt his gaze on her anyway as she sang that stupid song, her voice cracking and quavering more than ever, and did her dance, wiggling her behind for the boys. She'd rushed off the stage when it was over instead of taking a bow. And during the finale, when the two folk singers launched into the first chords of "Blowin' in the Wind," she knew she was singing in public for the very last time, and thank God for that.

Nobody was going to miss Little Mindy D.

Her face layered in goop, eyelids heavy with the false lashes, and skin itching from the spangly minidress she wore, she did her duty by mixing with the boys afterward, dancing with one after the other. This was her job, after all; the USO would send her the last paycheck once she got home. But all the while, she was thinking of Jimmy, waiting for her in that funky room.

Last night, there'd been no time for talking. But this morning the air was heavy with things to say, and there wasn't much time. Mindy and the others had to get to the Da Nang airport in an hour, to catch the transport plane back to Saigon. Then home.

"We should be back in a few days, depending on how long we have to wait in Saigon for a plane."

"Good. I'll sleep easier knowing you're not here."

"What about you?" Mindy knew she'd be leaving Vietnam both

lighter—her burden of the idiotic pursuit of fame lifted forever—
and heavier. Because now she had someone to worry about—last
night, as she'd lain in Jimmy's arms on that worn-out cot, she'd heard
bombs, maybe two miles away. "When's your tour up?"

"Six months," he replied. "Unless I re-up."

"Are you going to?"

"Should I?" His voice was barely a whisper. She didn't dare look at
him; hope, electrifying and terrifying, surged through her entire
body. When was the last time she'd felt anything like this—complete
happiness, happiness ever after, almost close enough to touch? She
didn't trust herself not to break down and sob, she was so overwhelmed.

"I wish you wouldn't," she murmured. Then she had to sit down
on her army cot, her legs were so weak with relief. Her breath came
in shaky shudders. Their shoulders were touching, but as if by silent
agreement, they kept their hands in their laps.

"Then I won't," Jimmy said, his voice strong and firm once more.
"OK, Mindy? I'll come home—to California, I mean. To you?"

She nodded, beaming, but her eyes were swimming. He reached
for her then, took her hand, and she heard him let out a sigh—a sigh
full of the happiness and satisfaction she was feeling, too.

A future. She had a future. A normal future with Jimmy. No need
to plan it now—where would they live, would they get married,
what about kids? Six months was still a long time, and anything
could happen, of course. In Vietnam.

But for this moment, she knew that if—*when*—he came home to
her, one gigantic missing piece of the jigsaw puzzle that was her life
would fall into place. The piece she'd been missing ever since Mom
left for Hawaii so long ago.

Someone would love her. Someone would think of her first.
Someone would hold her hand when she was afraid and trace her

smile with his fingers when she was happy. And she had someone to think of, too. Someone other than her sister, but her heart was so full she had room for Ginger, too. She had room for everyone. . . .

Maybe even Mom?

Jimmy Cho had done that; he had caused her miserly little selfish—and lacerated—heart to heal and regenerate enough to accommodate a family. Even one as messed up as the one into which she had been born. That was how it was, sometimes, she was beginning to understand. You came into this world with no say in anything, only endless opportunities to be hurt. But if you found someone like Jimmy Cho, you understood that there were opportunities for forgiveness, too. For healing.

For love, unconditional.

She laid her head on his shoulder, laced her fingers through his, felt his lips upon her hair, whispering her name. Then Miss Santa Monica ran into the room, shouting, "Get a move on, we're going home!" and everything sped up—the frenzied last-minute packing, racing to the jeep that would carry them to the airport, flinging her arms around Jimmy, telling him to stay safe.

"Come home to me," she pleaded, looking into that face that she would see in six months, and then every day for the rest of her life. He nodded, grinned, and kissed her so passionately all the other girls whooped and Johnny yelled, "Now, that's what I call going beyond the call of duty!"

Then she was gone, waving at Jimmy until he was swallowed by the dust the jeep kicked up. She clutched her purse so tightly her knuckles turned white as she tried not to cry, to give in to the terror she felt at leaving him behind. Couldn't she have stuffed him in her suitcase and taken him with her? Why hadn't she thought of that?

In four days, she was back in Los Angeles. It seemed like she'd

slept the entire way home; it seemed as if she were still in a dream—
the kind of sneakily wonderful dream that you try to hold on to by
going back to sleep when the alarm rings. If she could stay this way—
holding on to this dream, not allowing reality to intrude—for the
next six months, then she could will Jimmy home safely. She breathlessly told Paula all about Jimmy, about his coming home in six
months—no, make that five months and twenty-six days!—so Paula
would have to find another roommate then. She threw away the false
eyelashes and the shiny hose and the fake hairpieces. After applying
for jobs, regular jobs like waitressing or working in a store, she finally
got a position as a salesgirl in the junior section of Bullock's in Sher-
man Oaks. She had to admit to being Little Mindy D and the Girl
in the Curl on her application because she had nothing else, and that
tiny bit of glamour got her hired.

She got her first library card as an adult and checked out several
books of poetry, remembering how much she had liked that poem by
Emily Dickinson. Who she decided was still her favorite poet, because Anne Sexton made her uncomfortable and Sylvia Plath made
her sad and also reminded her too much of her mother. She started
reading other books, too, like basic accounting and rudimentary history. Maybe she could go back and get her high school diploma!
There were so many things she could do now that she and Jimmy
would be together. In the past, her image of her family was that of a
leaky dinghy and it was up to Mindy to plug every hole, and that
didn't leave time for anything like education. But now she saw her
future family as a sleek modern sailboat, and she and Jimmy would
take turns piloting it.

In her imagination, they were always sailing toward a perfect, rosy
sunset, both hands on the tiller, dolphins swimming playfully alongside.

Still, she breathed carefully, trod lightly, as the days went by; she'd never been superstitious before but now she avoided ladders and black cats, and took to throwing salt over her shoulder at dinner.

She put off going to see Mom. She'd wait until Jimmy was home. The two of them would go to see her, and tell her their news, and with Jimmy by her side, maybe she would find a way to repair her relationship—to redefine it—with her mother.

Then one day, the doorbell rang. When she answered it, her sister was on the doorstep. Ginger, with long, tangled hair, a threadbare maxi dress, dirty feet in sandals.

Mindy's mouth opened, ready to proclaim her joy, to immediately welcome her sister inside her hopeful bubble—*Ginger! Ginger was home!*

A little cry made her look down. Ginger wasn't alone. There was a basket at her feet, almost too small for its occupant—

A child. A chubby little girl flat on her back, her dimpled thighs up in the air as her plump little hands played with her bare toes. A little girl with brown eyes. Curly dark hair.

And a familiar smile that shattered the dream castle that Mindy had been so carefully constructing. The glass cracked, raining down in shards as she took in this child who possessed a smile exactly like the smile she'd last seen in Vietnam.

On China Beach.

13

Showing up on her sister's doorstep was the last thing Ginger had wanted to do.

She'd never stopped thinking of Mindy, not once in all these months. Never stopped missing her sister, but the missing was a familiar ache now; she was so used to it she'd have felt odd without it. But the missing was the least of it. From the first time Ginger's nipples had felt achingly tender, through the first bouts of morning sickness, counting the weeks on her fingers, the realization that she was carrying a child, and that child might not be Tom's . . .

Ginger had felt nothing but guilt; it was her shadow, sharply defined by the relentless California sun, from the moment she awoke until the moment she tried to find a way to fall asleep at night. Guilt about Tom. Guilt about her sister.

Why on earth had they done it, she and Jimmy? She couldn't speak for him—he hadn't even looked at her when they were done.

But she'd felt so *clean* that night, so restored to herself by the luxury of that shower, by the meal, by playing house with Jimmy in a real apartment with walls and a roof and running water. Hot food, enough of it. She'd allowed herself to look in a mirror and she'd been delighted, in a girlish way she hadn't experienced in so long, by what she saw—the shining curls, the glowing skin, her breasts filling out the borrowed dress.

Thus cleansed, adorned, she was ready. Ready for the moment

when Jimmy's absent-minded stroking became something more. She could have pushed his hand away. She could have reminded him about her sister. She could have reminded herself about Tom. But she didn't.

She shut her mind to any thought of those people whose happiness she was so used to placing above her own. She allowed her body to speak for her, to claim something, a little reward, perhaps, now that it had been attended to properly after so many months of neglect.

Later, though, she wondered. Was she so angry at Tom that she'd slept with Jimmy out of spite? She hadn't *felt* spiteful or small, in the moment, only blissfully aware of the athletic body next to hers, on top of her, inside her. The response of her own flesh, lean and taut because of the life she'd been living, yet pleasingly soft and pliable. Jimmy had murmured his appreciation of her breasts but then didn't have to say anything else; his body said everything she needed to hear.

But he wouldn't look at her, even when he was panting to his release, even when he cried out as he came; she felt him gushing into her, she strained her body to join him, she cried out, too. Her eyes were open. Jimmy's were squeezed shut.

After, for them both, it was all shame, all guilt, all apologies. All awkwardness.

"You won't tell Mindy, will you?" he whispered as he stepped back into his board shorts, concentrating intently on tying the drawstring in a perfect bow, anything to avoid having to look at her. She felt like crawling under the couch; she was beneath contempt.

"No—of course not. No."

They didn't say another word, and soon after Howie and Jen had come home, full of lively chatter about the movie they'd seen—*Two for the Road*, Audrey Hepburn was so glamorous, Jen sighed— effusively thanking them for having done the dishes. Then Howie and Jen shut the door to their bedroom, leaving Ginger to want to disappear into the cushions of the sofa, where she tried to get some sleep while Jimmy huddled on the floor in a sleeping bag, as far away from her as he could get. When she awoke in the gray dawn of morning, he was gone. She wrote a note of thanks to Howie and Jen on the back of a grocery receipt she found in the trash, with a postscript:

Tell Jimmy it was all my fault. He'll understand.

Then she crept away, hitching a ride back up to the chained lot. As she sat down with her back against the fence, she prayed that she wouldn't get pregnant because she hadn't been able to afford the Pill for months now, and everything had happened so fast, Jimmy had been too carried away to use a condom.

It was while she was praying that she heard the voice she'd been longing to hear for days; raising her head, wiping tears from her eyes, she saw Tom and a couple of the guys—Charlie and Russ—approach. Still wearing the same clothes, now stiff with filth, they'd worn when they'd left for Mexico, what was it? Four, five days ago?

"There she is," Tom said, his voice sharp with accusation. "The traitor."

"What? What do you mean? Where *were* you, Tom?" Tears came again, but this time they were resentful. She'd needed him; she'd kept vigil over this pathetic place for so long, alone and terrified. What did he mean by calling her a traitor?

"In a Tijuana jail, if you care to know." He plopped down next to her but didn't touch her. "Switchblade was an informant. For the Brotherhood. They tipped off the guard and we got thrown in a tiny cell full of cockroaches for a couple of days, to teach us a lesson. When I came back last night, you weren't here. And neither was the shack."

"I—I tried, Tom! I stayed here for days, but I needed to eat, I needed to bathe in the ocean. When I came back, they'd done this." She hit the back of her head against the chain-link fence, which rattled like a taunting wind chime.

"Where were you last night?"

"Didn't you see my note?"

Tom shook his head.

"Jimmy Cho—he let me stay at a friend's house. He saw me at the store, I was going to lift some bread and stuff. See—here it is!" She pointed to the wrinkled paper bag full of supplies that she'd remembered to take from Howie and Jen's this morning.

"That's a lot of stuff to shoplift," Tom said with a suspicious frown.

"I didn't. Jimmy paid for it—he was nice, Tom." How nice, she didn't dare explain.

"That gook? That chink? Nice? Jesus Christ, Ginger, how could you let him do you a favor? Stay away from him, I've told you—stay away from them all. You're pure-blood, honey, as white and pure as Eva Braun. You have no need of help from the likes of him."

"Tom, that's unfair. You took all the money! I almost passed out from hunger, and Jimmy saved me. Then we came back here and the fence was up and the shack was gone."

"Unfair? So let me get this straight—while you were hanging out with a gook, you let them take our home? Our stuff? You stupid bitch!"

She flinched, waiting for his hand across her face. But Tom didn't hit her, not this time. He sounded weary. Even defeated.

"I swear, you are the stupidest bitch I've ever met," he continued, but he remained slumped against the fence, watching cars zoom up and down the highway. The other guys had scampered across the road to the beach. "I don't know what I was thinking that day."

"What day? What do you mean, Tom?"

But he wouldn't answer.

"What do we do now?" Ginger was afraid to ask. But she had to know. "I missed you so much!" And she couldn't stifle the sob that pushed its way out of her belly, through her lungs, and up her throat—she had fucked up big-time, that was for sure. But she was Tom's girl. She didn't want anything else other than to be allowed to stay with him, take care of him, soothe him, no matter where he went next. Sleep beside him tonight, somewhere, *anywhere*. Let him make love to her, just in case . . .

Just in case.

She hooked her arm through his, stroked his forearm, leaned against him. He pushed her away at first. But then he relaxed a bit, let her reach for his crotch and allowed her to stroke him through the thin fabric of his ancient blue jeans. He was hard in an instant, groaning impatiently.

"I missed you, babe," he breathed, and she relaxed then. It would be all right.

"So what do we do now? Maybe—maybe we should call your mother?"

He slapped her hand away and stood up, not caring that she fell against the fence with a loud, rattling bang.

"Jesus, I told you before, that is never going to happen. Do you understand me? Never. Gonna. Happen. Jesus Christ, what is wrong with you? I will not take a penny from that bitch."

Ginger closed her eyes, swallowed hard, and nodded. She didn't tell Tom—she would never tell Tom—that she had phoned his mother once, the first time he'd gone to Mexico without her and didn't tell her where he was going. She remembered that Tom had called her, when he talked about her, by her first name—Rita. So she'd gone to a pay phone and looked in the book and found a Rita Riley listed, and called.

"Hello?" The voice was low and warm.

"Mrs. Riley? Tom's mother?"

"Tom! My Tommy—who are you? Where is he? Is he all right? Let me talk to him!" And Mrs. Riley's voice was so full of emotion, of fear and hope and longing, that Ginger couldn't bring herself to say any more; she'd placed the receiver down gently. This wasn't the voice of an icy-cold, money-hungry bitch. It was the voice of a mother— not in the Carol Donnelly mold but a *real* mother—who was hungry for only one thing: her son.

It was the first time she'd ever doubted anything Tom had said. She would never tell him about the call—or her doubts. So she kept quiet now.

"I can take care of us, you idiot. Give me some credit. So here's the plan. This is what's happening," Tom said, still pacing in front of her, scratching his arm, looking a little unhinged. "We're joining the Brotherhood, making it official, the bastards. I can't make enough dough by myself, and they have a stranglehold on everything in and out of Mexico. But I figure I can stiff them on the profits and line my own pockets."

"How much dough do we need?"

"I need a lot," Tom said shortly, suddenly plopping down next to her again. Now he rested his stubbly cheek on top of her head, like an affectionate puppy, and she was too relieved—and happy—to ask him more. But she did wrinkle her nose; he needed a bath.

"Where will we live?"

"Down in Laguna. With the rest. I hear they're all about happy families down there, so that's where you come in. I planned it all out on the drive back up. We'll pretend to be this devoted couple. They like couples, although they're into that free-love shit, too. Orgies, that kind of thing. But mainly peace and love and all that—not really my scene, as you know. I adhere to higher principles, namely me, myself, and the surf. But if we pretend to be together, all lovey dovey, we're in. I can get along with weirdos when I have to. Just watch me."

"Pretend?" She raised her head, nudging him away so she could face him. He was so handsome, so her type—not like Jimmy; she stifled a shudder remembering the night before. But Tom, he was so smart! So determined. So lean, with those sculpted surfer's shoulders and torso. His cheekbones were chiseled—he claimed he had Indian blood—and those gray eyes were always looking at the horizon, planning the next score, the next heist, the next big thing. "We don't need to pretend, Tom. We are together. Forever."

"Whatever." He put his arm around her, kissed her nose. Then he rose, stretching. "Damn, I'm all knotted up from that cell. I need a swim. I need a surf, I need a fuck—in that order. C'mon, let's go."

"Where will we sleep tonight?"

"Don't worry about that, my chosen one. Trust me."

And she did.

The first weeks in Laguna Beach, up on Woodland Drive off Laguna Canyon Road, were the best time Ginger had had in years.

Woodland Drive was a little dead-end street up in the hills that most people passed by without noticing, and it was crammed full of log cabins, trailers, rickety houses, and tents—the Brotherhood called it Dodge City. With nothing but the clothes on their backs, Tom and Ginger were welcomed with patchouli-scented open arms; no one asked where they'd come from. No one asked if they had any money. Tom was known by some of the men, and as soon as he made it clear it was his life's mission to work *with* the Brotherhood instead of against them, to make them enough money to continue cooking acid and distributing it to the entire world, spreading peace and love via mind-altering drugs . . .

They were invited to stay in a rambling red house with so many tiny rooms, it felt like a rabbit warren. Ginger was embraced by the other women—literally, clasped to so many unfamiliar bosoms, warm and welcoming, that she got dizzy at first. She couldn't believe that she and Tom were given their own room with a real bed, even a dresser in which to put their things. Not that they had any; Ginger had forgotten the hand-me-downs that Jen had pressed on her in her haste to leave that morning, and Tom had lost everything he'd taken to Mexico. But they didn't have that much less than everyone else.

Right away, Ginger was invited to the kitchen, where the other women explained that it was their job to feed everyone—including a horde of children running around, sometimes dressed and sometimes not, all with tangled long hair so that she had a hard time figuring out which were boys and which were girls. The kids didn't always seem to belong to only one set of parents, either; they were passed around from lap to lap, room to room, even, sleeping in packs, like a den of hungry wolf cubs.

After she was instructed in the preparation of the community meals, Ginger was led to the big round dining room table. There were canning jars all over it, and a big bowl of hash in the middle, along with joint papers.

"When you're not cooking, or blissing out, or fucking your man, you should be filling these jars with hash, not too much, only about a couple of inches. Or rolling joints. The kids take the jars and bury them way out back so the pigs can't find them. The kids take the joints, too, and run them to some of the dealers who go down to town and sell to the locals," the calmest of the calm women, Dearest, explained.

None of the names of the women she was introduced to—Dearest, Sunshine, Petal, Cocaine Candy—were real, of course, and when she asked why, Dearest shook her head full of frizzy red curls.

"A lot of the girls here are runaways, looking for a safe place. We don't want anyone to find them, so we all go by our new names, which are better, anyway. What name do you want to go by?"

"Oh, gosh, I don't know!"

"If you don't come up with one, someone else will and you might not like it," Dearest warned.

"OK, um . . . what about Blissful?"

"That's perfect! I can't believe someone else hasn't taken that. OK, Blissful, now, what about your man?"

"Tom? Does he need a nickname?"

"Let him figure that out," Dearest said, and one of the other girls—Petal—giggled. "What's his number, anyway?"

"What do you mean?"

"We've heard about him, you guys were up in Malibu, right? You have a sister who's kind of famous?"

"You mean Mindy? I guess she's famous."

"We're always looking for celebrities to join us, spread the good word. We had the Byrds up here last summer to play a concert. Do you think she'd want to do something like that?"

"No," Ginger said firmly, and Dearest looked at her in surprise, then shrugged.

"What about your man, then? You and he have been going over the border and dealing, right?"

"Yes, I guess—I mean, I went sometimes, of course. But it was only for a little spending money, nothing major."

"Uh-huh," Dearest said. She shook her head, put a hand on Ginger's arm. "I like you, Blissful. I'll be frank; I don't like Tom. I get a vibe from him that's pretty harsh. He needs to relax, be open to the experience of the Brotherhood. If he isn't, if he brings thunder down on us all, he'll be kicked out. And so will you."

"Oh, no—that won't happen, I promise! I'll talk to him, but I know—he's really into this, all you stand for." Ginger was lying, she knew it, but suddenly she didn't want to leave. She felt enveloped in a warm, seductive haze; the air was perfumed with patchouli and pot but also with lavender that grew outside the front door and a tomato-y soup bubbling on the stove. All the little kids running around, screaming their little-kid joy at the top of their lungs, filled her with happiness; she wanted to join them, scream her own delight. Dearest had such a kind and motherly aura about her, Ginger wanted nothing more than to sit next to her on the rusty porch swing outside, for hours at a time, doing cozy domestic things—knitting or mending or shucking corn. Maybe they could bake bread together in the kitchen. Maybe they could weed a vegetable garden.

As the days and weeks went by, she settled into the routine that wasn't a routine—there were no clocks on Woodland Drive. They all dropped in and out on one another—there were no locks on the doors or windows of the various structures that radiated out from the dusty dead-end street. Traffic went by on Laguna Canyon Road, people living their busy lives, never knowing about the community that was spreading out into the hills.

Ginger was invited to her first group grope about a month after they arrived. But she didn't go—she couldn't bring herself to—and nobody seemed to care or judge. She was being true to herself, Dearest told her with an approving smile before leaving for the cabin where the grope was going to be held.

"That's all anyone can be, Blissful. Be true to yourself."

Ginger smiled, remaining alone in the red house, canning hash. Even the kids seemed to have vanished and she had the queasy feeling they might be at the group grope. But she shut her mind to that and concentrated on her task, humming a little. She went to the kitchen to get an apple—she was starving, even though they'd just finished a lunch of lentil soup. Taking a bite out of the apple, which wasn't very crisp, she tried to swallow but suddenly felt her stomach rising up to prevent it; she ran to the one bathroom, relieved that everyone was gone. She fell to her knees on the filthy floor and puked into the toilet until her stomach was empty.

When she was done, her stomach cramping, she rose on wobbly legs. Splashing water on her face, she gazed into the scummy mirror over the basin. Was she imagining it, or were her breasts slightly fuller? She felt them, was aware that her nipples were suddenly more tender than they were even before her period. And then she realized she hadn't had her last period.

Like a zombie, she stumbled into the room she shared with Tom and fell down, face-first, on the rumpled bed. She wished she could shut the door, but there wasn't one. She lay there, eyes closed against the spinning world, and fell soundly asleep, only to awaken after the sun was down and Tom was shaking her shoulder.

"Hey, lazybones. Get up. The girls are wondering why you didn't help with dinner."

"Tom." She blinked her eyes, crusty with sleep; she sat up, and the room didn't spin. Her stomach was angrily growling; she was famished. Gingerly, she traced her nipples, and winced.

"Tom," she repeated.

"Jesus, what? What is it?" Tom was rummaging through one of the dresser drawers. He'd been gone these last couple of days, a typical run down to Mexico. But he'd been talking about going to Afghanistan for a big score; a handful of guys had done it a few months ago. They'd flown to Germany, bought a VW bug, driven it to Afghanistan, and bought the best hash anyone had ever smoked, the kind of hash nobody in California even knew existed. Removing the door panels of the car, filling the space with hash, and screwing the panels back into place, they'd loaded it on a freighter. Then they'd flown home with a few souvenirs — a sitar, some rugs and tapestry wall hangings to sell at Mystic Arts World—and picked the car up at the Port of Los Angeles a few weeks later. Those guys had had the vacation of their lives and were heroes now. Tom hated it.

"Tom, I'm pregnant. I think."

He stopped rummaging, stood facing the dresser for a minute.

"I don't—you know I use a condom, babe."

"Not all the time," she said, remembering the night he'd returned from Mexico and she'd jumped on him with an eagerness that left him no time to even think about protection. And his stash of condoms had disappeared in the rubble of the shack, anyway.

"It was just that once, right?"

"Once is all it takes."

"Fuck." He shoved the drawer into the dresser with a violence that made the rickety piece of furniture rattle. Then he plopped down on the bed and put his head in his hands. "Let me think."

She didn't dare speak. She hardly dared to breathe. She let Tom's mind—his brilliant, kinetic mind—whirl and spark. In her vulnerable hopefulness, she thought she saw electric charges in the dim room, emanating from the man beside her. The father of her child.

She hoped. No—she *knew* he was. He was the love of her life. Not Jimmy Cho. She could never have anyone else's child but Tom's. The universe wouldn't let that happen. Her own *body* wouldn't let that happen; it would have rejected any other sperm. Jimmy's sperm.

"I know a place in Mexico," Tom said finally, lifting his head. He wouldn't look at her. "A guy who can take care of it."

Too many questions fired through her brain—did he want her to *die*? Didn't he love her? The most insistent one of all—*why* did he know a guy in Mexico? But she took a breath, reached for his arm, hooked hers through it. She pressed all her softness, her fuller breasts, her curvy hips, against his rigid leanness. "Tom, oh, Tom. Think of it—our baby! We'll be a family. Like everyone here—we'll have our own baby to grow the Brotherhood. Everyone here likes babies—there are so many pregnant women! And everyone will help take care of it, too."

"Yeah." Tom still was like a man made of stone, not looking at her, not yielding to her softness. "I guess there's that. But Jesus, I never wanted this."

"Not even with me?" She smiled up into his face, so that he couldn't keep avoiding her.

He glared down at her, those gray eyes now shards of flint.

"God, no, especially not with you."

Willing herself not to run to the toilet again—her stomach was churning once more, even though it was so empty she thought she'd faint—she still kept smiling up at him. Hadn't she smiled, always, no matter what Mom did or said? Mindy had always told her to do that. Smile, always smile—always be pleasant, always get along, don't sass, don't pout, don't cry, don't be such a baby.

A baby. The baby. Their baby.

For the baby's sake, as well as for hers, Ginger had to win Tom over. Because if he left, she had no idea what she would do; she didn't want to be here without him, she'd be like any of the scraggly runaways passed around from man to man with no protector, relegated to the worst jobs, like scrubbing the outhouse behind where the tents were pitched. Hadn't Dearest said that if Tom got kicked out, she would, too? It didn't seem part of the whole vibe, the message they were sending out into the world of everyone loving one another, but Ginger didn't question it. Maybe it would be different, once they knew; maybe they wouldn't have the heart to kick out a pregnant woman.

But that wasn't important. It was Tom, it was always Tom. He was everything, everyone, her entire reason for being. She'd stopped asking herself why, long ago. He was simply the burning sun that gave her energy to keep going; without him, she'd wither and die, cold and alone.

But not alone, not now; her hand flew to her stomach, still so flat, but was that a faint ripple within, a butterfly wing's flutter of life? Her childhood, her abandonment, came flooding back. She wouldn't do that to a child; she wanted so much more for her baby. Two parents, not half of one. If she could stay here with Tom, her baby would have *dozens* of parents. How different—how much better!—it would be than her own experience.

"Tom, you can't mean that, not now. Look at me, please—look at me!"

He'd started to turn away but she grabbed his head with both hands and turned it toward her, trying not to flinch at his disappointed gaze. It was like he'd never loved her, never told her she was blessed among women to be his, the chosen one.

But he never *had* said he'd loved her, had he? Ginger had supplied it for him, forgiving him for not saying it, telling herself that only she could parse his emotions.

Then—miracle of miracles!—his gaze did soften. And she couldn't help the flood of tears cascading down her cheeks, her quivering lips. He sighed—a great, put-upon sigh—and pulled her to him.

"I guess you couldn't help it. It must be preordained, then. I am the Surf God, I am the way. This shall be the Son of the Surf God, destined to spread the message to the unenlightened. These idiots here—they will know me now. Even Griggs. Maybe finally I'll get to meet the emperor himself."

Ginger knew he'd been trying to meet John Griggs, the founder of the Brotherhood, ever since they'd arrived. So far, though, Tom had been treated like all the other foot soldiers. That was why he wanted to go to Afghanistan, she knew. To ascend into the orbit of the Great God Griggs.

"That's right, I heard that Carol Griggs likes to assist at all the births." Ginger felt even more nauseous, for the first time contemplating what lay ahead: giving birth here, attended by these women, and not in a hospital. There had been several births since they'd arrived, although she'd not attended any. But she had heard about one girl who couldn't stop bleeding, so they had to rush her to a hospital. Nobody ever said exactly what happened to her after that, although Cocaine Candy had said once, when they were all dropping acid up the hill under a full moon that lassoed the truth out of their souls—Ginger had seen the lasso, beheld it as a golden rope dropping down from the heavens—that the girl and the baby had died.

"Yeah. Well, I guess if I have to have a kid, this isn't the worst place in the world. But we're not here for long, Ginger." Tom lowered his voice, then got up, checked outside to see if anyone was in the hallway before returning. Facing her now, taking her hands in his—and all was right, all was going to be right, she felt it in her heart, felt his strength flow into her—Tom leaned in very close, whispering in her ear. "I'm going to score so big, I'll be able to steal right under their noses. I'm not the only guy doing that. Griggs is too caught up with Leary now to even know what's going on."

Ginger nodded. Timothy Leary had moved to Laguna Beach a few months ago with his wife. Everyone worshipped the college professor who urged the world to "turn on, tune in, drop out." The Brotherhood funded his never-ending legal battles, and in return, he blessed them with his presence. Ginger had seen him once down in Laguna, at Mystic Arts World, which the Brotherhood ran, where they sold incense and weird art, wall hangings from Mexico and now, increasingly, Afghanistan. It was yet another source of income for the organization. Leary was a handsome, middle-aged, lean man with white hair and pale blue eyes. He'd smiled at her, and she felt her whole body radiate energy; she told everyone about it at dinner and they all nodded solemnly.

"So when I score big—and I have to go to Afghanistan to do it— I'll light out. I'll have enough, finally."

"You mean we'll light out?" She searched his face anxiously; he laughed at her, smoothed her hair, took his index finger and rubbed away the frown lines on her forehead.

"God, you're such an innocent. Yeah, of course. I meant we'll light out."

"And do what?"

"That's for me to know and you to find out. All you need to do now is incubate that baby, OK? Let's go tell everyone."

Ginger felt her body grow limp with relief; her nausea was gone, for now.

"Can we go get some Taco Bell? It's a special occasion, after all!"

"Sure. Whatever you want. Today's a special day."

She ran after Tom, who was already out the door, calling for everyone to meet them in the dining room. But before she joined them, she dashed into the bathroom again. Not to puke, but to look at herself in the mirror. She hadn't imagined it—her skin *was* glowing, and she was softer, rounder, than before. She caressed her stomach and whispered, "It's OK now. Everything's OK, Tom Junior."

Because that was what she was going to name the baby, no matter what anybody said.

14

"It's a girl," Cocaine Candy said gently. A baby's cries pierced the air, shattering Ginger's distorted consciousness. The agonizing hours spent walking up and down a hall, in one of the larger houses with running water and electricity, the house they called the birth house; the final hour of torture on her back, knees drawn up, pushing, gasping for air, pushing again, the pressure unbearable, the pain a monster shredding her most tender flesh. Now came the joy everyone had told her about—*You'll forget the pain the moment you hold your child.*

They were wrong about that; the torn tissue around her vagina was burning, raw. But she held out her arms to receive her child, bracing herself for the onslaught of joy she had been told she would feel.

"Here she is, Mama," Candy said. She'd been a surprising midwife, gentle in a way Ginger had never seen her. And sober, not high. Some of the other women had been smoking joints and asked her if she wanted one, but she couldn't imagine inhaling smoke between the waves of pain. Even the incense they'd insisted on burning in the crowded room made her nauseous, and she'd thrown up twice. But overall, during those agonizing hours Ginger had felt as if she were in a womb herself, a cocoon of sisterly love, with feminine hands holding her, stroking her, folding towels, and placing cool washcloths on her forehead. And it made her miss Mindy more, not less; Mindy's were the cool hands, the calm voice helping, giving her strength, she'd wanted the most. Why hadn't she reached out to Mindy?

The moment her newborn was handed to her, she knew why.

"It's—it's—a girl," was all she could say. Candy nodded as if Ginger had said something profound. Neither of them said the obvious.

That this baby was dark skinned, dark haired, and in no way resembled a combination of her genes and Tom Riley's.

"A girl," Ginger repeated, overcome with exhaustion; her arms trembled as she held the squealing infant, naked, umbilical cord still attached, to her rock-hard breasts. "A little girl. My little girl."

"*Our* little girl," Cocaine Candy said reassuringly, as if she already understood the troubles ahead. Ginger shut her eyes, tears escaping anyway, running down her cheeks, dropping on her baby. Tom was away—he was in Afghanistan, finally. Scoring big, he'd assured her when he left her, eight months pregnant.

And alone, she reminded him.

"You're not alone," he'd replied with an exasperated sigh. "Jesus, Ginger, grow up. That's the whole point here. Happy families, remember? The guys score, the girls stay home and have babies and everything's peace, love, and understanding."

"But I'll need *you,*" she'd begged. "Promise you'll come back after Afghanistan? Promise?" She couldn't help her sobs; the hormones had driven her like she was a race car, careening from turn to turn. It made Tom crazy, but she couldn't help it.

"Why wouldn't I?" he asked. It wasn't the answer she craved, but she clung to it, clung to Tom, her enormous belly between them; he never did get used to the way her body had changed, and sex between them had become a pleasant memory, although she could still give him blow jobs, he pointed out. She let out a shaky breath when he kissed her on the forehead. Then he threw his clothes in a duffel bag and walked away. He didn't look back.

Ginger felt so unlovable in that moment. She'd turned into this whale of a machine, a huge farm combine that housed a baby and would soon expel it. She didn't feel like herself at all; everything about her was alien. Her skin had broken out in a way it never had when she was a teenager; her hair had lost its luster and was dull and coarse. Her fingers and ankles retained water no matter how little salt she ate. She hated everything about herself. She hated everything, period. She didn't blame Tom for grasping at the first opportunity to escape her enormous center of gravity. She was a black hole sucking all the lightness out of the world.

She prayed he would come back. That she would one day look in the mirror and recognize herself again.

It wasn't only Ginger, though, who was responsible for a new, tense undercurrent putting everyone in Dodge City, already paranoid from acid and pot, on prickly edge. The raids had begun.

She knew what she was supposed to do in case of a raid; they'd practiced it over and over, knowing it would happen sooner or later. At the first alarm Ginger was supposed to sweep all the roach paraphernalia into a pillowcase and stash it beneath a floorboard in the living room, then help Dearest with the jars of hash, running out back to stuff them into a hollowed-out old tree.

But nothing prepared her for the jolt of panic the first time a little boy came running into the house crying, "Pigs! The pigs are coming!" Up and down the dead-end street, kids were yelling the same, a platoon of barefoot Paul Reveres. Ginger—her belly tight and protruding, her ankles swollen—heaved herself up from her bed but then didn't know what to do. Her heart was racing, and the baby started kicking furiously; she felt a cramp and panicked, wondering if something was wrong.

"Get a move on, Blissful!" Dearest, running past the bedroom, screamed at her. "The cops! Hide the shit!"

Ginger stumbled out into the hallway full of people running back and forth; she tried to shield her stomach as they bumped into her with no apology or concern. She was just a cog in the machine, a worker bee with a job to do. Nobody cared that she was pregnant. She pushed her way to the table and started sweeping roaches and clips into the pillowcase someone shoved at her, then she pushed her huge way back through her panicked housemates to the living room, where she awkwardly kneeled down to pry up the floorboard. A splinter pierced her palm as she clawed at the wood; every inch of her was trembling, and she expected the cops to burst into the room at any minute with her still holding the pillowcase. Finally she got the board up, shoved the pillowcase beneath it, and heaved herself back up by holding on to a rickety chair.

"Get the jars!" Dearest yelled as she ran past the room again. Outside, police cars were whooping, red lights flashing, whistles being blown, as Ginger lumbered back to the dining room. Then she heard the gunshot—everyone in the room stopped, locked eyes, then began to run even faster. Ginger grabbed an armful of mason jars and ran as fast as she could, crying because she couldn't shield her stomach, outside.

Another gunshot, and she dropped two jars. Cocaine Candy stepped on the glass and swore like a sailor; she grabbed the other jars out of Ginger's arms and shot toward the hollowed-out tree.

"Don't let anyone else step on that glass, you idiot!" Candy hollered.

Ginger stood there, the bulky eye of the hurricane of illegal activity, as cops started swarming the house, the yard; one of them paused in front of her, looked at her stomach, shook his head, and moved on. Shaking, her insides dissolving, she felt a warm trickle of pee slide down her leg and her humiliation was complete. All around her, people were being cuffed and led toward the street—the kids had disappeared, there was a place they were supposed to hide, a little dip in the hill. Cocaine Candy was one of those arrested, and she shook her head at Ginger as she was led to the street.

The others—Dearest among them—slowly returned to the house as the cars left and the kids reappeared, all excited. One of the kids found a bullet hole in the front door; he proudly showed it to everyone. Nobody seemed to think it was terrifying, except Ginger; they all laughed and retrieved some joints, passing them around, pleased that most of the stash had made it to the tree.

Ginger couldn't join them; she went back to her room, took off her soaked panties, wiped her legs. Then she lay down on the bed, curled up in a fetal position. The baby kicked again, so at least that was all right. She didn't feel any more cramping.

She shut her eyes, missing Tom so much it hurt. She couldn't do this without him. This wasn't a home. It was a drug ring, pure and simple, and she had no idea how on earth she had gotten to this place that was even worse than the first time in Mexico when she'd been locked in the van with her own urine.

When Tom comes home, she told herself. *When Tom comes home, it'll be all right.*

Pregnant or not, and despite the raids—and as more happened, and one boy who had just joined the Brotherhood was killed farther down the canyon in Laguna, which did seem to sober everyone up for a while—she was expected to contribute, rolling joints and packing hash into jars. Other than that she stayed mostly in her bedroom; she was too big to trek up the hill, drop acid, and lie down, waiting for enlightenment.

The only enlightenment she desired was an end to the constant urge to pee.

. . .

"What is her name, Blissful?" Dearest had come into the room while Candy went outside to tell the others.

"I don't know." Ginger studied the little face, the milky eyes, the open mouth. Funny little bags beneath her eyes, making the baby seem both wizened and unbelievably vulnerable. She waited for some fierce emotion to grab her wildly beating heart, to calm down the panic coursing through her veins. Maternal emotion, the thing you read about—the desire to protect your child against anything. Anyone.

The emotion she'd never been able to imagine her own mother feeling but had been so certain that she would, when it was her turn.

Nothing. Nothing eased the panic. Nothing filled her mind other than terror at what Tom would say when he saw the child that was most certainly not his.

"Take her, please," Ginger whispered, struggling to raise herself with the child in her arms. "Please, take her."

Dearest ran to her, grabbed her daughter just in time. She made soothing, comforting noises to the baby. Noises that Ginger hadn't known how to make. Or had been too afraid to make.

She took refuge in sleep, all-encompassing. Anesthetizing.

Her baby—still nameless—was two months old when Tom was due back. Every day for those two months, she'd contemplated fleeing with her child. But to where? She couldn't go to her sister now. She couldn't imagine going to her mother. And the knowledge that, given a choice between her child and Tom, she would choose the latter, crept closer to her heart each day. Like a monster in a horror movie.

If Tom would still have her.

"Any day now," someone reassured her when the time came and went for Tom to rejoin the compound on Woodland Drive. They'd gotten the news that he'd shipped a VW bus from Istanbul. He was free to hop on a plane and come home. But days passed, and he never arrived, and Ginger couldn't sleep at night between feeding the baby and staring at the ceiling, gripped with terror that something had happened to him. Then her blood would turn to ice as she imagined how he would react when he saw the baby. Lack of sleep and appetite helped her lose the pouchy stomach, but her hair remained dull, her skin still an embarrassment.

The baby was a good baby. Was Ginger as good a baby as this one? Did babies who knew they weren't wanted understand instinctively that they shouldn't cry too much? That they shouldn't ask for anything—any kind of affection or concern—beyond food and clean diapers? All the young runaways fought over who could rock her or push her around in a rusty old carriage. The baby's dark eyes were calmly watchful and wary, and she only occasionally smiled. But when she did, her little face opened up like a dainty flower.

Ginger tried to picture herself standing between Tom and the baby, should Tom turn violent. She tried to imagine renouncing Tom, should he give her an ultimatum. But her imagination failed; she only saw herself crumpling to the ground on her knees, begging Tom to let her stay with him, to take her wherever he went.

Nobody *knew* her like Tom Riley did. Tom was the only one who ever came back for her, over and over.

And he would come back again. The thought filled her with both hope and terror.

The baby was three months old when Tom finally returned. "Let me see my old lady," he shouted as he strode into the house with a cockiness unusual even for him. Ginger was in the kitchen, helping Dearest make real jam for the mason jars—they sold it at Mystic Arts

World, not only for the money but to justify the huge amount of canning jars they bought, so nobody would be suspicious. She was stirring some blackberry juice, fragrant and sticky, on the stove. The moment she heard him, she dropped the wooden spoon on the floor, turned—but didn't run to him. Her legs had grown roots, apparently. She couldn't make them move.

He was tanned, his caramel-colored hair long and curly. A beard made him look statesmanlike; he'd always been clean-shaven before. She wasn't sure she liked it.

She smiled, shaking her head so her hair hung over her face. She was glad she'd lost all the baby weight; he'd never had to see her stomach still bloated, the pad between her legs heavy with blood. She resembled the girl he'd first met, she hoped; her hair and skin were better.

But Ginger didn't feel like the girl he'd first met. She felt as old as the hills they lived in. She had no idea how old she was anymore; she'd stopped celebrating her birthday a couple of years ago. But she'd lived too hard, been denied too many things that kept someone looking their age—the potions and lotions, the trips to the dentist. She had a broken incisor that she'd never been able to fix. Who knew how many cavities? Sometimes she had an ache in her lungs when she had to climb up to the top of the hill where everyone tripped.

But please, dear God, let her look attractive to Tom.

"Give me a hug, my old lady," Tom said, dropping a duffel bag, holding his arms out. She choked back a sob—he was obviously so happy to see her!—and then she ran to him, burying her face in his chest. He still smelled the same, natural, earthy but somehow also clean. He wrapped his arms around her, and she closed her eyes, wishing she could spin an iron web around them, binding them together, making time stand still. If only what had to happen next—didn't.

"Tom, I'm so glad you're back," she whispered. "I missed you. I missed you so much, you can't know how much!"

"I had to do a man's work, babe. And what a score! I'll tell you all about it. But Afghanistan, man, that is the place. Ugly mountains, beautiful poppy fields, bazaars—and the best hash you've ever had. They're getting wise to us, it's not as cheap as it used to be, but it's cheap enough. Everyone can be bought, so there's no worry about customs or that crap. And I'm taking my cut," he said, lowering his voice since others were beginning to trickle into the house to welcome the conquering hero. "Keep it quiet. There's plenty to go around."

Dearest had observed this touching homecoming while stirring the jam, taking over for Ginger. Her eyes narrowed as Tom whispered in Ginger's ear, but she kept a beatific smile on her face as she welcomed Tom home. Soon they were all seated at the dining table, which wasn't yet set for dinner, but someone gave Tom a bowl of soup, which he gulped down between exotic tales of escapades and acid.

"I spent some nights in a yurt with this magical family. They were from some tribe, like Gypsies. We all tripped together, even the kids. Like, it was the best thing ever because we were all one family, you know? Didn't matter that I was this white guy from America and they had names I couldn't begin to pronounce, we were all one family, and we all started loving one another, you know, because it didn't matter, nobody possessed anybody. We were there for each other, like our own tribe. I would have fought to the death to protect them. Crazy. But so right, you know?"

Ginger nodded along with everyone. Why had he shared this, first thing? Why had he told everyone that he'd slept with someone else, right in front of her? Despite her time on Woodland Drive, she still felt the chains of possession, of coupling. She knew it wasn't right, but she couldn't help it. She tried to relax her face, to look cool with it all. She reached for Tom's hand beneath the table, and he squeezed hers, and she felt a little better.

But then Tom dropped his spoon, turning to her in astonishment, letting his gaze fall on her flat stomach. "I can't believe—I forgot. I'm a papa! Where's the little sprout? I need to meet the fruit of my loins."

Chairs scraped the wooden floor as everyone found an excuse to leave the room, but Tom didn't seem to notice. He took Ginger's hands in his, searched her face. "You all right? I mean, you look great. I want to get you in bed right now. But—how did it go?"

She wanted to cry; he'd never been so concerned about her before. And was she imagining the boyishly eager gleam in his eyes? The pride? Had he finally embraced the idea of fatherhood—now that it was too late?

Never before had Ginger wished for an earthquake to strike Southern California—but she did right then. Anything to swallow them up, prevent the terrible thing that was about to happen. She rose, the room spinning around her, the voices of all the kids and women going about their days suddenly discordant, too loud, like a merry-go-round's music turned sinister. Somehow she walked to the bedroom. Somehow she picked up the wicker basket that held the sleeping baby. Somehow she carried it into the dining room.

Somehow, she picked the child up—not out of love, but out of fear. If she was holding a baby, surely Tom wouldn't strike either of them.

"Here," she said, her voice shaking as much as her legs were. She didn't know how she hadn't yet fallen down. "Here is—my daughter."

She couldn't look at Tom at first; she bent her head toward the baby in her arms, studying her as Tom surely was—the dark face with even darker eyes, almond-shaped; the thick, if curly, black hair. This was Jimmy Cho's child as sure as the sun shone too hot and bright outside.

The silence was unnerving, an abyss the two of them fell into, no end in sight. The only sound she heard was Tom's quick intake of breath, followed by panting, as if he'd just run a mile uphill. When she finally found the courage—not exactly courage, as her insides were contracting, meeting together in a knot made of snakes—to look at him, his face was pale beneath its tan, his lips pressed together, his jaw clenched. His hands were balled into fists, and she took a step back, put her hand over the baby's head, that mothering instinct finally flickering on but faint as a candle's flame. So easily extinguished—a puff of air, like the air that blew in when Tom turned and stalked out the door, could put it out.

And it did, because she practically dropped her daughter back in the basket and ran after him. Ginger needed her punishment as much as she needed him; they were one and the same, she couldn't have him—she wouldn't be worthy of him—until she got what was coming to her. She heard herself begging for it, begging Tom to punish her—

Before the sun disappeared even though there were no clouds, and everything turned dark.

Her throbbing head was in a soft lap and someone was speaking. Ginger's ears clanged so stridently she thought her head would split but then realized that it *had* split; warm liquid was running down her face and she tasted iron, so she knew it was blood. She tried to blink but one eye wouldn't open as she stupidly gazed at the face hovering over hers—Candy's face. Her blistered lips were moving, telling Ginger something.

"What?" Ginger tried to shake her head to indicate she couldn't hear, but the pain was like a vise, squeezing her temples together until she thought her brains would pop right out. She wanted to cry in frustration, and maybe she was, there was so much liquid everywhere, some of it congealing, sticky, some of it still viscous, dripping into her open eye, her mouth, her ears, which still rang.

"Charges," Candy shouted. "You can't press charges, you know. You won't. We can't risk that."

"Why would I?" Ginger's voice sounded hoarse, and her throat was raw. She remembered screaming, screaming for her very life—that was the first memory that came back. Her shrieks begging Tom to stop, and it seemed to take forever before anyone heard her because they were alone in a thick grove of bamboo, she'd followed him there and was at first grateful for the privacy as she did her best to explain—

"I'm sorry, I'm so sorry, it wasn't Jimmy's fault, it was all mine, I didn't know where you were—you have to believe me, it didn't mean anything, I'm yours, all yours, I deserve whatever you have to do to me—"

Then she was terrified of the seclusion as Tom whirled around and grabbed her by the hair, tearing at it, pulling it from her head as his other fist hit her left eye, he was kicking her knees, she fell but he still had a hold on her hair; it ripped from her head with a sickening tear. But his blows hardly made any sound. Because her ready flesh cushioned them.

"You bitch! You fucking bitch! You slept with that gook, didn't you? I'm gonna kill him. I'm gonna kill Jimmy Cho. Me—the Surf God—how the hell did this happen? You bitch, you're dead. *Dead!* That I ever let your chink-loving hands touch me, that I let you put those lips that touched his on my—I'm sick. I'm going to be sick."

But he didn't look sick unless rage was a disease; it distorted his entire face. His bulging eyes loomed at her, coming in too close, then zooming out, then in, as she raised her hands to shield her eyes, as her screams tore her throat as Tom kept coming at her again and again and again—until she blacked out.

And came to in Candy's lap, on her own bed. The baby—where was the baby? She tried to raise her head again, but now there was a film over her one open eye; her tongue was too big for her mouth and it pulsed with pain. She must have bitten it during the onslaught.

"This is too bad," Candy continued. She was wiping Ginger's face with a cool, wet washcloth. "Really too bad. He's a dick. I mean, I get it—that kid is not his. But he didn't have to beat you up."

Ginger took a breath, felt a stab in her right side, and moaned.

"Maybe you cracked a rib," Candy said almost cheerfully. "I don't think anything else is broken, though. We can wrap that up here, no need to go to a hospital. That's the important thing."

"Where . . ." Ginger tried to talk through her thick, immobile tongue. "Where ith he?"

"They took him up to Griggs; if anyone can cool him off, it's John. We'll keep him away from you as long as we can but you have to leave, honey. We can't risk any more violence, who knows what might bring the cops calling these days? Fucking pigs. But you know how they watch us. We can't give them a reason to start shooting up the place again, carting people to jail. So you have to leave."

"Where would I go?"

"Honey, Blissful, that's your problem. Not mine."

All Ginger wanted to do was close her eyes and sleep, but she fought through the fog closing in. Her mind wasn't cooperating, it kept tormenting her with pictures of what had happened—Tom's eyes, black with fury. His taunts—"You're just a stupid bitch. Nothing special. Just like my mother—just like your stuck-up *sister,* after all—a bitch who thinks she's better than me."

She'd never, not once, thought that.

"To think I took you with me that day after filming on the beach—you know why I did it? Do you?" Tom's voice kept screaming in her head, an anvil hammering her brain. What he said, she still couldn't understand.

"I took you because I wanted your sister, you stupid cunt! Do you understand? I only wanted you that day to take her down a peg, so she'd come looking for you and then I'd finally have *her*. The only Donnelly Girl I ever wanted, not you, you fucking cow!"

"You can't—you can't mean that!" Ginger believed she'd screamed it but maybe she'd only thought it. But his words lacerated her in a way his fists and feet never could.

"Yeah, I was sure she'd come after you. But she didn't. Turns out *she* didn't want you, either."

"Blissful? Did you hear me?" Candy's face grew closer; she gave Ginger's shoulders a little shake. "Blissful? You can't stay here."

"Yeth." Her tongue throbbed so much, almost more than her eye. She took a big breath—then cried out from the burning pain in her ribs. After it subsided, it was like the clouds had cleared, the pounding waves had calmed. She knew only one desire—one miserably overwhelming desire—and it was to remain with Tom.

Tom, who hadn't chosen her after all.

But he was upset. He'd been dealt a thunderbolt, and he hurt, and she couldn't blame him. She'd had three months to get used to the idea that Tom had not fathered her child—no, that wasn't right. She wasn't used to it, she'd never get used to it. But she didn't feel the staggering shock she'd once felt every time she looked at her daughter.

She had wounded Tom in a way she, a mere female, could never understand. She had betrayed him. He didn't know what he was saying—he was too injured. They both were.

That was why they needed each other. She'd make him see it that way. Somehow.

"If I—if I give the baby away . . . ," Ginger began, her battered brain slowly putting together the pieces of her own plan.

Finally.

"If I give her away," she continued. "If I do that, can I thtay?"

"I don't know. Do you think he'd take you back? Without beating up on you, which, I have to say, I don't think this was the first time, was it?"

Ginger tried to shake her head, but it hurt too much. Candy understood, anyway.

"That's between you two, I guess," she said with a weary sigh. "Only don't bring any trouble to us, you understand?"

"Yeth," Ginger said again as her eyelids—the one that wasn't swollen shut, anyway—fluttered. The fog was closing in. But before it did, she had one last coherent, terrifying thought—

She was like her mother, after all.

15

"Can I—can we—come in?" Mindy's sister asked as she picked up the baby, who had started to cry. She shifted her daughter in her arms, as if she could use the baby's wriggling little body as a shield. Ginger didn't meet Mindy's shocked gaze.

Mindy couldn't respond; all she could do was take in the sight—Ginger, barefoot in a threadbare maxi dress, a duffel bag and a wicker basket at her feet. And a baby—chubby, darling, with curly black hair and dark eyes and that heartbreaking smile—in her arms.

"Please, Mindy?"

"How did you get here? Are you alone?"

"Someone dropped me off. Look, the baby's heavy—can I come inside?"

Feeling numb, Mindy stood back while her sister tentatively stepped inside. Mindy picked up the duffel bag and basket and followed her into the living room. Ginger placed the baby on the carpet; the child pushed herself up on her plump arms and, head nodding unsteadily, blinked and gazed around, uttering a little cry of delight.

"What the hell, Ginger? What the hell?" Mindy tried but couldn't do it; she couldn't make sense of her sister with a baby who looked so much like Jimmy Cho.

"I know, I know, I'll try to explain. Mindy, I'm so sorry. I—

Jimmy—he and I, one night. It was right after he said you dumped him—that very night. He saw me at a store, Mindy—I was a mess. Hungry and dirty and I'd not slept much in days, watching over the shack. I almost passed out, and he gave me food and made me come back with him to his friend's apartment. Mindy, he was so kind."

Mindy nodded—what else could she do? And Jimmy *was* kind. But kindness couldn't possibly be the only explanation.

"He was also so hurt," Ginger said with a sharpness to her voice Mindy had never heard before. As if she was scolding her big sister, for the first time ever. "Anyway," Ginger continued, her voice now weary, resigned. "It happened. Just once. I was sorry, he was sorry—"

"He said the same thing," Mindy interrupted, remembering. "I saw him, a month or so ago. In Vietnam. I was on a USO tour."

"You were?" Ginger's eyes widened. "In *Vietnam?*"

"Yeah, I was. I came back a month ago. And I saw Jimmy—he'll be home soon, too—at China Beach. We made up—I mean, I thought we did. He's coming back to me when his tour is over. But he wanted me to tell you he was sorry. He wouldn't say for what."

Ginger nodded. "It was such a mistake. It meant nothing, Mindy. I swear."

"That's what everybody says," Mindy realized, thinking of all the stupid movies she'd been in, when—after kissing the Girl in the Curl—the lead actor would always go running back to his beloved, insisting *it meant nothing*.

She wasn't on a movie set. She didn't get to go back to a trailer and wash off her makeup and comb her hair. Bodies coming together, no matter the reason, always meant *something*.

Betrayed—that was what she was. The betrayed woman; she felt it keenly—like something had sliced away a layer of her flesh. How could Jimmy do that to her? Never mind that she'd dumped him first, told him her career meant more than him, all because of that stupid photo in the newspaper. But that he'd slept with her sister—that was the thing. The unforgivable thing. Anyone else, she would have probably learned to forgive and forget. But her own sister; it was too close, too icky, too something she couldn't wrap her brain around other than that it made her want to puke. Like he *wanted* her to find out—he wanted to hurt her that much.

And if that wasn't bad enough, there was also a child. A living, breathing—drooling, squealing—reminder of *all* their mistakes.

Her niece, she realized with a jolt. She was *related* to this mistake.

"Mindy, I want you to take her," Ginger blurted out, hiding behind her hair like she always did and had done ever since she was a little girl afraid of the world unless her big sister held her hand. Mindy had always hated it—such a baby, she'd always told her sister. A baby. With a baby.

"What do you mean? Like, hold her?"

"No, I mean—like *keep* her."

"For how long?" Typical Ginger—after dumping this bombshell on her, she was only thinking of herself. "Ginger, I am *not* going to be your babysitter, Jesus Christ! How on earth can you even ask that now? You need to grow up—besides, I have to go to work in about an hour!"

"No, no!" Ginger shook her head. "You don't understand! Mindy, I'm asking you to keep her, to raise her. Take her for me. I can't do it."

"What?"

"Raise my daughter. Please, Mindy. I'm asking too much, I know. But I can't keep her."

A baby. Mindy was being asked to raise a baby. *The* baby—the mistake of all colossal mistakes.

Dizzy—it was too fast, everything happening too fast, her feeble little scatterbrain couldn't take it all in, let alone make sense of it—Mindy plopped down on a chair.

"You can't be serious, Ginger. You can't ask me this. Me, of all people."

"I know it's asking a lot," Ginger continued, twisting the ends of her hair around her index finger, another annoying—familiar—habit that Mindy hadn't known she'd missed. "I know. I know I'm like Mom, I get it. But—I have to go back to Tom. He needs me. I can't bring her, he will never take me back as long as I have—her."

"*Her?* Doesn't she have a name?" Mindy couldn't help herself; this baby was a mistake but this baby was also a person, a vulnerable little lump happily shoving her own fist in her mouth and gurgling. Ginger blushed.

"I just—I never got around to it."

"Jesus, Ginger." Mindy turned to stare at her niece—Jimmy's child. Jimmy and Ginger's nameless child. Whom she was being asked to take in like a stray kitten? The baby lay on her belly, kicking her legs like a tadpole, grabbing at the shag carpet with her fist. Then she shoved the fist back in her mouth. Mindy watched dispassionately at first, then nervously—surely Ginger would make sure she hadn't put something dangerous in her mouth?

A spring uncoiled from somewhere within and Mindy leapt forward, grabbing the little hand, pulling it out of the mouth. The fingers were wet with saliva but Mindy didn't wipe them off as she retrieved a bobby pin. Shaking her head, she picked the baby up.

Jimmy's baby.

The child slumped against her with her dimpled legs straight out; she was wearing only a T-shirt that was too big for her, and a diaper in rubber pants. She looked healthy but not cared for—her hair was tangled, there was some crust around her mouth and in the folds of her legs. Her nails were too long.

Fury drove away all other emotion; she turned on her sister, still sitting there like some shy fawn who didn't know how to live in the world. How the *fuck* had Ginger never learned to do a single thing on her own? Always, someone had to tell her what to do, how to think, how to behave. For so long, too long, it had been Mindy. But look what happened when she left her to fend for herself! She needed to grow the fuck up, that was what Ginger needed to do.

"Ginger, this is insane. You're her mother. This baby is *your* responsibility. You can't leave her with me, she's not *my* responsibility. I don't know what to do with a kid! And I have a job, you know. I can't do this." Mindy shook her head, even as she began to rock the child back and forth in her arms—it just came to her, she didn't notice she was doing it until the baby started to coo happily, then she stopped, embarrassed. She'd probably seen it on TV, some perfect mother—Samantha on *Bewitched,* probably—rocking her baby.

This wasn't television. This was real life. This was the result of a one-night stand between her sister and her lover.

This was *fucked up*.

"I can't do it," Ginger whispered. "I can't be a mother. I don't know how—look at you! I never know how to hold her, she always cries and I always want to put her down. She'll be so much better off with you."

"How can you even think of doing this? Leaving your own child? Who on earth does that?"

Ginger laughed sourly, then Mindy did, too—she couldn't believe those words had popped out of her mouth. God, these Donnelly girls. They were such a disaster.

"I have to be with Tom, if he'll take me back," Ginger finally replied. "I know you won't understand."

The sisters stared at each other for a long moment. Ginger was sitting right there, in Mindy's living room, but it seemed as if an ocean were between them. They had lived in two entirely different worlds these last years. For the first time, Mindy realized that what she didn't know about her sister was vastly greater than what she did. That wasn't part of the Plan. Not at all.

Who was this stranger sitting across the room? But no, this was her sister—the same shy manner warmed by her pretty smile. But then she peered more closely—her sister wasn't the same, after all. Why hadn't Mindy registered the eye, swollen with purple and yellow bruises? The way Ginger placed her hand on her side when she laughed or took a deep breath? The patches of hair torn from her scalp?

"He beat you, didn't he? That bastard beat you up because this is Jimmy's child."

"Tom came home a few days ago—he hadn't seen the baby yet, he was away. Away on business."

Mindy snorted.

"And then he saw her, and he figured it out. He's a man, Mindy! His pride was wounded. I betrayed him—I betrayed you, too, I know, and I can never be sorry enough. It's me, it's all me, and I don't know what else to do now, how to make it all right for everyone. The only thing I can do is be with Tom, like it used to be—I have to be with him! You don't understand!" Ginger was crying, desperately. Great gulps, punctuated with gasps of pain when she clutched her side. Mindy should have comforted her, told her she was stupid, that over her dead body was her sister going back to that bastard, she and the baby were staying right here, Mindy would make it all right. Like she used to, back when they were kids.

But her lap was occupied by this gurgling, cooing baby that had no name and no mother. She did, however, have a father.

A father whose name Mindy spoke in her sleep.

Mindy wanted a drink more than she'd ever craved anything before. Or a cigarette. Something to inhale or imbibe that would dispel the panic—and rage—starting to burn within. She wasn't ready, she wasn't grown-up enough to be a *mother*. For the first time, maybe, she had a tremor of sympathy for what her mother must have felt at nineteen, presented with a baby—Mindy—that she hadn't wanted.

But Mindy hadn't asked to be born—

And neither had this little girl.

"Jesus Christ," she said again, defeated. "I don't know, Ginger— you can't go back to that lunatic. And I can't raise your child. Yours and Jimmy's—you can't ask that of me. That's not fair, you know. It's just not fair."

"What about Mom?" Ginger wiped her eyes and sniffed.

Mindy stared at her. Felt the guilt—which she usually held at bay by recalling the night at Makaha—whisper in her ear.

What about Mom?

For too long, she'd put it off, content to let DeeDee occasionally keep her apprised of the situation, although she hadn't heard from DeeDee in months. Hearing secondhand accounts of the rare Carol Donnelly sighting, now a shadow of her former self, but that was just age, wasn't it? No need to be alarmed.

And she was planning on seeing her soon, when Jimmy—

When Jimmy came home.

"Oh, God," Mindy moaned, looking down at the baby, who smiled up at her, so innocent. So like Jimmy. "Oh my God."

"I'm so sorry," Ginger whispered, but Mindy only shook her head. She had no solutions, no answers. Right now, she only had pain— too much of it, she didn't know what to do with it, it needed to spill out of her somehow. But before she could let it overwhelm her, she had to get rid of this child.

"Come on," Mindy said with a sigh. She stood up; the baby some- how fit herself so that she was nestled against Mindy's chest, con- tented, secure. *Alive.* Another Donnelly girl whose destiny was to screw up the things that other people seemed to do naturally. To find the most difficult, outrageously *idiotic* path and take that instead of the simpler, easier one.

"Get your things. Does she need to be changed?" Mindy nodded down at the child, whose eyelids were fluttering, sleep making a perfect rosebud of her lips.

"Probably. She always does." Ginger took her baby, did indeed hold her awkwardly, as if she was terrified of her, and probably she was. Ginger was terrified of everything. Except, strangely, the person who could do the most harm to her.

Her sister knelt down on the rug and began to change the diaper, asking Mindy where she should put the soiled one, and Mindy had no idea, she told her to put it in a wastebasket and she'd deal with it later. Mindy escaped to her bedroom. Plopping down on her bed, she put her head in her hands, trying to sort it all out—she was going to see Mom. Right this minute. She and Ginger. The three of them together for the first time in years. And they were bringing Mom her grandchild to raise. The woman who never should have had children in the first place. And the father of that child was Jimmy. The man Mindy loved—or at least, had loved, until this afternoon, and now she didn't know what to do with that love. Should she still love him, after what he'd done?

Should she still love her sister?

What about the baby—*Jesus, Ginger, how could you not name your own child?*

She stood up, made a quick phone call to work, babbling something about a family emergency, then grabbed her purse. Fit the three of them in her little convertible, Ginger holding the baby on her lap. Was that safe? She guessed it was. But she really had no idea.

They didn't say anything on the long ride down to Laguna Beach; the Coast Highway had gotten so busy, with too many stoplights and pedestrian crossways, a never-ending line of traffic. It took so much longer than Mindy remembered it taking, back when she and Ginger had driven it to and from filming the very first surfing movie. The sisters didn't even speak when Mindy parked her car on the street in front of the familiar, shabby apartment building consisting of two stories, each unit with a little balcony facing the ocean, but the building needed to be painted, and there was rust on the iron stairs leading up from the street.

As she rapped on the door to their old apartment, she couldn't help but notice that it, too, needed painting.

Someone opened the door. Someone Mindy didn't know.

"Excuse me, but—doesn't Carol Donnelly live here?"

The older woman with tightly curled gray hair who had answered their knock nodded, and she didn't seem at all surprised that two women and a baby stood on the doorstep. She held a lit cigarette in one hand, which she used to gesture toward a dark form on the other side of the room, framed by a huge, dirty window that faced the ocean. The form revealed itself to be a woman in a chair, binoculars up to her eyes as she stared out the window.

"Mom?" Mindy walked slowly across the dim room, lit only by the sun coming in from the big window. "Mom?"

The binoculars were lowered, and Mindy saw that they were on a string around the woman's neck. Then she saw that next to the chair was a metal walker, the kind old people used in nursing homes. The woman in the chair turned her head toward them, blinked rapidly for a few heartbeats, and answered in a familiar but weakened voice, "Who the hell wants to know?"

BOOK TWO

Carol

A social service meeting, an afternoon tea,
a matinee, a whatnot, is no excuse for there being
no dinner ready when a husband comes
home from a hard day's work.

Housekeeping accomplishments and cooking
ability are, of course, positive essentials in any
true home, and every wife should take a reasonable
pride in her skill. Happiness does not flourish
in an atmosphere of dyspepsia.

—Reverend Alfred Henry Tyrer,
Sex Satisfaction and Happy Marriage,
1951 edition

16

1955

"Are you ready for this?"

Carol Donnelly didn't answer; she couldn't. Her heart was in her throat—she put her hand up to her neck and felt the pounding. No words could get past it. For the first time in her life, she wasn't sure she was up to the task.

Was it fear that she felt? Fear was so alien to her in this setting, she honestly couldn't say. Fear was something that belonged indoors, in claustrophobic bedrooms or children's sour nurseries or cluttered kitchens. Fear was oppressive there; it blacked out any sun trying to penetrate the gloom. It made her small and mean, almost miserly with her movements, not to mention her affection.

Fear had no place outdoors, it never had; the sun chased it away, so did the wind, and most of all the water. Outdoors, Carol laughed and loved, ran and leapt and dove for a catch and swam and turned cartwheels and held her breath for long minutes and pushed her body to go that extra bit more—a higher dive, a faster sprint around the bases, another minute underwater. And it had never failed her.

It had taken a man to accomplish that, to turn her body into something that didn't do what she wanted it to. To turn *her*, Carol, into someone she had once had nightmares about.

But all that was *before* she discovered the surf. Already, she'd conquered miles of it back home. Which was why she was in Hawaii at this moment, desperate for something bigger than she was. Something that would pound some sense into her so she wouldn't make any more mistakes. Something *better* than she was, that would push her to be better, too.

She knew she could never find it back in California.

But here in Makaha, on the western shore of Oahu, she thought maybe she had. And so she could only gaze at the furious waves in wonder, not knowing, for the first time in her life, if she had even a fighting chance against them.

"Let's go!" The words kicked their way past the lump in her throat, surprising her and her companion. The fear—if that was what it was—had vanished; adrenaline kicked in. Carol grabbed her surfboard—ten feet long and twenty-five pounds of balsa wood—and started to run toward the water.

DeeDee grinned up at her in admiration; Carol knew that if she didn't go in, DeeDee wouldn't, either. Maybe it had been DeeDee's idea to go on safari in Hawaii, looking for the big waves people only whispered about in California—but DeeDee was more afraid of a thundering surf. And that was what lay before the two wahines, one tall and blond, the other petite and brunette, from the mainland: A surf more powerful than any they'd seen before. Waves whose thundering percussed their eardrums with a force they'd never experienced. The waves broke farther out from shore and were taller, twenty, twenty-five, thirty feet, so unlike the smaller, reliably manageable long breaks of Malibu. They'd studied these unfamiliar waves for an hour already, not enough time, Carol knew. But she also knew she was capable of just *looking* at waves for only so long.

Even more intoxicating, there was hardly anyone here at Makaha. Just a handful of guys who had at first glared at the two women, then ignored them. Carol and DeeDee were the only females present, which they were used to by now. It was such a remote stretch of beach, this fabled Makaha; they'd driven past it the first time on a sliver of road cut out of the green mountains. This side of Oahu was nothing like the tourist side, where they'd landed in Honolulu. It wasn't civilized, not in the manufactured way of Waikiki Beach. There were few swaying palms here, no hotels, a smattering of houses, and those only shacks or Quonset huts. There was a military base somewhere nearby, they'd been told, where ammunition was tested. But so far Carol and DeeDee hadn't heard nor seen a sign of it.

"Let's go!" Carol shouted over the crashing waves, and DeeDee started in behind her. They were together as they paddled out but soon it would be every man—every woman—for herself, each wave an individual kingdom that had to be conquered.

Which was exactly why Carol loved surfing.

"Do you miss them?" DeeDee asked that night in the van.

The waves had won, that first day at Makaha. Carol was a tall woman with broad shoulders, muscular legs. She had felt the difference in these powerful waves; her legs dug into the board so fiercely, it was a wonder they didn't leave dents. Her thighs had strained, her toes had curled; it wasn't so much riding the waves but rather holding on for dear life, like on the back of a bucking horse. She hadn't managed to ride one in or find a way to break out of the churning white water that arched over her head, a monster roaring at her back; each time, she'd wiped out. And each time, she'd been grateful for her stint performing as a mermaid in a show on the Santa Monica Pier during summer vacations, which had given her lungs of iron; this surf pinned her down in its swirling depths for far longer than the surf at Malibu, or Huntington Beach, or Laguna Beach.

Still, at the end of the day, eyes red and burning from the sun and the salt water, legs bruised from being kicked by her board, she felt as if she'd been slapped awake out of a stupor. She couldn't wait to go back out tomorrow.

"Miss who?" Carol asked as she absentmindedly rubbed calamine lotion on some sand flea bites near her ankles. She flexed her toes, nails painted a baby pink that matched the polish on the fingernails of her broad, powerful hands. Already the polish was chipped. Silly, she knew, painting her nails when she spent all her time scraping her toes on rocks or coral. But it was like dressing up in heels and gloves for the plane trip here from California; Carol wasn't nearly so unconventional as most people assumed. It wasn't like she didn't shave her legs or eschewed deodorant. She enjoyed a pretty dress, a fancy cocktail in an elegant restaurant, a manicure now and then. "You mean Bob and the girls?"

"Sure, who did you think I meant?" DeeDee wrinkled her nose. She was one of the lucky ones. DeeDee was the daughter of a famous head of a movie studio, and while she and Carol were close in age, DeeDee had found surfing before she'd found a husband—or rather, before a husband found her. So surfing could come first, no questions asked. No judgment pronounced.

It wasn't the same for Carol.

"Yes, of course I miss them." Carol screwed the cap back onto the glass bottle of calamine. There was no light in the van, other than a couple of flashlights propped up, casting weird shadows; no windows other than the windshield and rear window. It had a musty, grassy smell whose origin she didn't want to spend too much time contemplating, and the ceiling fabric was torn, hanging down like spiderwebs. But Carol didn't care; at that moment, it was more welcoming—more *her*—than the two-bedroom tract home back in Van Nuys. The home with the claustrophobic bedrooms and cluttered kitchen.

The home where her two girls were, at this very minute. The home she had left without a backward glance.

"I don't know how you do it, with kids," DeeDee said as she smoothed her sleeping bag and stretched out on it. Her legs were short but sculpted, tanned; she wore only a T-shirt over her panties, which were surprisingly fancy, pink with black lace. Carol grinned, supposing that you didn't really know a person until you saw what kind of underwear she wore. DeeDee's freckled face was open and kind; she did not look like the pampered daughter of a movie mogul. "You're like the anti–Betty Crocker. The *surfing* Betty Crocker."

"Yeah, I guess." Carol lay back on her own sleeping bag, folding her hands behind her head as she stared at the stained ceiling of the van. They'd rented it from the guy who shaped boards in Waikiki; he made a tidy profit renting the rusting bucket of bolts to pilgrims from the mainland who were drawn to the birthplace of surfing. Surfing safari, it was called; leaving behind all cares and responsibilities to spend weeks, months, traveling from beach to beach, sleeping in a car or on the sand, bathing in the ocean, occasionally grabbing supplies from a grocery store but often surviving on seaweed, coconuts, or the fish that you shared the ocean with. Living only for the waves. Letting them dictate the rhythm and purpose of your life.

It was rare, but not unheard of, for men to do it. But two wahines on a surfing safari? One of whom was a married mother of two? That made people stare. Already, they'd heard reports on the local radio station of the two mysterious maidens in the van. And when they'd grabbed their surfboards from the cargo hold of the plane, still wearing their smart dresses and gloves, someone had snapped their photo for a local newspaper.

"I don't know if I could just leave my kids like that," DeeDee said with a yawn. She rolled over on her side, adjusting her pillow. Carol felt the warmth of her body, the softness, pressing up against her, and she didn't mind it. Funny, how that was. When the double bed she shared with her husband sometimes seemed like a coffin.

"Do you think it's possible to be loved too much?" Carol whispered. But DeeDee was already softly snoring.

Carol brushed some sand off her pillow, closing her eyes. Soon she, too, was asleep.

Did she dream of Bob, of her girls, Mindy and Ginger? Did she think of them back in the suburban house? Bob sleeping alone in that bed, looking at her empty pillow, the girls in their twin beds, their room still painted nursery pink even though they were big girls now, Ginger eight, Mindy ten? Did she worry about whether they'd done their homework, if Bob had managed to heat the TV dinners without burning them, if he'd made sure they had fruit for dessert instead of the Hydrox cookies that were always in the cookie jar?

These were not Carol Donnelly's dreams or worries.

Carol's house looked like the others in the neighborhood: small and tidy, a green lawn mowed religiously every Saturday by Bob, who also kept the driveway swept and the garage in apple-pie order. But inside, the maple furniture was dusty, the beds usually not made (except on the weekends when Bob did them). The kitchen always had dirty dishes in the sink, and the linoleum was coated in sugary granules of sand.

"I'm never going to be a housewife," she had warned Bob when he finally caught her. They'd met in high school, junior year, in the middle of the war. She was a star athlete: track and field, swimming, softball. She had plans. *Real* plans. After high school, she was going to go east and try out for the All-American Girls Professional Baseball League. Her plans had once included qualifying for the Olympics, probably on the swim team, but the war had postponed the

Olympics for who knew how long. And she couldn't even complain about it, not with so many other horrible things happening in the world—the hellish world in which every movie, every song, every radio broadcast by the president, reminded her that *men* were making the biggest, the ultimate, sacrifices. How dare a *girl* complain about not competing for an Olympic medal in such a time?

With that dream shattered, the baseball league was the only option. Except for college, of course, but Carol had no desire to spend another minute inside a classroom even if it meant giving up the glory of the USC or UCLA athletic department. Which wasn't all that glorious if you were a girl, to be honest.

But this new women's baseball league—started up because all the male baseball players were away at war—was *professional*. She would be a star player—she'd been scouted, begged to come to the tryouts in Chicago. And she would earn money doing the one thing she was good at—disciplining and pushing her body. There was nothing else she wanted in the entire world; she had the train schedule and dreamed of a little apartment in one of the home cities that she could share with other girls on the team.

Would she miss the ocean, though? Carol had never lived where she couldn't plunge into the surf to wash away the cares of the world, where she couldn't lie on the beach being warmed by the sun. The league only played in the Midwest, which was cold, they said. She'd never seen snow. Still, to be able to play ball all the time, not only after school—how could that not be the best thing ever?

At high school, she was the Ice Queen, the untouchable Carol Murphy, earmarked for something great. She looked down upon the student body—literally, in some cases, given her height, five feet ten inches—and didn't give a hoot about their petty worries and hopes. Never had she gone to a homecoming dance or prom, even though she'd had multiple invitations. Never had she glanced twice at a boy who'd had the audacity to suggest she go for a burger with him after school. She lived at the track or the diamond or the pool instead. Every day. Her beaming face, framed by her bouncing ponytail, was on the cover of local magazines, in the newspaper as she won her trophies and cups and broke high school records; she hung around the swimming pools of Hollywood stars like Johnny Weissmuller and Cary Grant, whom she taught how to do a swan dive.

She heard the whispers, too. *Dyke. Butch.* Every female athlete heard the same whispers. The intramural leagues, the school teams, all tried to combat the whispers with ridiculous stunts like beauty pageants and charm school displays, anything to showcase the athletes' *femininity,* a word Carol despised and never did learn how to spell. How idiotic was it to mince around playing beauty queen after finishing a doubleheader? The dirt still embedded in your knees, thighs bruised from sliding, body pouring sweat, hair matted down from the baseball cap?

It was the rawness, the realness, of sport that she loved: The smells in the girls' locker room that couldn't be masked by sprays of Jean Naté. The frank talk about how to treat a bruise—raw steak or bags of frozen peas? The display of flesh, of breasts out in the open, taut bellies, glistening shoulders in the shower—it was all so simple. So natural, Carol thought.

Those beauty pageants were all about concealing or remaking; about being someone's idea of a *girl*. Already-flat stomachs girdled, firm breasts deformed by conical bras, stockings snapped into place by garters, everything beautiful about the body disguised or unnaturally enhanced—

Everything strong made to appear soft.

And charm school! Carol and her teammates had to attend charm school every Saturday morning. For some reason, it was deemed important that they learn how to pour tea and stand correctly, one foot slightly in front of the other at a right angle, stomach sucked in, smile, always a smile, plastered on a face disguised with the right amount of makeup. All of it—the pageants and the charm school—designed to reassure parents and boyfriends and impressionable children that being an athlete didn't mean you weren't proper wife material. Carol never felt ashamed of her supple body, except when she was forced to wear a modest one-piece bathing suit and high heels and a sash.

Her body was a thing of strength, to be marveled at for what it could do. Not for how it was measured—at one point in every pageant, she had to stand still with that smile and submit to having a measuring tape wrapped around her waist by a panting man in an ill-fitting suit.

But she put up with it; they all did. None of her teammates ever talked about those stupid pageants; nobody cared who was declared the winner. In the locker room, all they discussed was who missed that easy fly catch, who needed to work on her turn in the pool, what liniment oil was best for a sore shoulder.

It was only outside that they had to be someone else's ideal.

When Bob Donnelly—little Bob Donnelly—kept hanging around, pestering her to let him carry her books, offering to drive her home after practice or a game, she tolerated him. She wasn't totally immune to the gossip about dykes and being too butch. She didn't know if she was a dyke or wasn't and she didn't really care but her mother would, her father, too. And she needed their permission to go to Chicago to try out for the baseball league.

The spring of senior year, the tryouts only a few months away, she heard herself telling Bob Donnelly, "Yes, I'll go to the prom with you."

And afterward, when he drove her home, she said yes again. Yes, I'll let you do what you want with this body you worship so much you can't stop staring at it, touching it, marveling at my biceps, the iron flatness of my stomach, the long, lean muscles of these legs you say you want to have wrapped around you. Yes, I'll be your girl for the night, I'll let you tell everybody that I'm not a dyke.

"Don't Fence Me In" was playing on the car radio; Bob was finished before the song was.

And one more time—

Yes, I'll marry you, after the rabbit died and all her dreams with it. No taking the Super Chief to Chicago now, no getting an apartment with teammates, no playing at Wrigley Field. No being anything other than what her parents, her teachers, her grandparents and aunts and uncles and cousins and every magazine she read, every movie she went to, told her she really wanted to be—

A mother. A wife.

A stranger.

> Girls who will be happy in marriage enjoy teaching children and have a fondness for old people. They are not strong admirers of musicians and poets though they may like good music or poetry. They believe mates should be virgins at marriage and faithful thereafter.
>
> —*Modern Bride,* 1952

"I do," Carol said, then ran to the bathroom, falling on her knees in front of the toilet.

"Nerves," she heard her mother apologize. "Just wedding-day jitters."

It was a typical wartime wedding, held in her parents' living room the Saturday after graduation. Carol wore a tailored day dress and a little hat with a veil. She carried a white prayer book with an orchid attached; the room was so full of cloying lilies, she'd felt nauseous the moment she entered on her father's arm and saw Bob in uniform, standing next to the minister.

Or perhaps it was the morning sickness; she wasn't sure. But already her body was changing on her—her nipples were so tender, they chafed beneath her bathing suit. So far her stomach hadn't betrayed her, so they could pass the baby off as premature when the time came. But she studied her naked self in the mirror every day, touching her body, probing, searching for the inevitable changes— was that a millimeter of fat around her hips? Her breasts were certainly bigger; she could tell the difference when she swam or dived, her center was off. This body that she had sculpted with devotion yet also taken for granted was softening, morphing into something she could not refine by swimming or running a few more laps or skipping dessert for a week. And she despised it, for the first time in her life. Despised the thing that was causing it, this tiny embryo in her womb whose presence in a few months would shackle her indoors. That was what her mother told her, smiling, joyful. That was what her aunts said, too, once the ring was on her finger and everyone was told.

"You'll never want to go near a baseball diamond again, when the baby comes," they all sang, this monstrous chorus of femininity. "You'll see, Carol. Once that baby comes, you'll never think of anything else. And it'll take your mind off Bob, overseas."

Bob's letters arrived with regularity, never talking about his experiences. Instead, she was inundated with pages and pages of adoration, of astonishment at his good fortune. Once, he even confessed that he'd cried the night she'd said she'd go out with him. As if that were something she would want to know! It only made her pity him— when she thought of him at all. But she didn't, not as long as she could still squeeze into her suit and go to the beach, swimming against the waves. As her body grew and softened, she was so embarrassed by it she craved solitude. She was too ashamed to swim at the YMCA pool where she'd once trained.

Maybe she simply couldn't stand to see her own grinning face as she displayed the medal she'd won at the state championship, the photo hanging prominently in the front lobby.

> As the pains begin, you will be given an injection. When you wake up, with no memory of pain or distress because of the highly qualified skill of your obstetrician and his staff, you will be a mother, the fulfillment of your destiny. How happy you will be!
>
> —Hospital pamphlet, 1948

Lying on her back, wrists and ankles strapped to the rails of a narrow bed in a sterile room full of other women similarly splayed out, like chickens ready for the oven, Carol blinked up at the ceiling. The first pains hadn't been that bad—like menstrual cramps with some aching in her lower back. But now they were coming with more regularity, and she couldn't do anything to stop them; she couldn't turn on her side or sit up. All she could do was bunch up her legs or stretch them out, anything to relieve the vise increasing its grip on her lower body, that pain that started so stealthily, a drop in a pond that turned into a tsunami of agony. She wept with frustration; she knew her body, she knew how to relieve pain, she was an expert at it. Hadn't she played through any number of injuries over the years? But they wouldn't let her take care of herself; they'd lashed her to the bed like a biology specimen, and nobody paid any attention to anything she said. Or anything any other laboring woman said. Carol had the strangest sensation that the mothers-to-be were the least important people in the room. An assembly line of baby-making machines.

"My, my, what a fuss we're making." One nurse finally approached;

she had unruly eyebrows and a syringe in her hand. "You'd think it was the end of the world. You're getting everyone else riled up."

"It *is*!" Carol shouted through her parched throat; she was so thirsty but they wouldn't let her drink any water, or even suck on an ice cube. "It *is* the end of the world!"

"No, it isn't, it's what women do. The most natural thing, it's what they're made for. Now, close your eyes and start to count down from a hundred."

"One hundred, ninety-nine, ninety-eight—ouch!" A sharp prick, then a rush of cold invaded her body. "Ninety-seven, ninety-six, ninety-five . . ."

The next thing she knew, she was awake. How much time she'd been asleep, she couldn't tell. Although later she remembered strange dreams, of bells and whistles going off, little baby hands poking up out of the floor trying to grab her ankles, a plane going down in flames outside a window.

As soon as she opened her eyes, blinking until they could focus, and she realized she was in a different room and no longer strapped down, Carol Donnelly knew she'd been violated. Her body, whose every muscle, ligament, and tendon was so familiar to her, had been torn apart by someone's hands while she'd been asleep, and if that wasn't a violation, she didn't know what was. When she shared this with the same nurse, however, she was told, sternly, that she mustn't talk dirty.

"For heaven's sake," the nurse hissed through thin, colorless lips. "Have you no shame? I've never, in all my days, heard a lady say such a thing! First all that caterwauling, and now this!"

"But I know it," Carol repeated weakly, her hands automatically moving down to her shredded, burning vagina until the nurse, with a gasp, slapped them away. "Someone hurt me when I was asleep, someone took advantage of me."

"This one's still out of her head," the nurse whispered to another nurse, who was wheeling a bassinet into position next to Carol's bed. The two shared a weary look, then left Carol alone with the thing that was in the bassinet. The thing that had been torn out of her, or that had done the tearing, the violating—Carol didn't know, she didn't care, she was tired.

She fell asleep again, and this time she didn't dream. But when she awoke, the thing was still in the bassinet, and now it was crying.

The thing that was in the bassinet . . .

The thing that was in the bassinet was a baby. A girl. Her daughter.

Someone had named her Melinda. Who? Carol couldn't even remember being asked; when she was given the birth certificate to take home, there it was: Melinda Jane Donnelly. *Mindy,* that same someone must have decreed the child be nicknamed, because that was what the nurses started calling her. Maybe it was Carol's mother? Bob's mother? Somebody's mother, just not the baby's mother?

Mother. Carol was now a mother. Her mind knew this. Her battered and tender body certainly knew this.

Her heart, however—that was a different matter.

Even as she was holding the tiny red bundle against her burning breasts—the nurses didn't encourage breastfeeding except to relieve extreme pain; it was always followed by a bottle, no matter how full the baby was—she was thinking only of her body, how quickly it would heal from the indignities it had endured, how soon her stomach would lie flat again. She was happy to hand the squalling infant to the nurse between feedings.

Lying in bed when the baby was in the nursery, Carol was supposed to be reading all the pamphlets the hospital provided for new mothers: *How to Establish a Regular Feeding Schedule; What You Need to Know About Thrush.* But Carol put them all in a drawer, unread. Why did she need them? The birth seemed the end of something, not the beginning. The only thing she wanted to know was how soon she could fit back into her bathing suit. Fortunately, there were pamphlets about that, too: *The Grapefruit Diet for New Mothers; Why You Should Wear a Girdle to Bed*.

After she was released, and with nothing else to do as the war dragged on so that Bob seemed, more than ever, merely a bad idea she'd once had, Carol took to placing the baby in her wicker basket (How had she come to possess that? Was it a gift?) on the passenger seat and driving Bob's old station wagon—the scene of the crime— down to the beach. She longed to plunge into the water, to feel its cool, loving embrace once more—maybe it could wash away the feeling of being violated, heal the parts of her that were still raw and tender—but even she knew she couldn't leave a newborn alone on the beach. So she could only contemplate the water, studying the waves, the way they sometimes broke in a straight, powerful line, other times disintegrated into lots of smaller, harmless waves closer to shore. She took in the sun glittering on the water, the angry seagulls, the people bobbing up and down near shore, splashing one another.

Once, she saw a guy on a surfboard riding in, standing effortlessly on the narrow plane as it rushed toward shore. Years before, she'd seen Duke Kahanamoku, the Hawaiian surfing legend, giving a surfing demonstration for a bunch of Hollywood people in Santa Monica. The giant Hawaiian had maneuvered an enormous board through the waves. He was so tall that even when he dropped into his surfing stance he resembled a mythic god from an ancient civilization. Afterward he'd taken some people out to ride tandem while he surfed them onto the shore. Carol had longed to be one of them, but her father had held her back, making her let the movie stars go first. Then Duke had flashed his charismatic smile and waved goodbye before she could take her turn.

"I could do that," she whispered to the baby—*Mindy*—as she watched the surfer. "I'm only nineteen, you know." For some reason, her age seemed important. Important enough to say it out loud, even if to a one-month-old, and had there been anyone walking by, she knew she would have flagged them down to share it.

"I'm only nineteen," she repeated, running her hands down the contours of her body, feeling for the sharp hip bone that had gone missing these last few months. She could just make out its reassuring shape beneath her flesh if she pressed a little; she kept running her hands down her hips, needing to feel that solid reminder that she was more than doughy flesh and leaky breasts.

The baby started to cry, as if she didn't believe her. The wails grew louder, angrier, until Carol finally realized the sun was hitting the baby's face, so she threw a blanket over the basket.

"I bet I could do that," she said again as the figure skimmed across the water like a dragonfly, just in front of a breaking wave. He flipped the board up from the nose when he got close to the beach, maneuvered it back into the water, then flopped down on his stomach and paddled it back out to catch another wave. He repeated the whole cycle for about an hour, while she sat with the baby, now quiet beneath the blanket, and watched, fascinated. Sometimes he fell off before he could reach the shore, sometimes the wave died out and left him stranded; there was a long period when there were no defined waves, so he remained bobbing up and down with his board, calmly looking out at the horizon as if he had all the time in the world. He seemed so peaceful. Above all cares.

Carol envied him more than she'd ever envied anyone before. It was a new emotion, envy, and it unsettled her; in the past *she* was the one people wanted to be. She had never desired anyone else's life—until Bob Donnelly knocked her up. Sitting up straighter, Carol studied the surfer more intently. Unlike everyone else on the beach or splashing in the waves, he was one with the ocean, an instrument of it. The others were only bystanders whose lives were obviously elsewhere. He looked like he was home.

Finally he dragged the board up on the beach, where it made deep grooves in the sand, then hoisted it beneath one arm, walking along the edge of the beach until he disappeared around a bend. He had no beach towel or sand shoes or rucksack with supplies. He appeared to possess nothing at all except his surfboard.

Carol ached to run after him; a profound longing she'd never experienced before, so exquisitely painful she almost cried, filled her chest. She needed to know what lay beyond that cove; she was desperate to leave her burden on the beach—surely someone would find it and care for it?—and possess nothing, too. Except one of those boards, whose graceful curves stirred something in her; she'd never been so enamored of an object before. It was a work of art, golden balsa wood, not a superfluous line or doodad on it.

She could do it, she could! She could go with him! Carol's legs were shaky but she managed to rise. She took one step and she didn't fall down, the sand didn't swallow her whole, so she knew, then, that she could do this. She could disappear from her life and learn how to live another. She could leave everything, everyone, behind without a qualm.

She took another step—

The baby chose that moment to start crying again.

Carol fell, her legs crumpling with the weight of her anguish; she grabbed her knees, pulled them to her aching chest, and gave way to racking sobs that drowned out the baby's. It wasn't fair, this wasn't supposed to be her life. How on earth could she be responsible for another human being?

"I'm only nineteen," she sobbed.

The baby had stopped crying as soon as Carol began to; her blue eyes were round with wonder, and Carol had to laugh as she mopped up her tears with the sandy beach blanket.

"Aren't you the sly one? I guess I'll never be able to fool you."

Finally she was empty of tears, although she cradled her disappointment close to her breast, more tenderly than she'd ever cradled her newborn. Scrambling to her feet, Carol picked up the basket, holding it out in front of her like it was a tray full of food. She glanced down at the pink, wrinkled little face; the baby's eyes were wide open, studying her.

"How did you know?" Carol asked her daughter. "How did you know that I was about to walk away and leave you?"

The baby answered by putting her fist in her mouth, still looking at her mother with a wary gaze.

> Be a good listener. Let him tell you his troubles; yours will seem trivial in comparison.
>
> —Edward Podolsky, *Sex Today in Wedded Life,* 1947 edition

Finally the war was over—"Aren't you thrilled, sweetie? Bob will be home!" And after a few months, during which he was stationed in conquered Japan, indeed he was. Bob burst into sobs when he saw her and the baby waiting with all the other wives and babies—a field of wives and babies, planted before they left for war and now ready for harvest—at the Port of Los Angeles. He swept them both up in an enormous hug, his tears leaving the front of Carol's dress as soggy as her spirits.

"Aren't you glad I'm home?" he asked, and he didn't wait for her to answer. Because of course, it wasn't a real question. How could she not be glad a soldier had returned safely from war? Especially when she was surrounded by hysterical women proving how glad they were with screams of joy and floods of tears.

Now Bob Donnelly wasn't merely a bad idea; he was in her bed every night, at her table every morning. He caressed and groped and kissed and left his clothes for her to launder. He ate a lot and talked incessantly, making plans for the future, jabbering about schools and a country club membership, a car for him, Carol could use the old wagon.

He would not stop talking, stop needing—stop *being*. He was almost worse than the baby.

Bob got a job at the GM factory in Van Nuys; he bought a home—did he ask Carol's advice? Her input? Probably, although she must have blocked it out of her mind. But someone had to have picked out the apple blossom wallpaper in the bathroom, the pinkish-beige carpet in the bedroom, the red Bakelite drawer pulls in the kitchen.

All Carol could think about was that another baby was on the way, just as her body had started to belong to *her* again, a reminder of her past accomplishments and a promise of more to come. But now any promise was dashed once and for all; her only future was more diapers, more sour receiving blankets, doctor appointments, sleepless nights.

Her hip bones disappeared, once again smothered by layers of useless, mushy fat.

Before it all came crashing down on her, Carol escaped—to the ocean. Every day, lugging along her toddler daughter, who had taught herself not to bother Mommy when she was looking at the water. Instead, the little girl drew lines in the sand, dug in it with her tin spade and pail—and watched her mother. And when Carol ventured into the water for the rare quick dip, Mindy demanded to go with her instead of staying on the shore like a good girl. As if she didn't quite trust Carol not to swim away and never come back.

Bob insisted on coming along, too, on the weekends—"We'll make it a family day!"—and she seethed. The water was *hers;* the beach was, too. Now that all other avenues were closed to her, now that she was a *housewife,* the beach was all she had. She had made a few acquaintances, mostly men since she avoided other mothers with children, mothers who only wanted to compare diaper services and the merits of strained peas versus strained carrots. But primarily, she longed to be alone in the water, with the dolphins and sea creatures her only companions. She didn't fear them; there was room enough in the ocean for them all.

She'd even started to ride some waves in on her own, when she could convince Mindy to stay put on the beach. Carol swam out to where they broke, positioning her body toward the beach and letting the energy of the wave propel her toward shore. Helpless but power-ful, part of the ocean in a way she'd never imagined possible. The best ride of her life; a pure adrenaline rush that wiped out any other sensation—and reminded her that she could still experience joy.

Carol had grown resigned to accommodating Mindy's presence, but Bob was an intruder, the stranger at the communion service causing all other congregants to feel self-conscious, unable to find comfort in the ritual. He was a mistake, it was all a mistake, but she was trapped. By her own body—an outrage she couldn't let go of.

Another violation, and the new baby was born, a girl named Jen-nifer but called Ginger. Carol felt pity for this one, and even if it wasn't a happy emotion, it was an emotion. She'd felt nothing for her firstborn, although the little girl had made some inroads into her heart simply by being so quiet and obedient. And Mindy seemed to like the ocean as much as Carol did, plunging into the waves without fear when Carol held her hand.

But she pitied this new, squishy, crying thing bundled in hand-me-down pink. Pitied her for being born a girl. Pitied her for being

last, the runt, the lesser of the matched set of two sisters, because already Carol knew that the chance of having two model daughters
was nonexistent. And she was done with this business of babies.
She'd given Bob two daughters onto whom he could turn his oppressive devotion, and maybe leave her alone. And then . . .

Maybe all she had to do was—whatever she wanted to? What was
the worst that could happen? Divorce?

"Carol, you're not leaving these girls with the babysitter again!" Her
mother caught her one morning in 1953. The neighbor girl had arrived to sit. Summers were glorious; there was never a shortage of
teenage girls happy to come over and watch TV with Mindy and
Ginger. Carol was one of the rare neighborhood mothers who didn't
care if they used the phone or sat on the couch reading magazines or
even had their boyfriends over.

"Mother, they're fine. They're fed, they sleep well. They have all
their shots. What else do you expect me to do?"

"I expect you to raise them. How long do you think Bob will put
up with a wife who's never around, who doesn't fix him dinner, who
neglects her own children?"

"Till the end of time. I can't get rid of him." Carol stifled a sigh.
Maybe it was true that Bob was starting to question her—delicately—
about why she still drove out to the beach every day instead of joining the PTA, or why he was out of clean shirts, or why they had to
have bologna sandwiches for the third night in a row. At least he'd
stopped trying to get her to entertain his work friends and their wives
or join a bridge club. But he still worshipped her, never stopped
bragging about her past athletic accomplishments. He still sought
her out in bed each night—although she usually told him she had a
headache.

He still told her she was the best thing that had ever happened to him. Which made her question his life choices so far.

"You'd better be careful, my girl. Even a man as in love with a woman as Bob is with you—heaven only knows why—will realize the grass is greener, sooner or later. Especially when there are other women dying to give that man what you refuse to."

"Bob?" Carol tried to picture her husband coming home with lipstick on his collar or some other silly soap opera situation. She simply couldn't. All she saw when she thought of him was his brown, wet eyes, pleading, adoring. Or his manicured hands, too white for her taste, too soft—so unlike those of the surfing guys she saw at the beach, tanned gods with hands callused from waxing and repairing their boards. Or—absurdly—Bob's neckties. He favored abstract, modernist patterns, which seemed pathetic to her; it was as if he went out of his way to declare his kookiness to try to get her attention. When in fact it didn't matter if his ties mimicked Jackson Pollock paintings; he was still the squarest man she had ever met. He never left the house without an umbrella—in Southern California!

"Yes, Bob. He won't put up with your brooding and messiness forever. Now, put this casserole in the oven and you can tell him you made it yourself! And for heaven's sake, fix your hair! You're not fifteen anymore, you ought to be having it set at the beauty parlor. Then you should change the girls' clothes and meet him at the door in a pretty dress."

"Is that the secret to a happy marriage? Pray tell." Carol couldn't keep the sarcasm out of her voice; her parents' marriage, while it endured, was anything but happy. Her father, who helped coordinate stunts, spent all his time on film sets, and her mother played bridge and secretly drank.

"I regret the day I ever agreed to let your father put in that backyard pool and teach you how to swim," her mother said in icy reply.

"He made a tomboy out of you and you're too stubborn to grow out of it."

"I told Bob I'd never be a housewife. He shouldn't be surprised. Bye, Mom." Carol took the casserole, put it in the oven, and forgot to turn it on. But her mother had said one thing that made sense. She ought to enroll the girls in swim lessons, even though she'd taught them both a simple overhead crawl so she didn't have to worry about them when they had to accompany her to the beach. The thought occurred, fleetingly, that this could be her purpose: coaching her daughters to the Olympic glory she'd been denied. Was being the mother of swimming champions as fulfilling as being a champion yourself?

It should have been. According to everything she read, heard, saw, in those postwar years—Harriet Nelson beaming with pride when her sons brought home medals on their television show; Margaret Anderson of *Father Knows Best* wiping tears of joy when her TV daughter won the spelling bee—it *must* have been.

But in her heart, Carol Donnelly knew it wouldn't be. She was only twenty-seven. Her body, even though she hadn't trained like an athlete for years, was still humming, thrumming with energy and desire.

And when she sat on the beach by herself after a good long, solitary swim, the kind that wrung her out and cleared her head so that all she knew was the tugging of the surf, the reassuring ache of her muscles as she kept a straight line parallel to the beach, it seemed to her the waves kept saying, "It's not over, it's not over, it's not over." Whatever *it* was—life, glory, happiness, a taut belly, the pleasant ache after exercise, gold medals, trophies. Her own identity, maybe?

It was up to her to figure it out.

17

Ike runs the country, and I turn the pork chops.

—Mamie Eisenhower

The subsequent days at Makaha were days Carol knew she would never forget; they would be the template for all that might have been. If only.

She told herself not to think of the return ticket in her suitcase. The ticket Bob had forced her to buy, even when she tried to tell him it would be cheaper if she bought a ticket the day she decided to come back. He knew; the girls knew. The way they all three watched her when she waved goodbye at the airport. Mommy might not come back.

In the two years since she'd first taken up surfing in earnest, DeeDee—the only other woman Carol ever saw at Malibu who wasn't merely interested in getting a tan—helping her get her first board shaped by a guy she knew, Carol had learned a few things. More than a few things.

She learned to tell how a wave would break by lining it up with the horizon; if it broke in one straight line, it was a dud, closed in. She learned how to roll over with her board on her stomach when the white water rushed over her as she paddled out, so she wouldn't lose her board. How to pop up—timing it exactly right, paddling with all her might at the crest of the wave and then finding that one magic moment when the board was level for just long enough for her to jump up, legs bent, her right leg back, left leg in front, and then came the plunge, like going over the first hill of a roller coaster. The plunge wasn't very steep back in Malibu, but in Hawaii, it was completely different. Then the ride, the joy of both letting the power of the ocean itself propel her toward shore and the mastery of being in control of the direction of the board, eventually being able to walk up and down, lean on the rail to cut and change direction.

She learned to smile and grit her teeth when guys shouted, "Hey, girlie, go back to the kitchen," when she tried to maneuver into a lineup. She learned not to cry when they cut in on a wave or plowed into her on purpose.

She learned to plow into them right back, in retaliation. But smiling. Always smiling.

She learned that the thing she feared most wasn't being pounded against the rocks but being entangled in the slippery, insidious kelp. She learned that being caught in the churning surf after wiping out was like nothing she'd ever experienced; she was a helpless rag doll in a washing machine of swirling water, tossing her this way and that, her ears so full of water and pressure that her vision was heightened, always trained on that light above, getting closer and closer as she fought her way to the surface, and then the great gasp, the first gulp of new air in her lungs as her racing heart slowed down. It was like being reborn. Christened.

At Makaha, in late 1955, she learned so much more.

Thanksgiving. Every day was Thanksgiving, a humbling, abiding feeling of appreciation as she and DeeDee shed any mainland routine and convention, and simply let the rhythms of the ocean and the sun determine how they lived. When they ate, how much they surfed, how little. Sometimes, the ocean was stingy—the waves at

Makaha weren't always big and sharply defined, most of the time they were mushy five- or ten-footers—but those big waves were worth the wait. Carol and DeeDee didn't always sit around waiting; they'd slide down sand dunes on pieces of corrugated metal. Or they'd find a secret waterfall and dive off the top into cool, deep holes of water.

Carol and DeeDee were eventually absorbed into a small tribe of fellow surfers—men, mostly, although there were a couple of women who lived down the beach who also spent their days surfing, a mother and a daughter. But those two always returned at night to their own home; they weren't really part of the tribe. Many of the guys were from California but lived in Hawaii from November to February, when the surf was best. These included godlike, chiseled Buzzy Trent with his blond buzz cut, and big Greg Noll, already nicknamed "Da Bull." A compact, dark-haired local, George Downing, seemed to be the leader of the pack. They had been here first and they made sure the new wahines remembered that. Loudly they demanded that DeeDee and Carol cook their meals for them—the women, naturally, made them a meal of bowls of sand and palm leaves, which shut them up for a night or two until the grunts of "Woman, food!" started up again. These guys beat their chests, literally, like beasts of the jungle as they paddled out first for every wave, leaving the two women to fight to get in the lineup.

They weren't the only men on Makaha, however; there were native Hawaiians, too, of course; those whose beach this had been in the first place. They seemed to tolerate the California men, impressed by their skills and tenacity in the big waves, but then always quietly besting them with their own superb comfort in these waters, the ease with which they popped up, casually, as if a twenty-foot wave was no big deal. None of the Californians ever lost their awe of the Hawaiian surf.

After the first bumpy days, eventually the guys and the girls began to pool their resources, building bonfires for makeshift dinners that never tasted like less than the most sumptuous banquet to Carol, who was more ravenous than she'd ever been. Fresh fish caught and then immediately cleaned and panfried. A contraband chicken or two—Greg Noll was the master chicken thief of the outfit, but no one could ever truly get all the feathers off. Or they might be invited to dinner at one of the locals' homes, where Carol tasted poi for the first time, and was barely able to swallow a mouthful of the sticky, purplish paste.

"Mahalo," Carol learned to say, as she was lavished with kindness, goodness—happiness. What was it about this place that caused her to feel more herself than she'd ever felt, even back when she was part of a team, the sports star? Was it the unhurried pace, the camaraderie she and DeeDee were slowly developing with the guys, even if they still grumbled and grunted?

"I hate seeing chicks riding big waves," Buzzy once pronounced as they were all waxing their boards in the pastel morning light. "Chicks are delicate, they look great on those little waves in Malibu. But I hate seeing you two on those big waves. You can't look pretty on a board, riding these monsters."

"What do you think you look like?" DeeDee retorted.

"Like guys. Men."

"So women are only supposed to be decorative? That's all you require of us?"

"Hell yeah."

"Then take a picture and pin it up. But tell me the truth—don't we ride those monsters in as well as you do?"

Buzzy shrugged. "Sure, you two are fine, but you know what happens when one woman shows up. Soon enough there's a hen party out there on the waves and they'll all be needing rescuing and they'll ruin it. We can't have that." He said this last solemnly, as if his word were the law of the beach.

"Don't you think there are enough waves out there for all of us?" DeeDee waved her arm toward the ocean.

"There are some things girls can't do," Buzzy continued. Despite the evidence, every day, to the contrary. "You two are an exception but damned if you're going to be the rule."

"You hear that, Carol? We're exceptional!" DeeDee ignored Buzzy and flashed a smile at Carol.

"That's not what I—"

But the two women grabbed their boards and started to paddle out first. The guys had to scramble to catch up with them. Then the guys spent the rest of the day plowing into them, denying them even one successful ride in.

That night, Carol and DeeDee sulked in the van, refusing to respond to the drunken calls to come out and party a little, to stop acting like girls. They took turns rubbing Ben-Gay into the bruises that patterned their legs and arms.

"Sons of bitches," DeeDee grumbled as they settled down to sleep.

"I bet they're pissing all over the beach, marking their territory like dogs," Carol said. Thinking, for once, of Bob, and how he always kept his arm around her shoulder or waist whenever they were out in public.

"So what do you two do in that van?" Jeff Samson, one of the California guys, asked Carol a couple of nights later. The factions had made up, even though Carol and DeeDee knew it was only possible because the guys "allowed" them to share the waves. It smarted. But it was worth it to be back out there—and back within the golden circle.

They were all walking back from Jack Cho's house. Jack was one of the locals, a small man with a huge smile, a tall wife, and three young sons, the oldest of whom could zip around on his board like a downhill skier. Carol wasn't sure what Jack did for a living; she thought he'd once said he worked in a sugar cane factory. But then, *none* of them seemed to do anything for a living; who needed money? Who needed a job? A man—a woman—could live like this forever, it seemed to her, to all of them. The land, the water, had enough bounty. Their small group seemed like explorers on a new planet, a virgin paradise. There was no one else around. She felt a fierce desire to protect Makaha and this life they were constructing around its waves—she'd have put up a fence around the beach if she could. Frozen this moment, this place, these people, in time. Even with the guys' chest-beating antics.

"What do you mean, what do we do?" Carol wrinkled her nose, and then she saw it—that gleam in his eye. She burst out laughing, and the gleam faded. "What do you think we do in there, Jeff?" She couldn't help herself from lowering her voice seductively.

"Well, you know, I . . . I mean, well—" And the man who was afraid of no wave suddenly blushed and looked like he wished the sand would swallow him up. "Two women . . ."

"What about a group of men?"

"What?" His voice climbed two octaves.

"Well, what goes on in that nasty Quonset hut you guys share?"

"Nothing!"

"Then why do you assume something different for us?"

Jeff had no answer, except to grab her, pull her into an embrace, and kiss her. Right there on the beach of Makaha, under a full Hawaiian moon with the salty, earthy smell of surf and fish perfuming the air, and the sand, full of smooth, cool shells, between their toes. Carol stiffened at first, then gave in to the moment—two strong, healthy adults, muscles like cool statues but skin burning with desire. What the hell. Their bodies, pushed to the limit every day, deserved a little release, and besides, they saw each other all the time, barely clad, so Carol already knew that Jeff was not a compact man all over. According to Bob, Carol was not a highly sexed woman, but this was different. She was no longer a woman but a goddess—

A goddess of the water, of the waves, of the sun and moon. Mother Earth and Sea. She did what nature told her to do; she enjoyed a beautiful man enjoying a beautiful woman.

Enjoyment—it wasn't confined to the beach. Sometimes she and DeeDee did find that lying together, leg against leg, hip against hip, led to more. Touching, stroking, giggling, then more touching, more determined stroking, and then release. It was part of the natural ebb and flow of the island; that was what she told herself. Bodies doing what bodies wanted to do. They all *used* their bodies in the way that Carol had, back in her athletic youth—as their only form of expression. Words were useless in the water, muffled by the pounding surf. Bodies spoke more eloquently, in the water and out of it.

Every night, no matter whom she'd chosen to lie down with, Carol experienced a sleep more encompassing than any she'd ever known.

But she and DeeDee were just friends—not even close friends, not really. The relationships she was forging with these surfers didn't include sharing emotions and telling stories that weren't about what had happened on the water that day, or maybe tall tales of surfing exploits nobody actually believed, especially when they managed to scrape enough money together for a six-pack or a jug of cheap wine.

No, their bond went deeper than words and stories and emotions; their lives depended upon one another. Even if Buzzy still grumbled that women shouldn't be riding big waves and did his best to keep Carol from getting the best ones, she knew that if she ever got in trouble, he'd drop everything to help. So would they all. No one else understood the powerful, beautiful—dangerous—allure of the surf. No one else was living like they were. They were bonded together for life—but still, she couldn't imagine having dinner with any of them back home.

Home.

Carol had been in Hawaii almost a month when she left the gang to make her weekly call to Bob. It wasn't convenient; she had to drive the poky old van several miles down that barely carved-out road toward Honolulu before she could find a gas station with a pay phone. She was the only one of the tribe who did this—reached across the ocean to the mainland. They'd teased her about it the first couple of times she'd made the trip, joked that she must have a fella back there. She didn't say a word and managed a coy smile, while DeeDee just grinned. While she'd never intended to keep her family a secret, somehow neither woman had gotten around to talking about it. After all, nobody else talked about their other life; there were no other lives but this one on Makaha.

However, the third time she'd come back from her call home, she'd found all the guys staring at her as if they'd never seen her before, DeeDee looking guilty in their midst.

"You have kids?" they'd asked, incredulous. Then they couldn't help themselves; their eyes immediately went to her stomach, flat as ever, but still, Carol sucked it in as one hand automatically cupped a sharp hip bone. For the first time, she felt self-conscious about her body in front of them. Even though she was covered in a big T-shirt over her bikini.

"Yes, two girls." She felt defensive, crossing her arms in front of her breasts.

"You're a *mother*?" Greg's voice went up several registers, a preadolescent squeak. Suddenly he couldn't look her in the eye.

"How old *are* you?" Jeff asked uncomfortably.

Carol squirmed a bit, digging her feet into the sand. She glanced out at the water; the big, beautiful sun was low on the horizon, the sky purple in spots, faint pink in others, a delicate striation of colors.

They'd never asked questions like this before, any of them. Nobody asked, "Where'd you go to school?" or "What do you do for a living?" or even "Where do you live back on the mainland?" It was as if they'd all been born the minute they first set eyes on Makaha. Nobody had a past. Nobody talked about the future, other than where there might be bigger waves—there were rumors of a place even farther up the coast, a place called Waimea, with waves thirty, forty, fifty feet high.

Would they let her stay? It was absurd; how could they kick her out? Forcibly put her on a plane back home? But still Carol feared it. *This* was where she wanted to be. The little tract house in Van Nuys was fast fading in her memory, a yellowing picture of someone else's life.

"Twenty-nine," she admitted. Twenty-nine, thirty in a few weeks. Ancient. She had a fleeting memory of her mother at that age, a photo of her attending a bridge game in the thirties. Dressed in those longer, narrower skirts of that era, with tightly waved hair (which she still wore), spectacles. She looked ancient.

Carol wasn't ancient. There was no such thing as age here in Hawaii. She felt young and of the moment, capable of doing anything on her board. There was that time the surf had woken them all up with a different sound; they'd found themselves gaping at bigger, more urgent waves than they'd ever seen and all whooped and hollered and grabbed their boards and paddled out, the incoming waves so strong that Carol's arms ached by the time she reached the lineup. And one by one, the guys had taken the wave first—of course!—and one by one, they'd wiped out. All of them.

But Carol didn't notice the boards popping up out of the white-water, the frustrated bodies chasing after them. She only studied the incoming surf, and it was just this: Carol Donnelly, a surfboard, and a wave. Nothing else was present. No children, no Bob, no DeeDee. She felt ready for this—more ready than she had been for anything that had ever happened to her before. The surf didn't even seem as loud; it was as if she and the wave were in a glass dome. She pointed her board toward the beach and started paddling on top of the wave as it crested, then the golden opportunity presented itself. She felt the board hold steady and in that fraction of a moment she popped up from her stomach, her strong legs planting themselves on the board, and she rode it in. It wasn't pretty—her arms were wild things as they struggled to keep her upright; her toes dug into the board so hard she knew there would be grooves in the wax. She crouched, fought for the right position, had to change it several times. But she rode it in, and the force of the ocean, the mighty shove toward land, was not more powerful than she was, that day.

When she jumped off the board on her own terms, before it hit the rocks, she was greeted by hoots and hollers, cries of "Damn, Carol Donnelly! I've never seen such a sight!"

There was no feeling like it that she had ever known, and all she wanted was more of the same. Because in that moment, they hadn't seen her as anything other than better than they were.

She was terrified that it was all gone, now that she was somebody's *mother*.

Buzzy gave a low whistle. The other guys shook their heads.

"How old are you?" Carol whirled around on Buzzy. He scratched his head, genuinely at a loss; he had to take a moment to answer.

"Twenty-six."

"Twenty-five," George offered.

"Twenty," Jeff admitted, not able to meet her gaze.

"Eighteen," Greg said proudly.

Carol glared at DeeDee, who was thirty-one, but who remained silent.

"But a *mother*?" Greg repeated.

"So what?" Carol decided to take a different tack; defensiveness wasn't going to help her here any more than it helped her in the water when the guys started to go all Tarzan on her. She flashed her dimples, twirled her ponytail. Decided to do a few athletic flexes—twisted her torso, touched her toes, even did a series of cartwheels.

"Last one in is a rotten egg," she called, running toward her board. It was too late for decent surf but she needed to get in the water right then. Get in the water with her board, study the horizon, catch a wave; step back into this life before she was too heavy for it, burdened by children and age.

The guys joined her, so did DeeDee, and from that moment on Carol made an even more determined effort to close her mind to all she'd left in California. Maybe, before, she'd had guilty thoughts about the girls, particularly Mindy, who knew her so thoroughly that she felt uncomfortable in her daughter's presence. Mindy could read her mind, detect her thoughts and plans even before Carol knew them. Maybe Carol had wondered, truly, how much rope Bob would keep giving her. Maybe she thought of them not as the future but as the past, the people she would miss from now on because she was going to stay in Hawaii, she really was. The idea had absorbed more of her thoughts each day; she'd tossed it around and around, getting used to it until it seemed perfectly logical. Of course she was going to stay, live this life of waves and salt and sand and sun. She would never grow old—Peter Pan, she was; they all were. A tribe of Lost Boys—and Girls.

So when she went to town one last time to call home, she did feel the weight of what she was going to say, the impact on the lives back there. But she also knew that when she returned to the guys and DeeDee, she would be free. Lighter.

Nobody's mother ever again.

"Hello, Bob," she said automatically when the phone stopped ringing and someone picked up.

"Carol!" It was her mother instead. "Carol! You have to come home right this instant!"

"Did something happen to one of the girls?" Strange, how her stomach twisted in alarm, even after she'd come to her decision.

"It's Bob."

"Something happened to Bob? Is he all right?" Her stomach relaxed.

"He's gone. He left. He left you. There's a note."

Carol laughed; she couldn't help herself. Already she felt lighter. He'd done her dirty work for her.

"He did? Good for him." She hadn't thought he had it in him, and now—oddly—she respected him more than she ever had. "Good for him," she repeated, still laughing.

For a long moment her mother didn't respond. Then she growled into the phone.

"I don't know what the hell has happened to you out there, Carol Donnelly, but you have to pull yourself together and come home. Your girls need you."

"He didn't take the girls?" Now it was Carol's turn for silence as she absorbed her mother's words.

There was no scenario of her leaving—either before Hawaii or after—that included having her daughters with her. Of course Bob would want full custody. Of course the girls would stay with their father—the stable parent, she imagined any divorce court would say, and she would only agree. Bob *was* the responsible one. He would have the house, anyway—she didn't want it, she didn't want to live in any kind of building ever again. She was a nomad now. A surf bum, people were starting to call them.

She could never forget the ways the guys had looked at her when they found out she had children. Thank God they were over that now, but still—

"Carol! Carol, are you listening to me?"

"Yes, Mom, it's just . . . Bob left? And didn't take the girls with him?"

"Of course he didn't take the girls! Men never do when they leave—for heaven's sake, Carol, you're their *mother*."

Carol gritted her teeth, tried to swallow, but her throat had closed.

"So what happens now?"

"You have to come home. There are two hysterical girls here who don't have a father or a mother and I'm too old to take care of them. You can't do that to me. You have a responsibility. Come home. Right now."

"I don't know—my ticket isn't for another few weeks."

"Oh, for God's sake. You take it to the airport and turn it in for one on the next plane. How old are you, anyway? You're behaving like a child!"

"Twenty-nine," Carol whispered, even though her mother of course knew. But suddenly her age meant something else entirely. It meant she was a fool to think she could ever escape it, even here in Hawaii; that she would live beyond it, this label—adult. Housewife. Matriarch. *Mother.*

"Come home right now—" There was a shuffling sound on the other end of the phone, then her mother said, "All right," to whoever else was there.

Then Mindy was talking to her.

"Mommy?" Her voice quavered but Carol could hear her fighting to control it. "Mommy? Are you there?"

Carol gripped the phone tighter. She studied the dirty phone booth, the graffiti on the wall behind the phone—*Jimmy loves Sandy, For a good time call ——, Haole go home.* The small booth smelled like urine. A desire to bolt—drop the phone, run away, get back to the beach, and breathe the salty air—overwhelmed her. But still her hand held the phone to her ear and she could hear Mindy breathing shallowly.

"Yes, I'm here." When she said it, Carol felt sadder than she'd ever felt in her life. The manacles she'd thought she'd escaped suddenly brushed against her ankles. But they hadn't snapped shut. Not yet.

"We've been swimming a lot more, Mom," Mindy said in a rush. "Me and Ginger! We've been going to the beach—Annie next door takes us after school, when she's supposed to be sitting us—and we're a lot better swimming in the ocean now, and maybe we can take real swim lessons when you come back?"

"Maybe," Carol replied automatically.

"Wouldn't that be fun?"

"Yes, fun," Carol replied. Automatically.

Her mother took the phone from Mindy.

"Come home now. Right, girls? Tell Mommy how much you love her!"

"We love you, Mommy," the two girls chorused in the background, little Ginger's voice higher than Mindy's, softer, too.

"Did you hear that, Carol Donnelly?" her mother hissed into the phone.

The key to the van was in Carol's hand; she squeezed until the sharp metal dug into her palm. Her board needed waxing; she should stop and get some wax, get some for the whole crew. She ought to pick up supplies, too—how much money did she have with her? Five dollars? That would get some bread and canned soup, anyway, as well as the wax. If she hurried back—but no, she would miss the last waves. But there would be a bonfire to greet her, unless they decided to troop up to Jack Cho's house. They had an open-door policy, Jack and his wife—

Suddenly, her skin was itchy as a rash. She remembered having dinner with Bob at the club only a couple of months ago, before she'd decided to go on safari. All the talk about promotions and bonuses and who needed to scratch whose back to get them. And how about that new Chevy Bel Air? Wasn't *that* the car to have? Didn't a man have to drive a car befitting his ambitions? And wasn't it about time to look into moving up from that starter home, now that the promotions were arriving?

The wives drank sweet, sticky drinks—Manhattans—and gossiped about schools and beauty parlors and house cleaners, the latest book—*Bonjour Tristesse,* it was all anyone talked about, and based on the conversation, Carol thought it must be the silliest book ever. They'd looked askance at the pink ribbon tying Carol's long hair, even if they did appear to envy her figure. The dress—it, too, was pink, Bob's favorite color on her, with a wide crinoline that scratched her legs. She refused to wear stockings, which was scandalous. But her legs couldn't breathe when she wore them. The garters suffocated her thighs, the nylon was clammy. Her dress had little spaghetti straps holding it up, setting off her broad shoulders, her prominent clavicles—and her supple, muscular arms. She'd felt like a workhorse compared to the dainty fillies surrounding her. But when she'd confessed this to Bob on the way home, he'd corrected her.

"A thoroughbred. You're a thoroughbred, Carol Donnelly."

A thoroughbred he was happy to keep stabled forever, was what she thought. In a fancy new home, towed around in her trailer by a sleek new blue and white Chevy Bel Air.

"Carol! For heaven's sake, say something!" Her mother's voice pierced through her scattered thoughts, rattled her very core. "Your girls need you, Carol. I can't do this again."

"No, Mom, I know. I—I'll let you know when I'm coming back. I need to make some arrangements."

"Well, hurry up. Your poor girls—they'll cry themselves to sleep tonight."

"Do you know where Bob went? Can I get hold of him?"

"He left you a letter, I didn't open it. Do you want me to read it?"

"No—I'll read it—later."

"I think he's staying with a coworker, John something-or-other? He mumbled something about that when he called me."

"John Barkley, I suppose. OK."

"I cannot imagine what on earth Bob was thinking when he let you go to Hawaii to do whatever it is you're doing."

"I can," Carol said, a suffocating weight descending upon her shoulders, driving her into the ground.

As she headed back down the narrow, winding road to Makaha— after stopping for the wax but forgetting the groceries—she didn't notice the scenery, she didn't marvel at the setting sun over the ocean, the sweet air coming in through the open windows. Instead, she started to laugh—softly at first, then hysterically, until she almost couldn't keep the steering wheel straight and she got a cramp in her left side.

She knew exactly why Bob had let her go to Hawaii. To torture her. To let her get a taste of freedom. Before leaving her. Because he knew that in leaving first, he had done the thing he had tried to do since he first met her.

He had shackled her forever.

18

1960–1964

If you bungle raising your children, I don't think
whatever else you do matters very much.

—Jacqueline Kennedy

The apartment was small, only one bedroom and a pull-out
sofa, a tiny kitchenette, but it had a great view of Brooks
Street Beach. They didn't have a television, which the girls
had of course complained about at first, especially Ginger, but Carol
had pointed to the big picture window in response.

"Who needs a TV when you have that?" She'd indicated the ocean
view that was theirs for as long as they could keep paying the rent,
which was a nagging question but one she didn't have to contemplate
right now. They had a few months before she'd need to ask Bob for
an increase in alimony, now that the girls were older and needed
things that cost more money. Maybe college, even—though she
didn't think so, neither seemed inclined that way. If they were, they
hadn't said a word about it, and Carol sure wasn't going to. Who had
time for that?

Especially now that they were living across from the beach and
could be there from the earliest morning swells to the last ones at

sunset. Night surfing, even—holding a torch high above the spray while you came in on waves of undulating ink, toward cliffs of graphite, everything dark but the lights in the houses in the hills, the stars above, and the torch in your hand. It was dangerous but seductive; she felt like a true sea creature then, navigating through blackness, deprived of the sun. A mermaid.

The girls attended Laguna Beach High School for a time, but Mindy dropped out as soon as she could, at sixteen (Carol happily signed the papers), and of course, whatever Mindy did, Ginger followed. There hadn't been any fuss about leaving Van Nuys behind, no tears and hysterics over having to give up their friends. Funny how they didn't have many friends at school. Carol hadn't had to deal with birthday parties or sleepovers or the usual teenage-girl drama. She was lucky in that way.

Ever since she'd had to come back from Hawaii after Bob left, the girls had surprised her. It didn't make the wrenching destruction of her dream life at Makaha any less painful, but it did make life in California easier than she'd thought it would be. She was proud she'd brought up two such obedient girls. And two water babies, to boot! They were as happy to learn to surf, as eager, as she had been, and she probably should have predicted that they would be. After all, they were Carol Donnelly's daughters.

As they grew, as they improved on the water—Mindy a real natural, Ginger not so much but she certainly tried hard and looked decorative out there—Carol's pride in them, in the picture the three of them presented of a formidable, feminine wall of pure talent and athleticism, swelled. And allowed her to feel other things she hadn't been able to when they were small—worry, sometimes concern when Mindy tried something beyond her capabilities, fearless as Carol had been at her age. Or when Ginger, trembling with terror, nonetheless insisted on tackling a challenging surf, usually making a mess of it—

Carol always surfed near her in those moments. Protectiveness, too, when the idiots at Malibu were too obvious in their admiration for her beautiful teenage girls, or conversely got too prickly when Mindy started to outshine them on the waves. Carol loved that her oldest daughter gave as good as she got—plowing right into them in retaliation, doggedly staying in the lineup no matter how many times she was told to leave it to the real surfers, the men. Mindy's way was different from Carol's. Carol had always relied on her smile, her good nature, and now, surprisingly, her maturity. The Surf Mama, they called her, and it didn't feel like a slap in the face.

Not much, anyway.

Mindy didn't smile a lot. She answered back with her mastery of the sport—and her sharp tongue. The only person she never spoke sharply to was her mother. And, most of the time, her sister.

Mainly, Carol felt nothing but pride when she and her daughters made their way across the sand to whistles of admiration and the turning of heads—whether it was in Malibu, Huntington Beach, Newport Beach, or Laguna.

But not at Makaha.

She still felt bad about the way she'd spoken to Mindy at the bonfire. How to explain to her daughter what she was feeling, that stew of emotions only Makaha could stir up?

She hadn't been home—and that was what she called it, in her heart—since that first safari. She was relieved to see it unchanged for the most part, although the crowds were certainly bigger, but the difference was nowhere near as devastating as what was happening in California. Carol felt as if she were shedding layers and layers of scratchy winter clothing with each step she took on that soft Makaha beach. The sanctuary of knowing a place thoroughly, its every wave, every outcrop of rocks, each palm tree, those old Quonset huts still in use—it soothed her soul, made her feel all was right with the world. She vowed never to go away again. Even though she knew she had to and would.

Makaha was *hers*. She should have known what would happen when she brought Mindy and Ginger there for the contest. She should have known that she would revert to the bad mother again—the mother she'd been when she'd first come here.

The mother she believed she no longer was, now that her girls were older, more like friends than daughters.

"What do you think?" she'd asked Mindy and Ginger the first time the rented van—a different one, thank God, from the one she and DeeDee had shared!—pulled around a corner, revealing the majestic view of Makaha. The windows were rolled down so that the deafening barrage of the waves made conversation difficult. She had to shout.

"Wow" was all Ginger could utter.

"Cool" was Mindy's observation.

Carol couldn't believe that the girls were so underwhelmed. Didn't they know this was a sacred place? But they didn't, of course not. She'd never shared any of her thoughts and feelings about that time with anyone. They were hers alone.

Still, she was disappointed by the girls' reaction, and it ignited a long-dormant fuse beneath her skin, one she had managed to ignore.

Until her daughter won Makaha.

It wasn't fair—this was the tournament that meant the most to Carol. Hadn't she had to miss it the year she was here? Because of *them*? Watching Mindy take the podium, get the plaque, be showered with all the attention and adulation, was too much. Carol was only human; she seethed, thinking of the irony. That she'd had to go back to California that first time, missing the tournament, for *them*. That she had taken her girls under her wing, given them this life she had had to find on her own, shown them that women didn't have to dream only about marriage and cooking and babies and drudgery, that they could have the water, the sky, the birds of the air, the fish in the sea, that they could dream dreams perfumed with sea lavender and ocean spray. That Mindy and Ginger were better, bigger—*more*—because of *her*, the example she had given them. The template to live, really live—and not just be a paper doll like the ones Ginger used to play with, with frilly aprons and poufy skirts and high heels.

She had done all that, for her daughters. And what was her thanks?

Her daughter had bested her that day. She realized it watching Mindy ride that second wave. That was when Carol knew there was no way she was going to podium now, because Mindy was going to win. It wasn't pride she felt but resentment, watching her daughter—whose birth had been so traumatic, changing her body forever, yet still she had come out of *her*, been made by *her*—so young and nubile, the way her limbs naturally curved and bent like saplings in the wind. Carol's own limbs were getting stiffer, beat up too many times by the powerful surf she so craved. Her knees sometimes locked into place while she was on the board. All those years of taking her body for granted, throwing it around, trusting it would do what she told it to and not complain or betray her—

Those years were taking a toll. She was thirty-six now.

Mindy was seventeen.

She was jealous of her own daughter, and that feeling—that mean, miserly emotion—invaded her at Makaha. The place where she had never felt mean or small.

And that night, when they were all sitting around the bonfire, a lifetime of resentment and disappointment could no longer be contained by a plastic smile and perfect posture.

"I want you to know," she'd said to her daughter, her voice low but sharp, the finely honed end of a dagger she hadn't known she was still carrying around, weighing her down, "I want you to know, that should have been me. Up there, on the podium. It would have been me back in fifty-five. But I had to come home to you. The men didn't have to, DeeDee didn't have to. But I did. Because of *you*. I wish you'd never been born. You were a mistake, a mistake I have regretted every single day since. I never, ever wanted to have you or your sister."

And she'd turned away from her daughter, but not before she saw Mindy's face flush crimson, her eyes fill with tears—and pain.

Carol still couldn't forgive herself. She couldn't find a way to reach out to her daughter and say she hadn't really meant it. Because she had, and Mindy knew it.

The little apartment where the three of them lived started to feel both unbearably cramped and unbearably enormous. Too small for three women to live in harmoniously.

Too big for her to reach her daughter, who retreated in silence.

There were other surfing contests popping up now on the mainland— one at Huntington Beach, the one at Laguna—and despite the chilliness between Carol and Mindy (Ginger seemed blissfully unaware), the three of them were expected to show up, to bring some publicity to the sport simply by being a family trio of blond, athletic women. How they finished wasn't important to those looking to make these competitions profitable. Ginger never placed, but Mindy did regularly. She was a fierce competitor, as fierce as Carol had once been. Carol should have been proud. Maybe someday she would be.

After Makaha, Carol stopped competing. If she didn't have a chance to win, there was simply no point. And winning a surfing competition had never been the driving force behind her need to be on the water, not like winning a swimming competition or a ball-game had been when she was young. Surfing had *saved* her. No trophy or plaque could mean more than that.

Instead, she asked to be a judge.

"Chicks can't judge any more than they can surf." Of course there was resistance; there always was. Men pissing all over the beach, met-aphorically (and literally). What the hell were they afraid of? They were already gods, deified by the Beach Boys. They got the best waves at the competitions, the biggest trophies, the few sponsorships that were available, like Hobie.

"Have you ever seen me surf?" she would ask with that sunny smile. Some of them hadn't, of course—the dilettantes, the nonlocals (or "kooks," as Tom Riley insisted on calling them). But there was always someone around who had, and so she found herself the only female judge, high atop a rickety stand with binoculars in her hand and globs of zinc on her nose. Allowed only to judge the women, not the men. Because the women didn't count. They were only allowed to compete in order to drive attendance for the sponsors, to turn a one-day event into a weekend. The message was all too clear: Nobody cared about competitive female surfing.

But they certainly cared about the bikini contest that was held at every event. They loved their Miss Malibu, Miss Laguna Beach, Miss Coppertone. These were the girls who were plastered on the covers of the new surfing magazines that were sold up and down the coast—girls in bikinis, with tanned skin and sunny blond hair teased and stiff, lounging against surfboards. Girls who would never get their hair wet in the water. While girls like Mindy and Linda Benson and Joyce Hoffman, real competitors, were ignored by everyone except the actual surfers.

The days that the women competed were always an afterthought—attendance low, the trophies or plaques shabbily made, childishly small. The days that the guys—Greg Noll, new hotshots like Phil Edwards and Mike Doyle—were on the waves, the beaches were packed. Sponsor booths were set up—maybe the latest Corvette would be on display; Pepsi flags would fly patriotically as young, crew-cut college boys handed out soda bottles to one and all. The bikini contest winners would parade up and down, getting their pictures taken with the surfing winners. Occasionally a local television station would send someone out to cover the excitement. And always, some beach band would play after the competition was over—Dick Dale or the Beach Boys.

Nobody ever interviewed the female winners.

High atop her judge's perch, Carol observed it all. The Surf Mama watching her chicks come home to roost. Mostly, she longed for the crowds to go away, to have the beach alone again with just a handful of fellow fanatics. But the genie was out of the bottle; surfing was taking over California.

"Hey, Carol!"

She was climbing down from her judge's perch at one of the competitions in early 1964 when she heard someone shouting her name. She turned around, already smiling, and saw Chuck Gibson, an old friend of her father's. Chuck had been old when she first knew him— ancient. Yet she realized he had probably only been her age, in his late thirties. He must be almost sixty now.

"Chuck! It's been a while!"

"Yeah. The last time I saw you, you were making eyes at Red Skelton in that movie, remember?"

"I remember. That was the summer after my junior year of high school. I was underwater in that mermaid suit so long, I thought I'd grow scales."

"What have you been up to?"

"Oh, this." She shrugged, gesturing toward the waves, which were full of amateurs, now that the competition was over. Huntington Beach was a mass of humanity, the oil derricks, so big and out of place, visible about a mile off the coast. It was tricky to surf here because of the old pilings from when they used to pump oil closer to shore. There were oil fields just inland, although not as many as she remembered being there back in the forties. Such a messy, crowded, dirty beach compared to Makaha! But the surf was good—in some ways better than Malibu—and the town fathers were anxious to catch the surfing craze and make the place known for something other than oily water and sulfurous smells.

"Yeah, I heard that you'd become a surf bum. Always wondered what happened to you—thought you could be another Esther Williams if you'd wanted to. You're prettier than she is, that's for sure." Chuck's small, pale blue eyes took her in; she was wearing a bikini, but it was a modest one compared to what Miss Huntington Beach had sported. Carol's bikini bottoms always covered her navel, and her top was held firmly in place with thick, wide straps.

"Life happened. Kids. You know."

"Kids? You have kids? Say it isn't so!"

"Mindy—Ginger! Come meet someone!" Carol waved at the two girls, who were surrounded by the usual Malibu crew, including Tom Riley. Even though they didn't surf up at Malibu much anymore, that crew always seemed to find them wherever they were. It was like there was some kind of Donnelly Girl radar. Carol suspected it was really Ginger Donnelly radar; her youngest could have easily won any of these bikini contests, had Carol allowed her to enter.

Ginger and Mindy obediently walked over to their mother; they all—even Mindy—knew their strength was in the picture the three of them presented. It turned heads—and opened beady little eyes like Chuck's.

"Well, good job," was all he could say as he stared first at Mindy, then for a long time at Ginger.

"Girls, this is a friend of mine, Chuck Gibson. He's a stunt coordinator for—what studio is it now, Chuck?"

"American International. We're about to start producing a slate of movies all about surfing now that it's so popular. Pretty low budget, but we might get some teenage heartthrobs to headline. We're looking to find locals for the background. And to do some stunt surfing for the actors."

"Well, Chuck . . ." Carol began with a smile. She knew where this was going. "I could surely do some—"

"I think your girls would be perfect," Chuck broke in, not even looking at Carol. "The right ages, that's for sure. Can you surf?"

"Of course!" Ginger giggled. Mindy didn't answer, as usual; she raised her nose in the air with superiority.

"How about you?" Chuck asked her.

"She only won the trophy here yesterday, in the women's division," Ginger said with another giggle—and a slightly downcast look.

"Wow, a champion. Like your mother used to be."

Carol felt her face burn—and her skin sag. As if that were the moment time chose to steal her beauty and youth.

"Here's my card." Chuck reached into his shirt pocket and pulled out two cards, handing one to each girl. "I think you'd be perfect for both—as extras and surfers, at least this one—what's your name, sweetheart?"

"Mindy. And my sister's name is Ginger."

"Great. Just great. Mindy and Ginger. Got it. Well, if you're anything like your mom was when she was your age, you'll work out fine. Give my office a call. We're going to start the first picture in a couple of weeks, filming up at Malibu. Say, do you know anyone else who might want to do some stunt surfing, hang out on the beach for a few weeks, and get paid for it as well as a couple of meals a day?"

"Sure." Ginger pointed toward the Malibu guys, who were mocking the novices out in the surf.

"Great. Thanks. And don't forget to call that number, you hear?"

"Will do," Mindy said, her voice dry with skepticism.

"Yes, and thank you," Ginger said with another giggle, blushing as Chuck winked at her. Then he walked over to Tom Riley and the others.

"Well," Carol said. She didn't know what else to add. The girls hesitated, exchanging glances, before going off to find their friends.

Carol climbed up the ladder even though the judging was done. With each rung, she felt her knee crack, a joint protest. She flung herself down on the folding chair and gazed out at the water.

Too brief. Too brief a time, to shine in the sun. Especially if you were a woman. Especially if you were a mother. Of daughters. Like the perfect wave that ended too soon, the ride was never long enough. The world kept spinning, the waves kept coming, the sun kept shining, but always seeking new, younger faces to bathe in its white-hot glow.

And DeeDee was married with children and Jack Cho had died in a car accident and Bob was married again with new children—he never saw the girls—and her mother was gone and her father, too, and Chuck Gibson was a dirty old man.

The only constant was the sea, the reassuring regularity of the surf. It was the reason she'd picked up a board in the first place, to find a way to stay within its embrace longer. The surf was all she needed.

She drove home alone; the girls wanted to go up to Malibu and stay at that shack, even though Mindy often declared it was disgusting. But still she couldn't quite resist its lure, either—that masculine lure, the musky scent—Tom Riley's scent, Carol suspected. And of course, Mindy was always looking for any excuse not to breathe the same air as her mother.

They'd be fine there. Better off than with her. Although sometimes, Carol did worry about what might happen to them, two girls alone with all those animals. But no, there were other girls, the surf bunnies, hanging around, too. And the guys Carol had been with at Makaha hadn't put a hand on her unless she invited it; she assumed that same chivalry applied to this younger generation. The Malibu surf was best for Ginger, although Carol suspected Mindy was already tired of it but pretended not to be for the sake of her sister.

That was one thing Carol could count on: That Mindy would never leave her sister's side. That Mindy would be the kind of mother Carol could never be, had no desire to be.

She held on to that thought later that evening as she drove back to Laguna. All of a sudden, she didn't want to go inside that shabby apartment full of photos and reminders about her past. Instead, she hauled her surfboard out of the back of the wagon and walked across the Coast Highway. The beach was almost empty; there were a few bonfires, she heard some giggles and a guitar playing. But no one was out on the water, not that she could see.

Carol—a long-sleeved T-shirt over her bikini her only protection from the chill night air—plunged right in, letting the cool white swirls capture her ankles, then her shins, then her knees. Finally she flung herself on her board and began to paddle out. She was alone; no one was wondering where she was, no one was seeking her. No one was asking her to be in their surf movies. But on the water, it didn't feel like a punishment.

She hadn't brought a torch. She only needed the moon, because she could surf this break with her eyes closed.

But as she heard the surf suddenly intensify behind her, felt the board begin to lift with the incoming wave as the previous, pathetic waves petered out before they reached the shore, her skin pricked with adrenaline. *Good* adrenaline, that urge to run toward the danger, not away, that she had felt her entire life. What a gift—an unexpected swell at night; they hardly ever happened.

Sure as ever, Carol paddled into position. The dragon, invisible so even more exhilarating than usual, breathed down her back. She got to her knees, ready to rise to the moon on a sea monster even blacker than the sky. She laughed. She was one with the universe, the stars close enough to hold on to if she needed them. But she didn't. She never needed anything, or anyone.

She kept her eyes open the entire time, after all, so she could memorize this moment—the lights on shore rushing up to meet her, the stars winking at her, the moon that refused to hide behind any cloud. Her eyes burned from the salt spray, but she didn't blink.

That way, she knew, she would never forget what happened next.

BOOK THREE

The Donnelly Women

19

1968

Ginger hesitated at the door to her mother's apartment, struggling to hold the baby still; the child never relaxed in her arms. She squirmed and pushed herself away from Ginger's chest, but she didn't cry. Finally Ginger handed the baby to the woman who had opened the door—"Here, will you hold her?" And she stepped into the dark room, following her sister.

"Mom?" Mindy asked, as unsure as Ginger felt at that moment.

"Ginger? Mindy?" The woman in the chair, binoculars hanging around her neck, turned, with some obvious pain, to face them. Her blond hair was no longer shiny; it was coarse and shot through with gray, hanging in a blunt cut at her chin. Her skin was so leathery, peppered with sunspots—the typical older surfer's skin, the toll of years in the sun. But her smile was the same—practiced, picture-perfect. Devoid of genuine warmth.

This was their mother. Carol Donnelly.

The last time Ginger had seen Mom it must have been 1965, about a year after the accident. At first, it hadn't seemed that serious—Carol had smashed up on some rocks, gashing her head so that it needed to be stitched up. Someone on the beach saw it happen and got her to a hospital, where she was held for a couple of days for observation. Then she was sent home to their apartment, where she insisted she was fine, that the girls should go back up to Malibu and make that movie; it would be fun for them.

So they did. But they drove back down to Laguna most weekends to shower and do laundry and load up on groceries for the gang. Mom seemed like herself, mostly. Maybe a little shaky, still—she dropped her fork at dinner once or twice, she fell a couple of times simply walking across the little living room, where her surfboard gathered dust in the corner. Mom said she couldn't go out, not yet, she still felt a little weak—but of course she would, it was only a matter of getting her legs back.

Eventually, she and Mindy stopped going home to check in on her. Things got complicated: Tom made her his chosen one, Mindy embarked on her career—life happened. Mom would be fine. Mom was always fine—who was more independent than Carol Donnelly? Her daughters knew that firsthand. Maybe they did hear some talk about her not being quite right—someone saw her at a tournament and said she'd acted a little drunk, which sounded odd. Ginger had never seen her mother drink. A year went by, then another—someone else said they hadn't seen her at all lately, she hadn't been to any of the contests.

It was easy to find excuses not to go and see her, Ginger admitted. Hadn't Mom abandoned them, after all? Hadn't she always put her own needs first? They didn't require a mother anymore, she and Mindy. They were adults. They'd always been adults, but now their age matched their self-sufficiency. Besides, life was plenty challenging as an adult: It tugged you first in one direction, then another; it presented you with too many choices, or not enough—it required constant vigilance, or maybe none at all. Maybe it just pulled you along until you ended up pregnant by someone you didn't love and beaten up by someone you did.

"How long has it been?" Ginger whispered, and she meant it for Mindy, but Mom answered.

"Too long." Mom tried to laugh it off, but her voice quavered and she blinked her eyes rapidly.

"I'm Estelle," the other woman, still holding the baby, chimed in. "I live here, too."

"Roommates," Mom explained. "I needed help with the rent, and—other things."

Ginger and Mindy both nodded. Ginger glanced at her sister, who was chewing her lip, her brow furrowed. She wondered if Mindy felt as guilty as she did.

"So who is this?" Mom indicated the baby, who had quieted down in Estelle's arms.

"This is—your granddaughter," Mindy said. "Ginger hasn't named her yet."

"She's dark, isn't she?" Mom said, and Ginger was shocked; she'd not taken the baby out of the compound up the hill before, so she wasn't ready for the kind of reaction people would have to this child of mixed heritage. "Really dark."

"Half-Hawaiian," Ginger managed to say, and Mom wrinkled her nose.

"My grandchild, a hapa haole." Mom shook her head in disgust. "I never thought I'd see the day."

"Mom, you love Hawaii!" Mindy blurted it out before Ginger could. "I wouldn't think you'd be so bigoted!"

"I love Hawaiians but I wouldn't marry one. I never thought you would, either." She looked at Ginger.

"I didn't marry anyone, this is—the baby is—"

"A mistake."

"Which is something you should know about," Mindy said

sharply, before stopping herself. She exhaled, rubbing her face with her hands. "Let's all agree never to refer to this child as a mistake, OK?"

"So what brings you two—three—here?"

"I, we—we thought—but now I see, we were wrong about that. How long have you been—not well, Mom?" Mindy's voice was a fraction gentler now, although still frosty, as she pulled a beanbag chair next to the walker and plopped down on it. Estelle kept the baby, walking her around the compact apartment, bouncing and cooing. Ginger sat down on the beanbag chair next to her sister; it wasn't big enough for the two of them but she needed to be next to Mindy, to feel her flesh against her own. In an instant she was a little girl again, needing her big sister to hold her hand and lead her through the Grimms' fairy-tale forest of their childhood, where behind every tree lurked an evil witch or big bad wolf.

Or the ghost of a mother.

"A while. I guess—the doctor said I have something called Parkinson's? That accident, maybe it started it? I don't know, it's confusing sometimes. All I know is that I shake a lot, I lose my balance, and I'm stuck up here in this damn place. It's too hard for me to get down to the beach anymore. I can't do stairs. Funny, isn't it?" Mom laughed, but it turned into a cough that rattled her hunched shoulders.

Her mother seemed coarser now—Ginger wouldn't have been surprised to see her holding a cigarette in one hand and a can of beer in the other. She cursed, and Mom had never cursed. She wore a shapeless sleeveless housedress, but Ginger could make out her protruding tummy, the flesh dangling on the arms that had once been so shapely and strong. Her jaw wasn't taut; she had a soft double chin. But the nails of her gnarled toes were still painted that bubblegum pink she'd always favored.

All around the room, in picture frames or thumbtacked to the dirty beige walls, were reminders of Carol Donnelly in all her glory—the sunny California blonde with the ponytail, tall and splendid with her perfect posture. Posing with a surfboard. On a diving board, when she was in high school. At the plate, bat in hand—that one was new, Ginger didn't recall ever seeing it before.

So she had been right, after all—all those years ago when she was looking for her mother in her bureau drawer. Mom did miss that *before* life. More than she missed her daughters.

Oh, there were photos of the three of them when they were the Donnelly Girls, goddesses of surf and sea. Mom up in her lifeguard chair, judging Long Beach. The only picture missing was the one taken at Makaha, when Mindy won.

But there wasn't a single photo of just Mindy or Ginger, not even a school photo. Ginger remembered having them taken, every year, but where were they now? There wasn't a single picture of Mom with Dad, either. Ginger realized she'd only ever seen one photo of them together, their wedding photo, and it had been on Dad's nightstand, not Mom's. They were impossibly young, she remembered; innocent-looking teenagers, not the wary parents she knew. Mom's dress was just a pretty suit, not a gauzy confection. Dad was in his uniform. They stood in front of a fireplace, at Grandma's house, and Dad's smile was so big it was all you saw of him. Mom's smile was closed-mouthed. Her hair was brighter than her smile.

"I don't think it's funny," Ginger said softly, filled with an unaccustomed sympathy for her mother—it surprised her, and she didn't know what to do with her sympathy other than give it back. Mom stopped laughing and cocked her head at her, as if registering her presence for the first time. Then she smiled, and it was a genuine smile, one of kindness. And regret.

"Thank you."

"So I'm guessing you're not up to raising a child? Not that I really thought you were, based on experience," Mindy said, plowing ahead in her usual pragmatic, focused way, apparently not quite so sympathetic. "But that is why we came here. Get a load of this—your daughter doesn't want to raise her own baby. Sound familiar?"

"Ginger? What do you mean?"

"I need to go—to go back, to someone. The man I love. Tom Riley—you remember him, don't you?"

"That crazy idiot? You're still with that jerk? Who obviously isn't the father of this child?"

Ginger nodded, defeated by the entire situation; she was so tired, her ribs still ached, her head still rang with alarm bells if she moved it too much.

"Jimmy Cho!" Mindy blurted out, her face red, her hands in fists—the fury that she had so far managed to contain threatening to explode, a mushroom cloud about to obliterate Laguna Beach. Ginger suddenly regretted being on that beanbag chair. But Mindy took a breath, calming herself. "Jimmy Cho, you remember him?"

"Jack Cho's oldest?"

"Yes. That is who the father is. But the thing is, *I'm* kind of with Jimmy—oh, it's a whole soap opera, Mom! It'd really be a hoot if it wasn't actually happening." Mindy's shoulders slumped and suddenly she, too, appeared defeated by the whole situation. The air went out of the room and all three women sat in gloomy silence. The Donnelly Girls, who could conquer the waves, had been vanquished by a tiny baby whose happy gurgles and coos were an absurd accompaniment to the situation.

"Well, girls, you've gotten yourselves in quite a pickle," Mom finally said. "I can't raise this child, no. I can barely take care of myself and that's only if Estelle stays with me, and I'm not so sure she will. Her family needs her, she says." Mom rolled her eyes.

Estelle, still bouncing the baby in her arms, nodded. "Yes, they just moved out here from Georgia. They have a baby, too. A little boy."

"So you see," Mom said evenly, "I've got my own problems right now."

"Yeah," Mindy said. "You always do. Nothing's really changed."

"Mindy, please." Now Mom sounded contrite. "I didn't mean—we need to—"

"Never mind." Mindy abruptly stood up, causing Ginger to roll off the beanbag chair onto the floor. "I think I need something to eat before we continue this touching reunion. Anybody else hungry? Ginger, come with me, we'll get something to bring back."

"I could use some Taco Bell," Mom replied.

"No!" Ginger startled them all. "No—I mean, please, not that? It doesn't agree with me."

"Sure, whatever, then."

"Can we leave the baby with you?" Mindy asked Estelle, and Ginger blushed. *She* should have asked that, shouldn't she? She was about to walk out the door—anything to get out of that stifling place—without a thought for her daughter. More proof—not that she needed it—that she was doing the right thing.

Wasn't she?

She followed Mindy down the rickety metal stairs, which groaned with every step. They started walking across the highway, toward a burger stand they used to hang out at after school. Mystic Arts wasn't in this area—it was down by the Taco Bell. Which was why she'd nixed that idea; she didn't want to run into any of the Brotherhood right now, not with Mindy there. Mindy, who would ask too many questions.

"I don't know," Mindy was saying, and Ginger rushed to keep up with her sister, who was taking huge strides, determined to go somewhere, anywhere, except back to the apartment. "I don't know, what do we do now? How do I do this?"

"Mindy, stop!" Ginger panted. It was impossible to walk this fast and carry on a conversation; her ribs were burning, her head buzzing. "Stop, let's sit down, OK?"

They were at Main Beach Park, a flat, unsheltered lawn dotted with picnic tables and benches, and there were stairs and trails down to the beach. Ginger pointed to a picnic table, and the two sisters climbed up and sat on the tabletop, their feet on the bench, facing the ocean.

It was a clear day and Catalina was so visible, Ginger could make out the chalky cliffs on the south side of the island. There were sailboats out on the water, floating around like little pieces of paper. A few surfers, but this wasn't the main hangout, as she well knew. Orange bird-of-paradise flowers lined the stairs that went down to the beach; Brooks Street, farther south, was the best surfing. This was more of a family area than other parts of Laguna, so there were kids running around, tired parents chasing after them. Some couples on blankets, drowsily leaning against each other. This wasn't an area the Brotherhood frequented; too many cops patrolled it.

"Why were you so *mean* to Mom?" Ginger had to ask. Mindy was moody, she was abrupt. But she was rarely downright mean. "She looked so pathetic."

"I know," Mindy said, her hands still tense with fury. "I know. I had no idea she was like this. But seeing her again—it brought back some stuff. Stuff you don't know about."

"Tell me, then."

"No."

"You're mad at me, too." Ginger finally stated the obvious. Why was she even surprised by her sister's anger? She was the real reason for it, of course. Not Mom.

"You bet I am." Mindy shifted on the table, confronting her sister—Ginger had no choice but to accept her sister's fury. "I'm mad as hell, mad at everyone! But you! First you disappear, then you reappear and you sleep with my—with Jimmy. Then you dump his baby on my doorstep. And now I see Mom is—she's a wreck, she *needs* help, she can't *give* it. Just like before. And it's all on *me*, Ginger. Again! No matter what people say to me, or do to me, I have to just—do it. Fix it. Always."

"I—"

"And *you*! You still want to go back to that monster. After all he did to you, you want more. You know he hates you and will hate you forever for sleeping with Jimmy, and that's one thing I have in common with him, anyway."

"Mindy, please—you can't mean that, you can't hate me forever!" Even though Ginger wasn't going to stay, the thought of her sister turning her back on her forever was terrifying. Mindy was always there, her safety net. If things got too bad with Tom—although they had, hadn't they? What on earth would cause her to leave him now?

What Tom had said, that terrible day—he didn't mean it. He didn't want Mindy instead of her. So she couldn't be angry at her sister—and her sister couldn't be angry with her. No matter what happened to them all, Ginger had to know that Mindy didn't despise her, she had to know that somewhere in the world, her sister was thinking of her with love. Not loathing.

"Why am I not allowed to hate you? You slept with Jimmy! You had his child—not me! I can never be that to him now!" Mindy broke down, her body shuddering with sobs, and Ginger's heart tore for her sister. She hadn't thought of that; what she and Jimmy had done hadn't been an act of love. But it didn't matter; it had robbed Mindy of being able to give that to him, his first child. She'd never thought that mattered to Mindy—that either of the Donnelly sisters would be a mother had once seemed the most outlandish notion, as absurd as if they'd decided to become ballerinas or go to the moon. But apparently it did matter to Mindy. Ginger understood that now.

Because she felt the same way about Tom. She'd so wanted to have his child, she'd assumed that her body would reject anyone else's.

Ginger put her arm around her sister's shoulders. She'd never held her big sister like this before; always it was Mindy who comforted Ginger. It was about time someone comforted Mindy. "I'm so sorry, I am. I can't fix it. I can't go back in time. And now there's the baby—oh, I'm so sorry, I never thought it through when I asked you to take her. It's not fair to you, I know that. I'll find someone else, there must be another person—"

"No!" Mindy raised her head; her eyes were swollen, her face red and shining with unwiped tears. But she'd stopped crying, and now her violet-blue eyes were flashing with anger. "No, you can't do that. I can't explain it—I can't let you do that. If you can't raise your own child, I'll do it. I have to. I just do. Someone has to figure out how to be a mother in this family. I'm the last one standing. It's up to me."

Ginger nodded, still holding her sister, who didn't try to squirm out of her embrace. For a long time they sat like this, the little sister comforting the big one. Finally Mindy let out a shaky sigh, wiped her eyes, and gently shrugged off Ginger's arm.

"So tell me, Ginger. Please. I really want to understand. Why? Why Tom Riley? What is it about him that would make you do this—give up your daughter and let me, a known self-absorbed, shallow kook, raise your daughter instead of you?"

Ginger tried not to pay attention to the families on the grass, running after screaming children—one toddler fell down and let out a mighty roar, while her mother rushed to her, Popsicle in hand. She didn't reply right away; she had to choose her words carefully, so that she would remember them afterward. She knew she would; she knew this was a moment she would replay over and over the rest of her life. What she said had to make sense to both of them.

"When we were growing up," she finally said, grasping her sister's hand, "did you ever feel like there was a monster inside of you? A monster that you had to guard carefully, so it would never come out?"

Mindy squinted at the ocean, considering. That her sister didn't think this was a weird question only reinforced how close they were, even now.

"Yes," Mindy answered, nodding. "Yes, I did. Mom. *She* was the monster—the thing I didn't want to be. The thing I still don't want to be."

"Well, maybe she wasn't such a monster, after all. Did you ever think of that?"

"No, not once. Especially not after Makaha. I never told you— but it doesn't matter. But after seeing her now, after I found Jimmy in Vietnam—after seeing your daughter show up on my doorstep, unwanted—maybe." Mindy sat for a moment, her eyes searching the water. "Maybe now—I understand her. A little."

"I understand her more, I think. I'm like her. Mom—she followed her heart, didn't she? That's all she did, really. It took her away from us and that was the thing we couldn't forgive. Like my baby will never forgive *me*. But Mom had *passion,* Mindy. It's like that with Tom. He's my obsession, like surfing was Mom's. I can't explain it— I just am part of him. He's part of me. I can't be in this world without him—I'd die, I know it. I'd be missing half of myself. I know you don't like him—"

"Ginger, he *beat* you."

"I know." Oh, she was weak, so weak; so wrong. But she'd been overlooked too many times in her life. Tom would never forget her, never—you didn't hurt someone the way he had abused her if you didn't love them beyond reason. That was what she told herself, every minute of every day. "Even when he hates me, he still *needs* me. He's always seen me as my own person, and you never did. Neither did Mom."

"What do you mean, I've never seen you? Ginger, all those years, all I thought of was you, how to keep you safe, keep you from being adopted, keep you with Mom."

"Us. You had to keep *us* safe, with Mom. And finally, you decided to think about yourself for a change, put yourself first."

"I wanted you with me, Ginger! I begged you!"

"I know, but I was an afterthought. And that's OK, Mindy—you *should* have done something for yourself! I knew that. You always thought of me, I'm not saying you didn't. But I wasn't a real person, I was mainly your responsibility—and probably, too many times, your burden. Tom, he never thought of me that way. I'm never a burden to him, because he can leave me whenever he wants and he knows I'll still be there. You were never sure—you always thought I'd disappear without you. That's why you always looked back at me. Until you got tired of it, like anyone would."

"I don't know what to say to you anymore, Ginger. You've changed."

"No, I haven't. All I ever wanted was to be loved by someone. All I ever wanted was to be *necessary*."

"So what do I do now? You said I made my choice but now you're making it for me. You're making me responsible for your daughter, who, by the way, needs a goddamn name, OK? Jesus Christ, Ginger!"

"Mindy."

"What?"

"No, I mean—I just decided that her name is Mindy. The strongest person I know. I'm naming her after you."

"Great. Two Mindys. Great."

Ginger smiled, leaning against her sister's compact, athletic body. Mindy's body was strong—but her spirit was stronger. "So you'll take her?"

Suddenly Ginger's eyes misted over; her heart gave a lurch, as if a battle was taking place within it. And there was—unexpected sobs shook her so it felt like her rib was piercing her flesh. She couldn't stop; she cried messily, snottily, aware of a fresh, raw, gaping hole that would never be filled, the loss of the child she had carried for nine months, had pushed from her body, given life. The child who had her curly hair; she knew that. Everything else about her was alien—or so Ginger told herself. This was Jimmy Cho's child, not Tom's, and so—not hers. But the baby's hair was like hers, and there would be other things, too, that she would never see—would her daughter be shy, too? Happy at the simplest things, like pretty dresses? Sad at too many things, but so used to the sadness it felt like her best friend?

Would she like sunsets best, or sunrises? Chocolate ice cream or vanilla? Would she be good at sports or drawing? Be a leader or a follower?

Would she constantly be looking for her mother, like Ginger had when she was a little girl?

To do this to her daughter, to abandon her as she had been abandoned—no, even worse; Mom had come back, at least physically, and Ginger didn't think she ever would—was hard. It was almost impossible—but not as impossible as imagining a life without Tom. She was merely one person, one broken, damaged person, and she could only do the easiest thing, which was the hardest thing, but it was the only thing. She wasn't strong like Mindy. She wasn't strong like anybody.

She was only herself, and that had to be enough.

"I should go now," she said, wiping her eyes with her forearm. Mindy put her arm around her waist, pulling Ginger to her.

"Now? Not now—Ginger, you just came back to me! I'm still not finished with missing you from before, and now you're going to leave me again? We have so many things to talk about—there's Mom, and—"

"No, we don't. I'm sorry, Mindy. I know I'm awful, and I'm sorry I'm doing this to you. But I have to go. Now."

Because Tom might already have left—panic flooded her, drowning every other emotion. Where was Tom right now? Was he still up at the compound? Already on his way back to Afghanistan or somewhere else? She was desperate to find out. She had to tell him what she'd done, given up her daughter; he had to know she'd made this sacrifice. Like an angry god, he would see that he had been appeased. And then he would take her back. He *had* to.

And if he didn't, she'd follow him anyway.

"Ginger, what about Mom? We can't leave her like this. What about Jimmy? Have you even told him?"

"No. He doesn't know."

"So I have to do that, too? Write him a letter and say, 'Oh, by the way, I have something that belongs to you'?"

"You'll know how to do it. You're strong. I know now that there's no one else in the world I would leave my daughter—Mindy—with."

"But you'll come back? Someday?"

"I love you, Mindy."

Had she ever told her sister that? It was unspoken, wasn't it, the love between sisters as close as they had been? Or was it? Because Mindy's face was crumpling, tears flowing down her cheeks, as Ginger wrapped her up in a fierce embrace, imprinting the sensation of her sister upon her skin so that she could carry it with her, every day for the rest of her life.

Spoken, those four words solved the equation that had begun the moment Ginger had been born: two sisters minus one mother subtracted from one father equals—

Love.

Ginger slipped off the bench, turning quickly so she didn't have to see Mindy's face. She hurried up to the highway, where she crossed at the busy Broadway intersection. Then she trudged up the road, higher into the hills, as it turned into Canyon Road. It was a long walk, and each tired step took her away from the ocean, her sister, her mother. Her child.

But closer to Tom, at the top of the hill.

20

1969

The day Jimmy, fresh out of the army, came knocking on the apartment door in Laguna would forever be etched in Mindy's memory. Starting with the confusion on his face when she opened the door to the unfamiliar—at least to him—apartment.

"What are you doing here? I got your letter saying you'd moved."

She'd dreamed of his safe return for so long that when she finally saw him, she was almost annoyed—*Couldn't he have let me know ahead of time? Why didn't I put on any makeup today?* It was an effort not to snap at him, just showing up on her doorstep at four o'clock in the afternoon when she had so much to do.

Judging from the look on his face, he wasn't so thrilled, either—how could he be? There was a baby crying in the background and a woman in the chair by the window. Too many people—she saw it in his darting eyes. He was doing calculations, none of which came out right. *There are too many people here.*

"Mindy, what the hell—I don't—oh, *hello!*"

It finally occurred to him that he was seeing her for the first time since China Beach, and it occurred to her at that exact moment, and then they were two people crazily in love and all she knew was his smile that could make angels sing and strong arms that wrapped her up, lifted her off her feet. For that one moment she was purely grateful that he was home, no missing limbs, no scars that she could see. She allowed herself to wallow in this moment of uncomplicated happiness, forgetting everything else that she knew about him now.

Then she pushed herself out of his arms, smoothed her hair, and let him inside the little living room.

"Your letter said you had something for me? I hope that means what I think it does," Jimmy whispered in an unmistakable growl.

"I don't think so." Mindy smiled stiffly as he took in the shabby little room, which she'd done her best to tidy up after she and the baby moved in, but her mother insisted on keeping the ribbons and plaques and clippings where she could see them. Her mother's memories were the most vivid thing about her now. All Mindy could do was try to keep them from taking over the entire apartment, to create some space for herself and Melinda and the unknown future.

"Well, look who finally showed up," Mom said, her eyes glittering with something Mindy chose to label *amusement.* "So this is the father of my grandchild?"

"What?" Jimmy's eyes were huge; he looked at Mindy, looked at her stomach. "What?"

Forever, she was grateful that he seemed pleased at that moment. Shocked, but pleased—to think that she'd had his child. Then she had to laugh, because he was so terrible at math.

"I guess I need to introduce you to your daughter. *Ginger's* daughter."

Jimmy froze; his mouth opened and closed, like one of those funny banks she'd had as a child, a cast-iron clown you fed pennies to. He plopped down on that cursed beanbag chair Mindy couldn't get her mother to part with. For a minute she thought he might be sick, the way he clutched his stomach, his head. Then he slumped, hiding his face in his hands for a long minute. Finally he raised his head and met her gaze.

"I had no idea—she didn't tell me."

"I am aware."

"So now you know about—about Ginger and me. About what happened that night."

"Ginger told me, but I'd like to hear it from you."

"Maybe I should leave you two alone," Mom said, and her voice was surprisingly understanding and kind. In the weeks since Mindy and the baby had moved in—and Estelle had moved out—Mom had been as prickly as a sea urchin, unpredictable with her barbs and sarcasm. Mindy hadn't remembered her mother's being anything but aloofly pleasant before, that evening on Makaha being the exception. Now her sarcasm was totally unexpected, because Mindy had never thought of her mother as possessing a sense of humor. It was as if once she'd lost the use of her body, she'd acquired a personality. But not a particularly nice one.

"Thanks, Mom." And Carol got up with some effort, holding on to her walker. She pushed it, shuffling behind it, down the path Mindy had cleared by moving the furniture and clutter to either side of the room. Once Carol reached the bedroom, where the baby had stopped crying and was hopefully settling back down for her nap, she shut the door behind her.

"What happened to your mother?" Jimmy asked, after Mindy had filled a glass with water for him, which he gulped down.

"There was that accident—you might have heard of it. Years ago, she was night surfing here and got caught on some rocks. She hit her head. She has Parkinson's now."

"I'm sorry."

"Yeah, thanks. So, you were going to explain it all to me?" Mindy folded her arms, staying a good five feet away from this man whose body she had longed for, still longed for, the physical ache for him sharper than any kind of hunger she'd ever known.

She had convinced herself that she had forgiven him these past few months as she had cared for his child, learning how to diaper, how to haunt secondhand stores to buy a crib, a high chair, a wobbly stroller. How to find a job nearby so she could come home for lunch to make sure her mother was able to keep the baby from sticking her fingers in electrical outlets. Mom could cope, for now—and she seemed willing to help. Another surprise.

Ever since Ginger had shown up on her doorstep, Mindy's life had been nothing but a series of bombshells, large and small. A rearranging of how she looked at the world and the people she knew in it.

In those months—months of patting Melinda (never Mindy; it would be ridiculous to have two Mindys, and besides, she deserved a name she could make her own) on the back to bring up gas, of rocking her in her arms to get her to sleep, of discovering what made her smile, of singing "There Was a Farmer Had a Dog" a million times, of finding herself, unexpectedly, blowing raspberries on the baby's round little belly, of allowing that pure, joyful laugh to make the messy diapers and spit-up and globs of baby food on her shirt all worth it—she had thought of Jimmy. Almost constantly. She couldn't help it; Melinda looked so much like him when she smiled—which she did a lot. Far more than most babies. Mindy was sure of it.

And she had shifted the burden of the blame more evenly to her own shoulders, remembering how hateful she'd been to Jimmy, how singularly driven she'd been to have that silly career. Silly now, but vital then—vital to some stamp of legitimacy, of never again being the kid who wore the same outfit to school three days in a row, the kid whom adults whispered about, treated with pity masquerading as exaggerated kindness. She had been consumed with having that career, blind to how cruel it was—and how cruel it made her.

When she looked at it that way, she had to admit she was a lot like Mom. Focused, obsessed. With the wrong thing.

So she didn't really blame Jimmy anymore—that was what she told herself. And as she grew to love his daughter, she was almost grateful that he and Ginger had done it, that one night of regretful passion that had given the world this beautiful little girl, her niece.

But seeing him now for the first time in the same house as that daughter, all she could think of was that night and how he and her sister had come together. Her jealousy was so strong, the sense of betrayal so furious, she didn't see the baby anymore. She saw arms and legs and breasts—her sister's breasts—and Jimmy's penis and the face he made right before he came, squeezing his eyes shut, the drops of perspiration on his forehead, and she ran to the bathroom, the nausea bolting up, gushing from her lips just as she reached the toilet.

"Mindy! Mindy—are you all right?"

Her stomach heaved, she retched, she flushed the toilet. Splashed water on her face. Held on to the bathroom vanity until she felt some strength return. When she finally opened the door, Jimmy was standing right outside it, such panic on his face, such concern for her, that now she loved him again.

What the hell? Couldn't she pick a lane and stay in it? Those damned bullying emotions, knocking her out with expert blows every time she thought she had regained consciousness. She'd never thought of herself as an emotionally unstable person, but right now she sure was doing a great job of acting like one.

"Sit down." Jimmy put his arm around her, escorting her to the sofa. "I'll try to explain, if you want to hear it?"

She nodded.

"I was hurt, you know—well, we said all this at China Beach." He stopped, jaw clenching, and he took a couple of deep breaths before continuing. "I think I told you that right after you—after we broke up, I ran into Ginger. I didn't tell you she was a complete mess, and that later that night we—we were together. It wasn't like I was trying to replace you with your sister or anything, it wasn't that deliberate—that's what I told myself, anyway. Told myself that I just needed to stop thinking for a little while. But yeah, maybe I did want to get back at you. Maybe I did want to use your sister like I felt you'd used me—just for sex, for fun. And then—wham. Drop her fast, like you dropped me." Jimmy didn't look at her at all as he explained, but he did grip her hand. Tightly. "Like I told you on China Beach, I'm not perfect."

Well, who the hell is? Mindy wondered. They were all a fucking mess, the lot of them. That's why they belonged together.

She didn't say anything; she only squeezed his hand back, but that was enough. Suddenly he exhaled, falling back against the sofa.

"And now there's a baby." He shook his head, still trying to make sense of it.

"Yes, a little girl. She's almost eight months old now."

"Where's Ginger?" For the first time, it seemed to occur to Jimmy that there was a missing Donnelly Girl. He craned his neck, looking around the tiny apartment. As if Ginger could be hiding behind the one pathetic potted plant.

"Well, here's the kicker—she's gone. She left the baby with me. She went to Afghanistan, with Tom."

"What? Afghanistan—where is that, even?"

"Somewhere in the Middle East." Mindy sighed, remembering how she'd rushed to the library to find an atlas after she heard the news. She'd gone up to that compound—the Brotherhood—a few days after Ginger had left, after she had gotten the baby and herself settled with Mom. It was a creepy place, dirty, kids running around wild and naked, adults naked, too. Everyone was stoned out of their mind—it was like a horror movie with zombies. But some girl came forward—her name was Dearest, what a laugh!—and she told Mindy that Tom had gone back to Afghanistan; she didn't say why but

Mindy figured out it had something to do with drugs. And that Ginger had gone with him.

"He didn't want her to. But that chick, man, she has it bad for that guy. Even though he's an asshole."

And that was as apt a description of Ginger and Tom as Mindy had ever heard. So simple. So true.

"So she up and left you her—the baby?" Jimmy ran his hand through his thick black hair, still short on the sides in the military cut, but longer on top. Suddenly she remembered he had come home from Vietnam.

Vietnam, the nightly horror show she and Mom watched on the evening news. So many things had happened to Mindy since she'd been there, she felt detached from the images on the TV. Now Jimmy brought the reality back to her in all its bloody, vivid glory.

"Jimmy, tell me—are you all right? You didn't get hurt after I was gone?"

"Nah, I'm fine. We had some shelling, Charlie was always nipping around China Beach, but we were pretty safe compared to everyone else. I'm one of the lucky ones. The guys I rode home with, on the plane—they weren't. So many were shell-shocked, Mindy. Eyes glazed. One guy was on a stretcher, although there wasn't anything wrong with him that I could see, but he kept screaming unless he was zonked out on morphine. I got out clean, and I know I'm the luckiest son of a bitch in the world. I'm never going to forget that."

"I'm glad you're back," Mindy whispered, and for one moment the world stood still as she sat with her head resting on Jimmy's shoulder, his hand grasping hers, and it was only the two of them.

Then the baby cooed, and everything changed. Forever. It would never be only the two of them again.

"Do you want to—to meet your daughter?" Not for the first time, it occurred to Mindy that he might not want to have anything to do with Melinda. After all, in her personal experience parents didn't always feel obligated to stick around. And Jimmy was just a man, after all. A man who angered quickly, who carried grudges, who hurt and could be hurt.

A human being, in other words.

"Wow." He took a deep breath; his hands trembled a little. This was a lot for one man to absorb, that was for sure. "I guess—I mean, yeah. Yes. You two come as a package, I gather?"

Mindy nodded, unable to trust her voice. She wanted Jimmy to be besotted with his child for Melinda's sake, not her own. But she also wanted him to show remorse. More than anything, she wanted him for herself.

She wanted too many things. All her life, she had wanted too many things. She'd always defined herself by what she was missing.

Maybe it was time to define herself by what she had, instead.

"What's her name?" Jimmy asked.

"Melinda."

"Well, that's a good name."

"It was Ginger's idea, not mine."

"I'm glad. That's the name I would have chosen, too." Jimmy took her hand and held it to his chest; she felt his heart beating quickly, nervously.

"Thank you," she whispered, shutting her eyes for a moment, feeling only his heartbeat, thankful, once more, that he was back. Alive. Then she opened her eyes and stood on wobbly legs. "OK, let's go."

"Right." Jimmy rose. He smoothed his T-shirt, flattened his hair. "Do you think she'll like me? Do I look OK?"

Mindy laughed. It would be all right, it really would. For the first time since Ginger had shown up at her door, she knew it would be all right. She could do this, raise this child, take care of Mom. As long as Jimmy was by her side.

"She's eight months old. I doubt she's going to weigh in on your sartorial choices."

He laughed but clutched her hand like it was a lifeline as he followed her into the bedroom, where Mom was sitting on the bed with a surfing magazine and Melinda was awake in her crib, propping herself up on her dimpled little arms, gurgling and cooing at something only she could see—that baby vision, Mindy called it.

But she turned her precious little head toward them when they walked toward her. She smiled in recognition at Mindy and belly-laughed in that magical baby way, infectious, pure.

Jimmy laughed in response. He let go of Mindy's hand.

He picked up his daughter, and it was love at first sight. Mindy couldn't even be jealous; it was so right. This baby deserved a father like Jimmy.

And Mindy deserved him, too.

Soon after Jimmy came home, Mindy realized she was weary of California. It was too big, too sunny, too full of contradictions—mountains and beaches and canyons and fog and ambition and heartbreak, relentless in its beauty, expecting too much. Or conversely, providing too many opportunities to disappear altogether, to forget who you were, or at least the best parts of who you were. There were too many chances to disappoint the people who needed you in the pursuit of that special California glow.

As she was packing up all the detritus of her mother's life in preparation for the upcoming move, sorting through the faded glories of her mother's past, Mindy found a yellowed brochure for the Super Chief, the train that ran from Los Angeles to Chicago. It was a wartime brochure, plastered with warnings about troop trains taking precedence so arrival times might vary. But there was one train from Los Angeles to Chicago circled in red ink, the words *Baseball Tryouts* written next to it in a big, bold hand with lots of exclamation points.

"Mom?" She took the brochure over to where her mother sat. Always at the window, with her binoculars. Watching the ocean. All day long.

Sometimes Carol commented about the surfers she saw—she didn't like the wetsuits that were starting to be popular. She didn't like shortboards. But mostly, she didn't talk much when she had her binoculars up to her eyes.

And Mindy didn't talk to her much then, either. Or really, ever. They had avoided meaningful conversation, so life with Carol Donnelly now wasn't that much different than it had been when Mindy was a girl. They talked about food, the surf. The baby, of course. But Mom had difficulty meeting Mindy's gaze even as she accepted her help.

"Mom?" Mindy knelt down next to the chair, placing the brochure in Carol's lap. "Mom, look at this. Look what I found."

Lowering the binoculars so they fell around her neck, Carol gazed down at the brochure. She blinked a couple of times, held it out at arm's length, trying to adjust her vision, and Mindy made a note, one more thing to do: take her mother to the eye doctor. Where she'd find the money, she didn't know.

"What's this?" Carol squinted, her eyes watering. Mindy took the brochure from her.

"It's a timetable, for the Super Chief. To Chicago. It was in your things. What does this mean, 'Baseball Tryouts'? I knew you played in high school, but that was here in California."

"Ohhhh." Her mother sounded like a tire deflating. "Oh. That."

"What kind of tryouts?"

"It doesn't matter anymore."

"Mom, tell me. I'd like to know."

"You would? Why on earth?"

"Because I'm your daughter?"

"After what I said—that night, you still think of yourself as my daughter?"

"Well, not always," Mindy admitted, and she sat down on the floor, cross-legged. The tiles were cool beneath her thighs. The sun, coming in the window now that it was late afternoon, shone brightly on her mother, but Carol didn't flinch from the glare like Mindy did—not at first. Suddenly, she shaded her eyes, from both the sun and her daughter.

"I, uh, I'm not proud of what I said that night," Carol stammered, plucking at her polyester pants. "I didn't really mean it."

"People generally mean what they say, in my experience."

"Well, then, I shouldn't have said it."

"Is this maybe why you did?" Mindy held up the brochure.

"Maybe. That, and a hundred other reasons that had nothing to do with you as you are now, or as you were that day on Makaha. Reasons that weren't your fault."

"So what's this about?"

"I was supposed to go to Chicago, to try out for the baseball league. The All-American Girls Professional Baseball League—oh, it was a thing during the war. To make up for the men all being gone."

"And you didn't go, because of me." Mindy stated it; it was no longer a question.

"Because I was pregnant with you, yes." Carol nodded. "And then I had to get married."

Because that was what you did in 1944 when you got knocked up. Of course.

"So you always resented me." This, too, was not a question, and

Mindy was blinking hard, steeling herself for the confirmation of everything she'd always suspected was true.

"Yes, I did."

Mindy laughed shortly; she had to hand it to her mother. No sugarcoating the truth. Then she stopped laughing and wished she'd never brought it up. She'd had all the evidence she needed, all her life. Why had she pushed?

Because she wanted to understand her mother, she realized. Now that Carol was fading—now that Mindy had assumed the role of mother and Carol that of daughter—she simply wanted to understand it, all of it, *everything*. The smallest thing and the biggest thing. All the—things. Because she realized, beyond the pictures and trophies and newspaper clippings and her own childhood memories, she really didn't know anything about her mother's life. Not how she was as a girl—how she really was, not the pretty smiling blonde but the brooding girl in her bedroom as a teenager, because surely even the famously peppy Carol Donnelly had been a moody teenager once, hadn't she?

"Nobody ever asked me what I wanted to do," Carol said softly, her head hanging down, her entire body slumped. "As soon as there was going to be a baby, nobody ever asked me what I wanted. They all just assumed. Or didn't even care. Your father—he was the worst of them. He knew how he felt and he assumed I felt the same way, and all of a sudden—it was like I lost my voice. Like I had laryngitis; I couldn't speak up for myself. Well, we weren't supposed to, you know, back then. But I should have. I had, before, when I wanted to play sports. I told people, I told everyone I knew that was what I wanted! But suddenly, when I was pregnant, it was like my brain and my voice had been snatched right out of me."

"And then I was born."

"Yes, you were. And I—"

"You were stuck."

"That's about it." Carol sighed deeply. So did Mindy—until she remembered something.

"But you did leave, you know. You found your voice again, with surfing, before you came back."

Carol nodded. "It was the only thing that mattered to me. The only thing that made me feel like myself again. And even when you started competing, I never felt I was giving anything up, like I was giving myself up, like I had before. But then you won. At Makaha, of all places—*my* place. *My* home. And I couldn't help it—I was a bitch. A real bitch."

"Yes, you were."

Carol glanced at her then, and her gaze was sharp, shrewd—and appreciative. Like mother, like daughter.

"I am sorry." Carol finally said it—what Mindy had been waiting for years to hear. It didn't really make her feel as vindicated as she had thought it would. They were still a mess, a wrecked mess, the three of them—

No, the two of them. At least for now. Still a mess, these Donnelly girls. Apologies for the past couldn't change that.

"Maybe this is my punishment." Carol gestured toward her walker. "For that day. For hurting you. Now I'm trapped. And you have to take care of *me*—" Her voice broke; she put her hand over her heart, taking a big breath before continuing. "But I'm luckier than you were. You're a good mother. I see it every day. I don't know where you got it from, but you are. I don't deserve you, and neither does your sister."

"Thanks, Mom."

Was this the approval she had craved at Makaha? Should it still matter to her?

Whether or not it should have, it did. Her mother's praise calmed her, like a sleepy, warm cat on her chest. A cat named contentment.

"Do you want me to keep this?" Mindy held the brochure out to her mother, and their hands briefly touched. Mindy touched her mother a lot now—holding on to her arm to help her steady herself, helping to button up her shirts or dresses, tying her shoes. But as their hands brushed, it was like a little electric shock warmed her entire body. Because she remembered, all of a sudden, one of the rare moments from her childhood she had not trotted out to nurse a grudge over.

A moment when she was on the beach with Mom, just the two of them—it must have been before Ginger was born? Mindy couldn't have been more than two, but she remembered wanting to go in the water with her mother. The water looked so cool, so inviting, so she wobbled over to the edge, behind her mother, who stood so tall and still, knee-deep in the surf. Mindy remembered the shock of the cold water, the unexpected force of the wave knocking her over—

And then hands picking her up, carrying her. Warm hands, her mother's hands. Mindy was on her mother's hip and the two of them were watching the ocean. Her mother didn't say a word to her. Mindy didn't know how long they stood there; she didn't remember anything else about that moment.

All she remembered was the sand, the water, and her mother's hands.

21

1980

Of course, they went to Hawaii. It was Jimmy's home, so now it was Mindy's as well. And it seemed right; it was full circle. When she told Mom, her mother dropped the brittle sarcasm. She didn't say anything at all—only raised the ever-present binoculars to her watery eyes and gazed out at the ocean. As if she could see Hawaii from that shabby little apartment.

Mom never thanked her for taking her home. Her happiness in Hawaii was too full, too much. And as the years progressed, she stopped talking. The doctor said that Parkinson's could do that, could affect the vocal cords, and maybe that was what happened. But Mindy believed it was just that her mother was so happy, finally, to be back in this sacred place that she didn't need to speak. Mindy understood that kind of happiness.

Sometimes, when she and Jimmy and Melinda were out on the water together, or sitting at the dinner table, she was also too full of wonder to form words. Words were inadequate, after all.

She suspected her mother had always known that.

Out on the water, a young girl in a wetsuit surfed the waves of Makaha. Her hair was long, hanging down her back in dark auburn tangles. She surfed confidently, turning with ease, falling gracefully, always popping back up like a seal.

Mindy watched her, not too worried. Melinda was a natural, just like her aunt. Just like her grandmother.

Just like her father.

"Melinda! Mindy!" A voice from down the beach reached her ears; she turned, shading her eyes from the sun. Jimmy had his shortboard beneath his arm, ready to join them.

"Hey, Dad!" Melinda waved as she knelt on her board, bobbing up and down in the surf.

Dad.

The word still pierced Mindy's heart. Even after all these years. Melinda was about to turn twelve.

"How's the surf today?" Jimmy asked as he ran up. He'd left work early.

Jimmy's dream of having his own business had come true; he contracted out to several resorts down the coast, closer to Honolulu. He employed a dozen people—Mindy among them—to give swimming and surfing lessons, sometimes on replicas of original Hawaiian longboards. History lessons were always included with the surfing lessons. The resorts weren't thrilled about *that,* but Jimmy and Mindy and the others were in such demand that they were allowed.

Jimmy and Mindy alternated days so that one of them was always home with Mom and Melinda. They weren't able to earn much of a salary. Even if tips were extravagant, worth the occasional pawing that occurred when she took a beet-red vacationing businessman out on the board to tandem-surf the smallest waves, the money went back into the business. Jimmy had to put up with the same pawing from the wives, who were usually bolder than their husbands. Mindy had learned to live with a constant low-grade fever that was jealousy, even though she knew that Jimmy was faithful, as was she. But dear

God, he was a handsome man, and women noticed. Women wanted. Too much, like Mindy had.

In Hawaii, away from the rush rush rush of California and its highways, its who-do-you-know-can-you-read-my-screenplay-hey-didn't-you-used-to-be frenzy, their needs were simpler. No more sports car or motorcycle, the latest fashions, false eyelashes or hair. They lived in Jimmy's childhood home—his mother had welcomed the entire menagerie with no questions, never once complaining until the day she died, two years after they arrived. They were across the road from the beach but they had a view, and no apartment complexes or hotels yet threatened to block it. Land here wasn't that valuable; most people wanted to live much nearer Honolulu and Waikiki. Makaha remained a scrubby little area with trailer homes and wood shacks, the military the main users of the little road that hugged the coast. On occasion, the entire area rumbled like there was an earthquake when huge military convoys rattled along the road. The beach was still relatively empty except on weekends. But nobody really wanted to live this far north and west. The drive from Honolulu was too long.

More native Hawaiians lived at Makaha than in Honolulu. Here, the color of Melinda's skin would never be an issue like it would have been in California.

But there was another reason Melinda might be mocked.

"Aunt Mindy," Melinda said one evening at dinner, "why aren't you and Dad married? I know you love each other. I'm not a baby anymore, you know!"

This was the constant refrain these days—"I'm not a baby!" Screamed in frustration every time Mindy told her namesake to do her homework, brush her teeth, eat some breakfast, remember to put up Grandma's guardrails on her bed (a holdover from the period when Mom's dreams were so vivid, she tried to act them out in her sleep and often fell out of bed. They were past that now, but the guardrails remained).

"I know you're not a baby," Mindy said, sharing a glance with Jimmy.

Oh, Jimmy. Sitting across her table at night, still so handsome— a little more silver in that thick hair, a few more lines that crinkled around his eyes, like the rays of the sun. His smile still the thing that made Mindy want to get up every morning to see it. See him.

So why weren't they married?

"I just think it's simpler this way," Mindy said, repeating the mantra she'd been chanting ever since the first time Jimmy had asked her to marry him, soon after he returned home from Vietnam.

"What are you waiting for?"

That was what they both asked, Jimmy and Melinda (who, truth be told, mainly wanted them to get married so she could wear a long dress and put flowers in her hair; she'd enthusiastically described this in detail many times. Occasionally she also suggested that they could tie a satin ribbon around the collar of Petey, their dog).

Mindy's excuse was always her mother—it didn't seem right to upset her with all the fuss of a wedding. And who had the time, anyway? Where would they have the ceremony? The house was too small. Mom took up so much space with her wheelchair, walker, medicines, guardrails. Adult diapers now. A different wheelchair parked outside the door, with big plastic wheels that reminded Mindy of pontoons on a boat, to roll her across the sand.

It was a mistake in physics, how such a diminished woman—her muscles atrophied from disuse, her broad shoulders drawn up in a small hump behind her back—could take up so much room.

But it wasn't because of Mom that Mindy was reluctant to have a ceremony. What was she waiting for?

Who was she waiting for?

"Aunt Mindy, Grandma is slumping again," Melinda said, shaking Mindy out of her thoughts. She turned to her mother, strapped into her wheelchair but, indeed, slumping over to the side. Mindy gently pushed her upright, spooned some soup up to her, and the mouth opened obediently, automatically, like a child's. This was what her mother had been reduced to.

Carol Donnelly was near the end of the road—that was how the doctor put it, as if Mom were a beat-up old Edsel about to plunge off a cliff. Trapped in her chair, trapped in her mind. She'd had more years than she should have, he'd explained, thanks to levodopa, the miracle drug. But the medical profession was only now discovering that the body stopped responding to it at some point. And it hastened some disturbing symptoms—like the dementia that now encased her mother. The weeping fits, the depression, the confusion—all this was in her eyes, her voice long gone.

Still, they were a happy family. Wasn't that odd? No one would think that, given all their messy history. Mindy, taking care of everyone, going from changing her niece's diapers to changing her mother's. From feeding strained peas to Melinda to feeding pureed soup to Carol. It should have worn her down—that was what her friends at work said.

But she had Jimmy to help, to take the burden from her every other day when she escaped to the beach, even if it was tame old Waikiki. Even if she had to share her surfboard with sweaty, sunburned vacationers. She still found time, at the beginning and end of her day, to surf on her own—to feel strong and individual, legs planted on the board, to be a fierce warrior, to be free, one with the powerful, healing ocean.

To come home and be surrounded by the people who needed her—and who would never leave.

"We'll talk about it later," Mindy said decisively. And that was her mantra, as much as "I'm not a baby!" was her niece's.

The only thing that ruined her peace—this hard-won sense of joy in the little things, of happiness in caring for others—was the mystery surrounding her sister.

That was why she kept putting off a wedding ceremony. She was waiting for her sister. Whom she longed to see, whom she dreaded to see. Because if—when—Ginger returned, would she take Melinda with her? If she did, Mindy would have no right to stop her—and maybe that was why Mindy had never legally adopted her niece. She always wanted to keep the door open for her sister's return.

But if Ginger did want her daughter, Mindy knew she would shatter into so many pieces even Jimmy wouldn't be able to put her back together.

Sometimes Mindy woke up in the middle of the night with her heart pounding, her dreams invaded by terror. No! She could never let Melinda be taken from her. She would build a canoe out of a palm tree with her bare hands and paddle herself and her daughter—yes, her daughter!—all the way to Tahiti if need be. Because *she* was Melinda's mother in all the ways that mattered. In worrying and fretting and bathing and wiping and bandaging and signing permission slips and buying her first bra—God, how on earth had that happened so quickly?—and taking her out on the water for the first time, teaching her to float, then swim. Making doctor's appointments.

Watching Melinda while she slept—not so often these days, of course—and marveling at the curve of her lips, the long eyelashes. Searching for something of herself in her, something Mindy could only give her by example and trust. If she saw some of herself physically in the child—and sometimes she could convince herself she did, maybe in the stubborn set of her jaw—she was quick to attribute it to her sister instead. But other things—the confidence she observed in this girl who paddled right into the lineup of boys, faced their taunts with a shrug, even took a couple of swings at some idiots who tried to knock her off her board—weren't those things Mindy had taught her?

And love. Didn't love, finally, make someone a mother? The kind of love that filled you with terror when your child didn't pop right up after taking a spill on her board, or wasn't on the school bus when she was supposed to be—wasn't that a mother's love?

Yes. Yes to it all.

But always, in her dreams and during every waking hour, there was Ginger somewhere in the world. So Mindy never allowed herself to be called Mom, although her heart craved it—just once, she told herself. Just once, she wanted to hear Melinda say *Mom* instead of *Aunt Mindy*. But she held her heart at bay. "You have a mother," Mindy used to tell the infant Melinda every night before singing her to sleep. "You have a mother, my sister, Ginger. She has curly hair like yours, and she loves you enough to share you with me. You'll always be mine, but someday she might come back. And then you'll be loved twice as much. You'll be the luckiest girl in the world."

But eventually, she stopped telling Melinda—stopped telling herself—that Ginger might come back.

Two years after Ginger had left her baby, soon after they'd moved to Makaha, Mindy had gotten a forwarded letter. The stamp was an odd one, from Turkey. The return address was the American Express office in Istanbul, and Mindy knew immediately it was from her sister by the round, girlish cursive, appropriate for signing a high school yearbook.

Dear Mindy,

I know it's been too long. I hope you and Mom are doing well. And Mindy, too—the baby, I mean. I know she must be fine because you're taking care of her.

I'm in Turkey now. Tom's in prison here. I won't go into the details, because I don't know who else might read this, but something happened at the border and now he's in prison. Turkish prison. It's much scarier than what prison is back home, or at least I think it must be.

And I'm waiting for him. Every day I go to the front office, along with dozens of other people, fathers and mothers and sisters and wives. I've learned to take things with me to bribe the officials—cookies or cakes, wine, beer. Anything that might make them let me see him. But so far, they haven't. He's an American, and that's why. At least that's what they tell me.

So I spend the rest of my time at the consulate here but they won't help me, either. They say terrible things about Tom and what he's done, and I can't argue with that, but I still don't think it's worth being jailed forever. They've never tried or sentenced him, which I guess is the way they do things here. So I don't know when he'll be free.

He knows I'm here, though—I can sometimes see him in the jail yard, because I pay a woman to let me into a room on the second floor of a building across the way. I wave, and I know he's seen me, although he hasn't waved back. But he looks so small, so defeated. I've never seen him like this.

Before he was arrested, we had a fight. You might not believe it, but it was about you! He let me come with him to Afghanistan for business and for a while things were good between us again. But we had that argument right before we crossed the border to Turkey, where we were supposed to go to Istanbul, and he left the night before we were supposed to drive over. He took the van. I managed to get a ride a few hours behind him, which I guess is why I'm not in prison, too. He was taken away—I asked the border agents if they'd seen a man named Tom Riley. That's when they told me he'd been arrested.

I got a job in an American restaurant here—isn't that funny? That foreign countries have American restaurants just like we have Mexican or Chinese restaurants at home? I'm a hostess, I seat people. It doesn't pay a lot, but it's enough. And in my time off, I'm at the prison.

I never answered you, the day I left, when you asked me when I'd come back. I didn't think I would but I didn't want to hurt you right then. I was unloading enough on you.

But now you know, I can't. I have to wait here. I have to wait for Tom. And then, I don't know. I can't see past the day they finally release him and he finds me here, and he knows I waited for him, I didn't abandon him. That will be the best day of my life, and I'm not sorry about that.

So anyway, I know you're taking good care of Mindy. I hope Jimmy is OK, too, and he's a good dad. I can't imagine that he isn't. Tell Mom I said hi.

And kiss your reflection in a mirror, since I can't kiss you. I said before that you're the strongest person I know, and I stand by that.

But I've discovered that I'm pretty strong, too. Maybe because I learned from you.

Love,
Ginger

After the letter, even though Mindy wrote back right away, telling Ginger they were in Hawaii now with plenty of room for her, Mindy didn't hear from her sister again.

It was a few days after Melinda's twelfth birthday that they received the box. This time there was no return label. Only a brown box, taped and battered, addressed to Mindy.

"What's in it? Do you think it's a present?" Melinda clapped her hands and pranced around. Today she was a little girl, apparently. These days, Mindy had no idea who she would encounter on a daily basis—the imperious Not a Baby, or the loving, clinging child.

Today the child had decided that of course mysterious boxes showing up on your doorstep meant something magical! Something full of promise and enchantment! And Melinda always thought that every package or present was for her, not the boring adults.

But Mindy took a deep, preparatory breath before she sliced the tape; she knew better. Surprises were seldom pleasant.

Tape removed, she opened the flaps, and she and Melinda peered inside. It was chaos—bits and pieces of things, none wrapped properly, just thrown in as if whoever was packing was in a hurry. Some T-shirts, crusty with dirt or very old perspiration; a few pocketknives; an ancient can of surfboard wax; three plastic barrettes with the color worn off. A small tambourine, which Melinda immediately grabbed and started shaking, the tinkling of the jingles only ratcheting up Mindy's anxiety as she sorted through the stuff. There was sand or dirt in the corners of the box. When she lifted a small stack of old magazines out of it, sand fell into her lap.

The magazines were yellowed; some of the covers were missing. But as she flipped through them, a few pages were folded down.

On those pages were pictures of herself. The Girl in the Curl, in all her laughable glory—Mindy with that exaggerated black eye, holding a cigarette, the caption saying, "I'd rather fight than switch." Mindy pretending to surf in a fringed bikini, against a background as fake as her eyelashes. Mindy caught at the Whisky mid-Frug, her date someone handsome but his name long forgotten.

"Is that you?" Melinda stopped shaking the tambourine but Mindy's head still pounded as she looked at herself, confronted by the mistakes of her youthful past—but also, the glory. Suddenly she felt ancient.

"Yes, it's me—a long time ago."

"Oh my God, your hair!" Melinda laughed, clutching her sides and dramatically bending over double. "It's so huge! It's about ten feet tall!"

"Not quite," Mindy replied sourly. But she did look ridiculous. Nowadays she kept her hair short, only touching her jawline. She hadn't worn makeup in so long, the last time she'd even glanced at her little bottle of Cover Girl foundation it had been congealed, crusty. Staring at her painted face in the magazine, she wondered who that earnest, shiny young thing was. And what she wanted so very much.

Because what she had now was so—simple. So right.

"Who sent this?" Melinda was hanging on her back, her warm breath tickling Mindy's neck. She was so free, this one—free to be theatrical, free to be as affectionate as a puppy. Free to be whatever she felt like, because she never was afraid, she never had to worry about being left behind. She knew that every night Jimmy and Mindy would be there to kiss her good night, and every morning they'd be there to wake her up.

It hadn't been that way for her and Ginger—

"Ginger!" Mindy exclaimed, dropping the magazine, pawing through the rest of the box. This—all this—was *Ginger's*. And Tom's, too, judging from the T-shirts and pocketknives and bong. This box was full of their personal effects, what was left of them, anyway; there wasn't much. Mindy recognized that graying bikini that once had been white. And a charm bracelet with just one pathetic charm—a roller skate—because Mom hadn't realized she was supposed to add a charm for every Christmas and birthday. That was about it, but there was no question. These were Ginger's belongings.

But why? Why had these things shown up on her doorstep?

And who had sent them? She looked at the label again, but there was definitely no return address.

As she searched frantically for a note, a card, some explanation, the possibilities played tug-of-war with her heart—was it Ginger who had sent it? Tom? A friend of theirs?

The police?

"Are they—could they be dead?" Mindy wondered aloud, before remembering that Melinda was still in the room. The girl stopped pawing through the box and stared at her—

Mindy shut her eyes, shook her head. Shooing Melinda out of the room, she put the charm bracelet around her own wrist, tracing the tarnished roller skate with her finger. The bracelet was too small for her to clasp it, so it just draped over her skin. And Mindy mourned the shy, innocent little girl who had once worn it, even if she wouldn't allow herself to mourn the complicated woman that girl had become.

Then she quickly packed everything back in the box and hid it outside, behind a kayak at the end of the driveway. She couldn't say why she did this, only that she knew she had to keep whatever danger or tragedy it represented as far away from her as possible. But she also couldn't bring herself to throw it away.

. . .

"I think she must be dead," Mindy whispered to Jimmy the next evening, before the family set out for the beach like they always did after dinner. "I think that's why someone sent us that box."

"You don't know that," he whispered back. "She could have mailed it herself because she's coming home."

"But the awful thing is—wouldn't it be easier if she is dead? I can't let her take Melinda—we can't let her!"

"Shhh, honey, shhhh." Jimmy pulled her into an embrace, hugging her so tightly she could have lifted her legs and not fallen. He would have held her up. He always held her up. "Melinda is my child, too. I have a say in the matter, and do you think I'd let that happen? You are her mother, for God's sake. Let's just get married, OK? That would be one way to prevent Ginger from taking her, wouldn't it?"

"I don't know. I suppose? But I always wanted my sister to be there when we did marry, you know. I just wanted—I just want for all of us, and I mean Ginger, too, to be together. To be a family. But if she is dead, it would be—easier. But God—my baby sister!"

"I know, I know." Jimmy soothed her, patting her back, whispering into her ear. Then he released her, because Melinda was shouting at them to hurry up. Wiping away a tear, Mindy smiled up at him— her Jimmy, who gazed at her with such concern, such love. She would never grow tired of looking at that face, no matter how old they grew together. "Thank you. I just—that box. It's messing with me. People shouldn't get boxes with no explanation. It should be illegal. Although it would totally be like Ginger to—never mind." Mindy bit her lip as Melinda came capering up, accompanied by jingles; she was playing that tambourine. Ginger's tambourine, probably?

Too many questions, not enough answers—that box needed to be burned. Tomorrow she'd do it. Pour gasoline on it, light it on fire.

Get rid of it. And go on living their lives. Get married. Start the process to adopt Melinda. Ask her daughter to call her Mom.

Put the past behind her, once and for all—that would be the new Plan.

Mindy stifled a sigh as she helped Jimmy maneuver Mom into the funny wheelchair with plastic wheels that made it easier to roll her across the sand.

"Let's get the queen on her throne," Jimmy teased. Mom, of course, was unresponsive. Her face, lined and dotted with sun spots, was slack, her mouth slightly open. Her blue eyes were faded now, expressionless. Before she'd gotten this bad, she had come around to liking Jimmy. He flirted with her and Mom was positively girlish around him, and Mindy was reminded of when she was young, the way Mom got along with all the surfer guys, basking in their attention and teasing. She'd always liked men better than women. DeeDee had been her only female friend, but DeeDee had died of cancer in 1970.

Now, though, the flirting didn't matter. But Jimmy still did it, anyway—maybe more for the other two than for Mom.

Melinda asked to push her grandmother's chair, and she was big enough now, although she groaned a bit, panted exaggeratedly, making sure Mindy and Jimmy realized what a good girl she was being, how responsible, how thoughtful.

"She wants something, doesn't she?" Jimmy whispered to Mindy as he took her hand, and she nodded.

"Oh, definitely. I'm sure she'll spring it on us before she goes to bed."

They both chuckled. Two parents, bonding over the sweet duplicity of a soon-to-be teenager. But Mindy couldn't stop thinking about the box, and what it could possibly mean to her, to Jimmy—to this family she had managed to create, a miracle plucked out of the unpredictable surf they all were so drawn to. So she wasn't really taking in the view of the sun hanging low, like a ripe orange, in the sky, as they crossed the road to the beach accompanied by those tinny jingles, as if they were part of a parade. This daily ritual of watching the sun set seemed to help Mom sleep better.

The surf was louder now than it had been earlier, the waves churning more furiously.

"Looks like a swell is forming," Jimmy shouted over the thundering water beaching itself on the rocks. "Big waves coming. Want to go up to Waimea tomorrow?"

Despite her turbulent thoughts, Mindy's heart raced. She'd discovered big-wave surfing when she moved here; Jimmy had taken her up to Waimea. She was more suited to those waves, she discovered to her joy. Just riding them in, nothing fancy, fighting to be equal to the towering waves, to not let them overwhelm her. Just trying to survive.

She'd been doing it all her life. She was a natural.

"We can get the Not a Baby to stay with Mom." He moved closer, so he didn't have to shout so loudly. Mindy nodded, watching Melinda race down to the edge of the beach, where a couple of sea turtles were swimming near the shore.

"OK, that sounds great. I can get—"

She abruptly broke off. Because a car had just parked along the otherwise empty road, and someone was getting out of the driver's side.

A blond woman with long hair, plaited in a loose braid that fell over her shoulder. The woman was walking toward them, at first stumbling in the sand, but then she stopped, bent to remove her shoes, and proceeded toward them again more steadily, her heeled sandals dangling in her hand. She was alone, and Mindy couldn't tell if there was someone waiting in the car; the windows were too dirty.

Melinda came running up to Mindy and Jimmy as they watched the woman's progress. As the blonde came nearer, Mindy began to tremble. She recognized the shy smile, although it was bracketed by deep grooves now. The blond hair was darker. The curves were deflated; a gauzy dress hung loosely on the woman's body.

But the eyes, now that the woman was only a few feet away, were the same blue Mindy remembered. And that curly hair—was like Melinda's.

"Who's this?" Melinda whispered, tugging on Mindy's arm. "Who's this lady?"

Mindy couldn't move, couldn't speak. Neither could the lady now that she was so close, no longer sure-footed but hesitating before she finally stopped a couple of feet away from the three of them.

Mindy grabbed Melinda, grabbed her daughter—yes she was, of course she was, Mindy was her mother, she would make sure everyone knew that, especially the—

Especially her—

What should she say? What should she do? Run away with Melinda? Embrace her sister? Cry? Scream? A million questions fought to be the first out of her gaping mouth; the setting sun suddenly started to spin crazily, the beach was quicksand. She looked to Jimmy for help but his face was guarded, wary. He was also clutching Melinda.

"Melinda, this is—this is your—my—"

"Ginger." The voice was oddly clear and strong to Mindy's ears. She hadn't heard it in so long.

All of them—all *four* of them—turned to stare.

In her wheelchair, Carol Donnelly raised her head, and she looked first at one daughter, then the other, her tired eyes blinking, but see-ing, registering. For the first time in years, her mother was back, and Mindy gasped, not quite able to understand it.

"Ginger and Mindy," Carol said again in the voice Mindy remem-bered from her childhood, the pleasant tone so unlike the raspy, trem-ulous voice that had been her mother's before she stopped talking.

"Mom? Mom—are you—?"

"Say something to your sister," Mom instructed Mindy. Who was so stunned by everything—Ginger, her mother speaking, the sun setting, Melinda holding on to her as if she was afraid Mindy might float up to the sky, Jimmy looking at her with such love and concern—that she obeyed her mother.

"Ginger—I—how are you? Where's Tom? Are you—are you stay-ing?"

Ginger blushed, ducked her head—and Mindy's eyes filled with joyful tears to see the familiar gesture that used to annoy her so much. Why on earth had it? She couldn't remember now.

"Do you want me to stay?" Ginger asked, so softly Mindy could barely hear her.

Before Mindy could answer, Mom spoke once more. "Of course. This is where you belong. Where we all belong."

Then Mom turned her head back toward the setting sun. The only sound now was the pounding of the ocean—or was it the pounding of their collective hearts?

As Mindy took a step toward her sister, who burst into tears and held out her arms, one lone petrel swooped down over her, laughing joyfully before heading for the open water.

Carol gripped the smelly phone tighter; the phone booth was closing in, suffocating her. Come home, her mother said.

Then her mother said, Don't. Never mind. The girls are fine. Better off without you.

Then her husband got on the phone—her husband, she'd once had a husband, she vaguely remembered him, a high school boy, Bob. Bob Donnelly. Funny that they had the same name.

Stay, he told Carol, although she didn't ask his permission but some-how, she needed it. Stay, don't come home, the girls will be better off with me.

As she drove away from the phone booth back to the beach, her heart grew lighter and lighter until it fluttered in her ears, like it had wings. She felt the same way she felt out on the board—both powerful and ethe-real. Herself, completely. Not weighed down by anyone—those shackles she'd imagined, closing in on her ankles in the phone booth, had disap-peared. No more doctor appointments or breakfast tantrums, no more PTA, not that she'd ever gone to the PTA but every time Bob found out there was a meeting, he scowled at her in a certain way. No more dinners at the club, sticky drinks with gossipy housewives.

No more Mommy, honey, sweetheart. Mommy.

Just Carol. Just herself, and the water, and the people who were like her, the people who didn't fit in anywhere else but the ocean, which was between the earth and the sky.

And she lived there the rest of her days, surfing, swimming, taking care of her body, defying time and gravity, staying young. Strong, her legs never betraying her. Her legs were powerful and did what she told them and kept her on her board long after other people got old, got weak, got sick.

And one day, she would paddle out on her board as far as she could go. She would paddle out to meet the sun, and she would be swallowed up by the golden rays and shine down upon the ocean, showering her radi-ance upon them all.

Especially the two little girls at the edge of the ocean, holding hands.

AUTHOR'S NOTE

I can't believe that *California Golden* is my eighth historical novel. When I first started writing in this genre, with *Alice I Have Been,* I was certain I would never run out of actual stories to tell.

Thirteen years on, dear reader, I admit I thought that maybe I had. There are so many other wonderful historical novelists now, and it seemed to me they'd told all the good stories out there. What was left for me to write about? I was stumped, to be honest. Every idea I came up with didn't seem quite right for this moment. Or there were other books too similar. And, too, I felt I needed my next book to feel *younger,* somehow, while still exploring the past that I'm so fascinated by.

It also would help if this next book was a bit less tragic than my last one, *The Children's Blizzard.* I wanted to live in a world full of sun, not snow.

I won't bore you with how very long it took me to settle on this idea or how many people were involved in the search. I will say that the combination of sunny California in the early 1960s and the opportunity to learn about inspiring women who competed in what was then—and still is, unfortunately—a very sexist (not to mention racist) sport became irresistible to me.

When we think of that era—or at least, when I originally thought of that era—it is colorful, happy. Annette Funicello and Frankie Avalon dancing on the beach, the Beach Boys singing their hits. Endless sun, endless good vibrations. But there's always something darker beneath the surface of every historical or cultural moment, and that's what draws me in as a novelist. The 1960s were an intoxicating, turbulent time. My original idea for the novel was to keep it rooted in that early era of surfing, the late 1950s and early 1960s. But as I created my characters, and especially as I focused on Mindy and Ginger, I realized that I had to take them through the entire decade, from those early sunshine days to Vietnam, from Frankie and Annette to cults and drugs. Because that *was* California in the 1960s. And the upheaval of that era perfectly reflected the journeys of these two sisters.

But I also couldn't forget their mother's experience, that of a female athlete in the 1940s and 1950s, an era when women were not exactly encouraged to compete like men. A trailblazer, an icon of her sport—but at what cost?

While researching this era, I came upon a photograph of three beautiful blond women and their surfboards: Marge Calhoun and her daughters, Candy and Robin. It was a stunning photo that seemed to epitomize everything golden about that era. I quickly discovered that Marge Calhoun is considered one of the most influential female surfers of all time. And I was fascinated to learn that her daughters had competed, too. There was something about that mother-daughter-sister dynamic that made me want to explore it in fiction. While Marge Calhoun did go on a surfing safari in 1958, leaving her daughters for a time on the mainland, and both daughters grew up to compete, that's the end of the similarities between these women and my fictional creations. The personal journeys of Carol, Mindy, and Ginger are based on my own imagination and nothing more. I would say the professional accomplishments of the Donnellys are *inspired* by the Calhouns as well as other legendary women in surfing you should know about, women who had to put up with being knocked off their boards, denied the better surf, called names, and subjected to verbal, if not physical, abuse. The real Gidget actually did have a cross burned on her lawn, as I share in the book. So remember their names, look up their achievements: Linda Benson, Kathy Kohner, Marge Calhoun, Joyce Hoffman, Margo Oberg, and many others.

And don't forget Princess Ka'iulani. The story of surfing is the story of Hawaii. The story of surfing is one of cultural appropriation, too, and I hope I made this clear. Princess Ka'iulani was Hawaiian (actually half-Hawaiian, half-Scottish). Long after the missionaries declared that surfing, which had been part of Hawaiian culture for generations, was sinful, Princess Ka'iulani was a skilled waterwoman who represented Hawaii throughout the world, bringing attention to America's illegal annexation of the islands and overthrow of the Hawaiian monarchy in 1893. She is thought to be the first person to surf off the British coast. When we think of surfing, then, we need to adjust our mindset. It was not invented by the Beach Boys in the 1960s. *The Endless Summer*—while an excellent documentary—is not the perfect representation of the sport. The sport may have first gained worldwide popularity due to blond young men from California—that cultural appropriation—but if you want to know about the history of surfing, you need to know about the history of Hawaii.

To that end, here are a few of the books and documentaries that were helpful to me in my research:

Books: *Hawaii* by James Michener, *The Descendants* by Kaui Hart Hemmings, *Wave Woman* by Vicky Heldreich Durand, *Women on Waves: A Cultural History of Surfing; From Ancient Goddesses and Hawaiian Queens to Malibu Movie Stars and Millennial Champions* by Jim Kempton, *The History of Surfing* by Matt Warshaw, *The World in the Curl: An Unconventional History of Surfing* by Peter Westwick and Peter Neushul, *Barbarian Days* by William Finnegan, *Girl in the Curl: A Century of Women's Surfing* by Andrea Gabbard, *Gidget* by

Frederick Kohner and Kathy Kohner Zuckerman, *Orange Sunshine: The Brotherhood of Eternal Love and Its Quest to Spread Peace, Love, and Acid to the World* by Nicholas Schou.

Documentaries: *The Endless Summer,* directed by Bruce Brown, and *93: Letters from Marge,* directed by Heather Hudson.

I also subscribed to the Surf Network, which was full of fun shorts and documentaries. I recommend subscribing to the website Encyclopedia of Surfing, which again is chock-full of vintage film footage and reportage of those years. And I visited the California Surf Museum in Oceanside. As I was researching this during the omicron wave of COVID, I was not able to travel to Hawaii. I hope to rectify that soon!

One last thing—I've been asked whether I learned to surf myself for research. The answer is a resounding no. I always say my imagination is my most important tool as a writer. So I safely relied on that, supplemented by so many images of surfing that are available. I also spent a lot of time watching surfers off the coast of California. As a land-loving, more-than-middle-aged woman with a bad knee, I did not attempt to surf myself.

I want to be around a long time, so I can write many more books about inspiring, unconventional women swimming against the tide of history.

ACKNOWLEDGMENTS

Now the fun part—thanking all those who helped me during this journey!

My heartfelt thanks to my agent, Alexandra Machinist, for steering me through this process and being such a fan and supporter. This is our first book together and I look forward to many more.

To my editor, Susanna Porter, all I can say is thank you, once again, for your insight, warmth, and steady hand—and for graciously giving in to my argument for Mindy's Mary Jane shoes!

To my team at Penguin Random House—Gina Centrello, Kara Welsh, Kim Hovey, Karen Fink, Allison Schuster, Gina Wachtel, Susan Corcoran, Quinne Rogers, Jennifer Hershey, Leigh Marchant, Allyson Pearl, Elena Giavaldi, Pam Alders, Benjamin Dreyer, Loren Noveck, Anusha Khan—my heartfelt gratitude.

A big thank-you to Christie Hinrichs and the team at Authors Unbound, who make it possible for me to visit so many readers around the country. And thanks to Maddee James and her team at Xuni.com for coming up with a great website redesign.

I am grateful to be friends with so many wonderful authors, and I want to single out those who were particularly helpful to me as I navigated some professional changes and tried to figure out what to write next. Edward Kelsey Moore, Christina Baker Kline, Kate Quinn, Renee Rosen, Sarah McCoy, Elizabeth Letts, Quinn Cummings, Nicole Hayes, and Greer McAllister.

I'm a huge fan of the dedicated Penguin Random House sales reps and can't name them all here; just know I'm grateful for your enthusiasm and support over the years. Ditto to all the bookstore owners I've visited and hope to see again soon, in real life! A particular shout-out to Bridget Piekarz for being a sounding board as I decided what to write next.

And to my family—Dennis, Ben, Alec, Emily, and Mavis—thank you so much for your love and support.

Finally—but most important—I am eternally grateful to all you readers who have followed me on this journey. To infinity and be-yond!

ABOUT THE AUTHOR

MELANIE BENJAMIN is the *New York Times* bestselling author of *California Golden, The Children's Blizzard, Mistress of the Ritz, The Girls in the Picture, The Swans of Fifth Avenue, The Aviator's Wife, The Autobiography of Mrs. Tom Thumb,* and *Alice I Have Been.* Benjamin lives in Chicago, Illinois, where she is at work on her next historical novel.

melaniebenjamin.com
Instagram: @melaniebenjamin_author
Find Melanie Benjamin on Facebook.

ABOUT THE TYPE

This book was set in Garamond, a typeface originally designed by the Parisian type cutter Claude Garamond (c. 1500–61). This version of Garamond was modeled on a 1592 specimen sheet from the Egenolff-Berner foundry, which was produced from types assumed to have been brought to Frankfurt by the punch cutter Jacques Sabon (c. 1520–80).

Claude Garamond's distinguished romans and italics first appeared in *Opera Ciceronis* in 1543–44. The Garamond types are clear, open, and elegant.